DREAMS
OF
ANTIQUITY

The Awakening

a novel

JOE HEHN

"I dedicate this book to Grief, the Guru of Compassion."

This story was inspired by love. And love has the power to take a person to celestial heights as well as deep, grievous valleys... and every space between. This tale will most likely stimulate emotions tethered to the highs and lows of love, which can be a beautiful, though unpredictable, experience. Like any roller coaster worth riding; hold on tight, buckle up, and enjoy the ride.

PROLOGUE

As the great city of Babylon stirred itself awake, the meditative swoosh of a broom sliced into the morning's stillness. Rich ambered rays slipped through the sparse cloud cover that lined the horizon as birdsong serenaded the couple. The old woman was draped in a faded, plum colored shawl, a disheveled braid nestled under her tattered scarf. She crept along the stone flooring inch by inch, methodically brushing dirt free from the stoop. "They say she's quite ill… some are even saying she won't live through the month," her squeaky voice rang out as the broom strokes mimicked a subtle tide.

Her husband's reticence was typical. After decades of constant chatter this was how they conversed. The old woman waddled in place as she turned, redoubling her efforts back down the slight pathway.

The old man finally regarded her with an "mmhmm…" leaning the rickety chair back on its hind legs.

Half a century of rocking in place had chiseled two coin-sized notches into the stone.

"Some say nonsense, others are worried. She's recovering slowly, but the illness has… Ha-Hem!" she coughed into her hand; he ceased rocking. "Too much dust, it must have been a windy night." She looked up to the trees as her elongated nostrils smelled the air, "Where was I?" Her face squished together in confusion.

"The Queen, her sickness," he croaked, rocking again.

She continued sweeping, "Oh yes, yes I've heard it's taken a toll not only on the Queen but on him as well." Her honey-colored pupils scanned for any lingering debris as she spoke.

"Mmhmm…" He scratched a white beard as thin as a dusting of snow, only half listening to his wife. His milky, blind eyes, once as green as the sea, cast a steady gaze outwards as he perked an ear up with any new sound.

"What will happen to him if she passes?" she asked, then sighed. The woman melted into consideration, her wrinkled hands clutching at a broom handle thinned and glossy from wear. "They share such a rare and bold love… I wish it could live forever." She peered up to the sun, watching tangerine rays stretch skyward like a young girl's arms upon waking.

The thought of it all brought forth a smile as old as Babylon as she reminisced over her own tale of love.

Her hand, freckled and wrinkled with time's unabating influence, moved to rest on his. His knotted fingers wove themselves into hers, holding fast to the moment. As they exchanged several reassuring squeezes, each of them vaulted into the past, returning to memories so long ago they could have been prior incarnations. They both dreamed of their shared antiquity until the melody of sweeping bristles resumed some moments later. Within that simple gesture was an eternity of hidden sentiment. Or maybe it was something more powerful than sentiment, something closer to faith; a faith brimmed with devotion and belief in not only mere love, but their love.

"Time can only tell what will become of the King. And time…" he took a deep breath, gave a knowing smirk, then exhaled, "*will* tell." The old man's baritone rang true as his Beloved began humming an old Babylonian tune.

Her song melted him into serenity as the chair steadied and his eyes closed.

ONE

Gracien watched Ayadonna's breast swell like the ocean's tide – breathing life not only into her own being, but his as well. He approached their bed, reaching out to touch her face before hesitating and stopping just short of her cheek. His hand hovered near the Queen's face like he was trying to pet the wings of a butterfly. For a split second Gracien worried about waking her up before remembering that even his touch would not wake her from her slumber. Though she had slipped into a coma three days prior, the months of taking care of his sick wife left him with unshakeable behavior; encouraging her to sleep when she could, holding his breath when tiptoeing around, and speaking in hushed whispers. There was no need for any of that now, but it still felt like the right thing to do.

The hair of his knuckle grazed the fuzz of her cheek before sliding down her face. The texture of Aya's skin was bumpy and creviced, yet it radiated with the familiar, tender warmth. Her concave cheeks were reddened and freckled from either the disease or from the various side effects of herbs, medicines, and salves. Grayish-black blots encircling her puffy eyes flaunted exhaustion from scores of sleepless nights. Various scars, stitches, and lacerations from a multitude of treatments raked across Aya's arms and torso. Holding back tears, Gracien stood over what was left of his wife after ten months of battling this relentless disease. The

Queen's weight must have been half of what was normal. Muffled, labored breath fought its way into her lungs, then escaped with a gasp as if being chased. This was the only sound she made. How he missed the affection of her voice and the joy of her boisterous laugh. Tears pooled in his sea green eyes before dribbling down his cheeks and escaping into the safety of his full, black beard. The bedroom chamber was eerily silent without the typical bustle of healers, family, and handmaidens. His only companion these last few days was the sheer, white curtains billowing around the bed as a breeze blew through the window.

The King's sobs echoed through the room as a palpable agony throbbed within his heart. Gracien tried swallowing his grief as a sole finger dragged across Aya's skin. What was once a bronzed, olive sheen now looked yellowed and translucent – the crisp white bedding only defining it further. Gracien's fingers migrated up her neck, sliding over her barren scalp. He could feel the ghost of her rich, raven-colored locks spreading around his fingers as they had done a thousand times before. Just then, the echo of her laugh resounded from somewhere deep within his mind, pulling him into the embrace of a memory.

They were resting on a cool, shaded patch of grass beneath the canopy of a seasoned fig tree. Leaves rustled and branches swooned as a spring breeze whipped about, whispering secrets through the expansive gardens. Gracien pushed himself up, careful not to disturb his dreaming wife before scanning his surroundings. The royal gardens embraced the couple in every direction, with an endless array of trees, shrubs, and flowers mapped out to create pathways, common spaces, and secret nooks. Pristine marbled benches lay scattered about the sprawling grounds with a few wooden replicas in the less frequented parts. With several fountains featured in the more impressive sections, the hum of trickling water could be heard in nearly every corner. Beyond the secret hideaways, the gardens were mapped out with exacting precision until spilling out into a natural field just beyond the border. The beautiful meadow extended for a hundred paces or so before merging with a collection of pines. These towering timbers graduated into thickened density as the forest climbed up the mountainside - ultimately thinning just shy of lightly, snow-capped peaks cradled by opal-colored skies.

Gracien dipped his head back, holding the stretch as his slight, squared off nose inhaled the fresh spring aroma. Two pops sounded out as he cracked his neck on each side. His dark hair that fell just below his ears shimmered in the sunlight piercing through the branches above the royal pair. Gracien swiped a strand of hair behind his ear, a habit which Ayadonna adored. His fingers continued down to the bottom of his dense, coarse beard, giving it a pinch as he considered whether to wake her or not. The thick mane shielded his cheeks and squared jaw but accentuated a radiant smile and gleaming white teeth. A fit, lean physique lay hidden under his loosely bound, white linen shirt and olive-colored pants. Both of their shoes were kicked over to the side next to their rich, royal cloaks swaying like dried sheets on a branch.

Gracien inhaled, smiling at the perfect afternoon. His contented eyes scanned the gardens for a moment longer before returning to Aya. Her thick locks flowed down her back like a dusk lit stream. Even with the slight, natural weave, her hair fell all the way down to her lower back. A beige, intricately laced dress hugged her curvy, slender physique. Suddenly an extended yawn departed from her face as she rolled to her side. He chuckled, placing a strand of hair behind her ear, and blowing gently on her face to see if she'd wake.

Her perfectly pitched eyebrows lifted for a moment as her dream swayed off course. Those eyebrows were one of his favorite features, a telling precursor to her uttering a single word. They could approve or disapprove, admire or deny, inquire or ignore, and, of course, extend a welcomed invitation. Aya's small mouth doubled in size with the help of her distinct smile lines which bordered a gleaming grin. Smooth, bronzed skin accentuated the whiteness of her perfectly aligned teeth. As was common for the women of Babylonia, Aya bore a slightly larger nose, which only helped to balance her natural, but beautiful, appeal.

Grass blades popped under shifting weight as Gracien scooted himself over the earth, nestling around her frame like a big spoon embracing a little one. A slight moan escaped her lips, followed by an incoherent whisper and then a sigh. With her eyes still closed, she gave a pleased smirk while scooting herself back into the fullness of his embrace.

"Eye - Ya - Don - A," he pronounced slowly with affection. "Time to leave your dreams... be here with me," his thick, heavy voice resonated deeply, tickling her ear and stirring consciousness.

Aya's subtle chest heaved with an inhalation, expanding her body beyond the fetal position as she whispered back. "Gray - Sea - In," she mimicked with sarcasm before releasing a dramatic exhale. "When I wake up to you... this is the dream," her voice rang out with embellished femininity.

"Pouring it on a little thick, huh? Is it my birthday or something?" Gracien chuckled as he nudged his chin into the cove of her neck.

Aya giggled in return, turning into him, and wrapping her arms around his waist, her fingers weaving through his hair before brushing her lips on his. "I just thought a little flattery would go a long way." Their exhalations mingled before sharing a kiss.

"You flatter me just by being yourself... always so sweet," he whispered. "*So gentle.*"

She looked him over, examining her lover with a tilted head while a sole finger coiled his beard. "I wonder what you'd look like without a beard. You know I've never seen you with a bare face." She began humming softly.

"It's not very, um, becoming, for a man of my position to be without one. Supposedly it makes me look older, wiser even – like I know what

I'm doing." His fingers and thumb pulled at the bottom of his beard as he smirked.

His eyes opened, a teal vibrancy resembling shallow seas gazed into Aya's hazel pupils.

"Well then, you should keep it." Her hand swept his aside as she pinched his chin, wiggling it. "Because you need as much help as possible convincing everyone..." she held back a giggle then mimicked his deep tone, "that you know what you're doing." A full smile replaced the smirk as she held her breath with anticipation.

Gracien inhaled, his gaze peering up into the canopy of the fig tree. "It's interesting..." he paused, searching for the right words as his bottom lip curled with consideration, "that this, supposedly, intelligent woman would taunt the very person who just so happens to have his arms wrapped tightly around her body. Especially... considering how extremely ticklish she is." Aya's frame tensed.

"Since when can't a Queen tease her husband?" Her nose drove into his neck as his grasp tightened.

His firm, capable fingers walked themselves over to her ribcage as she squirmed, fighting him off while pleading. "Gracien please, you know how much..." she wailed in laughter, her back instantly arching in rebellion as his rigid fingers prodded her ribs.

The booming laugh startled a fleet of sparrows from the depths of the fig tree. "Pa-Lease! My. Love!" she screamed between roars of delighted torture.

Moments later his fingers slackened as his arms brought her exhausted frame in closer. Gracien buried his face into the softness of her neck and kissed it repeatedly as she squirmed.

"I cannot breathe! You monster!" She repeatedly slapped him on the arm until his ironclad grip released.

"Okay, Okay," he panted. "I surrender... I surrender."

Gracien rolled them both over the grass. A childlike giggle escaped Aya's lips as they settled. He positioned his face just in front of hers and they listened to the stillness, allowing the silence of the moment to deepen; staring, smirking, and trying to pry a laugh from one another with funny faces.

"I love you," he whispered.

"And I…" her head bobbed forward with her words, "love you… My Beloved."

They each held a smirk as their heads approached with glacial speed. It wasn't just the kiss they celebrated but the moment leading to it. Gracien wrapped her small frame into his own, merging them in an impassioned embrace as their kiss held. After a short while their lips parted and Aya rested her head on his chest. He scanned the space between branches and leaves, watching as the sunlight fanned, splintered, and scattered, feeling it's warmth, and inhaling one deep, perfect breath. His mind stilled, settling into nothingness and peace, into happiness. Or perhaps it was something beyond happiness. With Aya safe and sound in his arms, Gracien felt utterly fulfilled. Through his love for her and hers for him, he was complete – for their love was his liberation, his enlightenment, his God.

The perfect memory faded as his eyes focused back on reality. Gracien leaned in and whispered. "What I wouldn't give to hear your laugh or feel your whisper tickle my neck." Closing his eyes, he placed a kiss on top of her head.

He held the kiss as well as his breath for a moment before his usual negotiations. "I'll do anything. Please spare her. I beg you; I'll do anything you ask."

Dreaming like a child after a full day's play, Aya didn't stir. Gracien's head shook side to side as his throat swelled and his eyes teared over. He clasped a hand over his mouth, suffocating his cries. What confused him was that these tears were not from sorrow, agony, or grief.

Rather, they came from a place of awe. "I'm so blessed, so fortunate to have found such a love."

He reflected on how throughout her battle, Aya's courage never wavered. She grew fearful at times of course, but she never lost her courage. She was a warrior unlike any he had ever known. Vile medicines, constant vomiting, various infections, sleepless nights, agonizing pain, and all the while, vitality seeped from her like wine from a spout. Aya was determined and dedicated but given enough time, even granite is stripped away by the wind. His tears flowed freely as he imagined how hard it must have been for his love to watch her external beauty wither away, a rose shedding one petal after the next until she was left with nothing at all.

The back of Gracien's hand stroked her cheek as he considered her bravery; how it didn't fade but grew stronger through her battle. Ayadonna's heart guided her, telling her to find the light and reside within its embrace each and every day. She reminded them all: the healers, the family, the palace, the Kingdom, Gracien, and most importantly herself – that life is a gift. One not to be taken for granted and not to be shrouded in fear. Life was meant to be embraced, to be cherished, to be shared, and to be celebrated.

Somehow, this disease had eroded her external beauty and yet he had never found her more beautiful than in this very moment. "Stunning. Absolutely and impossibly stunning." His heart swelled with a stew of love, agony, awe, and fear.

His free hand wiped away tears as he gathered himself before kneeling beside her. "I'm just so grateful to have found you my love." His lips quivered with ache as his fingers grazed her cheek with the softness of a spring breeze.

A slight knock rang out on the chamber door. "Your Excellency?" Tudor, Aya's healer, stepped through the opening then turned around to close it.

His lanky fingers lingered on the thick wood as he took a long, deep breath before turning to face them. Tudor's tall, thin frame spun and moved forward only to falter. He was taken aback by the scene before him. Beauty and impermanence danced like lovers as Gracien knelt next to Aya, his hands clutching hers, light spilling into the room from the windows and a gentle breeze teasing the ivory sheer curtains enveloping the bed.

Tudor's once young, healthy face was now gaunt and weathered. He had aged a decade while caring for his Queen over the past ten months. Rolling his hands within one another, he stepped forward as if walking on splintering ice.

With his head hanging low and his hands now in a pleading, prayer-like position, he nearly cried the words this time. "Your Excellency?"

He was a child plagued with a looming punishment, his large Adam's apple failing to swallow his guilt and grief.

"Her Excellency," his voice broke. "She's... she's not *in* there anymore. There's nothing left to be done." He swallowed again, his gaze slicing into the floor before his feet. "Except, to say goodbye."

He couldn't bring himself to look at his King, who was still kneeling beside Aya with his hands holding hers.

Gracien's spirit was torn from his being with what he knew was to come. Hearing the healer's words was a living nightmare. The sharp silence filling the room was excruciating. A flash of blind fury erupted as he suppressed the urge to choke the life from Tudor right then and there. Seething with rage, he tore his gaze from Aya and mauled the healer with a murderous glare. But upon seeing Tudor entombed in grief, his rage receded. Gracien returned his attention back to Aya and exhaled, his face reducing back into anguished disbelief. It felt as if his own death approached, and he welcomed its arrival.

"It would be best... it would be best if we gave her something to ease her passing," Tudor staggered through his words.

The subtle sound of a small vile sliding across the table screeched throughout the bedroom like a dying vulture.

Gracien stole a gaze away from Aya, freezing his empty stare on the elixir for a moment before returning his attention back to her. Aya's chest rolled with gradual breath as a great wave would traverse an endless ocean. He adjusted his hold on her, trying to take more of her into his hands.

"Her passing could take days... possibly longer. This will allow her to withdraw in peace. A mere swab placed on her lips," Tudor wept freely, "and the Queen will be set free."

Tudor stood for what seemed like hours awaiting Gracien's response.

Without removing his gaze from Ayadonna, Gracien whispered, "Leave us."

Gracien patted away the beads of sweat forming on his forehead as he flashed a forced smile towards his guests. His and Aya's family sat patiently as the unabating Babylonian sun beat down on the late afternoon. Everyone was donned in their finest attire and surrounded by an array of white flowers. A grand staircase, also adorned with clusters of flowers, led down from a loft to an intimate terrace below. Several rows of seats were fully occupied with guests, including Gracien's parents, the King and Queen of Babylonia. Two perfectly white columns stood on either side of a pristine pool which seemed to hang over the edge of the cliff-side. Framed between them, Gracien paced back and forth like a caged tiger as he waited.

"She's always late, but today? As if today would be any different from any other day... It's not like it's special or anything," he whispered to himself while trying to keep his composure.

His pristine, deep blue tunic gnawed at his flesh as the hot sun baked it like dough. Gracien shaded his eyes with a hand as he peered into the Heavens. A sole, meager cloud glowed in the sky. He turned, flashing a partially hidden smile towards his parents and siblings, who reciprocated with sympathetic smiles of their own. Women cooled themselves with elaborate fans or makeshift versions for those less prepared. Men blotted the perspiration buildup on their cheeks and foreheads, smiling to one another as if everyone enjoyed the relentless heat and unbridled sun.

The sheen of Gracien's decorous robe refracted the sun's brilliance with each pivot of his agitated feet. Even with the heat and the nervous prince pacing about, the energy throughout the terrace was nothing short of magical. A royal wedding was a rare and illustrious occasion and the streets and paths that wound through the mountain were filled with thousands of people waiting to see the newly married couple. Gracien tugged at his collar, twisting his vein riddled neck free from the constricting garments. He inhaled deeply, annoyance maturing into frustration.

"You would think *at least* today she would... *could* be on time," he negotiated with himself, sounding like an old married couple. "No. Let her be, she's getting ready. She's nervous."

His feet edged the lip of the pool, the water glimmering with a teal vibrancy. The sun was an hour from setting into the sea, making it glitter like a diamond. The light illuminated the forest surrounding the terrace, painting it a golden hue. Even the wildlife understood the importance of such an occasion, as exotic birds sung out while hawks circled above.

"Aya please, this is getting ridiculous my love. I can't wait here forever," Gracien mumbled to himself as he glared at the empty staircase.

It was absolutely stunning with all the bundles of jasmine, lotus, roses, and lilies - but all he saw was what *wasn't* there.

He spun, exhaling into the sea as his gaze penetrated as far along the horizon as possible, his chest gradually filling with air like sails catching wind. He seemed to lose himself within the beauty and mystery of the expanding horizon, experiencing his first moment of peace since the beginning of the festivities. He turned towards the staircase only to find Aya waiting on top like a resurrected angel. Gracien's breath was sucked from his body as if his spirit had suddenly departed.

"Oh - my - God," he whispered.

At the sight of Aya's teary eyed smile, he felt weak in the knees and lightheaded. Ayadonna prepared to descend, and felt her bottom lip quiver with the effort of suppressing joy as her eyes glanced down the stairs then back to Gracien.

As the toes of her bare foot reached towards the first step, a harpist began serenading the moment. The celestial sound liberated Gracien from his entranced state. With a deep, quickened breath and a shake of his head, he left the living dream and stepped into his assigned position. No matter how insane it seemed, he couldn't help but think that this feeling of pure love was exactly how he would feel after being brought back to life after dying.

Aya took a step and then another, her feet gaining confidence and her pace quickening. Her breath was labored, her golden eyes beaming at the beauty of the moment. But with a deep breath and a nod to herself, she slowed and settled her excitement. Scintillation rippled over the strapless, pearled gown as sunlight embraced the fabric. Aware of her clumsy nature, Aya placed trepid weight on the tips of her toes before fully committing to each new step. Her fingers clutched at the vibrant bouquet like a makeshift railing. The pop of color against the canvas of white was mesmerizing. Swirls and loops of thickened hair stood atop themselves, a sole strand dangling over the corner of her forehead. Aya gleamed, her makeup shimmered, and her elation dazzled the entire audience. She mingled glances between steps, guests, and Gracien as the terrace neared. The setting sun bathed her in a nectar so ripe with radiance she seemed to shine of her own accord.

Suddenly her footing faltered, sending her teetering to one side. The crowd gasped and Gracien jolted towards her but stopped himself as Aya immediately recovered. She unleashed an eruption of laughter which sent a wave of glee through the crowd. Aya's hand shot to her mouth as she blushed with embarrassment. Gracien stepped back into place, extending a prideful smile and a slight nod of relief as everyone relished the moment.

Aya's final step settled, and she raised her eyes to meet his. In a flash of palpable energy, their gazes merged, sending tickles of delight through the air. Gracien and Ayadonna both fought back tears while their smiles collapsed into trembling frowns of euphoria. The moment was one of absolute purity, a childlike innocence beaming from them both. Gracien attempted to maintain his composure but as Aya neared, he couldn't control himself for a moment longer, moaning a sob as he wiped away tears. They stood a few feet from one another as a handmaiden approached and claimed the bouquet of flowers from Aya. The soon to be princess took a deep breath and flashed a self-encouraging smile towards her parents before turning towards Gracien. By the raw look exchanged between the two, the crowd could see that it was much more than just a royal union; it was a soulful one.

They stood before the cliff-side pool, hands and gazes united as the dwindling sunlight melted into a banquet of color. Hawks continued circling as bird song replaced the harpist's tune and winds ferried the sounds of waves breaking up the mountainside. The picturesque view was framed with white columns on either side accompanied by palm trees swaying in the breeze. The cliff-side plummeted down to the awaiting sea which sparkled like golden mesh. Standing at the edge, Gracien and Aya felt as if they were floating towards the Heavens – two souls returning home.

Aya inhaled, the guests straightened in their seats and Gracien looked at her as if they were the only two people there.

"As your wife, I swear myself to you and to our love for all eternity. Through all that may come we shall face it together, always and forever," she spoke with resolve and without flaw, standing taller as she continued. "Our love is eternal. An everlasting dance between day and night, moon and sea, life and death - without end, without beginning. Two flames *reuniting* within one Source." She paused, allowing the depth of her words to settle.

"I will always abide by this one truth, this faith... I will always believe in us and in our love." Her brow furrowed with emotion, her words striking a chord in them both as well as everyone in attendance.

Gracien swallowed, exhaling his awe before beginning his vows. But Aya interrupted, throwing him off with this unexpected change.

"Never forget this my Beloved, have faith." As she spoke, Aya's face began to fade as if blending her beauty with the scenery behind her.

Gracien felt her hands become lighter, like they weighed nothing at all. He looked to the crowd then back to Aya, his panic surging.

"Remember this vow, this belief, and use it as a constant truth throughout your journey. No matter what happens... you will always have this one truth." Her final word lingered and time slowed.

Aya's form continued to fade as Gracien grabbed for her hands, but it was as if he was trying to catch the wind. "AYA!! NO!!! Please don't leave me!" he screamed.

Aya's form lifted and began floating above the terrace floor before moving to hover over the pool. Gracien had no choice but to follow.

Before he could think he was jumping in, pulling himself through the water in a complete frenzy.

"AYA! PLEASE! NO! Please don't leave me!" He vaulted to the edge of the cliff-side, his hands clawing and grasping at the air as she floated further from him.

Her transparency increased as she drifted further away, Aya's form slowly merged with rays of light from the setting sun. Gracien looked back to the guests for help only to find an empty garden. The entire setting looked like it had been rotting away; no decorations, no flowers. The stairs were in ruin and the outer forest had consumed the terrace. He quickly returned his panicked stare back towards Aya, whose expression embodied absolute serenity. She moved to speak before fully merging with the fading light of the setting sun.

With the chill of a crisp winter wind, Aya's words rang out one final time, "Believe in us…"

Their bedroom was a lightless, frigid void. Gracien rolled over, extending a hand to Aya's side of the bed only to be met with the chill of desolation. His hand tapped and patted the emptiness like one frantically searching for a lost jewel. Then it all came back to him.

She's dead.

His spirit was wrenched from his body with the remembrance of her passing. Anguish suffocated him as he gasped for breath. Gracien pulled his knees into his chest while releasing a silent moan. A palpable ache swelled in his heart, spreading through his arms and legs until his entire body tensed with the torment. He was a man petrified by fear.

Gracien had never experienced such deafening, desolate silence. Nothing existed but an ocean of suffering. His Aya, his soulmate, his best friend, his wife, his bride, the future mother to his children, all she ever was, and all she would ever be, was gone forever – never to return. Ache congealed in his heart. His hands began tearing at his chest as if trying to wrench the pain free.

Total fear – a darkened, incomparable loneliness possessed his mind like shadows emerging at dusk. Then a wave of paralyzing dread swept in. Abandonment, denial, guilt, regret, anguish, hate, and betrayal battled for dominance like demons clamoring over the throne of death. Suddenly his body revolted against the anguish, uncoiling itself with a tremendous gasp for air. He moaned out – his weakened frame lengthening as his lungs filled to the max. Then all at once his body compressed, coiling into itself as if constricted by a python. With his final contortion Gracien unleashed a wail of anguish, expelling any desire to live without his Aya.

"Whyyy… hy-hy-hy… " he cried.

His eyes bulged with ache as he began weeping so grievously, he found himself praying for death just to be with her again. His hollowed frame writhed with torment as exhaustion mounted, building strength, and finally overtaking him after a lengthy battle. He retreated into sleep; the sole respite from a reality which only nightmares could subdue.

Footsteps echoed in the royal gardens as Gracien's most senior advisors strolled through.

"The people mourn with such genuineness, it's quite moving." Tamuza's deep blue eyes heightened his conviction, giving him a younger appearance than his clean-shaven face portrayed.

He was taller than most other men his age and towered over his companion, Shenbar. Tamuza's grayed hair danced in the breeze as his face brandished a somber expression.

He plucked a jasmine flower from one of the blooming bushes. "Even the gardens seem to have lost some vibrancy since her passing. I swear it… this flower would smell better if she was still with us." He moved to place the flower in the lapel of his very handsome, sapphire colored tunic before thinking better of it.

He inhaled the aroma one more time then twisted the stem between his fingertips, watching as it spun into the wind and flew away. This was the first time he could recall *not* smiling at the small delight.

"It feels like the entire royal family died in a tragic accident." Shenbar, a short, almost comically spherical man waddled in place of walking, favoring his right leg.

He bore a pointy, burnt orange beard which just so happened to match the rich, exuberant robe wrapped over his nearly non-existent shoulders. His pale blue eyes protruded through his wrinkled skin. The highlight of his face was a rather bulbous nose, reddened from decades of plum wine. Several resilient strands of grayish, orange hair stretched across the top of his head like the remnants of an abandoned spider web.

"The writing was on the wall, but no one wanted to believe she really could die – or we were just too scared to speak of it." Shenbar released several heavy sighs. "The people mourn for Aya, and they mourn for Gracien too. I guess we all mourn for the end of their love story. His absence from the public eye proves the immensity of his grief."

Shenbar's words faded into silence as the two continued to stroll aimlessly.

"I'm unsure of this whole situation… I'm unsure of what I'm unsure about but something feels… *grave*. Something beyond Aya's passing." Tamuza's hand cupped his mouth in thought before looking to Shenbar. "Still no word from him?" His expression froze in anticipation, then dampened with Shenbar's dismissive nod.

"Three weeks. Three whole weeks and he has yet to leave their… ehem, *his* chambers. I expected, and I know you did too, for him to attend her life ceremony," Shenbar spoke to himself before looking to Tamuza with a childlike innocence. "Should we umm… should we be worried? Three days ago, he demanded that the chamber guards leave and not come back." His gaze pleaded for consolation.

Tamuza patted his old friend on the back. "I can't say. I wish I could muster up the strength to encourage us both. But time will tell. Time will tell if our Gracien is strong enough to live on and be something without her." He sighed as the two exited the garden, making their way towards the royal chambers.

Minutes later their steps softened as they approached the doorway and Tamuza's forefinger hovered before his pursed lips, "Shhh…"

Shenbar nodded as they tiptoed to the door. Both men's expressions melted into heartbreak as Gracien's wailing could be heard through the door. They eyed one another, shaking their heads with grief before making a hasty retreat.

Several paces away and they still spoke in hushed whispers. "Any update from the servants? Has he eaten anything today?" Tamuza asked.

Shenbar shook his head. "Nothing. Not a thing in over two days. But the wine jugs need constant refilling. Well not all of them, not the ones shattered to pieces in the courtyard terrace." He frowned, "I hear every time the servants try to bring food or check on him, they're met with some explosion on the other side of the door."

"Time. Time will tell. We must give the poor boy… time." Tamuza sighed again as the two were swallowed up by the hallway's darkness.

Just as the men vanished down the long corridor, the door of the royal chambers squeaked open a sliver's width. Gracien's sole eye glared through. His overgrown fingernails pierced the slit, rounding the edge and pulling the door open. Gracien didn't leave, but kept to the shadows, listening for life beyond the door's threshold.

The sparse light entering the bedroom sliced through a score of slashes and tears in the curtains. The room looked like it had been ransacked by bandits. The blades of light revealed what was once a charming and sacred atmosphere, but now lay disheveled and smelling of rot. Gracien's head slipped past the edge of the door, stopping to reveal half an eye peeking out. Like a tortured prisoner finding his cell door unlocked, he looked battered, barren, and wild with fear. His frame was frail and boney – his face was gaunt and empty. He had aged a decade in a mere three weeks. What was once a thick mane of hair lay ragged like that of a crow's nest. His beard was cut from his face in some parts and torn in others. Gracien's pupils bulged with the afternoon radiance then retreated, adapting, and slinking like a snake.

The only sign of his Kingship was the tattered remnants of his royal robe. This too was covered in stains and tears. Instinctively he pulled it closed around himself, cloaking his underwear and pale skin. Gracien's eyes twitched as they peered to the right into the depths of the west corridor and then the east. He slipped from the door and began creeping down the hall to his left. Soiled fingertips grazed the wall as his stained feet half-walked, half-ran along the cold stone, reminiscent of an escaping convict.

He sensed movement down in the courtyard. The sight of a servant made him jolt upright – freezing like a deer. Her eyes fell on him and with a gasp her as hands shot up to muffle her mouth – an armful of plates crashing to her feet. The clash sent Gracien sprinting down the corridor, his bare feet thumping over the hardened stone as the royal robe flailed in his wake. A guard ran up to the woman, shaking her to attention as her finger rose, pointing in the direction of the King's retreat.

Gracien heaved breath like a predator on the hunt, placing his footfalls with stealth-like precision as he stalked about. Suddenly the drum of another's footsteps rang out as a man strolled down an intersecting corridor. Gracien jumped towards the wall, hiding in the shadows with his back and palms glued to the stone. His bloodshot eyes narrowed as he recognized Tudor. The healer paused, looking in his direction but one of the corridor's many columns concealed the King.

Gracien peeled himself from the wall and scurried towards the courtyard-side of the corridor. Tudor's eyes skimmed a parchment as he walked, unaware of Gracien darting from one column to the next. The healer paused a second time, looking up with a curious gaze. He walked over to the railing, looking up to grayed skies brewing an ominous storm, then down into the courtyard below.

"Oh!" he gasped as three mourning doves leapt from hiding, their calls and flustered wings booming over the silence.

Tudor jumped back, his hand clutching at his chest before giving a sigh of relief. He bent over, picking up the dropped parchment as the clap of bird flight melted into the sound of subtle footfalls. He rose, bringing his head up to find Gracien standing just a few feet away.

A bewildered expression washed over him as his eyes went wide with realization. "Your Excellency!" he shouted.

It happened in less than a second – Gracien lunged at him, choking him by the neck as the two men slammed into the railing. Tudor nearly toppled over it, but Gracien's grip was strong. Throwing him to the floor, the King fell on top of his prey. Tudor's knees buckled under the weight of them both crashing to the ground. His hands wrapped around Gracien's, trying to pry the iron clad fingers from his throat. Gracien's overgrown fingernails pierced the healer's neck, drawing blood as he squeezed with all his strength.

Gracien pulled Tudor's gasping face mere inches from his own. The King's lifeless gaze glared into the healer's helpless gawk. Tudor's eyes streamed with tears as his feet kicked and writhed in desperation. His fingers clawed at Gracien's hands as the veins of his face and neck bulged in rebellion. Gracien bared his teeth like a wolf, spit jutting from his parted lips as his face trembled with fury.

With a flash of rage, he slammed Tudor's head against the stone. "BRING!" he raised it up only to bring it back down again, "HER!" and again, "BACK!"

Gracien's thumbs sunk deeper into Tudor's neck as his fingers strangled the last breaths from his lungs. Tudor's eyes began to roll into the back of his head as a sudden revelation broke through Gracien's murderous revenge. His fingers released their hold of Tudor's neck and utter shock washed over the King. The abrupt force of his retreat knocked Gracien backwards as if he had been tackled off the poor man. Curled up on the stone, Tudor gasped for life through choking gags. Gracien stared blankly at the healer as the horridness of his crime crystallized.

As Gracien was shocked out of his desperate attempt to avenge his Beloved, he was overcome with a wisdom not of his own mind. It dawned on the King that men take the life of another driven by fear. He sat on the stone floor in horror as he listened to the origins of his wrongdoing. Men are compelled to inflict unimaginable horror by the mere shadow of fear. But when men kill for revenge, especially one driven by love, a part of their love dies along with that which they destroy. And so killing this poor man only meant that he was in fact killing a part of Aya, a part of their love.

Gracien shook himself to reality before crawling backwards as Tudor's crippled voice moaned for help – coughing, choking, and gagging precious breath as blood streamed from the many puncture wounds in his neck. Gracien stood, he himself panting for breath as he looked from

Tudor – to his blood-stained hands – then back to the healer. He stumbled, searching for sure footing as Tudor's crumpled body shook with each deep, throaty cough. Terror washed over Gracien's face as his eyes widened with the realization of his crime.

Tudor rolled over to his back and mustered a huge inhalation. "HELPPP!" he bellowed a raspy, feeble call.

Gracien shook his head in denial, retreating from his crime while wiping his hands on the tattered robe – his mind began to torment him for committing such an atrocity. "No… no… why, I couldn't. No-no-no…" His lips quivered as he tripped over himself, falling to the ground before scrambling along the stone, a frantic cat desperate for escape.

He somehow recovered. Turning, he scampered along the stone before bursting to his feet and darting down the corridor and into the darkness beyond.

His hands and fingers dug into the earth and rock mixture, pulling his frail body up the mountainside. Rainwater slickened the surface and tested his grip. A streak of muddied crimson dribbled down his forearm as the elements coalesced with Tudor's blood. As he climbed, strong gales of wind hammered down on him, violently whipping his hair and robe about. An especially strong gust flung Gracien sideways, a sole hand and bare foot were his only anchors as he hung on for dear life. The wind tortured his senses: stealing his breath, stabbing his eyes, and smothering his ears.

"Nooo!" his muffled scream tore through his throat as he blindly swung himself back onto the cliff-side.

He hunkered into the stone and mud like a bat waiting out the wind's torment. As the gusts dwindled and finally retreated, he gritted his teeth and got back to work. Deep grunts and angered moans rang out with each new step as Gracien made slow but steady progress up the steep incline. His muscles ached, screaming out in rebellion as they were pushed to their limits. Suddenly, a deceptive stronghold broke away, the loosened stone plunging downwards, ricocheting off the mountain and disappearing into a blanket of fog. He failed to maintain his hold on the mountain. One moment he was climbing, the next he was falling. His hands flailed about, his body plummeting towards the earth until his fingers caught hold of a tree root snaking through the stone, snapping his body to a halt. Gracien dangled, undaunted, as if nothing could frighten him now. He peered down the steep cliff-side before snarling at the setback and pulled himself back onto the stone.

"It will take more than that," he growled.

This climb was the only way to the top. A great storm some years prior had caused a massive landslide, blocking off the road they had used on the day of their wedding. It wouldn't have been too difficult for an average man, but Gracien was starving, barefoot, drunk, and deranged with grief – and Tudor's near lifeless face was imprinted over each and every climbing hold.

He neared the summit and the cliff-side rounded out, but again his footing slipped, causing his hand to scrape down the rock face and tear a fingernail from its bedding. Blood oozed down his hand as the nail fluttered in the wind. His expression grimaced before the relief washed over his face, as the physical pain momentarily muted his internal agony. His eyes closed as the comfort of this new sensation banished his grief. As the pain in his finger settled, his eyes opened, and his gaze narrowed on the summit. No moan of discomfort escaped as his bloodied finger dug itself back into a holding, pulling himself up to the mountain's peak.

His mud-soaked hand slapped the wet rock-face. Stained and blood-ied fingers clawed for support, pressing into the stone and pulling his body up over the ledge. He tugged himself far enough beyond the cliff-side before deflating, his face falling into the wet earth. Heavy exhalations riddled a puddle with bubbles as he regained his breath. His feet dangled over the edge for a few breaths before his knees bent underneath his shaky frame, pushing himself up into a wobbled stance.

He stumbled forward, grappling at the overgrown plant life as he made his way through the forest. Thickened vines and tangled branches crisscrossed his path as Gracien ripped apart gaps wide enough to slink through. The numerous talons of vegetation scraped and cut his exposed flesh as the humid, forest air smothered his breath. Ten minutes later his destination appeared, revealing a grayed horizon that was interrupted only by towering trees and wildlife. A few final steps and he was through. A blast of mountain air welcoming him into the clearing, cooling his sweaty body as his feet stumbled forward.

As his tattered robe flailed in the wind, Gracien examined himself for the first time since Aya's death. He was splattered with mud, a streak of blood cascaded down his leg from his finger, and numerous scrapes raked across his arms from both Tudor and the forest. But he had made it. And there he was, standing in the exact place he and Aya had exchanged their vows only a few years prior. Weathered by time, the terrace had aged quickly, as had the man examining it. Escaping beyond the forest line, the wild had swallowed up the perfectly manicured garden. The vines crawling along the stone and climbing up the columns. The once immaculate staircase now lay soiled and battered from the mountain's unsettled slumber. Gracien's expression was unmoved as he turned from the clearing, gazing out into an ominous sea and dreary skies. A deep inhalation mounted as he recalled Aya's death and like a rogue wave his grief crashed onto him.

"Why!?" his voice ripped through his throat and echoed amongst the ruined marble, shaking the memory from the dense forest that covered the sacred space. His bare feet sunk into the mushy earth as he slowly approached the cliff-side. Gracien's face twisted with emotion, morphing with hatred, anguish, and disbelief. The edge of the cliff-side approached, instantly dropping off and unveiling an agitated sea crashing into fractured stone some three hundred feet below. The roar of colliding elements blasted up the cliff-side like brawling lions. Gracien's teeth clenched unknowingly, tears bubbling up as he stared out into the shrouded vastness.

"Why… Why did you leave me Aya?" He fell to his knees, slumping into himself and burying his head in tarnished hands.

The deep ache incapacitated his breath, stealing air from his lungs for so long that his vision began tunneling before finally unleashing a great gasp. "Whyyy!!!" he screamed again. The echo of his terror billowing out then fading into the vast horizon.

His emaciated physique, a shell of its former self, flexed and strained as veins protruded from his colorless skin. "Why would you leave me?" he wailed through mumbled words, searching the Heavens for consolation.

In a flash, his eyes blackened into nothingness as he leapt from the ground. "You! You took her! You stole her from me! Why!" Drool trickled from his mouth as hatred boiled over.

Again, he collapsed, falling to his knees, and sinking into the mud. "Do you hear me? Please, Aya, answer me!" he pleaded with his hands in prayer as his body swayed with grief. The wind only howled in return, wrapping itself around the poor bemoaned man like a cloak.

Tiny droplets of rainwater pattered the ground as Gracien's shoulders shuddered with grief. "I can't…" His words lingered as crying moans overwhelmed his speech. "I… I can't live like this… Not without her." He pushed himself to his feet as the rainfall escalated.

Turning to face the terrace he gestured to an invisible audience. "This is not life… This is death," he cried, trying to convince the derelict space. "So then what awaits me? It can't be worse than this... Than a living *death*." He stepped backwards, his heels nearing the edge.

"Please Aya my love, my sweet Ayadonna, my Queen... my everything," he sobbed, then screamed. "I'm a King!" Turning back towards the sea, "a King banished from his Kingdom! Help me! Help your King to live *in* life... not... *in* death." He pulled his shuddering body fully upright. "I believe, in our eternal love," he spoke through trembling sobs as he straightened, his toes extending over the cliff-side. "And I'll find it once again. I'll search Heaven and Hell until our love is reunited!" His fingers curled as he roared at the skies, his face a mask of fury and hate.

"I hold you to your vow Aya, because eternity has no end." His hands rose from his sides with his mounting proclamation. "So I ask you to save your Beloved, to save him from this torment. Aya, my sweet perfect love, help me, save me... Save me from myself," he pleaded as his left foot snaked over the edge of the cliff, his arms and hands reaching outwards, his back arching as his arms spread even more.

Violent waves battered the cliff-side below as the fullness of the approaching storm intensified. The winds pressed him backwards, causing him to step back from the cliff's edge with the force of the gale. Gracien's body shuddered with grief, his head dangling from his neck as it bobbed with agony. He pressed forward, not stepping but attempting to slide his foot over the earth and towards the edge. The wind intensified, fighting back, and whipping rain in his face as his hair lashed about. Gracien countered, leaning into the force as his feet scraped over the earth until one snaked back over the ledge.

"Save me Aya... Reunite us." He straightened, his gaze penetrating the Heavens as he spoke and then suddenly, the winds died. "For I... believe in us."

And with his final words Gracien leaned forward, titling himself beyond the edge of the cliff. His senses raged, his mouth gaped open, his eyes filled with terror, and his hands flailed backwards as he tried to reverse his forward progress. Only it was too late. His momentum tipped him beyond the mountain's edge like a great falling oak. In an instant, the sea's mild gust escalated into utter violence, tearing through his flailing body as Gracien plummeted, screaming in terror. The roar of the fall was deafening, leaving him in total silence. But then, time slowed as a thousand raindrops floated alongside him, each reflecting the impossible: Ayadonna was there with him. A thousand reflections of his Beloved ceased his screams as a sense of peace overcame him. Gracien accepted his fate and closed his eyes.

TWO

Struggling under the unbridled radiance of the afternoon sun, Gracien's eyelids fluttered open. A hand rose to rub his eyes before returning to his side and exploring the barren space next to him. His fingers stumbled along the emptiness like a lost traveler. Ayadonna's void stirred an instant storm of grief, abandonment, rage, and anguish as his heart succumbed yet again to the pang of her death.

As his hand revived the chilling reality, a new realization formed. *Sand?*

The peculiarity of grabbing a handful of sand stole him from his torrent of grief. Watery with sleep while adjusting to the sun's brilliance, his eyes tussled with clarity. The blurriness made it difficult to comprehend the steady stream of sand pouring from his open palm as he rapidly questioned reality. Gracien rolled over and sat up. His sand covered hand moved to shield his narrowed gaze from the rays of sunlight as he examined a tranquil beachfront.

Too real to be a dream? Nodding in confusion, his sea-green colored eyes poured over the shore. It looked familiar but somehow new. *Where am I, what... What happened?* Even the tone of his inner monologue sounded off.

Dreamlike visions and vexing thoughts ricocheted in his mind like bottled wasps. His face flushed with panic as a flood of memories stormed his consciousness with a near palpable force.

Falling. I recall falling… But why? Why was I falling?

Overcome with bewilderment, his eyes quivered in panic. He became lightheaded and his breath receded into short, violent bursts.

The mountain. I fell. His eyes widened with utter confusion. *But… But I chose to die, to kill myself. How? How am I still alive?*

His heartbeat exploded like a drum of thunder as he noticed the lack of something which would have been guaranteed with such a fall: Pain.

How could I have survived without a sting of hurt? It was so high… and such a violent shore. The sea… it must have swallowed me up… a wave maybe… a giant wave. Panic accelerated his thoughts. *Yes, yes… a wave… and it caught my body just before, just before I was smashed into the rocks.* He swallowed repeatedly as his delusion mounted. *…It knocked me unconscious. Yes, YES!*

Another thought emerged. *Impossible, what are the odds of that… No one could have survived that fall… You're delusional.*

He countered his own thoughts. *No, it must have caught me, and… and… spit me out far from shore!*

Anxiety infested his skin like a horde of ants, stealing him from his thoughts as he looked to the beach for answers. His mind raced with one rebuttal after the next until the realization of his attempted suicide overshadowed them all like an instant storm. He sank into himself, wanting the only thing in all his life that could provide comfort.

"Ayadonna… My poor Aya. My Beloved… She's…she's…" he murmured under his breath as his mind trailed off.

His spirit had drained from his body but with a flash of rage, it breathed again. "She's dead!"

His fists pounded into the sand, deepening the hole with each new strike. On the final blow his hands stayed at the bottom of the newly formed pit as he grated his knuckles against the coarseness of the sand.

The hot, tearing sensation provided a temporal release, suffocating the agony of his loss. He dragged his hands from the hole, sand falling free from his ebony skin.

Air launched from his lungs with a gasp as shock erupted. *This... this can't be.* He peered down at the sandy hands as they ascended, grains dripping off and revealing the unimaginable beneath.

"Impossible." He finally heard his voice, realizing it sounded very different than if the words had been spoken from the lips of a Babylonian King.

Gracien stared down at the hands of a young woman, soft and unseasoned, replacing the fingers and palms he had known so well. Chocolate skin stretched across his dainty fingers as they fanned in the afternoon sun. His wide-eyed gaze scanned his tiny wrists, forearms, and elbows, then up his now small, thin arms as the heartbeat within his breast erupted with panic. Gracien felt beads of sweat fall from his dark hairline, leaving long streaks between the stripes of dusty white paint swiped across the girl's brow. His panic soared, his face framed in horror and disbelief. Tears streamed downwards, slicing through the Aboriginal paint. The nostrils of his wide, bulbous nose quivered as he reigned back tears. His lips were cracked from hours of dehydration and unabashed sunlight, and were even bitten apart by the constant gnaw of perfectly white teeth. He bore the amiable cheeks of the young woman's clan: generous and splattered with dark brown freckles. His deep-set eyes bore an intense gaze, bearing the same vivid, sea-green pupils of his previous life. Filled with a mixture of earth and grayed tones, his hair was as thick as sheep's wool and was only thickened further with sand and dirt. Falling just below his neck, his hair stabbed downwards with a slight weave like vines that reach for the floor. His boney shoulders jutted up and down as his hands and arms hovered in front of his face, studying the bizarre ligaments which he had never seen before.

As Gracien's insanity festered, he wrapped his arms around himself and wept like a child in mourning. Trembling with desperation, his hands fell, grasping at the animal skin encircling his small waist while attempting to swallow reality. "Aghh!" a sudden gasp rang out like someone surfacing for a final breath. The air was expelled outwards with such violence that his throat burned with fire as a coughing attack ensued. Through aching gags, he rose from the sand slowly as if he were lifted by another being. As he attempted to retreat backwards, his fingers curled and his face twisted in horrid shock.

"This! Can't! Be! What's happened to me?!" he screamed through panting gasps of terror, only deepening his fear as the voice that escaped from his throat was at least an octave higher than he was used to.

His two small feet stumbled backwards through the sand, the heel of one catching the buried knob of rock. The next moment he was falling and everything slowed to a stop.

SMACK! His vision darkened, tunneled, and blurred.

The crack of flesh reverberated over the serene beach as the back of his head bashed into the rock face. Blood oozed from the wound, pouring out onto the sand. As he passed out, his eyelids fell closed.

Gracien came to, his eyes parting slowly for a moment, then shooting open with panicked realization. As a surge of terror rippled through him, he launched up from his prone position. "Krshhh!"

"Ohh!" he yelped as his wound tore itself open, ripping the dried blood away from the rock as his hand shot to the back of his head.

Blood trickled down his neck as his hand prodded the partially dried, gooey mess of flesh and hair. Several consecutive winces hissed through his grimaced face as his hand wandered about his torn scalp. Gracien's fingers tapped closer to the epicenter of the wound, his middle finger pushing the grinding bone and flesh together. The inner sound of shifting flesh accompanied by the strange, painful sensation pulled him into an instant state of vertigo. His vision tunneled and his mouth pooled with saliva as he prepared to vomit. "No… keep it together… no… stay here Owanna." he pleaded with himself, the name of his new life falling from his lips without effort as he swallowed the urge to retch.

"Sit… just breathe Owanna, just breathe." His eyes closed as the chill of shock swelled further. "That's it." He swallowed again. "Just breathe and remain calm." His body settled with the sound of his encouraging whispers, gradually cooling from an intense heat to the chill of cold sweats.

"I am a King… *the* King of Babylon. How could this all have happened? How was *I* placed into the body of this woman?" he pleaded while examining his hands with disbelief. "It can't be possible…"

As the moments passed, he felt the chill of his brow recede as the build-up of saliva also retreated. His eyes fluttered open and three deep breaths later, his vision cleared. Gracien tried pushing himself up before catching sight of the protruding rock. Seeing the blood-stained hairs mashed onto the stone caused his knees to weaken. He collapsed onto himself, weeping into his red stained hands.

"What… is… happening?" he sobbed, the sound of his unfamiliar voice causing him to moan with disbelief.

Gracien shook his head and exhaled a quick, fierce blow.

"Calm yourself… calm down… I need to calm down," he whimpered, sitting up straighter while breathing like he was in labor. "I need to relax… and I need to figure out what's happened…what *is* happening to me." His mind was chaos, raging with unimaginable thoughts and delusions while he shakily wiped tears from his eyes. "This doesn't make any sense, this can't be." He inhaled a deep and prolonged breath before closing his eyes with an equally long exhalation. "Slow down. Relax and breathe... that's it... just breathe. Good." His voice soothed him into tranquility. "That's it... keep breathing." His pulse and vision had finally settled.

From a distance it looked like a sole girl merely enjoying a beachfront meditation.

"Ok... now think. What *has* happened? How did I find myself..." it was impossible for him to even say it out loud. "...in this body, in this life? Ha!" He drunkenly snorted at the notion before careening and squeezing his eyes shut, searching what felt like an eternal depth for answers. "Wake up, wake up, wake up!" He rattled his head, overly exhausted.

Gracien shook his head back and forth, his little body fighting off his reality. His emotions raged, swaying from anger to pity, from guilt to betrayal, from anguish to denial. All overshadowed by surges of abandonment, anxiety, and a deep terror of the unknown. His body trembled with a grave burden, feeling as though the life-force within his heart was drying up into ash before being blown into nothingness. His mental torment was suffocated by the sound of shouting from the brush behind him.

"Ooooo - Waaaa - Naaaa!" The call echoed through the forest and over the beach.

He spun in his seat, the turn sending a dash of pain through the back of his head. Worry erupted at first, but the familiarity of his brother's voice immediately settled his nerves. A young man's head popped through the brush down the beach, two hands splitting the branches as if he was preparing to dive through the middle.

Jiemba scanned the beach. "Oowannaaa!" He drew out the last syllable, sending shivers down Gracien's spine.

His tone meant one thing: Owanna was in trouble.

"Owanna! There you are!" Jiemba yelled, pushing the bush apart with a quick shove then jumping between the branches.

The young woman's older brother's footfalls quickened as he raced over the hot sand, his walking stick bobbing like a spear down by his hip. Gracien moved to stand, but a surge of dizziness and a dash of pain flared. With a bracing hand, he pushed himself up only to fall back on his seat. Gracien shook his head, trying to escape the surreal state as the sound of Jiemba's annoyance neared.

Gracien's pulse quickened as he attempted to stand yet again, but fell once more as his brother's words cemented reality. "Where have you been! Mami is worried sick!" he began berating his little sister, his strong hand clasping around her arm. "Owanna." He froze. Anger spilled from his gaze as it landed on the wound.

He dropped his walking stick, kneeling beside her. "Your head!" His fingers moved to touch the wound but hovered over it instead. "This is serious, very serious," he whispered to himself. "Owanna…" His tone was much softer now. "Are you alright?" His other hand wrapped over her shoulder.

Still in shock from both the wound as well as the insanity of this situation, Gracien didn't respond. Jiemba stood about a head taller, his face nearly identical to Owanna's but with more pronounced cheekbones and thinner lips. A thickened spread of freckles resided below his eyes and bumps of acne covered his inflated cheeks. He too bore white painted lines and intricate designs along his face and frame. A slight animal skin covered his privates and a large pendant of carved bone dangled over his neck.

Jiemba spoke in slow motion. "We must get you… get you back to Mami and Dadi. To Mulungwa," his voice comforted her, causing tears of exhaustion and defeat to cascade down Owanna's face.

"Nht, nht, nht," his tongue clicked the roof of his mouth. "No, no, no… don't cry. Grab my arm," his voice deepened as he heaved her to her feet. "Yes like this, let's go little sister." He wrapped Owanna's arm over his shoulders, grabbing her wrist with his left hand then securing his right around her small waist.

"Nht, nht, nht," he repeated as if prompting a horse. "Just like this, very good, Rrrr… " He strained as he pulled her back along his arrival tracks but they sank further into the sand with the added weight. "Good-good-good," he sputtered off as rust-colored pupils glanced back at the wound to see blood trickling from the crimson gob of flesh. "We must hurry." His eyes teared over with panic.

Jiemba's lean, ebony muscles flared and flexed with the strain as the pain continued to surge in Gracien's wound like a wind-fueled flame. His vision narrowed yet again, his eyes only able to show him the ground before him as the cold sweats returned, saliva pooling within his arid mouth.

"I feel sick," Owanna blurted out as her head bobbed up and down.

"Hold on Owanna, tell me when the sick comes… and we will stop." He continued to drag his little sister.

"Now, now!" she pleaded just before heaving off to the side as her dizziness doubled.

Now carrying all of Owanna's weight, Jiemba didn't even pause. "We-must-get-you-back! They…" He gritted his teeth with the mounting effort. "They will know what to do." His words were dense and spastic.

Owanna's toes dragged behind her as Jiemba carried her. He scooted her sideways between the brush as the terrain graduated from sand to forest bedding. The new terrain proved even more difficult, as dense vegetation covered the earth. Owanna's foot immediately caught on a vine.

"Agh!" Jiemba yelled, fighting to prevent the sudden pitch sideways, but with Owanna's added weight, his attempt was fruitless.

Both toppled over, tumbling down to the forest floor.

"Aghhh!" she yelled as the pain screeched.

Her fingers stabbed her temple as Jiemba jumped up, pulling her back to her feet.

"Wait!" she yelped.

"Owanna! We must get help!" He knelt, grabbing her shoulder. "We need help, should I leave, and return with help?" He spewed out laborious gasps between stealing glances between Owanna and a labyrinth of brush. "Or can we try again?" A frantic expression riddled his face. "We're not too far. Soon they'll be able to hear us! Let's go, let's go!" He made the decision himself, pulling Owanna back up to her feet.

"Ughhh!" she screamed as he hauled her arm back over his shoulder.

"Good! Good! Let's go, little sister. All mooossttt... there!" he growled.

Owanna squeezed her brother's body with all her might as a pulsing agony rippled through her head. Throbs of anguish surged as intermittent flashes of white mauled Gracien's vision. He pressed his temple with such force that the bone beneath seemed to divot with the force of each new step. As the two trudged through the cluttered forest flooring, he couldn't help but hope this was yet another nightmare.

"A dream, this is a dream... just a dream... wake up Gracien. Wake. Up," he mumbled as his head bobbed lifelessly.

Jiemba glared at his sister from the corner of his eye before both went wide with terror.

"Stay awake Owanna! Stay with me, your brother Jiemba!" his voice quivered as he quickened their steps. "DADI! DADI! HELP!" he screamed as sweat poured from his brow.

Gracien retched all over himself, the pressure from vomiting blurring his vision as pain no longer came in waves but with constancy.

Jiemba ignored the vomit, continuing his panicked charge through the brush screaming, "DADI! DADI!"

His steps gained momentum as the brush thinned into a flat, manageable terrain.

"Tudor. Tudor... he will help me..." he slurred as his head bobbed. "Poor Tudorrr..." Gracien spoke like a weeping drunk. "Aghhh," he moaned, his loose arm flailing at his side.

"DADI!" Jiemba's frantic screams deafened the forest. "Help! US!!" his shouts raced through the thinning vegetation.

Off in the distance a faint rumble of commotion returned his calls.

"Almost there... They're coming now, Owanna! Almost there... Hold on little sister... Hold on!" he commanded through bursts of breath.

The distant cries grew stronger, the space between the two parties shrinking.

"Hommm... home," Gracien slurred as darkness crept in from the corners of his vision, swallowing the light while Jiemba's screams for Dadi seemed to echo from a dream.

"Yes, little sister we're going home, hold on... Holddd onnn Owwannaaa..." his words deepened and slowed, evaporating into nothingness as Gracien's eyes rolled into the back of his head.

Gracien's swollen eyelids peeled open, the crust of sleep crackling apart. The bed of straw snapped and popped as he rolled over to his side.

"Where... Where am I? What happened?" his voice wheezed.

As he took in the hut, his senses were kidnapped by a swell of mystery. Sunlight poured through several windows and cracks along the walls as fascinating aromas filled his nose. His nostrils flared, sucking in air so heavy and thick with exotic notes he could taste it. He looked over to the side of the bed, finding a batch of dark green, oily goop in a wooden bowl.

Gracien leaned over. The smell extinguished the fresh breeze, causing him to pitch backwards. "Whoa," he said before grimacing with the ache of movement.

Gracien's feet, scratched and sore from their recent trek through the forest, plopped to the earthy ground, sending a shockwave up his small frame and mushrooming pain within his head.

He reeled. "Aghhh!" a moan fluted from his mouth as his fingertips pressed into his temples.

Gracien's face winced with the familiar pain, releasing a series of groans through his dry, cracked lips. His face held the wince while slowly sucking in air as if trying to manipulate the flow of pain. Gradually, he pulled his aching body to an upright position. His small feet were not steady beneath him and he struggled to remain steady as he stood, clinging to the table beside him.

Three fingers of each hand rubbed circles into his temples, but the bandage of leaves wrapped around his head made it difficult. His timid fingertips followed the veins of the leaves towards the back of his head where a large lump of organic dressing shielded the wound. Some gooey, sticky paste seeped through the cracks and onto his fingers. His hands retreated as he rubbed the salve together then took a sniff. The scent physically knocked him back two paces.

His face contorted in revulsion. "Ohhh…" he gagged, mimicking a cat coaxing hair from its throat.

He looked to the bowl next to his bedding, doing his best to not inhale the medicine at all.

Gracien wiped the paste off his hands as he regained himself, taking a step towards a bowl of water. The mounting soreness and heavy ache frustrated his progress.

"Ouhff," a little moan crept out before the coolness of the water drained down into his belly.

As the bowl came down from his mouth, so did his examining gaze, looking himself over to discover that he was washed, free of any body paint, and wearing a different animal skin.

Flashes of vomit, blood, and rolling in the sand played out in his head. After his second bowl of water, Gracien used his thin forearm to wipe the wetness from his mouth. He flinched, tonguing his bruised and swollen upper lip.

I must have banged it on the ground when we fell, he thought. *Jiemba!* He looked to the door as if he would find his brother waiting there. The cover of the hut flapped in the wind, beckoning him to leave as a shiver of fright tingled down his spine.

Next to the straw bedding were several polished tree trunks made into stools from Owanna's family's hut. Her mother's interlaced stitch of animal skin lay at the foot of the largest of them. He didn't question the memories of his current life that slowly seeped into this conscious-ness. Gracien knew that Owanna's family, his family, had been waiting by his bedside – and most likely devastated with worry. His heart tinged with pain at the thought of them suffering because of him, as if they didn't have enough to worry about.

He examined the angle of sunlight darting through the hut. "It must be early, early afternoon. I've been out for an entire day at least," he said while poking the purple of a newfound bruise.

His attention moved to the hut. "This place, it's strange... but kind of familiar."

Gracien surveyed his surroundings with intrigue, picking up ran-dom items and examining them like an amnesic traveler. Lines and fans of sunlight sectioned off the space as dust particles floated about like miniature sea creatures. His stomach groaned out for food as his head leaned all the way back to investigate the ceiling. Eerie straw dolls slowly spun from decaying strings that hung from the beams above. Their faces caught the light as they rotated, giving them a lifelike appearance, and sending shivers down his spine.

Creepy.

Some sort of petrified dog's head, or maybe it was a dingo's, looked as if it was stuck in the wall with its body trapped on the other side. A collection of shield-shaped masks painted with various emotions aligned the doorway and three long pipes that could only be didgeridoos leaned up against a nearby wall. A plethora of bowls, organic trinkets, and various utensils glimmered under the beams of sunlight as his fingertips aimlessly glided over them. Owanna recalled never being inside but remembered peeking through the doorway when she was a very young girl as Mami writhed in pain while delivering Owanna's little brother, a birth which nearly took her life.

Gracien shook the memory from his head before examining a table displaying an array of ceramic pots and containers hosting various ointments, potions, salves, and liquids. There must have been some kind of order masked within the chaos of the salves, as there was a graduation of color running from reds, to oranges and yellows, then to greens, blues, and purples. Bunches of herbs with dirt still clinging to their roots lay beside a strange, blackened bark, the sap of which oozed yellow. Several other herbs and leaves lay scattered next to a mound of oddly shaped green and yellow beans. A wooden muddler lay perched on the edge of a mixing bowl which contained a green batter, hardened, and darkened into blackness as it thinned up the bowl's curves. Gracien bent over, taking a quick stab at the smell before making a hasty retreat. The horrid scent was the same as his bandage. He made a disgusted face with his tongue sticking out before moving on.

Over to the left awaited another table with an opening in the wall above it. Sunlight poured through the window, drawing Gracien to it with an unknown force. His head tilted as the surrealistic, unknown familiarity embraced him. He approached the counter as a palpable presence moved in and around him like a converging, chilled wind. Gracien's hand extended outwards as if he was navigating a lightless room. Dainty fingers slid over the mound of mixing bowls, cups, and assorted tools like a blind person mapping out a space. Birdsong rang out just outside, a rustling sounding out from a nest resting up against the outer wall. Gracien's head tilted as he listened and his feet sidestepped, entering a blade of sunlight as he progressed along the table. Like bubbles popping upon a pond's surface, something stirred within his being. His mind drifted and his eyes stared blankly as his hearing dulled. All his senses then shifted from reality and into the memory. Gracien transcended time and space, taking himself back to another place, ceasing to exist in his now feminine form and merging with remembrance. He closed his eyes as his hand ceased being Owanna's, transforming into the man he used to be within his memory.

Aya had swayed side to side while humming a familiar Babylonian tune, her hands busy rinsing grapes in a bowl of water. Like dusk sliding over the landscape, Gracien eased in behind her then embraced Aya's hips. Birds chirped out as the wind whistled in the background. The tremble of branches and rustle of leaves just outside the window broke up the beams of sunlight. Patches of flickering rich, golden light pattered across Gracien and Aya's faces as they savored the simplicity of this beautiful moment.

His hips in line with hers, he caught the sway of her body like two autumn leaves synching into a swinging descent. Aya's hum continued, unwavering as it vibrated through Gracien, sending shivers up his spine and uncurling the hairs of his neck. His fingers walked down her ribs before reattaching to her swaying hips.

Aya flinched, the hummed tune faltering for a moment as her smile extended. Gracien's coarse beard tickled her neck as his chin anchored in over her clavicle. Her weight eased, tension pouring from her frame as she leaned back onto his strong body like an uprooted oak resting on another. Patches of sunlight danced over them as rays of sunlight darted around the shifting leaves. A cool breeze merged with Aya's hum, vibrating not only from her lips but her chest. Gracien's eyes closed, and his face muscles softened as he let out a contented sigh, which snaked down her neck and clavicle, making her shutter with delight. Aya's eyes closed, her hum purring through their bodies as they swayed like stalks of wheat on a breezy afternoon.

The Queen's aroma swept through Gracien as if Ayadonna had been right there in front of her. The scent of Aya's jasmine hair monopolized his senses, his own hips swaying as her small hands clung to the table. A slight hum stirred within, growing with the gradual intensity of a rising sun as she fully exhaled the tune. A vibration born ages ago rippled through Gracien's being as he, now the young woman in her family's hut, swayed within its harmonic embrace. The resemblance was exact, as if Aya had occupied the space between Gracien and that old wooden table. The delight of such intimacy ran through him like a thawing stream washing away winter's chill. With his eyes still closed, Gracien's head lay off to the side, as he was lost not only in the memory, but in the love radiating through them both. His hands released the table, slowly rising and then holding himself within an embrace. The young woman's petite frame swayed within itself as if persuaded by some invisible force. "Mmm, mmmMmm, MmHmHmMmmm..." The ancient Babylonian hum rippled throughout his being as well as the hut.

Something startled him from the trance-like state, pulling Gracien from the vision as a strange, gargled voice spoke from behind. "Witjuti, emu bush, kakadu plum."

Gracien tensed, slowly turning to look at the woman standing in the doorway.

The shamaness coughed, spitting a bounty of gargled phlegm into a small bowl as she approached the workbench. The sunlight engulfed her, highlighting a dozen scars and tattoos. An enormous, disheveled mane resembling clumps of dried seaweed hung from her head. Shrouded in a mixture of fear and embarrassment, Gracien stood in frozen disbelief as the old woman swished her own spit within the bowl.

Stone and wooden bracelets clattered together as she scowled with one good eye at the swirling contents while releasing a low pitched, "Hmmm."

Owanna had of course seen the shamaness about the village but the two had never spoken before. Everyone knew of Mulungwa through her various roles: village healer, fortune teller, mediator, and counselor. She even delivered most of the newborns, including Owanna and all her siblings. But most of the younger villagers never spoke directly with the woman, sometimes out of respect but mostly out of fear. The village children spoke of her many tales and legends in secret, darting off to safety once they heard the shamaness's laugh tumble down the village pathways. Though she somehow never followed the echo of her laughter.

Mulungwa snapped some dried sticks in half and threw them into the mix. She added a dollop of a crimson-colored glob as thick as tree wax, then sprinkled in a pinch of tangerine-colored powder.

"Eeeee..." she hummed with interest as a sole finger first mixed then sorted the contents. "Agh-ha... haha!" she groaned out, proudly presenting the bowl to Gracien as if proving a point.

As she twirled towards Gracien, her robust mound of hair lacked any fluidity, miraculously staying in place. She wore a garb of yellowed animal skin with dark brown spots speckled throughout. It hung and pitched from a soiled weaving strung about her neck alongside a heavy bone necklace. The husk covered just the top of her breasts allowing them to swing about, grazing the top of an animal fur encircling her waist. As Gracien examined her, the captivating designs and patterns of the older woman's tattoos drew him into a sense of security. Gracien felt like he had known this woman all his life, that she was someone he could trust. Mulungwa stood a full foot shorter than Owanna, yet her presence was nearly double.

"Aghh ysss, ysss," Mulungwa's gruff voice confirmed as she worked.

Hands that looked two decades younger than the rest of her body flashed about as they prepared the concoction. She smashed ingredients, adding a muddy looking liquid, then strained the entire mix through an interlaced weaving of leaves. Bowls clattered off to the side after serving their purpose.

"Nearly, nearly," she whispered into the belly of the brew.

Gracien, wide-eyed and mouth agape, ogled the old woman as she danced around the hut with her deteriorating feet. The shamaness turned, encouraging Gracien towards the brew with a toothless smile. Her left eye was pearled over with blindness and the other bore a striking shade of indigo. Gracien stepped back as the woman approached, knocking into the table and causing it to groan out in dispute.

Both of Mulungwa's hands offered up the bowl "Take," she nodded, curling her lips and smiling again. But Gracien still hesitated, clearly frustrating the shamaness.

"Owanna," she said abruptly. "Take," she repeated.

Gracien felt safe, assured.

"Here… gumbi gumbi, herbs… Help swelling, honey, honey too, good for tongue…" She dipped her finger in the gooey mixture then sucked off the paste, her face flashing a soured expression. "Strong, strong." She smelled the contents with a deep, embellished inhalation. "Taste like young flower." She attempted another smile as Gracien's stomach groaned out in hunger.

His hand extended, taking the bowl from the woman. "Thank you," Gracien whispered as he hoisted it up to his nose. "Jasmine?" he inquired.

"Good," Mulungwa pointed to her own nose, tapping a few times before gesturing for Gracien to eat.

The shamaness then paused as if absorbed by a memory, her gaze gliding from Gracien to the roof. Her attention held there for several moments before she began peering around the hut, rotating her head and body as she searched for a hidden sound.

Mulungwa's gaze then returned to Gracien, staring not at the girl but through her. "Curious... curious," she whispered before waddling towards her. "Spirit... with us." Her gaze drove through Gracien, whose own gaze peered up to the ceiling then back towards Mulungwa.

"Aghhh..." Mulungwa took two steps back, closing her eyes and furrowing her brow with focused concentration.

She inhaled deeply as one hand covered her heart, the other facing outwards as if commanding Gracien to be still. "Strong, strong... singing," her voice, inflected with a deep and distant tone. "Smiling... big smiling." Mulungwa's own smile lessened with the gravity of the moment growing stronger. "Love, strong-strong love." Then she was silent for nearly a whole minute before speaking again. "Sick, bad sick." Her smile fully retreated as her good eye teared over. "Lost... bad sick... dying." She melted, looking to Gracien with crumbling sympathy.

Both of their eyes welled over as Mulungwa moved closer, her hands extending towards the girl as if she was pleading for mercy. Gracien's throat swelled as an anxious, itchy sensation rippled over him. Dropping the bowl to the ground, his hands shot up, cupping his mouth. He wanted to scream, to run from the hut but he was frozen with horror and grief. It felt like his spirit was fleeing his body and he began to fall, but Mulungwa stepped in, catching him within a loving embrace.

Gracien's legs buckled under a tidal wave of grief and the pair fell to their knees. Mulungwa's presence felt so much larger than what her petite frame portrayed. Her arms were like that of a goddess; strong as tree trunks, her hands radiated warmth and compassion. Within the cocoon of security, Gracien's heart melted under the agony of not only Aya's death, but of his own as well. Like a siren's song, his eerie cries wailed beyond the hut. Mulungwa squeezed tighter, wringing the pain from the poor woman, like soiled water from a rag.

His calls of grief beckoned others, darkening the doorway with the arrival of Owanna's parents. The two larger and older versions of Jiemba and Owanna hesitated for only an instant, briefly looking to one another, before wordlessly darting towards their daughter and Mulungwa. They enveloped the weeping pair within a joint embrace. No questions were asked as they melted into a pile of lamentation. Their hearts, their empathy, and their love merged with Gracien like ice melting into water. They had no reason to join in such sorrow, yet deep down within, they knew an unspoken truth: what they didn't know and what they couldn't know, was reason enough to love her. Their purpose was to grieve the unknown, to share in the sorrow of something unimaginable and incomprehensible, and to mourn this something with their beloved daughter. Gracien began to exhale as he felt this immense wave of love wash over him, embracing the love of *his* family.

More shadows clogged the entrance as Jiemba and five other siblings arrived. Their expressions of confusion morphed into ones of worry, then anguish. A cry only a child could make rang out from the youngest as Jiemba cradled his brother, and with it the children poured through the doorway, falling onto the sobbing heap. The huddled mass released a chorus of grief which rang throughout the village. The alarm caused other villagers to creep towards Mulungwa's hut with caution only preserved for a hunt. The anguish pouring from the shelter beckoned grace and sympathy from the entire village. Gracien could feel the presence and love of his family and community surrounding him as he slowly slipped away to a distant dream.

Gracien felt his feet walking, but realized he was not putting effort into his steps. His body lacked the usual bounce of his gait, gliding rather than strolling as he advanced. His head tilted to the side while examining his hand, the fingers of which were being tugged by another. The hand held within his was somewhat transparent, like a winter's fog concentrated within form. Gracien scanned upwards seeing his hazy love before him. He watched as the sleeve of her equally translucent gown flowed about her wrist. Wavy, strands of ink black hair hypnotized him, flowing within her wake like seaweed being pulled by a river's current. His chest ebbed with breath, yet he neither inhaled nor exhaled. Gracien smiled, and within his mind a sentence formed, but not of his own accord.

Hello, my love, Aya's voice reverberated in his mind.

And with the arrival of this extrinsic thought, Aya peered back at Gracien, unveiling a smile as he moved to speak.

Only he was interrupted with another thought; *just think, there's no need to speak here.*

That was your voice… in my head? And now… it's my own? Gracien asked with a look of uncertainty.

Aya's laugh echoed within him, sending shivers down his spine just before his own internal laugh rang out. Her eyes glowed with an unearthly power, simultaneously beaming with pride and sympathy. She continued pulling him, turning her entire form around, floating backwards with both hands embracing his.

This is incredible. Where are we Aya? Are we going to the gardens?

The palace gardens are a different time... and we're going nowhere because we're already here.

Gracien examined his surroundings to find them roaming about a different garden than that of the palace. It was fascinating and dreamlike, yet oddly familiar. *I know this place,* he thought.

Yes... Yes you do, Aya responded.

The earth appeared as if it had been frozen over by a gentle winter, yet it pulsed with the fluidity of an underwater garden. Plants stood still when Gracien looked directly at them but began oscillating as his attention scanned elsewhere. The size and presence of the shimmering garden seemed to continuously grow, evolving before him but without enlarging or expanding. Flowers of all sorts blossomed as seedlings bloomed, growing outwards but at the same time remaining within the same space. Great pines swayed, rotating in all directions without movement. The landscape unfolded, extending itself without expanding beyond its current perimeter, which simultaneously seemed very close and impossibly far. Various sized orbs of light fluttered about like falling snowflakes. As the orbs drifted near the plant life, they revealed a geometric, emerald-colored pattern on their surface, which seemed to scintillate from an internal life-force. The orbs emitted a melodic noise, drifting by Gracien and bestowing a soothing vibration. The hum wavered at times, like the orbs were communicating not only with one another, but with the garden as a whole.

Incredible. We love it here, don't we? he thought.

Yes. Yes we do, Aya's voice followed as she continued to lead him forward.

But why did you bring me here? he inquired as Aya pulled him into her embrace, the two drifting about like slow-dancing apparitions.

So that you remember... Aya's voice dimmed.

Remember what?

Her voice softened. *Love is not bound by time... or by anything at all.* Her words echoed inside of him, drifting through the plants and flowers rather than around them.

As they glided about, the radiant orbs passed around and through the couple. Their vibrating song escalated in pitch as the orbs merged with the two, sending them a surge of radiance and energy like a strong gale inciting the glow of embers.

Of course I remember, Aya. He smiled.

Aya's lips remained unmoved, yet beamed with affection. *You remember this here... but not there,* her voice was fainter now, trickling into the depths of his mind.

There? Gracien inquired, curiosity washing over him as the garden began to radiate with an intensifying, opalescent glow.

Aya's form also intensified as he gazed into her eyes, *Gracien, never forget. Believe. In. Us."* Her voice was now a hushed breeze over a winter landscape as the hum of twilight awoke.

Gracien woke to the chirp of crickets as his eyes popped open with the rush of anxiety one gets when realizing they've overslept. He found himself curled up in a fetal position, still within the safety of Mulungwa's hut.

His mind struggled with defining the details of the dream. "Aya... She was there, wasn't she? She said something... Told me to remember something... What was it she said?" Gracien murmured just above a whisper.

But the dream as well as the message faded into obscurity like ripples melting back into the surface of a pond. A familiar sound pulled him from the mindful investigation, the deep breath of his father's slumber seemed to shake the hut. Gracien peered over the edge of his bedding, finding both Mami and Dadi sound asleep just below. His attention shifted towards a third sound, the creak of a netted hammock swaying on the other side of the hut. Gracien gasped, his heart skipping a beat as he coiled into himself. Illuminated by a sliver of moonlight, the sole, pearled eye of Mulungwa glared back at him.

Gracien's body tensed as he held his startled breath. He leaned in for a closer look as his eyesight adjusted to the darkness. Mulungwa let out a snort as her unblinking eye held fast to Gracien.

"She's asleep." He let out a sigh as relief flushed out the fright.

He hesitated, gazing suspiciously at Mulungwa for a moment more until his attention diverted to his brother, Yarran, stirring in the corner of the hut. An infantile murmur squeaked out as the boy negotiated with a dream. Gracien's eyes narrowed on the jumbled mass of interweaving limbs. His siblings slept together like a pack of cubs, their subtle exhalations puffing out from various parts of the pile.

Tears welled up as he realized his entire family slept, uncomfortably so, *just to be here in case I needed them.* He exhaled with the realization, his brow furrowing with affection.

Gracien couldn't prevent the tears from dripping down his cheeks. His throat dried, swelling with the deep appreciation and love for his family, and theirs for him. He sobbed, wiping away tears and swallowing emotions as he considered climbing down and joining the slumbering mass. His inspiring moment was short lived, because in the very next, something within him spoiled like half-eaten fruit baking in the sun.

The emotion quickly matured, overwhelming him with a weight of guilt and resentment he had never before experienced. Banishing the gratitude he had embodied a moment ago, the gravity of this force dragged Gracien into itself.

His sorrow morphed into anger, into scornful contempt. *I can't allow my grief and suffering to consume them. Their grief, could never, ever compare to my own...* His mind trailed off as he pulled his knees into his chest, hugging and rocking his tiny form as the greed of his grief possessed him.

"I know they love me... but they can't know my pain. They can't understand it, and they'll never truly know the depth of it," his tone heightened, his heart rate rose. "Because I won't and can't share that with anyone, for their own sake," he whispered to himself, becoming protective of his grief like a thief sorting through the day's spoils.

His mind began justifying what he knew was to come. *It's an infestation... a disease, a sickness which like any other, can and will spread. And I can't allow my anguish to infect them.*

His teeth gritted and with the surge of pressure, a tremendous stabbing pain erupted from his wound, spilling out into the rest of his head.

"Aghhh...." His jaw clenched, and his hands pressed in over his ears like some awful creature was screeching from within.

He held his breath, holding out for the pain to pass. Several moments later it did. His breath and pulse steadied as the pain simmered, tension seeping from him as he surveyed the room. No one noticed or moved an inch, they all basked in the moonlight seeping through the cracks in the walls. He realized he must have held every ounce of torment within. He couldn't make that mistake again.

Gracien felt the onset of a familiar foe, panic, stir within him like a rousing dragon. Birthed from the budding emotional darkness, a slow and steady self-mutiny mounted as he considered his future. Gasping for breath he shoved the dark presence from his lungs while his skin rebelled with irritation. Like a prisoner clawing at the walls of his confinement, Gracien's spirit scratched at his inner shell for liberation. The veins in his neck spasmed, sending a wave of pain into the back of his head. The pain temporarily muted the panic but this time he groaned out before quickly covering his mouth with both hands.

I can't do this. I can't be this in front of them. Go Owanna, go away and flee from them… for them, his mind cried the anguished words his lips couldn't.

His heartache doubled as he gazed at Dadi, Mami, then his siblings. He didn't want to leave but knew he couldn't stay. The immense love he felt for his family astounded him. Love that was rooted in years of community and memories that continued to pour into him.

I can't let them watch me die. This striking truth, which had been neglected up until now, erupted like a volcano.

The searing thought bore through him like a blaring funeral gong, filling him with ominous shivers and horrific delusions.

"Aghh!" he gasped as Mulungwa's hands tightened around his bony shoulders.

"Breathe my child," her words were the spell of an alchemist, blanketing Gracien in a cloak of instant relief.

Mulungwa's soft hand swept down Gracien's arm and to his wrist, pulling the young woman from the bed. "Shhh… step, step." A sole finger hovered in front of Mulungwa's lips as her head gestured towards the others, cautioning Gracien's step.

Gracien slunk from the bed, a ripple of pain and a spell of vertigo engulfing him. Mulungwa steadied him, squeezing her hands while pressing up against his body for support. The witch whispered something inaudible and with it another wave of relief washed over him.

"Breathe. Breathe. Breathe again. Now step, step," Mulungwa instructed and Gracien obliged as the woman quietly guided the girl past her family.

Gracien swallowed heartache as he examined his tribe. The image of them all huddled up in such a peaceful state seared itself into his soul.

The pair passed through the hut's blanketed doorway, the welcoming chill of twilight cooling Gracien's skin and sobering his spirit.

"Breathe deep, like ocean." Mulungwa's face exemplified her advice as she exhaled air from pursed lips like she was guiding an expectant mother.

Unchecked by the sleeping pack, her tone was confident yet soft as her hands rubbed circles into Gracien's shoulders. The shamaness's divided gaze glowed under the moonlight, drilling through Gracien's chest as it continued to settle his abating panic. Mulungwa's stare shifted towards the moon's brilliance, her smile extending as both eyes closed like one taking in a gentle, spring shower. Gracien looked up, discovering a blushing moon just as his face cringed with torment. The sudden movement had sent a fury of pain through his head, his hands shooting to the source and patting his bandages. Mulungwa's hands tightened around Gracien's shoulders as her silent lips quivered a spell. An instant later her sluggish eyelids popped open with urgency.

She brought Gracien's hands up to her own chest and pressed down on them. "Love... love." The instant her words escaped, the winds howled through the village.

The unannounced force seemed to shake the entire area, rattling the trees and straw roofs with such strength that Gracien tore his hands away, looking over his shoulder as dogs howled in the distance. Mulungwa grasped Gracien's hands back into her chest, pulling the young woman's focus into her unsuited gaze.

"Not alone," her voice deepened, and her head nodded as if Gracien should understand.

"What do you mean, not alone?" Gracien begged, shivers tingling up his spine and over his skin.

The witch inhaled, closing her eyes as her head dipped back while she paused for an extended breath. "Message, message." She inhaled and exhaled several times. Gracien searched Mulungwa's face for answers before the shamaness whispered, "believe... in... us."

Gracien shook his head in denial as he tried pulling his hands away. "No... you couldn't, it can't be... How could you know?" He tugged violently, ripping his hands away before noticing they were covered in blood.

Mulungwa looked to her own hands, bringing them up into the moonlight and smelling the blood. She reached for Gracien's hands, quickly examining them before spinning him around and checking the wound. A crimson stream oozed from the leafy bandage and ran down his neck.

She spun Gracien around again, gesturing for him to wait with pacifying hands. "Mend-mend, mend-mend," she rattled off before fleeing towards the hut.

As if braced by an apparition she paused three paces away, turning back towards Gracien and closing the distance with her gaze.

"Not. Alone." The sweetness of her words rippled over the moment as she looked up to the heavens, exchanging a grateful nod.

Mulungwa inhaled deeply before bounding back into the hut like the last of a disappearing flame. The shamaness's departure chilled him to the bones, but Gracien's head and face were suffocated with a feverish heat. The pain muted for the moment as he mouthed out those impossible words. "Believe in us." He continued to repeat the powerful phrase, though the sentiment lost fervor with each echoing wave.

A palpable force of exhaustion washed over him as bloodied fingertips prodded the faulty bandage. Wincing with pain, he pulled a leaf free from its bond. "Aghh," his vision tunneled as he heaved an empty gag from both the pain and the smell of the repulsive ointment.

He turned to the hut, stumbling forward a few paces before stopping himself as commotion swelled within like an angry beehive. "I can't...

not again, no…" He stepped back, looking to the hut, then to his bloodied palms, back to the hut, and finally to the wall of brush bordering the village.

The darkness beyond it beckoned as he muttered, "they won't understand, they can't… I can't." He stumbled, falling to the ground as the temptation for escape shrieked like a banshee.

An instant later his bloodied hands slapped branches from his path as his feet stumbled, recovered, then stumbled again while Gracien somehow charged blindly through the brush. The canopy above masked the sparse light of a crescent moon, leaving him in the shadows. His chest throbbed with heartache, his lungs burned for relief, and his head wound screamed for air. But this wasn't the worst of it. His fear was utterly crippling. Gracien felt as if he was somehow running from the fear more than anything else. It didn't make any sense and he longed for help, but not from those left in his wake. There was only one person he desired.

"Why! Whyyy… did you leave me, Aya!" he screamed, pouring anguish out into the night as he barreled through the dense brush. "Come back to me Aya… please! I beg you, come back. Agh-ha-ha… Take me with you!" he cried through gasping pants for air.

Protesting the physical strain, his body begged for pause. Gracien's steps slowed as his body began shutting down. His feet tripped over one another, causing him to collapse into the trunk of a massive eucalyptus tree. Leaning against the base with a heaving breath, Gracien slumped down into a soft body of moss ascending from the base of the trunk. The organic bedding cushioned him as the severe pain from his wound rebounded, mounting another attack, and crippling any attempt at flight.

His fingertips stabbed into his temples. "Aghhh…." he moaned as they slid over the bandages.

They pressed and prodded the mass which oozed dark, thickened blood at an alarming rate, dribbling all the way down his back and onto the moss. "I don't care anymore… Let it bleed out…" he moaned, pressing his face into the moss's spongy coolness as his weakened fist battered the tree trunk. "COME BACK! Take me with you Aya! Pa-Lease my love!" he begged as his vision blurred with the mounting misery.

Gracien's hands, neck, and back were covered in blood, while the rest of his body was soaked in sweat and lapsing into a convulsing chill.

The distant village ignited as muffled voices and blazing torches danced like fireflies.

"Oh-On-Ughhh!" Shouts for Owanna vaulted through the impenetrable thicket like rumbles of thunder. "Ow! Wan! Aaaa!" A choir commanded as the calls grew nearer.

His mind raged like two opposing armies. One side screamed *call out to them you fool, let your family love you! You'll die out here!* The other countered, *run. Run, dammit run! Save them from yourself!* Gracien's eyes went wide like a crazed beast.

He clawed at the tree trunk, pulling himself to his feet with a sudden surge of adrenaline and launching into a full out sprint. An instant later his vision tunneled and blurred, the pain from his wound swarming through his entire body now.

"You must escape! Run!" he screamed, his hands ripping through the brush like he was fighting off wasps.

The further he ran, the darker it got. Like a doe eluding a stalking death, he bound from one pocket of treachery to the next, branches scraping and stabbing his body in defiance. Distance consumed his family's cries as Gracien's gasping breath muffled everything but his frantic footfalls. Bloodied hands pushed, pressed, and braced his agile frame through the labyrinth as his lungs and muscles screamed for pause, but his relentless will whipped him onwards.

WHACK! His head slammed into a toppled tree trunk.

Gracien's body hit the forest floor so hard it sounded like he had been dropped from twenty feet above. The combined blows stole any chance of breath as his body bowed with agony. His shallow gasps echoed through the night like baneful spirits.

Gracien's being ached for air as blood openly poured from not only the initial head wound but a second as well. A python of fate squeezed him into nothingness as realization cemented.

I'm going to die.

The thought was a shriek of terror, veiling any chance of hope like an instant twilight. Never had his soul known a fear such as this. No thought, no sensation, just complete horror as his vision darkened into an eternal void.

"Guhhh!" a surge of gasping breath washed into his breast. "Aghhh-ha-ha-aghh!"

His piercing scream rang out, costing him the very last speckle of life. Gracien heaved one final breath inwards, an immediate exhalation hissing out. A light flickered within his internal, fleeting darkness as the words, "believe in us," sang out, gleaming like a lone, distant star. The terror of death retreated into the shadows as a pearl white figure materialized, taking Gracien by the hand as Owanna's eyes closed.

THREE

Heavy with the weight of slumber, his eyelids fluttered open like the wings of a butterfly. Olive colored fingers fanned the gaps of reality gracing his line of sight. His hand seemed distorted and blurry, like he was looking at it underwater. As it spun, his fingers fanned and twirled before suddenly dropping down to the earth beside him. A barren patch of dirt, dewy and cold from the night, caught the dead weight as it searched for life. Aya's missing warmth doubled the morning chill and Gracien's heart panged with ache as he remembered, Aya is dead. His heart sank once more upon the realization of the loss of his family. Mami, Dadi, Jiemba and the little ones; all were gone, lost in another life as he woke up in who knows when. But there wasn't any time to stew in grief as he was accosted by the racket of a rousing street market. Compared to the serene, beachfront awakening from his previous life, this was a blaring symphony of commotion.

Gracien found himself rolling back into a fetal position, his arms cradling his head, fingers yanking at his mane as he moaned out, "aghhh!"

"Shut up girl!" the fruit vendor spat. "Always crying, laying around like worthless dogs and crying! As if it's not bad enough, I'm in the worst spot! No light, rot piled up, good for nothing dogs…" his voice trailed.

The vendor's hands scrambled to prevent a tower of papayas from tumbling over, causing his headscarf to come undone and throwing him into a further fit of frustration.

Gracien peaked from the gap above his elbow. The tension in his arms dissipated as his eyes examined the surrounding scene. His pudgy, well-fed frame uncoiled as the elements of the stirring Memphis market came to life.

The Egyptian marketplace stoked embers of curiosity before berating him with unimaginable confusion. "Howww? No… It can't be." His eyes widened with shock, fingers shooting up to his lips as if to prevent the change in his voice.

"Dalilah, Dalilah," the seventeen-year-old spoke her own name as if testing a ram horn used for slave auctions before retreating into the shadows.

Stockpiled with rotten fruit, stale nuts, and pitted shells, and her lonely corner was still a better comfort than being out in the open. The hideaway reeked of death as a torrent of buzzing flies pelted the mass of rot. Gracien receded, squishing himself back into the mess without concern. His face washed over with trauma and panic, making him look more like a veteran warrior than an orphaned girl.

"Not again… No, no, no, not again please no… Not again. This can't be, this just can't be." Lies berated his unblinking gaze as his hand lifelessly patted the emptiness beside him.

Rags draped over the girl, covering most of everything except where the weathered fabric thinned into holes. His hand ceased patting the ground, moving up and around his shoulders as the other joined in unison. As he held himself tightly, his clenched teeth shone through skin darkened by the filth of living on the streets. Sea-green pupils radiated through a hooded brow which nearly swallowed his eyes when smiling, making them look like two black slits. His embedded dimples winked regardless of expression. His brow was bordered by generous cheeks, rosy and creased from awkward sleep. A tiny mouth with pursed lips sliced just below a narrow, subtle nose – the nostrils of which flared with angst. Filthy, somewhat pudgy fingers pulled at his messy, dark brown hair, soiled, and tangled from weeks without a wash. Lumpy knees tucked themselves into his chest as she began rocking back and forth within the rot.

Aya, why… Ayaaa… whyyy would you leave me, he silently screamed as the buzz of flies swirled.

"You, there! You! What have I told you? Every goddamn day I tell them!" He looked around to the other merchants, pointing to Gracien, then to the bazaar and then back to Gracien as coins spilled from one hand to the other. "But they never listen – do you, dog? Hey DOG! Don't ignore me!" he screamed, reaching for a papaya.

It smashed up against the wall behind Gracien, chunks of orange exploding into the stone and chasing away the cloud of flies.

"YOU DOG!" he screamed while walking around the rickety cart with malice stretched across his sun-beaten face. The other vendors grinned, nudging one another with excited anticipation.

"Damn dogs hanging around my stand," his voice growled just above him. "Scaring off all my customers with their crazed dog faces!" He spat to the side, kicking dirt at the girl in a pile on the ground.

Gracien scrambled, trying to get to his feet before slipping in the muck and falling back down. He recovered just as the man's chubby, grime-soaked fingers swiped for his collar. Gracien rolled underneath his claws, causing the older man to lean forward and lose his footing in the slick of rot. His feet whipped upwards as if someone had pulled a rug from under him before slamming back down into the filth.

"Goddammit you, you DOG!" he moaned, clutching his lower back with one hand, and reaching to adjust his headscarf with the other, all the while the other merchants roared in laughter, pointing, and keeling over with delight.

Gracien backpedaled, his eyes blinking life into focus while swatting flies from his face. He looked to the other merchants. The younger ones clutched their stomachs with delight as the veterans shook their grin laden faces. His own grin began to extend for a moment before a sole word rang out from the merchant's mouth like a siren.

"THIEF!" he screamed for all to hear.

"Thief! There! A thief… There! There!" The vendor shouted, pointing with his hand as the other held fast to his ample back flesh.

Some of the other vendors booed, dismissing him with a wave of their hands.

"Thief?" Gracien questioned while walking backwards in a daze.

The vendor continued shouting the word, his finger stabbing the air in the once King's direction.

But I didn't steal anything. His thought died with the sight of a crowd dividing just ahead.

A handful of vendors and the morning's first customers spread like the Red Sea as the city enforcers barreled through it. "Patrolman," he whispered to himself while bumping into strangers as he backpedaled.

"Watch it… Ughhh, you stink like death girl." Gracien looked up to a woman who was holding her nose while swatting away the stench.

"THERE! OVER THERE!" He heard the vendor's familiar scream. "The fat, rancid dog! Just over there!"

Two turban wrapped heads bobbed above the surface of bystanders as the patrolmen headed straight for him.

Run! The thought breathed life into him, sending a pang of anxiety and an explosion of adrenaline through his chest.

Like a startled deer, his muscles tensed for a mere instant before launching him into retreat.

"Stop HERRR!" Their words roared throughout the market as

Gracien tore off, leaving a mass of chaos in his wake.

Everyone's heads spun, watching Gracien as he ricocheted off carts, pushed through patrons, and slapped away virtuous hands as he barreled through. Dalilah's muscle memory kicked in as Gracien continued to soak up his new world, his new life. The homeless dogs went insane with all the action. The shyer ones cowered under carts while the more courageous gave chase, nipping at his heels and barking like lunatics.

"Grab! Her!" Shouts and confusion followed in his wake as he pushed, squirmed, and bounded through a narrowing alley adorned with textiles.

Muffled roars gained momentum as the patrolmen closed in. "That one! That one!" They yelled as their mandarin-colored turbans bounced over the crowd, leaping upwards trying to spot the thief.

"Get off!" Gracien screamed, prying clutching fingers from his arm then skidding around a corner into a thinner stretch of the market.

He sprinted for as long as his lungs could manage before checking his wake.

Gracien sighed with relief just before his eyes went wide. "Oh shit!" He hurdled three children playing dice then crashed into an old man serving tea.

He spun off him. "Sorry!" he yelled back into the uproars before rounding another corner.

There he barreled into a mound of unattended woven baskets, rolling over them and rebounding to his feet before diving behind a silk cart.

His lungs heaved breath as his mind raged with horrors of captured orphans and their cruel punishments. A grand commotion erupted, blowing past like a downhill boulder and billowing the silks.

He held his breath, "...nine, ten, eleven, twelve." He counted as the turbulence faded before ejecting a breath and immediately gulping down a new one.

Gracien poked his head through a gap of soft fabrics hanging from wooden poles above. His panicked eyes scanned for any signs of his pursuers with his hands clenching at the silks like prison bars. He felt the fabric slacken, sliding off the pole from his unaccounted weight before spilling over and showering down on top of him. His head poked through the pile like a sand rat. Blowing hair from his face, he couldn't help but smirk.

After removing a pipe from the corner of his mouth an old, scruffy merchant cleared his throat. "Now would be a good time for you to run." He popped the pipe back into his mouth then blew out a perfect smoke ring.

The old man hadn't moved an inch since Gracien ducked for cover under his silk stand.

"It sounds like they're returning. If you had waited a bit longer before spilling out, they wouldn't be."

Smoke slithered through his rich, raven colored beard as his eyes narrowed on the budding ruckus rolling back down the alley.

Gracien peered along the upside-down alley before thrashing about in the scarves like he was wrestling a baby boar.

He bound to his feet. "Thank you, thank you," he blurted while backpedaling as the merchant nodded with a smirk.

And then he was off.

The thunderous pursuit of patrolmen stormed after him, their footfalls and shouts having doubled. "Stop herrr! Halt! Thief!" Various cries merged with one another as Gracien kept just ahead of the chants.

There! Slide under! he encouraged himself through the blaring, mental panic.

A stubborn donkey stood smack dab in the middle of a mob of people as a small boy tugged at the reins while another pushed from behind.

Shoppers yelled, vendors roared, and the donkey rebelled, launching himself through mini hops of his front legs. All the while a towering mound of tapestries stacked atop his backside began leaning to the side like a tilting oak.

"Whoa! GET! Move IT – Move IT!" A tussle of shouts rang out ahead as, "thief! Grab that rat thief!" Approached from behind.

Gracien sliced between the thickened crowd before dropping to a crouch and then to his knees. A forest of limbs denied him any light as he scurried along the filthy path. He scrambled around the legs of surprised bystanders then right up to those of the stomping donkey. The creature's stressed footfalls fell in dramatic fashion as he, and it was definitely a he, threw a tantrum in the middle of the parade.

"One... twooo..." He inhaled deeply, holding his breath.

"Get back here!" A hand grabbed him by the foot.

"Aghh!" he screamed, his fingers clawing at the ground as the patrolman dragged him backwards.

Gracien panicked, grabbing someone's ankles. The patrolman's grip was iron tight, pulling him along the dirt, but in a flash he rolled over and kicked with his free foot. It smashed into the guard's face, instantly releasing his hold. He scrambled, rolling back to his belly, crawling up to the donkey, and shooting himself under its legs like a frog.

After springing to the other side, Gracien kept to his knees while scurrying through the congestion. The raucous from those around him muffled the patrolmen's shouts. He dragged himself through a mob of legs until the crowd thinned enough for him to jump to his feet. Glancing backwards while pushing through, he coughed up dust and wiped his eyes free of dirt. His footfalls slowed to a casual pace as he rounded a corner, then another, before checking for any more trouble.

I think... I lost 'em. He sighed with relief. With a smirk and nod of his head, Gracien turned down another alley.

As his breath settled, his head rose as the scene before him came to life.

Gracien's feet stumbled down the alley, his dazed glare pouring over an unlimited array of products. An endless lane of merchants outran the extent of his vision. Their shouts, barks, hoots, whistles, calls, songs, and cries beckoned all the perusing customers.

A soliciting parrot squawked, "Nuts 'n seeds! Nuts 'n seeds!" as it plopped down to a lower perch.

Gracien reached out, gently petting the colorful creature as its eyelids fluttered with delight.

"Buying or not?" a throaty voice inquired.

A long-bearded merchant stepped out from a mound of cashews as the parrot launched itself to his shoulder. Gracien shook his head while quickly stepping onwards, continuing his stroll like a tourist exploring far and distant lands. Aromas of tea varied from one cart to the next as veteran merchants sat around upturned baskets and hollowed wine drums. Dice rolled, coins danced, and tempers flared as they argued philosophies over a shared hookah. The women cleaned while the children, the true labor-force behind each sale, advertised goods between impressive tricks and tense negotiations.

"BESTTT pricing! Best work in Memphis. In all of Egypt!" a young boy shouted.

He jumped to one of the cart's poles, careening from it like a sailor. A meager hat dipped to his waist as he bowed, rising, then shooting Gracien a wink. His vest was too small and his pants too big, but the boy's smile gleamed with pride. Gracien retreated into himself like a turtle while the young boy resumed his song and dance.

Gracien carried on, his fingers grazing the fronds of meticulously woven baskets. Free from stains and glistening like fresh bread, they were from a life of luxury that he would never know in this life. As his dirty fingers enjoyed running over the delicate weave, Gracien snickered at the thought of mauling a stack of baskets just ten minutes ago. A lanky merchant wielding an eye patch approached, his broken smile gleaming with ambition. His charming demeanor deflated as his sole eye fell on the dirty orphan pawing over his lovely baskets.

"Ntt Ntt!" His finger wagged.

Gracien's hand withdrew as the merchant fell back to his seat, resuming a verbal tussle with his wife as if they had never been interrupted.

While retreating, Gracien caught a vibrant orange speck from the corner of his eye. His fingertips plucked the piece of papaya from his frizzled hair before flicking it to the ground. He caught a whiff of the sweet smell, the aroma which raised an awareness deep within, reuniting him with a memory long forgotten.

Prince Gracien had found himself perusing a popular bazaar in the Tangeru district. Vendors offered every imaginable good and service while flanking one another without a breadth between. Lines of booths, tables, carts, tents, tubs, and makeshift displays snaked through the multitude of streets like vines racing along the mortar of stoned walls. An array of aromas mingled with one another like festive dancers parading through the streets. Colors graduated as vegetables bled into fruits, which spilled into spices, which overflowed into meats and fish. And like an exploding rainbow, the food burst into a textiles section so vibrant, it stung his eyes. Merchants roared, squeaked, chirped, bellowed, whooped, and begged. All either singing their own praises or boasting those of their goods. The cacophony swirled in and around Gracien like autumn winds. He wasn't shopping for anything in particular, merely relishing the exotic experience as he navigated the jungle of commerce.

His fingertips prodded the multi-colored fruit in search of ripeness, crawling over one mango then another. The generous hood of a dark green cloak sheltered his fame as the sun illuminated the bottom half of a sparse beard. Gracien nodded to the vendor, tossing a sole coin into the teetering scale plate. It banked off the edge, spinning around the border like a top as the old man eyed Gracien with a hint of familiarity. He raised his finger, wagging the short stump as he motioned to speak. Then a strong gust of wind blew through, whipping up dust from the street as vendors slunk into hiding. A moment later they began peeking out like prairie dogs as loose wrappers swooped back down to earth. Three bites into the peeled fruit, Gracien had already disappeared into the masses.

The mango pit thudded into the dirt as the prince kissed leftover juice from his fingertips. Suddenly a boy tripped, clinging to Gracien's leg to break his fall. His playmates paused their chase, mocking him with cupped giggles and pointing fingers. Gracien raised his cloaked hand, his fingers tapping the open air and halting the hidden guard's advance. As if from thin air the trio materialized from three separate pockets of the market. With an obedient nod their muscled frames deflated before falling back into obscurity.

"What's your name, little one?" Gracien lowered to a squat before the boy, his gentle hand patting the tiny shoulder as the boy's fright morphed into amazement.

The child swallowed in response before exploding to his feet. Two quick glances shot over to his pack of friends before returning his attention to the prince.

The boy's finger rose, pointing to Gracien's face. "Pwince Gwayson," he whispered.

Gracien smirked, pushing the accusatory finger down. "That's right, Prince Gray-sea-in," he pronounced, chuckling as the boy's face lit up.

"Ohhh… Prince Grayyy-seee-inn! Is Prince Zerious here too?" the boy shouted, excitedly searching for Gracien's more famous older brother.

Gracien couldn't help but laugh, shaking his head. "Shhh-Shhh-Shhh… Prince Zerious isn't here but he wanted me to give you this." He placed a gold coin, one bearing his brother's face, into the palm of the boy. "Shhh this is our secret, okay?"

The boy's jaw dropped as he nodded profusely while eying the glimmering treasure.

"Now run along – and try using your feet this time." He patted the boy along while rising to his feet.

With his mouth still agape, the boy stumbled backwards. His finger pointing back to Gracien before hesitating and launching back down to his hip like a sheathed dagger. Three other boys encircled him, berating him with questions while poking him back into reality between glances at the cloaked figure. Gracien's smirk extended as he adjusted his hood and turned away from the children, entirely unaware he was about to be overcome with awe.

His hand shot up to peel back his hood, freeing his line of sight from any obstructions. Gracien perfectly played the part of a man witnessing something not meant for earthly eyes. His Adam's apple bobbed as if he were swallowing a stone, for it seemed to him that an angel stood some thirty paces away. Anxious whispers built around the prince as merchants and buyers alike began to recognize him. He was unaware of the commotion he caused, as the most beautiful woman he had ever seen was casually conversing with a seed merchant. She seemed to be negotiating and doing a poor job at it too. The merchant patted his ample belly and gave a chuckle while balancing scales stacked with pumpkin seeds. Frustrated, the woman blew a long, weaved strand of hair from her face before extending a smirk and nod of consent. The coins she dropped into the merchant's hands fell as if time had slowed. He must have told a joke because her free hand pressed on her clavicle as her laugh boomed out, slicing through the market like a sole thunder strike. Gracien's austere nature crumpled, his own laughter building then exploding into the surrounding bustle. He couldn't look away, considering a mere blink too much a risk at tempting the gods into snatching her away.

Like startled pigeons joining in flight, bystanders chimed in, their laughter merging with Gracien's. But no one knew what they were laughing at. Taking in their princely sovereign who stood in the middle of the Sunday market roaring with laughter was reason enough. The chorus of laughter grew, fanning out like a contagious wave through the streets. Only the guards held their cool, their veined fists clenching sword hilts as they scanned the area for threats.

The woman's laugh simmered into a smile as her ear perked with curiosity. Her delicate hand moved up to it, repositioning a long, ink black lock of hair as she turned towards the cheerful chorus. The top tier of her pearly white teeth bit down on her bottom lip with the fascination of a child. It took only a moment before the crowd's infectious laughter urged her into a budding giggle. This blossomed, her eyes squinting from her smile as everyone looked to one another with confused merriment. Her full laugh returned, booming like a lion's roar. Gracien redoubled his amusement as her laugh resounded back towards him. A gap emerged between Gracien and this amused beauty. Their eyes met, their gazes merged, and that once in a lifetime feeling swirled within them both. A nudge from God, an inner Source demanding complete presence, for this very moment is one which will forever alter the course of life.

Breath retreated from her chest as she gasped. Gracien settled into the embrace of her gaze, his grin softening into charm, into wholeness. Her head dropped with shyness as his smile returned. Her chin raised back up as if lifted by his hand. Those eyelashes of hers dipped like palm fronds, the gesture tugging at his feet. Gracien's foot scraped forward across the dirt path, his body leaning with confidence. Then somebody grabbed him by the arm.

"Your Excellency, what, what an honor it is…" the man mumbled.

Another hand grabbed Gracien by the shoulder, spare arms wrapped around his waist, hands tugged at his sleeves, and children pulled at his fingers.

"Your Majesty!" echoed throughout the market in a chorus of rejoice. "Please help us!" unsynchronized shouts rang out. "Here Your Grace, over here please!"

His panic swelled as he tried pulling his hands free.

"Our Prince has come to grace us with his presence!" The screams built quicker than the infectious laughter from moments ago.

In the confusion, Gracien lost sight of the woman and the fear of losing her cemented. He screamed, "BACK! GET BACK!" His roar thundered through the frantic masses, subduing the hysteria as everyone froze.

Gracien's guards tore people from the huddled mass surrounding the prince as they too shouted commands. Gracien peered through holes in the crowd, stretching his neck, standing on his toes, and fighting his way forward as if wading through mud. Like ducklings fastened to their mother, the crowd surged with his efforts.

"Get BACK!" the guards roared, instilling panic into the crowd while tossing them aside like children.

Gracien continued swimming forward, wrenching fingers and hands from his arms and shoulders. "Please don't leave us Prince Gracien!" people begged, pulling at him and tearing at his cloak.

"STOPPP!" Gracien thundered and everyone, including the guards, froze as if time itself had stopped.

"Please, listen to me! I'm looking for a girl! A girl that stood just there." His finger pointed across the mass, and everyone turned to look at the fat merchant wearing an expression of utter shock.

The merchant's lips began to tremble as a sole finger rose, pointing towards himself. "Ma-ma-ma-ME?" he mumbled.

Gracien rolled his eyes, shaking his head dismissively as the crowd looked back to him with confusion.

"No, not you. I said a girl. A beautiful girl. With long, kind of messy looking hair... but beautiful hair! Very beautiful!" He backpedaled with his hands waving about, pleading with the audience.

The people standing next to him backed up, giving him room to breathe.

Gracien inhaled, scanning the area for this hidden beauty as he resumed moving forward. "Her hair was, umm large, and big... with a scarf, a green scarf covering part of her head. And she had teeth, white ones," he explained in broken sentences as he craned his neck while standing on the tips of his toes.

He used the shoulders of a bystander to steady his teetering weight. "Her laugh, did you not hear her laugh, it was... well... the loudest laugh I've ever heard. And it was kind of, obnoxious... but in a good way." He shook his head while pushing off strangers and scouring over the sea of people.

The silence faded as people began mumbling to one another. "No wonder Zerious is the favorite." One merchant nudged another.

"The girl, the girl just over there! The one with the seeds." He pointed back towards the fat vendor who gestured to his assortment of seeds with a smile.

The crowd's expression crinkled into consideration as they imagined exactly what this woman with black hair, a loud laugh, and seeds would look like. But just then Gracien's hand felt the warmth of another. He turned towards the sensation as his gaze slowly scanned up her hand, then her arm, snaking along her breast, up her neck, pausing at her mouth, and finally falling into her eyes. In a heartbeat, those rich, golden eyes owned him. Their gazes merged, his fingers wrapped around hers and he pulled himself towards her. The crowd backed up, their smiles extending with the gravity of the moment.

"I feared I'd lost you." Both his hands embraced hers, pulling them into his chest as he stepped closer.

She remained silent, a serene smile extending before her gaze broke from his. The woman scanned all the attending eyes, her head dropping with the unwanted attention. Gracien's knuckle caught it, pulling her head up and meeting her eyes.

"Your name, please, tell me your name." Again she had glanced towards the peering eyes of everyone watching with anticipation before returning her attention to Gracien.

She had held his gaze with confidence, with a warmth unlike anything he had ever encountered before quietly revealing her name. "Aya-donna." she spoke with the grace of a princess.

"Watch out!" a man shouted after nearly barreling the young girl over.

Gracien recovered from his trance, blinking the Egyptian market into focus, and pulling over to escape the mass of traffic.

The weight of grief closed in, but he knew this was no place to melt-down. "No... Keep it together. Not here, not now," he encouraged, keeping his demons at bay while pulling himself together.

Gracien cleared his throat, shook his head, rolled his shoulders back, and took a deep breath. Yet Aya's gaze lingered. His stomach rumbled out loud as the aroma of street food rolled through.

"The others... they must be hungry." Suddenly, he remembered the orphans were waiting for him.

Catching the scent of food, Gracien's head turned like a dog. "Jas-mine rice... and lamb," he moaned as his nose sniffed the air.

He scanned the street hosting an endless assortment of food carts, all of which billowed pillars of smoke. Mounds of yellowed rice glowed with an almost unnatural appeal as steam surged from the summit. Spits hoisting huge legs of lamb, whole chickens, chunks of beef, and strips of goat meat dripped grease into celebratory flames while hovering over glowing coals. Tables were completely overrun with food: piles of seeds, grains of every color, heaps of nuts, mounds of glistening olives, and infant pink beans blending into elderly grayed beans. Thick stalked vegetables with itsy bitsy leaves and thin stalked ones with leaves bigger than her head. They had bread for days: twisted bread, rolled bread, crushed bread, fluffy bread, hollow bread, disc bread, triangle bread stuffed with a different kind of bread! And of course, there was bread for the most meager of budgets, yesterday's bread. The smell was a hungry girl's dream.

Gracien's pace quickened, trotting through the alley as he looked three carts ahead, scanning from one to the next. *He'll do just fine,* his gaze narrowed on a newer cart as he rounded the corner, checking his sides and wake for any attentive glares. *The good thing about being an orphan is that most people don't notice you until something's already missing,* he snickered.

The smell of freshly baked bread seduced the stomachs of every passerby. The sumptuous loafs basked in the open air, stacked on top of one another and showcased like artwork on a large table extending from the bakery's wide doorway. A skinny merchant man was collecting coins and doling out the bread.

Must be a brother-in-law or something because I never knew a skinny baker. Gracien chuckled as the man picked at his thumbs.

He walked past his mark, glancing at the skinny merchant from the corner of his eye. Gracien scanned the alley for what he would need before popping over to a mound of garbage. His soiled hands picked through the mass for several moments before nabbing a tiny pile of partially rotten blueberries. He walked back towards the bakery, stopping just short of the corner. He peeked around the stone, shooting a rapid glance towards the oblivious merchant. The man stood slightly beyond the reach of an awning that protruded off the wall. Gracien's grimy fingertips launched a berry from the corner of the stand to the top of the weathered textile that formed the canopy.

"Two... three... four..." he counted as he tossed another blueberry, repeating this process several times before pausing.

Some of the berries splattered on the awning. Others bounced then rolled down the arched fabric, dropping through a tear and bopping off the merchant's head, causing him to look up and inspect the skies for rain.

"What the..." He rubbed his head.

One hand covered Gracien's gleaming smile, holding in the giggle as the baffled man looked around. He investigated the awning, then the ground, then the awning again before leaning over and picking up the rotten berry.

He rolled the paste between his thumb and forefinger. "Hmmm... blueberry?" He gave a sniff.

Three consecutive berries fell on his head, startling the oaf into a sunken crouch. Just then Gracien's hand swept in, swiping three loaves from the table, and placing them under his shirt. Moments later he was skipping down the alley looking like an expectant mother. Gracien rounded a corner and stopped, picking up a half-buried scarf that lay in the dirt.

He swat it against his leg several times. "This will do." He gave it one final smack before dumping the bread in the middle and tying a knot.

He flung the makeshift satchel over his shoulder, gave one final peek back down the alley then headed for the camp flaunting a satisfied grin.

Gracien tossed his bounty of bread over an old, wooden gate then climbed up the stone wall, plopping down to his feet on the other side with feline grace. The gate moaned as it settled back into place. He placed a hand on it, stilling it to silence while listening for anything abnormal.

His arms snaked through the next obstacle. "This damn hole, it's getting smaller," he cursed while squeezing through the secret entrance.

His chest rose and he sucked in his stomach while pulling his body through the small crevice. Once through, his hand slinked back, snatching the scarf full of bread.

Gracien's foot began moving forward before pausing. His mind shifted to Aya, to the surreal nature of the moment, to the insanity of his existence. "What's happening... How did... how did I get here? Why am I all alone?" His lips quivered.

"Why? How? I don't understand. I wake up one day and somehow recall another life, my past lives?" he questioned.

"This is madness, why... why me? How can I be here, in this body, living this life then have this... this awakening... Then deal with not only everything here, but grieve everything from before as well?"

He knew deep within himself that the same soul which lived as Gracien was within Dalilah now, within this life. He knew that somehow, on some random day, he woke up being able to recall his past lives like a candle igniting itself. It had been the same with Owanna, and this was now the second time it had happened. All these lives had just blended together, merging all memories, emotions, strengths and weaknesses. On the surface, he had a life up until this point living as Dalilah, with all her complexities, character, and intimate life experience, yet the current of her spirit was Gracien. His soul had incarnated into this new life but he was able to remember all his past lives. Whether or not this was a curse or a gift remained to be seen. Right now, it felt far from the latter as tears streamed down his generous cheeks.

His hands tore at his heart. He felt the familiar itch of anxiety rise up his chest and neck as his breath shallowed further. As he gulped down air, an existential pressure entombed him like he was being crushed by a stone.

A barrage of questions poured from his trembling lips. "It doesn't make any sense, how am I the only one to remember my past lives? Who or what is my soul? Can I tell anyone? Will there be someone who can help me? Help me with what? When will this end… How will this end? Why can't I just die? Why can't I be dead like my sweet Aya and leave… this?" He gestured wildly.

With the final question, a hammer of grief smashed down upon him. He backpedaled as a new force appeared with it: guilt. He had completely forgotten about Aya's death over the morning's events. Any distraction veiling the gravity of Aya and his death was an insult to both. Gracien couldn't believe himself. How dare he complain about having a life to live, or lives to live, while Ayadonna's was stolen from her. He had his entire life ahead of him and she was cheated from living hers. How dare he complain, how dare he wallow in despair because he had to live life while Aya suffered death.

Moments ago, he was laughing and smirking, enjoying his clever antics in the bazaar as if he wasn't navigating this cataclysmic existence. He may as well have been spitting on Aya's grave. Gracien leaned back, the chill of the stone wall trickling down his back.

His guilt frothed and bubbled like a witch's brew. "I'm sorry… I'm so sorry for forgetting," he pleaded, looking up to the Heavens while gesturing with raised palms to anyone who may have been listening.

After several moments bathing in confusion, guilt, tears, and apologies he felt as if a temporary penance had been paid.

"Okay now pull yourself together Dalilah. Keep it together, for them. Don't let them see you like this." His silent whisper matured as it pulled confidence from his past.

He remembered having to maintain strength, courage, and hope for Aya as they battled her illness. Gracien's lips extended, blowing out the heavy breath and doing his best to purge the budding panic.

"Stand up, shake it off... Center yourself, Dalilah. Center." His spirit heeded the spoken commands. "For them, breathe in and be strong. For them."

He took in a massive breath, holding it for a moment as his head nodded with silent approval. He pushed off the wall and stood with an ejected huff before approaching the entrance.

A murmured conversation wavered with the intensity of an argument as it rebounded towards the entrance. Gracien stood taller, building himself up to present the inflated identity he thought the children not only needed, but also enjoyed and valued. His exhale escaped like a howling wind. He pulled his shoulders back, picked his chin up, brandished his best practiced smile, and made his entrance.

"Dalilah!" He was greeted with an echo of cheer.

An authentic smile replaced the practiced one as Gracien enjoyed the sound of his name being sung every time he returned. Their welcome was a rare and loving embrace, and one he allowed himself to enjoy. At only four years old, the youngest of the bunch, Amira, ran up and collided with Dalilah's legs then squeezed with all her might. Amira's modest grip latched around the back of Dalilah's knees as her tiny face squished with blushing delight. Her sparse nose and perky mouth were centered within her round face, bordered by two rosy, overbearing cheeks. Amira's large, beautiful eyes warmed the coldest of hearts with a mere glance. They always maintained a wide, teary-eyed appeal that shone with the zest of gold. Neck length, bark-colored curls bounced several moments after she ceased moving and her high-pitched giggle delighted everyone into a fit of laughter.

"Missed you!" she squealed.

"I missed you too," Dalilah returned.

"What took so long? From the looks of it, seems like you were wrestling street dogs again," Sheena said.

Sheena, the third oldest at fourteen, was a short, meaty girl from a small village much further south. She brandished her pleased half-smirk while brushing dirt from Dalilah's tattered shirt. Rust colored freckles lay sprinkled along her face, with a concentration between her hazel eyes and the bridge of her nose. Sheena walked with the confidence of boys twice as large and let out annoyed huffs while blowing her matted, auburn-colored hair free from her face. Her hand couldn't help but dole out dismissive gestures like some grumpy, old merchant blaming everyone for everything. She was endearing, loyal to a fault, and had a mighty bellow for a laugh. Nobody had more fun laughing at their own jokes than Sheena.

Dalilah shrugged with a shy grin. "Ran into some trouble."

"Whoa you stink worse than normal. What kept you last night?" Kaleef's deep, adolescent voice rumbled behind him as he leaned in over Dalilah like a teetering palm tree.

Kaleef's throat bulged from his neck, with his Adam's apple bobbing like an acorn plopping into the river. Ink black hair as fine as spider's silk swept down around his ears. His large ears curled in towards his temples as if they had been baked in the sun. Kaleef was the most sensitive creature of the bunch, allowing his emotions to run free at the first sign of affection. He theatrically sniffed above Dalilah's head three times before plucking something from it with tentacle-like fingers.

Razor thin nostrils flared as he smelled the pulp between his finger-tips. "Papaya?" He popped the shrapnel into his wide, sharp mouth. Bearing such an array of features gave him a polite, amiable charm and a temperament matured well beyond that of a sixteen-year-old.

Chestnut-colored pupils shone with playfulness as he chewed, giving a satisfied nod then laughing, "huh-huh-huh-huh-huh," like a wood-pecker hammering away.

Dalilah moaned. "Gross... Ugh! You're weird," she spoke while un-wrapping the bread. "Because it got dark too quickly and I was too far... Didn't want to risk trying to make it back with the curfew and all."

"Ohhh!" A chorus of pleasure rang out as the freshly baked bread grew back into its full form as she pulled out the loaves.

The triplets ran over, hauling two kittens and a caterpillar with them. The first kitten flaunted an inky black coat, the sheen of which gleamed like moonlight off the Nile. Its grayed brother was spotted with brown streaks fanning across the tail.

They dropped the cats before crashing into Dalilah. "This is fresh! Wow!" Shuna buried her face into the bread then gradually withdrew while giving a nice, deep sniff.

"Let's show Dalilah our game!" The trio picked the cats back up then placed the caterpillar on top of a pile of stones.

The seven-year-olds were nearly identical with only their hair, gen-der, and a few features telling them apart. Rouna, who bore short, spiky hair, was born first, a fact she constantly shared. Malek's hair was more feminine than that of his sisters, cascading down over his face and behind his ears, even on his filthiest day it had a midnight sheen. Shuna's was curly and robust, like she bore the leftover hair laying at the feet of the schoolchildren after a fresh cut. All three had frail frames, cleft chins, and expressions which made them appear more serious than they really were.

Their smiles were exact replicas, small but packed with charm and misaligned teeth. Matching, wheat-colored pupils, squared off jaws, and protruding cheekbones set the tone for their perfectly symmetrical faces, a prelude to guaranteed beauty in adulthood.

The trio freely spoke their minds, as most children do, but with the triplets it's as if they shared the same mind. "The gray one – he'll pounce first – yeah – jumping and batting – at the caterpillar – before the black cat is able – he's the quickest." This sentence was spoken by all three of them, each speaking more than once as they readied the felines.

"Later, later... My stomach is moaning out like a deaf beggar," Kaleef complained, tossing two pebbles at the kittens, and chuckling as they retreated.

"Heyyy!" Shuna frowned.

"Me too, let's eat." Gracien opened the scarf.

Like feasting wolves devouring a fresh kill, the children tore into the bread. Resembling toppling dominos, they plopped down to the ground right where they stood as their mouths worked over the doughy pleasure. They were all settled around a cozy fire pit, which also served as the hearth, family room, and nap stations. A pile of wood, borrowed from ever-changing sources, lay stacked a few paces from the fire's reach. This makeshift hearth was circled by seven nests composed of blankets, bedding, ragged clothing, and old food sacks. Tattered awnings, unwanted or stolen from unsuspecting merchants, cast down precious shade over each of the dwellings. A small collection of trinkets and collectibles lay hidden in several nooks and crannies throughout their respective nests. Several ceramic basins of water lay off to the side, leaning up against the stonewall of the abandoned building that edged the camp. The latrine was just a deep pit with a wooden board and a very dirty hole cut out in the middle. It was seventy or so paces from camp, just beyond the various makeshift walls enclosing the space. Their home was as charming as an orphan camp could be. Flaunting a quaint herb garden, a collection of cooking ceramics, makeshift furniture, a busted harp, and a few oil lamps hanging about, though good burning oil was difficult to steal. Insects, rodents, and various other critters migrated throughout. Plants grew where they could, and wild dogs sought shelter during the cooler months. The cats liked the critters but didn't take too well to the dogs. All too often there'd be a sudden eruption of hisses, groans, and chaotic scattering and next thing you know, there's a stray pup trotting into the camp like he owns the place. People, however, were rarely privy to the camp. It was tucked away behind a few rows of derelict structures located a good half mile east of the largest migrant settlement in all of Memphis.

Their favorite aspect of the camp was a massive olive tree settled in the corner. Each evening the children were lulled to sleep by the rustling of its leaves. Every morning northern winds blew through, painting the camp with that fresh, earthy aroma. On some days, especially the un-bearably hot ones, they'd lounge in the sturdy limbs or swing about in the makeshift hammocks. The olive tree was not only the cool spot in the camp, but it was also their sanctuary; a place for reflection and peace. As large, old trees often do, it bestowed a paternal and protective influ-ence over the children. They loved it for that. And each year or so, their love was rewarded with a harvest of savory olives.

"Easy, easy… you'll choke. Chew it slowly, try to make it last, you'll feel fuller after, remember?" Gracien advised as the triplets nodded with cheeks stuffed like squirrels.

They all laughed as Amira pushed the bread further into her mouth with a sole finger. "Mmm…" she moaned.

"Yes exactly, good point," Kaleef returned, everyone giggling with stuffed mouthfuls.

"Remember to share. Kaleef needs more as he's bigger," Gracien said before releasing a drawn-out exhalation. "And I need to rest as I'm tired from this morn…" his words trailed off as he lost himself looking into the distance. "Well I'm just tired is all."

Shaking himself back to reality he stood, brushing the dirt from his backside before backpedaling from the group. "I'll see you all later," he whispered through a forced smile. Kaleef responded with a nod and a smirk.

The moment he turned away, the light within him extinguished. Expression poured from his face as if a mask was removed, revealing anguish beneath. The urge to cry, to moan out in exhaustion and to scream with fury boiled over like a hateful geyser. His steps quickened as he dashed over to the darkness of his makeshift bed, crashing onto it like a corpse.

The dam containing Gracien's suffering broke as he fell into the confines of his bed, burying his face within the dirtied fabric. A deafening scream tore through his insides as well as the fabric, but it was barely a squeak to the outside world. His chest expelled air from his lungs like juice pressed from sugarcane. Panic poured through as he fought for breath, but none would come. His eyes widened, pulling for air as his mouth gasped for refreshment as an unknown heat seared his throat and chest. Taloned fingers clawed at the bedding, suffocating his cries as his body writhed with internal ache. He looked as if he had been scared to death, his face holding the frozen expression for what seemed to be an eternity.

Like overdue rains, air finally swept into his chest, extinguishing the ache as his body slackened with the fleeing tension. The purge built momentum as he sobbed through waves of guilt, regret, depression, and denial, all of which were accompanied with a physical ache. He trembled through the cries, his shoulders bouncing with each rapid exhalation as his hands wrung the blankets for relief. "Ayaaa..." his extended moan rang out like a warning horn blasting over an endless desert. The poor soul continued in this fashion until his breath settled into subtle cries and exhaustion overwhelmed him into sleep.

Birdsong tugged at his consciousness and Gracien's eyes flickered open with dusk's approach. His hand lashed over to the side, striking the wall as he sat up with startled confusion.

Aya's gone. The thought echoed within his mind as a rapid, panicked breath returned.

Gracien examined his surroundings as if he had been transported somewhere else in the dead of sleep.

A wave of reality crashed in around him as the grief intensified. "I'm so sick and tired of waking up to this despair. This pain... It's a predator hiding in the woods, a monster waiting to pounce as soon as my eyes open," he spoke out loud as if describing his pain to another.

Arms sore from idleness pressed his sluggish body up from the bedding. Gracien scanned the camp for the others through eyes heavy with sleep and grief. All six of the other children lay close by, buried in their bedding to escape the chill.

I slept through the entire day, again, he noticed while wrapping an extra blanket around his shoulders.

A small bowl of water waited next to his bed. The threading of a smile normally would have extended in discovering the kind gesture from one of his adoptive siblings, but he just stared blankly at it. Gracien had lain dormant for over a day and a half, not always asleep, but dead to the outside world.

"Kaleef," he coughed, the irritation of dryness spilling down his throat. "He must have told them to leave me be." He took the bowl and sipped the water, the wet chill a welcomed relief.

"So much kindness and yet they have next to nothing, less than that even. No home, barely any food, and no family, but still they think of others."

He pressed himself up, his body unbinding like tree limbs after a heavy snowfall. His arms shook off the weight of hibernation as he walked towards the fire pit. The birdsong continued, bringing back memories of mother's morning hum as they both prepared for the day. It was as if he could hear it then and there, as if the birds themselves chirped out the very same tune. Dalilah's memory always painted the same image each morning, ever since the fire.

Her mother had stepped about the modest kitchen with such grace; one hand preparing breakfast as the other had cradled a belly swollen with a child. Dalilah's own giggle rippled through her mind, the joy of a child ignorant to the struggles of life.

Her mother's eyes widened as a fingerful of yogurt delighted her senses. "Ohhh! Yummy!" she mumbled with her beautiful, bold eyes rolling backwards.

Every morning she tried to convince her daughter that whatever she was about to eat was going to be the most delicious thing ever. Dalilah didn't need to be convinced. She loved watching her mother's overly dramatic expressions and so feigned disinterest.

Gracien's happy expression poured from his face as a new memory of thickened smoke and burning lungs ensued. It had been over a year since Dalilah's mother, her future sibling, her home, and life as she knew it had been engulfed by a reckless ember. Gracien shook his head, blinking his reality into focus. The birdsong returned as his hand stirred the fire's embers with a stick. He knelt, fanning the flames with deep exhalations before sitting back and losing himself with the flickering dance of fire.

But as the fire crackled, he only thought of Ayadonna.

He whispered, "I miss you. I don't... I don't know how I've ended up here… It's all so surreal Aya, so confusing… As if I'm living one end-less dream bleeding into another. How did I get here, my love? Why have you left me all alone… In such despair and to fend for myself?" he spoke in a matter-of-fact kind of way, as if negotiating with Aya, while defiantly stabbing the glowing embers with a stick.

"I cannot go back to the life we had. This… this I know. And I don't want to die, to suffer through death… but I don't want to live either. Not like this. I just can't live like this anymore Aya. Every day, from one moment to the next your death swallows me into darkness." He was cry-ing now. "And… and I just don't know what to do anymore. I feel so lost, Aya." Gracien looked at the flames as if Aya was hiding within them. "Please, please guide me… Show me what to do. Please, I beg of you… Help me, my love." His eyes streamed with tears as he pleaded with the fire.

"I want to leave this life. I feel as if I am constantly fighting for breath like something is wrenching at my feet… trying to pull me under the surface and into an awaiting darkness. I want to be free of it, to escape… to be back with you. Please my love, help me to escape all…" with an open hand he gestured to his surroundings, "this." He moved to wipe away tears as the sound of footsteps approached.

Amira's sweet voice rang out, "good marwm-ing, you swept a wong time, so wong time. But, but I tried to wake you, to go wake you up so you woulb not sweep so long," she teetered on her tiptoes while extend-ing her neck and fidgeting with her fingertips, "but Kaleef, he told me 'NO!'" she made a mean face. "He puwled me. He said you are sad. Dawiwah? Are you sad?"

Gracien had been attending his small companion with a slight, mindful smile until Amira uttered her question. Suddenly he found him-self looking through Amira instead of at her.

Amira's small hand shook Gracien's shoulder. "Dawiwah?" Amira questioned.

Gracien's eyes widened, shaking his head, and inhaling deeply as he forced an enormous smile. "Yes... yes, I slept too long. But I'm awake now," his voice was pitched with enthusiasm, as was typical when speaking with Amira. "Wide awake and I think it may be time for *annn...*" Gracien paused, cowering down as his words settled into secrecy.

Amira's eyes widened, crouching her frame next to Gracien's. "Time for what?" She whispered back.

Gracien looked over his shoulder and then the other, before returning his gaze to Amira and whispering, "An adventure."

Amira gleamed her biggest possible smile, her hands cupping her mouth for an instant before shouting, "AN ADBENTURE!"

'Shhh, Shhh, Shhh..." Gracien pulled her down while chuckling. "Not so loud... not so loud... we don't want everyone to know do we? Just you, me, and the others, right?" Amira nodded, her hands curled up under her chin.

"Now go wake them. Tell them about our adventure," Amira darted off to complete her task. "Psst. Amira?" Gracien called after her.

She turned back, trembling with excitement, and tiptoeing back towards Gracien. "Yes?"

"Wake them slowly, no jumping on them, okay?" Gracien's brow rose and Amira returned with a crazed smile, which caused Gracien to fight off a hearty laugh. "Good. Be gentle."

And like that Amira was off, leaving Gracien to consider their next adventure, a distraction he hoped would still his grief.

"*Last* time we *almost* got caught... If it weren't for that herd of goats.

Why would we try again?" Sheena questioned the group, her words dripping out like honey.

"*Last* time we didn't succeed because we *almost* got caught, so that's why," Kaleef returned, matching her sarcastic tone.

"But why take the chance? It's dangerous!" Sheena returned, looking to Gracien.

"*The climb* is not dangerous..." Kaleef rebutted. "Getting caught is dangerous. That's why this time will be different. Last time we went for sunrise, that was our mistake. So, this time we'll go at dusk and watch the sunset! It will be easier, the guards won't be able to see us climb up as the daylight fades. Harder to see us, and um... catch us," the two teenagers argued like newlyweds as the other five hung about the olive tree like napping monkeys.

Kaleef placed his hands on Sheena's shoulders. "I've done this several times now, and it's going to be okay. But we must work together, keep an eye on Amira and on each other. If we do that... then, then we'll be okay. I promise Sheena." Kaleef held her gaze until she acquiesced with a nod.

SMACK! He clapped, startling the entire group. "Okay so here's the plan!"

Everyone giggled with delight, even Gracien, as Kaleef began pacing back and forth like an army general. Their clandestine little abode was unusually silent as the group attended Kaleef's riveting instructions.

"Last time I was stupid. *Thisss* time," he paused, looking to them and wagging a finger, "I'm *less* stupid!"

SMACK! He clapped again, startling everyone once more. "We must set out two hours before dusk. That should give us plenty of time. It will take only ten or so minutes to scale the south wall." Kaleef spoke towards his feet, spinning on his heel then pausing to consider Amira. "Maybe fifteen or twenty. The stones are larger in some parts, and we'll have to lift her," he looked to Gracien who nodded in understanding.

"We must wait until thirty minutes or so before the sun sets, so that the light is as dim as possible. *Anddd* we have to give ourselves enough time to climb. We must-must-must be as quiet as possible, like crawling statues. This…" He wagged his boney finger again. "This is why we won't get caught. Others try this at sunrise. But with all the rising light it's too easy to be noticed. That's why we must be up top and settled as the light is fading with the setting sun."

Shuna whispered in Malek's ear. "What's aiding mean?" Malek asked.

"Fade - ing," Kaleef pronounced.

"Oh, okay," Malek said, still perplexed.

Kaleef resumed, "so as the sunlight…"

"What's fading mean?" Rouna interrupted.

"What? Going down or becoming less, like going away," Kaleef sputtered out.

"I told you," Shuna said with a slap to the back of Malek's head.

"Ow! What was that for?" Malek rubbed his head as Rouna smacked Shuna on the shoulder.

"Owww! What was THAT for?" Shuna returned to Rouna.

"Shushhh! I want to hear da adbenture!" Amira shouted.

"THENNN… Then we'll escape under the cover of darkness!" Kaleef shouted, his hands slamming together as he jumped towards the tree trunk. "Rawr!" he roared.

"Don't do that!" Sheena yelled after being startled.

The triplets laughed and Amira began to tear up.

"See! You're scaring her!" Sheena growled.

Kaleef swept in, pulling Amira down from the tree and tossing her into the air. "Are you ready for an adventure, my little warrior!?" he shouted as Amira's gleeful, tear laden face giggled with delight.

Kaleef caught her one final time then plopped her over his hip like a mother of five. "Are we ready? It's going to be a bit of a trek just getting there so let's get going!" His elongated grin awaited everyone's response.

One by one they looked to one another before nodding in approval and laughing in agreement. They all jumped down and closed in around Kaleef and Amira with a group embrace. Enthused by all the excitement, Gracien delighted in the communal joy until guilt once again pierced him like an arrow. He tried swallowing the dread while attempting to keep it all together, his pulse racing as panic surfaced like boiling lava. He nodded a fabricated smile, turned, and fled for his bed.

The children were huddled up in the empty stall of a stable. A camel's head hung over them from the next stall over, chewing away on grass. The stable was located just outside the pyramid grounds, next to a small strip of merchant carts selling last minute supplies for desert voyages.

"So, we need to keep low. I'll give the signal and once I do… keep close to the ground like you're trying to hug the stone. Most of the guards will be scanning the bazaar exits for thieves or fights. We'll enter on the eastern side, so we'll be hidden under the pyramid's shadow." Excitement poured from Kaleef as he shared the plan.

"The day guards finish their shift at dusk, so they'll be preparing to go home, and the night guards always start their shift sharing tea as the sun sets. So, this is the best time. Here," Kaleef pointed at a square drawn in the dirt with a piece of hay. "This is where we'll wait. We come out here and, on my signal, we'll start the climb. Then it's straight up from there... a silent climb." His smile gleamed with pride.

"One other thing, we can't get caught. They won't climb up the pyramid to capture us, instead they'll wait for us to climb back down. So, if we see torches, we run and meet back at the camp. Got it?" His gaze narrowed at the triplets. They were old enough to understand consequences but still young enough to forget the important stuff.

The gravity of what they were about to do suddenly sank in. Amira began humming a bedtime tune as she drew shapes in the dirt with a stick – seven stick figures holding hands.

Sheena remarked, "I take that as a good sign. If we're together, we'll be okay."

They all nodded, smirking toward one another.

"We'll wait a little longer." He looked up to the sky, shielding his gaze with his hand before returning his attention to the group. "The sun has to come down a bit further still." Kaleef patted Sheena's shoulder. "You're ready, right?"

"Ready for what?" She shot back, making Kaleef puff his chest with annoyance.

"I'm kidding." She winked, picking Amira up, "now this sounds like an adventure, doesn't it?"

Sucking on her thumb, Amira nodded with delight.

Kaleef stood, bumping his head on the camel who moaned out in surprise and then disappeared.

Rubbing his head, he couldn't help but pace around, rethinking any points he may have missed. "Remember, we have to be patient, we have to keep hidden, and we'll use the cover of darkness..." he rambled on.

Gracien's head popped up as his eyes narrowed, not on Kaleef, but the echo of his final three words, *cover of darkness*. The phrase hit him square in the chest, knocking him off the deck of reality and dragging him into the depths of a cold, dark memory.

Gracien's boney hand had scraped along the tunnel's stone walls. They were slick and chilled with moisture from being buried deep below the palace. The walls glowed, then glimmered, then shone with an amber glaze as the torchlight illuminated the narrow, arched ceiling, crumbling walls, and Gracien's gaunt, grief-stricken face. The sound of his heaving breath and heavy footsteps bounced ahead, echoing down into the awaiting darkness. He hadn't traversed the secret passage alone since he was a prince when he would sneak out of the palace to have some fun outside its walls.

A pang of anguish rippled through his heart as he thought of how sweet her excitement had sounded as they trekked through the passage all those years ago. His emaciated throat swallowed the memory of Aya's excited giggle rippling down this very same tunnel the first time he had guided her through it.

"Are you sure about this? It leads somewhere, right?" She had questioned with more than a sliver of worry as he led her by the hand.

"Of course. I came down here as a kid all the time, my brother showed me on my ninth birthday. The bastard told me to close my eyes then sprinted off, taking the torch with him. He left me alone in total darkness until I found my way out. It took forever..." He looked back to Aya, "and I think I pissed myself."

"Awww, wittle Gwaycien... you were probably so cute. You sure nobody will catch us?"

"Yes, adorable... and covered in pee. There's only one way out, it just takes a bit of time, and we're using the cover of darkness... trust me my love." His hand had squeezed hers reassuringly.

"Ohhh... the cover of darkness, eek!" she squealed.

He couldn't help but get lost in memory as his determined gait propelled him down the cold tunnel. The beloved memory faded as the exit neared. He placed the torch into a slot in the stone wall, its flame rebelling as the breeze intensified into a howling gust that ferried a swirl of leaves down the middle of the passage. The sound of dripping water echoed behind him as the chirp of crickets and buzz of twilight came alive just beyond the doorway. Gracien took a deep breath, preparing himself for the impossible challenge awaiting him on the other side. His bony hands pushed through the thick, rigid blanket of vines cascading over the small enclosure and he stepped through.

The instant his eyes fell on the scene, his heart plummeted into the hollows of despair. His knees almost buckled at the sight of the landscape, making everything all too real. "No, no, no, nonononono…" he mumbled, forcing himself to step forward into the eerie embrace of the royal cemetery.

Ayadonna's stark white obelisk seemed invulnerable to the darkness as it glowed in the twilight. It lit up the other burial shrines, their luster dulled from the elements and passing of time.

His footsteps struggled over the mushy ground as he approached. "Whyyyy… not my poor, poor Aya," he sobbed, pulling a charcoal-colored cloak in and around his boney frame.

The air was heavy and as cold as a stone. There was a faint light coming off the glowing, crescent moon. The wind howled, stirring leafless branches into a tremble. He fell to his knees, the chill of dampness soaked through his cloak as his fingers grazed the sharp engraving.

The Beloved – Queen Ayadonna.

A warm cloud of breath poured from his mouth as if it were his last. "Whyyy! Why did you leave me Aya?" Words slurred forth as spittle dripped from his lips like he was a delirious drunk.

His hands clawed at the earth, digging, and ripping roots from the bedding.

"Aggghhh…" he moaned out, sitting up with two fistfuls of slopping earth dripping from his hands. "I want to die… to be here with you, to be free of this endless suffering. Couldn't you have taken me with you? Why did you leave me!"

Suddenly the crickets stopped their song, the wind abated, and the branches stilled. Gracien felt a warmth fall on him as if the sun had torn through a cloudy sky. His head popped up as he listened for anything other than silence.

A comforting presence rippled over his chest and head. "Ayadonna?" Saying her name out loud doubled the intensity of the sensation.

All his body hair stood on end and he dropped the fistfuls of earth. His hands moved towards his chest, overlapping just over his heart. The silence surrounding him intensified as the strange but comforting sensation strengthened, reaching the warmth of a sunburn, and holding.

"Are you there… Aya? My love?" His mind immediately rebutted, *you're insane, she's dead.* He ignored the thought, instead picturing Ayadonna embracing him from behind with her hands placed over his heart.

The imagery seemed not to come from him, rather it was placed in his mind by another.

"It can't be, it's impossible." His hands pressed harder into his heart.

His eyes trembled from side to side as if he'd somehow lose the feeling if he blinked. He wanted to believe it was her. He wanted so bad to believe but it all seemed too insane. One thing could not be disputed; this sensation, this feeling wrapping him up, felt real – at least realer than anything he had experienced since her death.

The chirp of crickets had resumed as the breeze regained confidence.

The branches had swayed as he stood, backstepping away from her grave with his hands still pressed upon his chest. "It can't be, it just can't. Aya, was that you?"

SMACK! "Okay! Let's do this!" Kaleef clapped, startling Gracien back into reality.

His eyes focused in on Kaleef while nodding automatically, his hands unknowingly pressed upon his own chest, just over his heart.

After a few hours of trekking, the group found a good starting spot to scout out the Great Pyramid of Giza.

"Now, now! But remember, be as quiet as a shadow," Kaleef whispered as they all raced off to the base.

After a full out sprint, they each slid next to the huge stone base, keeping themselves crouched down like readied cats. The pyramid's extensive shadow chilled the air at least ten degrees as well as provided cover from the guard's watchful eyes.

"Climb up and then I'll hand Amira to you. We'll continue passing her up from there for the first dozen or so blocks until they get a little bit smaller. From there she'll be able to do it herself." Kaleef stuck his head out, glancing to the three children on his left and then to the three on his right.

Everyone nodded in agreement. The triplets sprang into action, quickly ascending a huge base stone encased in shiny limestone. Sheena then Gracien followed suit, turning to pluck Amira from Kaleef before he bound up too. They fell into a natural rhythm – climbing, pulling one another up, then climbing again as the stones shrunk in size the higher they ascended.

"She can manage now. Right, Amira?" Kaleef questioned through gasping breath.

Knowing she wasn't supposed to talk, Amira nodded with a hand over her mouth. Unburdened from the task of hoisting Amira, Gracien found himself able to take in the tangerine horizon and humbling landscape. The desert went on forever, its massive presence extending a warm embrace towards the first few flickering stars. He already felt as if he was floating towards the Heavens, and they were only a quarter of the way up.

The wind intensified the further they ascended, muffling any sound beyond his rapid breath. His fingertips scraped along the rough, inner stone in some places and the smooth outer shell of limestone in others. The familiar wear on his fingertips dragged him back to the memory of his final cliffside ascent, his first death. Dread and angst rumbled in his belly like spoiled food. Along with it came the exact flurry of grief he had endured while heaving himself up the mountain side on that fateful day. The inner rumbling migrated out of his belly and into his chest. It was crude and sinister, like hosting an ominous stranger in your home. He swallowed, keeping mindful of each new hand hold as the unease rippled out over his skin. A shriek rang out as a murder of crows circled the pyramid's summit, blanketing the mighty structure with their foreboding shrill.

"Stay here, stay present and keep climbing," he encouraged.

His fingertips dug deeper, scraping the stone with unnecessary force as his heartbeat stuttered with the budding anxiety. Catching sight of the other children from the corner of his eye reminded him to center. The last thing he wanted was to lose control in front of them, especially in this situation.

His breath intensified, not from the labor of the climb but from the escalating dread. The fear was like a tantrum-throwing child; completely unconcerned with anything but itself. He kept his head down, focusing on the small window that his line of sight revealed as he ascended each ancient stone. The sound of the wind faded as his heaving breath muted everything else. His mind's concentration was no match for the budding dread. The panic boiled over, disabling his entire body. Gracien collapsed into the meeting point of two stones, gasping for breath as fear swallowed him like quicksand.

Hide...must hide, the terrifying thought echoed, doubling his mental chaos.

He scanned his surroundings for somewhere to flee, somewhere to hide, somewhere to curl up and die. They were already two thirds up with nowhere to retreat and the thought of descending back down wasn't even a consideration. His mind was incapable of conceiving a solution as it navigated the dense, violent waves of a full-blown panic attack.

Trapped! I'm trapped! he screamed within his mind as the living nightmare grew darker. *Escape, run, hide!*

The words repeated themselves as if shouted from the lips of some infernal creature hidden in the darkness. Gracien peered down the endless stream of massive stairs, standing with the urge to escape, compelling his feet towards the edge. He desperately longed to end it all – and so another thought rendered the solution.

Jump.

His chest heaved breath as his heart felt like it was about to explode. His hands and arms extended outwards towards the open air as if he was reaching for an invisible ledge. The tips of his sandals brimmed the stone edge then scraped beyond it as his terror mounted.

Jump. Just... jump and it will all be over with.

Stillness. A minuscule pause, and within that small space a new thought took form, *this is insane! What's putting these thoughts in my mind?*

The confusion disrupted not only the thought to jump, but also the urge to do so. Within that space, the lens of his mind was cleaned, opening a window into reality. He couldn't help but wonder what caused such self-sabotaging encouragement as his sandals slid back onto the fullness of the stone, for this thought was different than the others had been. This felt pointless, simple. It wasn't to end pain, rather a temptation placed in his mind simply because the ledge was so close and so tempting.

A vile, wicked thought. But not mine, not from me… It came from something wounded, something frightened. A mind that urged death a moment ago now struggled to find the right words for describing this sinister, secondary presence.

Just then a disturbance sounded out – Amira's angelic giggle. The sound reached out, seizing Gracien's spirit like a fishing net. Gracien looked up to Amira, finding all six of the children peering off into the distance, each of them displaying wide-eyed, awe-inspired expressions. He watched them for a moment, his breast ebbing with stifled breath before turning to see what held their fascination.

As he turned, he gasped, his lungs holding the sole breath like a deep-sea diver. All but a small portion of the setting sun peeked out from the top of a bulbous cloud pattern. Radiant beams of light speared the landscape like a giant, golden rake. Peach and purple tinted clouds expanded, morphed, and intensified as the entire color spectrum raced across the expansive sky. Like a blind person suddenly granted sight, he was dumbstruck with awe. Gracien knew he had of course seen color, but he had never *felt* color. The significance of nature's most beautiful occurrence banished his internal dread like dawn dispelling darkness.

He stepped back, falling to his seat with tears streaming down his cheeks as the experience overwhelmed his every thought and sensation. Aya's abounding presence was so strong and immense, it annihilated his identity. The emergence of a new thought bloomed like a sprouting seed.

I want to live.

The sentiment rippled over his skin before sending a bubble of promise up his spine and into his innermost being. Conceived by the union of something so impossibly beautiful and the peace of a silent mind, a revelation was born. Gracien knew he needed to speak the thought out loud in order to breathe life into it.

He drew in a long, deep breath, swallowing the ache of dryness then exhaling.

"I want to live. I know that I'm not a King anymore, I'm no longer that man, living that life. Not only did I bury my sweet Ayadonna, but I also buried my past life with her. I must…" He wept, searching for the strength to continue as sobbing breath thwarted his speech. "I must let all the bad of that life go and remember the good. I need to look forward and discover a new way to live… create a new version of myself." He whimpered like a child but the sincerity of his words poured forth with sage-like fortitude.

Gracien then sat in silence, marinating in the sentiment and gravity of his words. Another realization surfaced along with a new feeling. He wasn't sure he had ever experienced this feeling, it was a still as a morning fog rolling over a silent lake while amber sunlight spilled over the horizon. It wasn't joy and it wasn't exactly peace either. Whatever it was allowed a gap in his grief, a pause in his suffering. Breath. Silence. Awareness. An unknown beauty, an ethereal experience, or perhaps the unification of both, had banished his grief and created a temporal void in time and space. The opportunity allowed Gracien to come to terms with a truth, and to clearly consider his situation for the very first time since Aya's passing.

As the sun dipped below the horizon, Gracien unraveled one new realization after the next. He knew with certainty that he could never get back to where, who, and what he once was or recapture what he once had. Aya was gone. Yet Gracien didn't feel her to be dead, not in the way he once considered death; a place void of light and warmth, a place of eerie finality. He couldn't make sense of this faith, this belief growing stronger in his heart. Gracien believed, or rather knew, that Ayadonna was alive, albeit somehow beyond his understanding. Like a beaten and bloodied warrior shedding his armor, this realization helped Gracien shed a layer of his suffering. The mere absence of such a burden rejuvenated a portion of his spirit.

For if Aya was not truly dead, not gone forever, then this meant something more. It meant that life had reason, life had purpose again. What reason and what purpose, Gracien didn't know just yet. But he did know that given enough time and exploration, he'd discover the reason. He also knew that ending his life was no longer an option. He'd just return in some new body, living some new life, with all the same grief still weighing down upon him. There was no escaping that. For whatever reason, his soul kept reincarnating while Aya was somewhere else, but she had the ability to influence and guide him in each new life. This was the only truth he felt comfortable accepting at this point.

The only other fact he knew was that his life as Gracien, his life as king, was the only true death to be born out of Aya's. Gracien, sitting on top of the largest tomb ever conceived, laid to rest not only his desire for death, but also his desire to salvage a life which no longer existed. Tears born of understanding streamed down his face as his heart embraced this new, liberating choice. Everything that was chaos moments before seemed to make a lot more sense. It felt good to know that something mattered again. He felt like a sprout that had bloomed into a flower, without any passing of time.

This choice of his laid the foundation for something much larger than itself: possibility. If he knew nothing about what death was but a little about what it wasn't, therein lied the possibility.

And with it a new idea presented itself. *Ask Aya for a sign.* His mind immediately dismissed the idea as nonsense. *But what could I lose by asking?* it countered.

Gracien swallowed then cleared his throat. "Aya, my love. Show me, prove to me that I'm not crazy. Show me that you're still with me, that you're still somehow…" He inhaled, closing his eyes and whispering, "alive."

A long seeping exhalation hissed out before Gracien gulped in a giant breath and held it. He felt anxious but also doubtful. He didn't know what to expect but felt like he should watch for something. As if he needed to be an eagle surveying the landscape, his senses ingested everything before him. He felt a tingle of desire or maybe it was hope. He wanted to be right, he longed for the confirmation his soul seemed to already have. After almost a minute he exhaled slowly, as a ripple of defeat washed over him. The last of the sunlight sank into the desert's clutches as the winds picked up, pelting him with sprinkles of sand. Gracien moved to get up and join the others before catching sight of some small speck of movement.

A stark, blue vibrancy flickered about as the wings of a butterfly fluttered towards him. It rose, encircling Gracien a few times as he extended a finger with the innocence of a child. Out of nowhere his mind filled with the sound and imagery of Aya's laugh. It flooded his being, sending a shockwave of vibration and energy over his skin. The echo dwindled as the celestial creature descended, stopping midair to hover just out of reach before retreating to the Heavens. The encounter was brief but the impression, eternal. Gracien, not realizing he had held his breath for the entire experience, quickly dumped it before the shallow inhalation of astonishment swept in.

He had received his sign. Ayadonna had awarded him a slight gift, yet one which would forever alter his spiritual journey. The confirmation he sought overwhelmed his physical form, emboldened his spirit, and nourished this new, yet infantile faith

"Dalilah? Are you okay?" Sheena softly inquired from several steps up.

Gracien wiped his eyes before turning with a genuine smile. "Never better." He wanted to share the experience but the possibility of looking insane swept the magic rug from under his feet.

Sheena smiled in return, sitting down beside Gracien as the others approached from a few levels up.

"This was a special one," she mentioned, making Gracien's face wash over with confusion.

Sitting on her hands, Sheena gestured towards the sunset with a nod of her head. "I've been up here a few times for the sunset," she said quietly as she looked back towards Kaleef. "Don't tell Kaleef. I don't want to spoil our adventure," she bumped Gracien's shoulder with her own as they both chuckled.

"It was special," Gracien's voice sounded worn and raspy. "Definitely more of an adventure than I expected." He sighed.

"Are you sure you're alright?"

"For the first time... in a very long time... yeah, I feel okay." Gracien smirked, nodding in appreciation.

"Good, just making sure. We should head back soon, before it gets too dark."

The pitter-patter of the other orphans sounded out as all five lined up on the edge before plopping down next to Sheena and Gracien. They squished into one another as the chill of nightfall swept over them.

"That. Was. Intense," Kaleef said, shaking his head back and forth. "Wow."

They all looked to one another, Amira yawning like a lion cub after a full meal.

"Well, I don't see any torches yet, but keep your eyes peeled and be careful on the way down. Climbing down can be trickier than climbing up." Kaleef jumped down from one level to the next as he carried Amira, whispering instructions as he descended. "Take your time and try to be really, really quiet. No talking until we're free and clear."

And as they trickled down into the thickening nightscape, Gracien felt as if he could have fluttered all the way down. While unraveling his newfound love of life, he noticed something was missing and an internal void developed. It was true that he no longer wanted to die, but the uncertainty of how to live began sending ripples of angst through his center.

They made slow and steady progress, taking longer when they reached the bigger stones on the last several levels as they passed Amira down. The open desert wrapped them up in its chill, urging them to hurry as they approached the last level. Gracien jumped down to the soft, warm desert earth, a welcomed relief after the unforgiving stone. He turned back, taking Amira from Kaleef as Sheena and the triplets plopped down, buzzing with satisfaction. None of them noticed the mob of approaching torch flames.

The torches swept in and around them, hovering in a circle around the children while illuminating the stern, unamused faces of the guards. With the pyramid behind them and the guards in front, there was nowhere to run and no chance of escape. Gracien's voice lodged within his throat as a crippling sense of terror disabled any chance of flight.

A deep, disturbing voice spoke from behind the curtain of torchlight, "don't try to run. You've been caught scaling the Great Pyramid, an offense punishable by dea..."

"No!" Kaleef interrupted, yelling back, "we were..."

But Sheena cut him off, "you great pack of fools! She could have been killed! I thought you were here to protect the Great Pyramid and our people! And yet a child, no less than four years old, walks right by your protective shield and CLIMBS UP! And you're blaming us?" She grabbed Amira by the arm, shoving her in front of the guards. "We've been looking all over for her, only to discover she was halfway up the pyramid already!"

Utterly terrified and thinking she was to blame, tears and screams gushed from Amira as Sheena continued. "All the while you fools sip tea while taking in a sunset." She sprung towards them with her accusations, her gaze glistening with rage.

Deflating with sympathy, the guard's faces softened. The torch circle seemed to grant Sheena a wider berth as her fury washed over them.

"Quiet child! You should have notified us," one of the guards shouted.

"There was no time to get your attention!" She was screaming now.

Concerned her behavior may worsen their consequences, Kaleef eyed her then coughed. Sheena ignored him.

"One misstep and she could have fallen to her death! We acted fast, scaled the pyramid, and saved her." Her tone softened as she knelt beside Amira before embracing her. "It's okay, it's all going to be okay. Shhh, shhh, shhh…" she consoled.

A deep, angry voice beyond the torches rang out, "you're quite clever… for a *filthy* orphan. I have no patience for children's games. You may have convinced my men, but I see flaws in your story. Nevertheless, we're not here to imprison children for playing *near* the Great Pyramid." The voice stepped into the torch light, his scarred face growling, "let this serve as a warning, a final one at that."

The head guard grabbed one of the torches and leaned down directly in front of Sheena's face, the sharp slice of an unsheathed dagger ringing out. "Next time you won't be able to deliver such a story, without a tongue. Now go." He gestured with the dagger.

A gap in the torch light swung open and without missing a beat, Gracien swooped Amira up into his arms before making a hasty retreat.

"And then Sheena was like, 'You fools!' she actually called the guards a pack of fools!" Malek looked around to the others, reenacting the confrontation as if Sheena had jumped down from the tip of the pyramid and landed on the guard's head.

"Unbelievable. Unbelievable! Can you believe it?" Malek was so excited he paced about the fire pit gesturing wildly with his hands.

The others laughed, enjoying the change in expressions as only half his face lit up each time he pivoted.

Sheena, who was still too rattled to sit still, took a dramatic bow then wove her hand like a pharaoh being ferried through the streets. "Thank you, thank you my loyal consorts."

"What's a consort?" Shuna questioned, warming the bread over the fire's edge.

Kaleef gave a bellow of laughter, his mouth filling with shadow as the firelight flickered about his face. "It means to twist around, bending your body, kind of like…"

"That's not what it means," Sheena interrupted, "that's *contort*. Consort is like a friend."

Kaleef's eyes widened as he nodded, "oh."

"Friend?" Rouna asked.

"Mhh-hh," Sheena confirmed while picking rot from the bread and tossing it to one of the cats hiding among the darkness.

"I always thought we were family. Because you know, we don't have any," Rouna spoke hesitantly, stoking the embers of the fire with a stick as Amira slept in her lap.

Silence dangled on a string before Malek snatched it up. "Me too," he mumbled with a mouth full of bread.

"I do too, it's just a word I heard someone say once. You are my family," Sheena responded, plopping down next to Rouna, and wrapping an arm around her.

Gracien sat just out of reach of the fire's light as well as the conversation. Lost in reflection, he swung in a hammock while rolling an olive over his knuckles.

Kaleef tore a small piece of bread from the loaf. "Me too," he said as he approached Gracien. "Here, you should eat."

"I'm not hungry, nerves still ricocheting about... from the guards and all. I think I'll just head to bed." His voice was raspy.

He cleared it while pulling himself up from the hammock.

"But you haven't eaten all day."

He tried to smile but fell short. "I know, long day... too much excitement for me, I'm going to get some rest. Make sure Amira finds her bed before you find yours. Goodnight."

He spun from Kaleef, flashing a glance towards the rest of them before making a hasty retreat.

He looked down to his feet, watching as the most subtle of silvered waves passed through his legs. As he stared down, he saw the strong legs of a king, ones that lead to the familiar body that he knew so well. A band of moonlight stretched over the glassy surface of the Nile, beginning at the opposite shore, and leading across to where he balanced himself on the shifting sand of the shallows. Gracien's gaze scanned his surroundings, taking in the opposite shore as everything but the oscillating stripe of moonlight seemed veiled in a dense darkness. The sound of the gentle waves lapping on the shore had a rigid, almost scratchy note to them, like two rocks rubbing together. Gracien watched the reflection of three ibises soaring over the length of the river as cricket chirps rang out like an untuned flute. His head popped up to witness their flight, only to find the sky free of anything but the moon.

"So cold." A chill embraced him as if he had stepped into a winter's storm.

His hands clutched his elbows, pulling them tighter. "So cold... and so dark." He looked around like an abandoned child. "Why is it so, so dark here... I can barely see, and this weather is frigid. I feel like I'm choking on it." His feet began to squirm under the river's surface.

The noise of his legs wading through the water sounded out like the ripping of cloth. Every sensation his senses took in seemed angry, laced with oppression.

"What is this place?" He swallowed, rubbing his arms as he peered about.

"It's what you've made it." The reply sounded out like the pluck of a harp chord amongst the moan of dogs.

"Who's there?" Gracien stumbled backwards, his head spinning from side to side as he searched for the source.

"It doesn't have to be this way, Gracien... You can leave the darkness anytime you want." A warmth thawed him from the inside.

"Where are you, who are you?" His voice was riddled with fear as he stepped backwards.

"Here, on the other side," Aya's voice stirred the water, dispatching tiny ripples outwards as she spoke from below the surface.

Gracien paused, his hand reaching for the moonlight glistening on the river's surface. "Aya?"

Aya's form, radiant and complete, somehow hovered both within the moonlight and under the surface of the river.

"Yes, I'm here. I'm always here with you. You don't need to be afraid... Your fear only feeds the darkness."

Gracien's fingers grazed the surface. "It's warm... How is it so warm right here? Everywhere else it's so cold and lifeless, so cruel." He peered about, his hands returning to a self-embrace as the darkness around him intensified.

"It doesn't have to be... and it will change for you. But you must believe. You must know that where I am now... there is no darkness, no cold... only light and warmth, only life and love. I no longer suffer... I'm free from all that now. And here, here I'm able to help you, to guide you to a place where you too will no longer suffer." The tip of Aya's finger poked through the surface of the river.

Gracien watched with astonishment as Aya's hand reached up through the river. Her entire form was moonlight compressed into form. As she rose, she pulled the moon's reflection from the Nile's surface like the train of her wedding gown. She rose to her full, impressive stature, her lovely form radiating with the brilliance of a full moon's reflection as her height matched Gracien's. Her aura glowed like moonlight and everything around her, including Gracien, was glazed in silver.

Aya started towards him. "Come to me." Her tone sent a wave of warmth over him, breaking off the chill of darkness like a wolf shaking off the snow.

"I can't!" He stepped back, his fear welling up. "I can't leave this place." His eyes bulged as he clung to himself like a forgotten prisoner.

"*Gracien?*" she spoke as delicately as a feather's kiss.

"I just can't, just can't leave," he began repeating like a crazed fool. "Can't escape... I cannot esca..."

Aya hovered a few paces in front of him. "You must believe." Her fluid, serene tone had a palpable gravity to it.

Gracien's rambling immediately ceased as if his ears were just turned on. His gaze locked onto Aya's moonlit form, shuddering under the weight of her grace and glory. His hand extended towards hers, their fingertips hovering a breadth away as he inhaled one long, deliberating breath.

"It's okay my love. It's okay. Let go of the darkness... Just let it go."

He knew it would be okay as their hands embraced. Moonlight poured into his fingers, spreading up his hand and into his arm. The enriched warmth migrated through him like warmed honey. It banished the chill from his body, and he stood taller, rejuvenated, reborn. Aya began sinking back into the water, slowly descending as the moonlight pushed back out across the river's surface. Their hands clung to one another as moonlight continued flowing into Gracien.

"I will always be with you, Gracien. It cannot be any other way. Go towards the light my love and believe in us..." Her body continued sinking, with her torso and shoulders dipping below the surface as her hands still held his.

All but her hands were fully submerged, but they too began pulling Gracien down into the river. His instinct was to pull back, but the warmth and light traversing throughout his entire body dispelled any reluctance. Aya's spirit permeated his own, casting out the darkness as Gracien melted into the sensation while slowly sinking into the river, into Ayadonna. The water line swallowed his knees, and hips, then his torso and shoulders until it reached his neck, and he closed his eyes – fully entering the light on the other side.

Gracien shot up, leaning back on his arms with his legs tangled in the bedding. His shallow breath quickened with excitement and vented from his hollowed lips. Perspiration beaded across his chest as he repeatedly swallowed. His tired eyes fruitlessly searched through the veil of sleep as the symphony of twilight stirred. Exhaustion swept in. Gracien closed his eyes, tipped his head backwards and sunk back into the warm bedding. The dream lingered for a while longer, radiating over his skin like a sunburn until thinning with his settling breath. A slow, steady breath filled his lungs and his eyelids peeled apart. His pupils expanded then settled, taking in the fullness of a radiant moon shining directly overhead. The silvered moonlight poured into him while sleep slowly tugged him back into its welcoming embrace.

Gracien and the others carried on living and providing for themselves one day at a time for many months to come, each of them pulling their own weight to make ends meet. Being safely tucked away in the clandestine camp, their main concern was filling their bellies from one day to the next. Different approaches of getting money or supplies were necessary as none of the orphans were able to produce a steady stream of coin. The triplets continued to tweak the craft of distraction.

"We're just borrowing the food... until we have money to pay it back." Sheena winked with a mischievous smile, then tossed several apples towards Rouna who fumbled with the deluge of fruit.

The triplets were decent thieves, but they had a lot to learn still as they were sloppy and took unnecessary risks. Kaleef did his best teaching them different techniques as they strolled through the market but he, Sheena, and Gracien were so good – it wasn't worth putting the triplets at risk. Sheena and Gracien took turns bringing Amira to the market.

Like a well-trained actor, she played her part perfectly. "But pa-pa-pa-pwease help feed my tummy... is so emp-tee." She patted her little belly while flaunting those puppy eyes.

Amira's unmatched cuteness and toddler speech made donations pour in without the whole song and dance.

Kaleef must have inherited a strong will for business. "Either you have it or you don't! Ideas for making money, well they just kind of float into my head from time to time and I put them to the test," he stated when explaining to Sheena how he always seems to land his odd jobs.

Whether it was running deliveries for merchants, cleaning and sweeping up various shops, or filling in for a random apprentice, Kaleef always found some small opportunity and wrung it dry. But he also got itchy after spending too much time at the same job and always reverted back to thieving. He must have also inherited the generosity gene, as he was rarely selfish with his wages and plunder, often splurging on rare culinary delights for the whole crew.

An alluring aroma beckoned the children as he conquered the multiple gates into their dwelling. "I give you, Mahshi: Peppers stuffed with spiced rice, eggplant, and grape leaves!" he proclaimed while jogging into the embrace of the awaiting group like a village champion.

On the rare occasion Kaleef spoiled them with something truly special: lean strips of roasted goat with garlic and onion or chicken kebabs glazed with lemon and rosemary. Shawarma was also a favorite, but it was usually cold by the time he returned. But they didn't mind waiting for Malek to reheat the meat using a thin, flat stone placed directly on the fire. The amazing smell acted as an invitation to all nearby strays because suddenly there was a lot more commotion among the fringes of camp.

Malek and Kaleef would hover over the sizzle, oohing and awing as they stoked the fire and poked the searing goat loin. "Ohhh yeahhh."

"Here, try a piece." He pinched a small, perfectly cooked portion, placing it into Shuna's mouth.

Her eyes rolled into the back of her head as she over-chewed the savory treat. "Ohhh myyy…" she moaned while fanning the heat.

On the especially rare occasion, Kaleef returned with a plate of kanafeh, an uber sweet dessert the children clamored over like vampires.

"No one is ever tall enough to reach it… Maybe I'll keep it all for myself!" he teased as the plate hovered over outstretched hands and pleading cries.

All the children boasted full bellies. Well, all of them except for Gracien. This however wasn't due to a lack of food but rather a lack of appetite. Much had changed in the many months since his pyramid revelation. Fleeing under the watchful eyes of a dozen guards had him feeling anxious of course, but also a little optimistic – a feeling he hadn't known in a very long time.

Upon returning from the pyramid, if someone had asked him a simple question, "is everything going to be okay?" he would have taken his time in answering. Furrowing his brow with consideration, exhaling a deep sigh, allowing a gradual nod to gain momentum, then extending a half smirk of confirmation, "yeah… yeah, it's going to be okay."

That convinced person was a far cry from who he was today. His time mingling fireside, playing games, and telling stories thinned over the past few months, as did his physique. He flaunted a bony rib cage, gaunt cheeks, and hollowed eyes. What was left of his muscles hung off his bones like wet laundry and his hair had thinned into spider's silk. Gracien's emaciated appearance had helped fill the camp's donation fund, but it did little for his ailing health.

Gracien's revelation of not wanting to die was a monumental step in his spiritual journey, but that didn't mean he knew how to live – or with what purpose. Gracien lived for Aya and Aya alone. And now that Ayadonna was somewhere else, a place of love and light, he felt utterly abandoned. And he hadn't the least idea of how to escape his own darkness. This was a whole new layer of grief he wished he had never discovered. It was a charcoal blanket stitched to his soul; a coat of chainmail welded to his spirit.

He did his best to hide the constant suffering with disingenuous smiles, fake laughs, and his go to response, "yeah, no… I'm fine." But it was getting harder to keep up the "normal" routine while everyone was getting more concerned.

And he wasn't the only one battling demons. Each of the children, other than Amira, as she was still too young and pure, struggled through their own particular grief from one day to the next. Sometimes the pooled grief would consume them, causing a full day or two of communal withdrawal. Everyone knew about one another's circumstance enough to show a bit of sympathy, but that was like feeding a lion a mouse sized meal. One empty well cannot fill another.

Silence was a constant companion on these darker days, as they avoided discussing the particulars of their struggles. For none of the children had the know-how, nor the life experience to speak openly about grief, depression, and anxiety. They did their best to cheer one another up as well as themselves by just trying to have fun, a child's right in any other environment. They'd play games, sing songs, copy dances from the festivals, and mock the grumpy merchants. A favorite pastime was to share a set of old wives' tales while hanging about in the olive tree, one true and one make believe, then voting on which was which. Campfires were perfect for swapping stories, sometimes turning into group therapy sessions for those bold enough to open up. Each of them had their own way of comforting one another, but Kaleef in particular, was better suited to lift the veil of melancholy.

Somehow, he knew how, or at least when it was possible to break up the pity party with that ever-reliable question, "who wants to go on an adventure?"

Like plunging into the Nile after three weeks without a bath, the mere idea of a new adventure cleansed their spirits and lifted their moods. The excitement of some new thrill, usually sprinkled with a bit of jeopardy, always had a way of distracting them just enough to forget about their troubles for at least a day or two. The instant Kaleef uttered that question, while flaunting a mischievous smirk of course, excitement swirled about the camp as they prepped for whatever precarious thrill lay ahead.

And so ensued a gauntlet of adventure: chasing fireflies through the abandoned caverns – breath holding competitions in the Nile under a full moon's light – sneaking into the migrant camps and watching holy festivities where women danced about roaring fires as troops of musicians performed – investigating sacred sites under the cover of twilight – playing hide and seek among towering, desert dunes – counting shooting stars on a clear night – scaling faulty rooftops without getting caught – sword fights in the cemeteries, the loser left behind all alone until the howl of a dog rang out – and the most dangerous of all: sneaking into the temples and looting the lamp oil. But their favorite of all adventures was the obstacle course, a foot race from one point in the market to another. The triplets were given a generous head start of course and Sheena, Kaleef, and Gracien each had to steal something to make it fair. Break the rules and you were on dish duty for a week. You couldn't take a shortcut, it had to be on the busiest of days, no hiding, and most importantly, don't get caught.

As adventures ensued, Gracien's understanding of how they functioned as an escape from his grief crystallized. The profound adventure on top of the pyramid proved more beneficial to him than he had initially realized. He discovered something which had been buried deep within himself: the ability of introspection. His mind began watching and observing itself, delayering his mental tendencies like an onion. He discovered that each new adventure was an exciting distraction, a high of sorts which captivated his mind and spirit long enough for him to temporarily forget the darkness. Like a sailor focused on a sole patch of sun peeking through a storm-filled sky; eventually he needed to prepare for the ominous weather or suffer the consequences. And not only did he observe how his mind perceived reality during, as well as after, each new adventure, he also came to understand that with the completion of each thrill, there'd be an emotional crash to follow. Like an opiate addict running out of funds, he witnessed the withdrawal that always ensued, leaving him feeling worse off than when he began.

His pyramid realization marinated as he spent countless days curled up in the safety of his nest deep within self-reflection. "Since I'm no longer a King... I'm no longer anything. Everything I was, every aspect of my identity that I invested in establishing - a husband, a best friend, a lover, a soulmate, a businessman, and even future identities like a parent or a grandparent... They're all dead. My entire life is dead."

The loss of all he was, and all aspects of his identity not only required, but deserved, more reflection. With it came the suffering of losing everything he'd ever held near and dear. And so, for many, many months Gracien curled up into himself, continuing to mourn not only Aya's death but his as well. Before long, he even found himself mourning Owanna and her family. For Gracien, the appeal of adventure dwindled over time, as it no longer held weight substantial enough to balance the scales of his grief and suffering. His only respite being the asylum of dreams granted to him by sleep.

"And den, and den she flied up to me, giving da most stwongest hug. It was warm, like sun when it wakes up... when your nose is stilled cold with sleep." Amira pointed to her nose as she rambled through her story.

"Uh-huh... and then what happened?" Kaleef responded while cleaning her face with a wet rag as she sat on top of a stack of old crates.

Amira leaned in, speaking quietly. "She whispered in my eaws, but not so soft like I am doing now. It... *felt*... loud but it was not... loud?" she questioned herself as Kaleef smiled, nodding in understanding.

Gracien walked up to them, his body feeling sore and lethargic from a full day in bed. "Good morning." He yawned.

Large dark circles hung from his eyes. His cheeks had all but vanished, sinking into themselves as his gauntness looked over Amira and Kaleef. Scrawny fingers bawled up into fists, rubbing the sleep from his red eyes.

"Morning. Amira was just sharing her dream," Kaleef responded while wiping Amira's face as she tried to squirm free. "Almost done, keep still."

"Ohh, can I tell Dawiwah?" Amira pushed the towel from her face, jumping down from her seat then pulling at Gracien's fingers.

Gracien leaned down, his smile fully extending. "Tell me what?"

Amira looked to Kaleef with hesitancy, fingers nipping at her lip before leaning in and cupping a hand over Gracien's ear. "Da woman from my dweams, da one in da white, she told me to tell you... Don't. Be. Afraid." Shivers rippled down Gracien's spine as his eyes immediately teared over.

His hands shot upwards, grabbing Amira by the shoulders. Amira tensed as if she was in trouble.

Kaleef stepped towards them. "Everything okay?"

Gracien ignored him as he stared into Amira's eyes, swallowing then forcing a smile. "I'm sorry, I didn't mean to scare you. Did she..." He cleared his throat. "The woman in white... Did she say anything else?" His watery eyes begged for more.

The tension poured from Amira's body as she relaxed, looking to Kaleef then back to Dalilah. "Yes," she nodded dramatically.

"Can you... can you tell me what she said?" Gracien sputtered off while pulling Amira closer.

Amira whispered ever so softly. "Da woman in da white... She says dat... she says dat she is always here." Her little finger poked Gracien square in the chest.

Gracien's head turned to the side, his gaze lost in nothingness as Amira's words settled. His trembling hand released Amira's shoulder, cupping his own mouth as he cried before uttering a slight moan of disbelief. Thinking she had said or done something to upset her adoptive sister, Amira began to cry.

Kaleef squatted down beside them as Gracien inhaled deeply, wiping the tears from his eyes, and bringing Amira in for an embrace. "Thank you, thank you, thank you... You did such a good job telling me." He squeezed Amira as if he would never see her again. In a flash he pushed her back to arm's length, looking her square in the eye. "And I'm so sorry for making you cry. Do you forgive me?"

Amira nodded slowly, rubbing one eye with a balled-up fist. "She-she-she... was... she was... bery beaut-i-ful. And her hug was so-so... so warm and fuzzy," she stuttered between stifled breath.

Gracien chuckled, wiping happy tears, and bringing Amira back into an embrace. "She is beautiful, isn't she?"

Amira giggled as Gracien melted into the moment – and Kaleef, into confusion.

"There," Rouna gestured towards the merchant with a nod of her head.

Kaleef shook his head while slithering through a mass of people. "No, he *looks* like he's sleeping." The seemingly negligent merchant, with arms crossed over his chest and a head scarf dipping over his eyes, leaned back, resting in a nest of fabric.

"But he's like a cat, he's probably more aware with his eyes closed than the younger merchants are with eyes wide open. See. See that there... see what he just did? I think he heard us," Kaleef picked up the pace as the merchant peeked over to them with a watchful eye before squirming back into his seat.

The market was insane. The children had never seen it bursting from the seams with so many hordes of customers and new vendors. Lines of shoppers navigated through and around all the vestibules, carts, shops, and sole solicitors like endless streams of army ants clearing out a thicket of forest.

A week-long festival, showcasing various archery and wrestling tournaments, brought in the masses from several outlying villages. This was good business for everyone because money spilled into the city from every corner of Egypt. And the local merchants wanted their fair share. They doubled their stock, gave unheard of discounts for buying in bulk, used outlandish advertising, and called in aid from their extended families to help meet the inflated demand. Various performers, local and visiting alike, did their best to encourage donations from the pockets of the meandering crowds while the thieves just took it for themselves. And this of course, meant more patrolmen.

Kaleef had to yell his observations as they passed by a band of belly dancers backed by a trio of men thumbing their lyres. After walking beyond the cacophony, Kaleef paused, encouraging the gang to crouch down. Pedestrians poured around the huddled group like they were boulders in a raging river. The heat was especially brutal today. He swiped his brow as sweat trickled down it before scanning the area again.

The entire group peered through the masses at the sleeping spice merchant as he rocked back and forth to the tune of the music. "This is what I mean, stealing from them when they look like they're sleeping is always a risk." Kaleef sounded wise beyond his years, patiently speaking to the children without looking towards the merchant. "You cannot control when they wake up... so their distraction, sleep... it's something you can't control, turn, or twist, and..."

"Manipulate," Gracien said.

"Yes, manipulate," Kaleef said as the group resumed scoping out the market for an ideal target.

Kaleef motioned to speak before returning his attention to Gracien. "Dalilah, have you... When's the last time you've... Ummm..." Frustration washed over him. "Are you hungry?"

Gracien looked to him, utter exhaustion stretched across his face. "I'm fine," he said, too low for him to hear.

Kaleef had read this statement on his lips a hundred times before, and on cue his gaze narrowed with uncertainty.

"I mean... we're all *hungry*... but you look..."

"I'm fine Kaleef. What about him?" Gracien interrupted, gesturing towards a potential mark by casually rubbing his chin with one hand while holding Amira's with the other.

"Too many people around him, too many eyes to see," Sheena said.

"Yes, exactly. This guy looks good, but there are..." Kaleef's nose poked the air as it counted, "five, six, seven. Seven additional people, all with two eyes and two ears to see and hear us." He looked down towards the triplets and Amira who returned wide eyed, attentive gazes.

Kaleef got down on one knee. "He is very busy attending to all of his customers... but they too can see you steal, catch you, and turn you in before the merchant realizes what's happened."

Malek nodded in realization. "Ohhh..." he moaned out, putting the pieces together as to why he was nearly seized by a customer some weeks prior.

Amira let go of Gracien's hand so that she could hear Kaleef, inching herself just behind the triplets.

"They need to be thoroughly distracted, preferably by one of us... so that we can have more control over how long they're distracted for, *and* the younger the merchant, the better."

"Why?" Shuna asked.

"Because they have... they have..." Kaleef pondered the right answer.

"An unseasoned eye," Sheena blew a strand of frizzy hair from her face, rolling her eyes at the heat.

Malek motioned to ask a question, but Gracien interjected. "Untrained, like he hasn't seen enough yet to be good at spotting thieves and distractions."

"Oh!" Malek said as his sisters looked to one another nodding in understanding.

Kaleef nodded. "Yes, they have less experience looking for thieves because they're younger. The old ones, the seasoned merchants, the ones who look calm and they're never worried about anything... those are the ones to avoid if you can. And most importantly!" His finger stabbed the air as all four children held their breath. "Never, ever go for the expensive stuff. It's not worth it, it's not worth losing a hand or worse... dying for." His somber eyes considered them until they each nodded, gulping down understanding.

"We steal to eat, not to sell what we've stolen for money. Remember this rule and you'll live a longer life. Jewelry, gold, silver, expensive spices and medicines, pricey lamps, fine linens, and silks, all that and more. Leave it for the experts... or the stupid ones. You see..." he continued, speaking with his hands as much as he did with his mouth.

Gracien stepped away from the group, a line of people slicing between them as he walked. The spice alley, the best smelling street in all of Memphis, extended in one direction as the sprawling fabric section veered off down another. He strolled towards a merchant's cart, it was a newer one, probably an out of towner with all the exotic scarves and linens. Gracien's eyes went wide with the sight of a coral scarf flapping in the wind. Pulling him in like a snake charmer, everything around him faded into the background as the coral vibrancy breathed life into a slumbering memory.

His eyes no longer peered at the scarf but envisioned Aya standing just before him, adorned in a beautiful gown displaying the exact coloring. The memory was deafening with color, expression, and beauty, yet without a single sound – mimicking the newfound silence surrounding Gracien within the bazaar.

As Gracien listened, Aya spoke, laughed, then spoke again. Her words were lost on him and they fell on deaf ears while Gracien's unblinking gaze glared into the past. His hand extended towards the merchant's scarf, fingers pinching and rubbing the tail like one who had never experienced the sympathy of silk. Gracien's head tilted in adoration as Aya's smile beamed. Ayadonna pursed her mouth closed with the pleased look of an unabashed yet delighted child. Her rich, bountiful locks fanned out as she twirled, showing off the whimsical flow of her coral gown as it spun along with her. Her performance was thick with embellished femininity, bouncing on her toes and flicking a hand through her long, lush hair. She pinched the fabric on both sides of the gown, twisting back and forth and giving a slight, alternating buckle of her knee with each slight pivot. Gracien's fingers continued to massage the silk between his thumb and forefinger, his stare penetrating beyond all of reality. Ayadonna's laugh rang out. Gracien experienced only the look of her laugh and not the sound, but nonetheless it rebounded through him like a drum. Aya hunched over in delight as the exchange between her and Gracien proved overly entertaining. Gracien couldn't remember what they had discussed, nor did he care. He was as captivated in the memory as he had been in the moment.

SLAP! "Get your grubby little fingers out of here, girl! Get lost!" The merchant screamed.

Her hand moved to strike again but Gracien jumped back while rubbing his own hand. A befuddled expression spread across his face like someone waking from an unplanned nap. The woman followed him, stepping so close that her swollen, speckled nose was an inch away from Gracien's.

"I said Get! Lost! Or it'll be your face next!" She spat off to the side.

As the woman retreated to her seat, Gracien's frail body continued its dazed walk backwards. His eyelids fluttered and he rattled his head with a few swift jolts, shaking himself back to reality as the coral scarf billowed in the breeze. He looked down to where he felt a tug on his shirt. Amira's golden, prideful gaze looked up to Gracien as her cupped hands lifted upwards.

"What have you got there?" Gracien questioned, wiping sweat from his brow.

His smile extended as Amira's cupped hands opened like a blooming flower.

Gracien knelt, pinching the vibrant, burnt orange spice between her fingers. "Saffron…" His smile vanished as an explosion of screams erupted just a few paces away.

"Where did you get this? Where? How?" Gracien scooped the expensive spice from Amira's hands then tried to nonchalantly scan their surroundings.

Like an ominous chill preceding a sandstorm, the atmosphere curdled with tension. Amira's eyes began to tear over as the yelling in the background crystallized.

"There! There she is! Stop that thief!" the merchant shouted.

Gracien's eyes locked onto Amira's as he pulled her in. "Walk back to Kaleef and Sheena as slowly as you can. Do you understand?" Gracien spoke as clearly and quickly as possible while what felt like a wave of heat surged from behind him.

"Go, now." He blew any lingering spice from Amira's hands then stood without uttering another word.

Amira heeded Gracien's instructions, vanishing into the mass of limbs like a bunny fleeing into a thicket. Knowing escape would be nearly impossible, Gracien rushed towards the screaming merchant.

"There! The little one! She was just there!" Shouts from the hefty man preceded his mass, bursting through a group of people pointing and shouting in the direction Amira had fled.

Gracien stepped right in front of the merchant, lifting the handful of saffron before his face like a child flaunting treasure.

Entirely caught off guard, he stopped dead in his tracks. "Get out of my…" and just like that Gracien blew the spice all over his unshaven, sweaty face.

Bystanders clamored for the saffron as it rained down around them. The merchant stumbled backwards, coughing, and swiping at his face as if being attacked by bees.

"Get over here!" he screamed after recovering, clawing his arms outwards and coming up empty handed.

Gracien was already gone, distancing himself not only from the danger, but from Amira and the others. He heaved the hot, humid air through his weakened lungs. Only a few hundred feet in and his muscles already screamed out in rebellion as he leapt between shoppers, carts, performers, and panicked dogs. The typical clamor of pursuit followed in his wake, and it was catching up a lot quicker than normal. As he bounded over a circle of chanting monks, he searched through the sea of people for any sign of Amira, Kaleef, or the others.

Watch out! Turn left! Duck! Roll underneath! Full out sprint! His mind fired off commands like lightning strikes.

"SHIT!" His footing slipped as he tried rounding a tight corner, sliding over the dusty earth, and slamming into a wall.

"Gotcha!" a patrolman screamed, his fingertips grazing Gracien's shirt as he shot past him, missing by less than an inch.

Gracien scrambled on all fours, recovering then blasting off just as the patrolman lunged back around the corner. The alley was a labyrinth of obstacles: hookah circles, dice tables, caged animals, and dancing children. The patrolman's breath clawed at his neck. He was a charging lion, a belligerent bull, a rabid dog. Panting and grunting like a wilder-beast, he leapt at Gracien. His fingers grabbed the collar of his shirt just as Gracien ripped a tower of crated chickens to fall right on top of the soldier. The collar of his shirt tore off as an explosion of feathers, shrieks, and howls erupted. He risked a glance back. The patrolman's legs tumbled overhead in a mesh of cages as a sole chicken thrashed above the thicket of dust. Success began pinching at the corner of his smirk as he recentered.

No. All celebration died with the sight of him.

Another patrolman stepped into his path. WHAM! His arm clotheslined him right across the neck. Gracien's legs snapped forward as his neck wrapped itself around the patrolman's arm. The momentum of his legs continued forward while the patrolman slammed him down onto the unforgiving ground. Several cracks popped off in his ribcage. He clutched at the muscular forearm as a swell of fiery pain tore through his lungs.

He knelt on top of his chest. "Stay down!" he screamed as if Gracien had any other option.

Air refused to enter his lungs. His mind raged with panic as if he was being sucked down a whirlpool.

"Over here! Got her!" He rolled Gracien over, pushing his suffocated face into the dirt as the shade of two more patrolmen enveloped them.

A set of ironclad fists dragged him to his feet, displaying him like a fresh kill. His lungs relented, gasping in air which fueled the pain all along his chest and back. They dragged him through the alley with his head bobbing like a dead chicken's. Unsettled feathers swirled above as the fat, sweaty, saffron merchant limped into their path.

"This the one?" The patrolmen asked out as their vice-like grip crushed Gracien's muscle into the bone.

"Yes! Yes, that's the one!" he wheezed. "But there was another one, a smaller runt who stole it."

"Good enough for us," two other patrolmen chuckled as they resumed dragging Gracien, kicking chicken crates from their path.

They walked right past the merchant, who limped around trying to keep up.

"What about... what about the other one?" Still wheezing, he doubled over.

"Good luck finding the other one." The patrolman snorted while Gracien's chest screamed for a proper breath of air. "What'd she steal anyway?"

"Saffron, two handfuls."

One patrolman whistled. "Expensive taste for a bag of bones."

They dragged Gracien from the alley and onto the main passage. Saliva dripped from his lips as he groaned for breath. The bobbing thrashed his bruised throat, so he picked up his head. A crowd of onlookers watched as they carted him forward. He scanned their faces, absorbing the judgmental expressions and hostile glares. Suddenly his teary eyes met Kaleef's – they were black with horror. His worry-stricken gaze was camouflaged within the crowd. The triplets slid through the mass of limbs. Their faces were wrecked with worry and silent screams of terror. Malek looked to Kaleef, who shook his head dismissively in return. Sheena was off to the side, doubled over and sobbing into her arms.

"Amira?" Gracien gasped, holding his breath as dread overwhelmed him.

Relief washed over him after spotting Amira clinging to Kaleef's leg, her sobbing face buried in it as he patted the back of her head. Gracien exhaled, dropping his head back down as the vision of his family seared itself into his soul.

"Thank you," he whispered.

The cold, wet stone of the cell extinguished any lingering warmth he had brought into it. Gracien's feeble frame trembled and convulsed as he lay curled up. The cell wasn't tall enough for him to stand up in and barely wide enough as he lay curled up. The ache of starvation, coupled with a deep and penetrating depression, disabled any movement. His head pounded with anguish so intense it felt as if it was being crushed from within. A crimson gash raced along his temple and through his hairline, a gift from the guard escorting him to the cell three days prior. Flies bounded back and forth from pelting his wound to the spoiled food lying near the cut-out of the old wooden door. He hadn't touched his water bowl since arriving. The chill emanating from the wet, tomb-like enclosure didn't compare to the one in his chest. The only warmth in the cell came from three spears of sunlight slicing through a puny hole in the wall. Other than the occasional scrape of a food bowl, the only other sound was the echo of footsteps. Occasionally though he'd hear an eerie moan coming from another inmate, or their departing spirit.

His mind however, was a circus of chaos begging for mercy. *Aya-donna, I just can't anymore. This life, any life, it's just too much. I'm not strong enough my love. I want only one thing... To be reunited with you, to be done with this cruel existence, the fear, the torment. Please my love, help me. Help me find my escape so that we can be together once again.*

This plea, and many versions of it, had repeated like a mantra over the past three days. Over time though, his prayers sunk into a whisper as Gracien's life force dwindled like the flame of a fleeting candle.

He knew his fate was sealed long ago – before his imprisonment and even before Amira's ill-fated mistake. It had been sealed the moment he knew he didn't want to die, which was the very same moment he discovered he didn't know how to live. Gracien had given up on himself. His health wasn't ever a priority, for the burden of moving on was too great an enemy. And here, dying on that cold stone floor, the boom of failure sounded out in his soul – casting out any lingering will to live. This, coupled with the now familiar, yet still terrifying, presence of certain death, was too much to bear. He had not only let himself down but had also disappointed the children and, most importantly, Aya. It didn't make any sense, but he knew it was his burden to somehow honor Aya's death through living life. That guilt was a powerful enough force to crush the strongest of spirits, and therefore found no challenge in extinguishing Gracien's.

As his breath quickened with life's culmination, those three beams of sunlight began flickering on the wall. The anomaly of this stole him away from the agony of self-loathing long enough for him to peel back his eyelids. Bloodshot eyes watched as the light harmoniously expanded then shrunk like the reach of a bashful tide. He followed the beams from the wall to the window, and in an instant the pain and torment poured from his heart as the silhouetted form of a butterfly darkened the cell. The vibrant blue wings billowed, showing off a gleaming scintillation like that of a morning dew. Gracien's throat swelled with the arrival of this unrequested sign, a very clear gift from his Beloved. It wasn't the butterfly which had bestowed the gift of knowing but rather the thought which arrived after.

"She's encouraging me to pursue life. My time here, or in the next life, is not meant to be wasted away. I have purpose. What purpose, I don't know yet. Maybe at the very least my life could be spent honoring Aya, honoring our love."

The radiance of this newfound truth rose like the sun in all its brilliance. His gaze locked onto the indigo glitter reflecting off the wings of the butterfly. The reflection of sunlight expanded, surging, and filling the cell with such whiteness it was blinding. Warmth and light cradled him like a newborn as the hand of an angel grazed his cheek. Dalilah's body shuddered with the departure of her final, stifled breath and her eyes closed.

FOUR

"Gray...Sea...En," Her words echoed in his mind like a rippled wave.

He gasped, his eyes popping open while shooting up from his prone position. "Aya? Aya?" His chest heaved air as he attempted to gather himself.

Still drunk with sleep, he strained to see through the veil of darkness suppressing the hillside. Gracien pressed his hands to the coolness below him, pushing himself up off the coarse, wool blanket that separated him from the ground.

He came to his knees, drawing a hand up to rub his eyes. "She was close. She was here with me... Right here in camp," he whispered while shaking his head in confusion.

The change in his voice, the alteration in the pitch and tone shocked him into awareness, his eyelids widening further as he frantically scanned the darkness.

His hand tapped the grayed blanket, the material foreign and the ground below it padded with grass. "Grass... Why?" He gasped, "Kaleef... Amira, the triplets, Shee-na-ha-ha..." he moaned while falling to all fours.

Gracien examined his surroundings like a burglar avoiding detection. "Where... How?" His chest heaved as panic soared.

The boy's eyes began adjusting to the darkness and he scanned the surrounding terrain. The landscape rolled like colossal, ocean waves just before a storm.

"This can't be! What happened to me? Where... where am I?" His ears pitched as they caught a slight hissing coming from several paces away, he froze.

His heart exploded with the thought of snakes before immediately dismissing the idea as nonsense, the sound was too sweet, too warm. It was closer to something like snoring children. Snow covered mountain peaks blushed as dawn approached. He crawled off the blanket, his hands sliding over the dewy grass as he investigated the sound. Suddenly a loud cry sliced through the morning silence, stirring a large mass of creatures into awaking. "Maaahhh" rang out followed by a chorus of similar greetings from his flock of goats. The entire herd began standing and stretching their front legs, welcoming the new morning with the jingle of their collar bells, exaggerated yawns, thumping hooves, and drawn-out cries.

"Ohh." His head dropped down between his arms "Yeah." He didn't know what else to say as a flood of remembrance poured into his consciousness, the name *Ish-a-yu* ringing in his ears.

"But why... whyyy," he sobbed into the earth, his body slowly sinking into itself as the will poured from him. "Not again, not again, no, no, no." Dribble dangled from his lip as the boy purged his anguish into the cool, grassy hillside.

"Aya... Why? Not again... Not again..." He groaned trying to form words before collapsing backwards, tucking himself into a fetal position.

The goats, curious and concerned, encircled the boy as he lay curled up sobbing on the damp grass. Their tiny bells chimed as they neared, some walking over Gracien's blanket that was stitched from their very own wool. One hovered over him, staring down for some time before offering a nudge. Gracien was too entombed in grief to notice. The goat retreated, joining a few others standing a few paces away. Their pearl-gray coats encircled the darkened wool blanket that held Gracien balled up in the middle. From overhead their formation resembled an eye, one which gazed up into the Heavens with great anguish and longing.

As if he had only blinked instead of falling asleep, Gracien's eyes popped open before jumping to his feet. By the sun's height, two or so hours had passed, and the goats had wandered about. The boy, standing and panting like a lunatic attempting to evade some unknown threat, scanned the hills for answers. Like a well trained shepherd, Gracien instinctively began to count his herd.

His tanned, young face bobbed with the numbers rattling off in his head, "... 18, 19, 20 anddd 21. They're all here, they're all safe." He exhaled relief and for an instant his mind was as still as a windless day.

He raised one of his hands, stopping just short of his face. Gracien twisted the hand, evaluating it like a warrior looking over a new blade. The hand of a young man with the wear of a veteran fell on the top of his head and the other followed suit. A thick, short, disheveled mane of dusty black hair filled his prodding palms. Like an exhausted hiker washing himself in a river, Gracien's hands swept over his forehead and down his face, poking and dabbing at cheekbones, eye sockets, nose, lips, jaw and then chin before dropping to his side. He exhaled, looking over the rest of himself with utter indifference.

The body housing Gracien's soul was that of a young man seasoned out of adolescence. Sunny afternoons had turned his exposed skin into a rich, teak color while the unexposed parts were faded and speckled with birthmarks. Bulbous, well-defined cheekbones, a wrinkled brow, and a modest but crooked nose were painted over with rosiness from too much sun. Sea green pupils gleamed from abnormally large eyes which mesmerized any onlooker. The beginnings of a beard graced his squared jaw and bordered bulky lips, which were cracked with dehydration. He was tall for his age, but his frame had yet to receive any muscle, highlighting several layers of weathered clothing hanging on him like a coat rack. The fluctuating climate of central Nepal always had him either putting on or taking off a layer.

His shoes were worn, tanned leather with wool padding on the interior. They were too big for his feet, so he strapped them on tightly as if someone was going to steal them while he slept. Beige colored pants speckled with stains and dirt hugged his legs with twine wrapped around his shin and calves to keep in the warmth. A garment of grayed wool encased his torso with a linen shirt underneath to minimize the itchy texture. Twine was tied around his forearms as well and a generous, midnight-colored scarf swaddled his neck. Most evenings, and on especially gloomy or sunny afternoons, the boy used the scarf like a hood, shielding himself from the temperamental weather.

Emotion began pooling in Gracien's eyes as he scanned the great expanse like some lost, dispirited pilgrim accepting a looming death. The sun was two measures above the highest foothill, illuminating the vast wonder laid out before him. His hair whipped about as the winds provoked the youngest of the flock, inciting high pitched bleats of angst. The expansive hillside embraced the shepherd and his flock like an endless, turbulent sea hosting tiny fishing boats. Looking north, rice fields climbed towards the heavens like staircases made for giants. The rows bore an almost unnatural neon green, dulling the rich, deepened green of the jungle butting up against the vivid crops. The jungle vegetation thrived throughout the impressive landscape, growing more robust and vibrant as it neared the sapphire water that slithered and weaved through the base of the valley. As wide as fifty men, the river raged under the sun's unabashed radiance. Flares of water sprayed into the air, interrupting the gleaming surface as it collided with colossal boulders and sharp bends. As they never strayed too far from the river, Gracien's only other companion was its constant lull.

His face squished over with despair as thoughts of the children bubbled up. Gracien missed his orphaned companions, wondering what came of them after his death. Did they live full, rewarding lives? Or like him, did they succumb to the hardship of their circumstance and grief? Amira's sweet voice echoed in his mind, sending a pang of hurt rippling through.

Their makeshift family, albeit temporary, lived on in his heart. "Everything is temporary, nothing lasts... As if it's not meant to." He inhaled deeply, attempting to swallow this difficult truth as a lump of guilt swelled in his throat, "I could have been more... I could have been better. There must have been a way," he exhaled, deflating as a memory surfaced.

Returning from his trek to the village and back, Ishayu had entered their hut feeling overly exhausted. Having finished the errands his father sent him out to care for several days earlier, he called out for him.

"Buba!"

The strange echo of his hail was the first thing that struck him. Twine tied to a rucksack of supplies slid off his shoulder and down his arm, the thud of goods hitting the wooden floor sounded out louder than it should have. He scanned the barren hut. Nearly everything was missing, not that they had much in the first place. The next thing he noticed was the uncommon chill. Ishayu walked over to the hearth, placing a hand above the lifeless ash. The cool pull of wind tugged at his hand from the passage above as he stared into the blackness for a long time before finally yelling.

"Bubā... Bubā... Bubā!!" he called out without removing his gaze from the blackened wood.

He wished he hadn't as the empty echo cemented his truth. Bubā was gone. His young hands poked at the ebony-colored remnants within the hearth, occasionally stealing away to wipe his tears, leaving traces of ash. After trying to gather his courage, the boy rose, spinning ever so slowly with his head hanging down. Ishayu knew what to expect, catching sight of it before investigating the cold hearth. Framed in ash, his teary-eyed gaze had locked onto Bubā's final gift glaring at him from the empty corner: his shepherd's staff.

Standing on the hillside and navigating a stew of emotion from that fateful day, Gracien's hand clenched at the staff. It was smooth and polished over with wear from decades of use. His hand rested on a knot two thirds of the way up, squeezing it as if he was wringing out the pain of abandonment. He could sympathize with and even forgive his father for succumbing to the mountain of grief he had endured after mother's death. But he could not forgive him for abandoning his one and only child. The boy's grief-laden eyes hardened under the weight of betrayal as they searched the landscape for understanding.

Ishayu had lived off the land and tended the flock on his own ever since father's desertion. Every so often he slept inside the hut, but most nights he preferred a starry sky and twilight's chill over the eerie silence of the hut.

Suddenly the sound of a distant bleat stole him from his reverie. Gracien's eyes narrowed as he tallied the animals. Several responding bleats rang out from the others scattered about the hills before the tribe began grouping back together.

His count came up short. "20... only 20" he confirmed as the distant bleat resounded again. "Oh no." The boy dashed over to his blanket, grabbing his rucksack of supplies before chasing after the distressed call.

Over an hour passed as he scoured the landscape, going the wrong way for far too long before getting back on track. He could barely concentrate as his mind rifled through an endless stream of scattered prompts and anxious thoughts. The march of the herd followed in his wake, and they were being rather rebellious today, needing a bit more encouragement than normal.

"They seem bothered by something today," he said out loud as his frustration mounted. "It must be near, I just heard it... How can this be! Keep looking, just keep looking and you'll find it. Such a fool, you should've been paying attention instead of daydreaming!"

His ears perked up as the bleat sounded off again. "There! It's close!" His head swiveled in the direction of the call, and he took off, leaving the herd behind then sprinting up a steep hill.

Gracien didn't even know why he was pressuring himself to hurry, he had lost many goats before, and so had his father. This was a common ordeal, but the stress of the situation seemed to overwhelm his mind and body. Completely out of breath with sweat beading across his brow, the boy overcame a summit to discover an unobstructed view. It took only a moment for him to locate the young doeling stuck within a small, dense thicket. As soon as she saw him, her cries poured forth as if she was being swept away by a river. Gracien sighed with relief before growling under his breath. He slowed to a trot as he approached but then something caught his attention as it sailed over a nearby hill. The black mass was traveling fast and heading straight towards the doeling.

"A wolf," he gasped.

He began sprinting down the hillside, but the grass was slick and the earth sloppy from recent rains. He stumbled three paces then fell as the forward momentum proved too much. He rolled, unknowingly losing his rucksack but using his staff to recover and launching back into a run. It was a footrace now. The wolf was much quicker but had more distance to cover. Gracien gained too much speed, causing his arms to flail as he tried keeping upright. He slipped and stumbled again before regaining his balance and diving feet first, sliding over the grassy terrain then crashing into the entangled animal. The tiny creature shrieked out in terror as Gracien shook himself, looking back along his wake and seeing a fifteen-foot mud streak. Wrestling the claw-like branches, he was able to quickly free himself, but the doeling rioted against her imprisonment, shrieking so loud it stung Gracien's ears.

"Shut up, dammit!" he growled through clenched teeth as he worked at wrenching her leg free from the mess of twisted branches.

She kicked and writhed trying to free herself. "BAA! BAA!" her screams were constant as Gracien's hands tore at the stubborn weaving while pressing his body against hers.

He instinctively went for his knife, finding nothing at his hip and looking back to see the little speck of his leather satchel back on the hillside. "SHIT!"

"Grrr…" His body froze as the deep growl bathed him in fear.

As the doeling thrashed and shrieked, the wolf's jaws snapped shut, spittle ricocheting from his mouth. Gracien's hand reached for his staff through the thicket, his head turning ever so slowly as his fingers inched over the ground. Fully outstretched, they clawed at the grass, but the staff was too far away.

Dive for it, his mind demanded.

He swallowed; the menacing growl was right on top of him. Gracien screamed as he launched himself towards the staff as the wolf lurched. Gracien's fingers wrapped around the weapon as he dive-rolled over it headfirst. In one fluent motion, he finished his roll and landed on his feet, twisting his body towards the threat and swinging the staff with all his might. He was shooting in the dark but hoped to be lucky. He landed his blow as the wolf's open mouth caught the flimsy attempt like a dog playing fetch with a stick. Its yellowed fangs sank into the wood as its momentum launched them both over the doeling and back into the thicket.

Gracien screamed, emboldening himself for battle like a charging warrior as he pulled the staff up over his head, using the wolf's momentum and sending the beast sailing over his head and back out of the thicket. Unharmed beyond a few scratches, Gracien sprung to his feet then jumped from the bush. He faced off with the massive predator as it instantly recovered, spinning towards Gracien with a quickened snap of its jaws. It held its attack, their glares uniting as the wolf resumed its deep growl and snapping jaws. Their tumble must have freed the doeling, as it fled up the hillside towards the herd. Gracien knelt down and observed the wolf's thick, raven-colored hair bristle as it crouched towards the ground, preparing to launch. With lips pulled back, exposing bright pink gums and sharp fangs, its mouth splattered saliva between snapping bites and rumbling growls. Gracien's eyes narrowed as he stepped in closer, wrenching his hands around the staff and warming it for battle.

Gracien circled, his heart nearly exploding with adrenaline as his body tensed for war. "Come on… Come onnn… Make the first move," the boy growled back while stabbing the staff forward and provoking the fight. "Come onnn…. Get on with IT!" he screamed.

Each time the staff stabbed outwards, the wolf leapt sideways, snapping, and barking at the empty space left behind.

"COME ON!" Gracien screamed while stomping the ground.

The wolf paused, then launched with jaws readied for attack. Gracien sidestepped, simultaneously swinging the staff overhead like an axe while using the full weight of his body. His feet lifted off the ground before landing with the staff hurtling towards the wolf's head.

CRACK! The thick wooden mast smashed into the side of the wolf's skull.

The violent force caused the beast to yelp out a piercing cry as it tumbled sideways, twisting, and writhing on the ground for a moment as if it were entangled in invisible netting. Gracien spared no time, stepping in and twirling the staff off his initial strike before slamming it down on the wolf's head.

CRUNCH!

The second strike offered no yelp as the beast twitched lifelessly. Gracien heaved breath like a man with his axe stuck in a tree. His eyes went wide with disbelief as he stared at the scene below. The staff's mast was lodged in the wolf's skull, causing one of its eyes to pop from the socket.

"Whoa," he said, stepping in to pry the staff free.

Even with that lifeless glare and its tongue hanging from the side of its mouth, the wolf looked just as menacing as it did moments ago. Gracien stepped on the wolf's neck, then in one quick motion sprung the knot of wood free.

The third sound was the worst of them all. A disgusting SCHLOOP! with a crunch.

"Ugh…" Blood and brain matter spattered across Gracien's face. "Grow-oh-oh-oh-sss." He wiped it away with a forearm. "Disgust-inggg!" He swept the fleshy muck from his face.

A chorus of distressed bleats rang out from the herd. "Ughhh… I'm coming…" he groaned before the heavy patter of quickened footsteps approached.

Gracien was tackled to the ground in a fury of snarling, barking bites. The staff went flying as the two crashed to the ground. They rolled over one another before this second wolf landed on top, ferociously biting and clawing at the boy's arms while trying to barrel its muzzle into his neck. Gracien screamed in terror as one fist punched upwards while the other defended his face and neck.

His father's words rang true: *always go for the eyes, boy. That's your only chance.*

The brawl was a nightmare of terror as the wolf thrashed and tore while Gracien shrieked in horror. All life outside of the struggle ceased to exist. Gracien's hands searched for the eye sockets but instead took hold of his jaws. Then his thumb found an eyeball, pressing down on it with all his might as he screamed out in rage. The wolf yelped out, thrashing about, and biting down on his fingers. Gracien pressed into the fleshy socket, piercing and rupturing the wolf's eyeball. It squealed and raged, lashing its head sideways before jumping backwards.

RIPP!

The sound occurred first, then the swell of pain swept in. The wolf's hysterical yelps and whines dwindled as it retreated up the hillside. Gracien moaned out, his back bowing with pain as he clutched his three fingered hand. Blood gushed from the mangled stumps and down his hand. The wolf's distant yelps were replaced by the familiar sound of barbaric roars and quickened footfalls closing in on Gracien. He inhaled, holding his breath, and tensing his whole body in preparation for certain death as his eyes closed and the creatures fell upon him.

"Boy! Boy!" The man shook him by the shoulders. Gracien's breath released through pursed lips as the tension of fear deflated.

And with his breath's escape, pain poured back into his hand. "Aghhh," he groaned.

"He's alive! He's alive!" the man yelled as his hands tried rattling him awake.

The stranger rolled Ishayu over to his back, bracing his neck while making the move. The boy inhaled, holding his breath as he cradled his injured hand, wincing and groaning out. Both of his hands were covered in blood, and he had several puncture wounds along his arms. A few scratches crisscrossed his face, and he was sure to discover a few bruises in the coming days.

"Ohhh… well actually it's not all that bad, we can manage this. It could have been far worse," he spoke gently to Ishayu before turning to another with an equally tranquil demeanor, "give me a rag or two. Even a spare shirt will do."

Ishayu's eyes opened with hesitancy as he winced. "Who are you?"

"Just a friend. Let's sit you up." The old man positioned his hand behind Ishayu's back. "Ready?" The boy nodded before being pushed upwards as he winced through a clenched jaw.

"Well done, well done. Okay now let me have a look," he continued speaking very calmly before calling back to his companion. "Bring water too."

As the stranger searched Ishayu for additional wounds, the boy looked him over. His head was balding in the upper front section with dark gray spikes of hair creating a crescent moon on the back half. The old man's cheeks were cratered and sunburned, which made his bushy gray eyebrows glow. He mumbled through dehydrated, cracked lips, revealing a large gap between his two front teeth. The man's face was the picture of austerity as he concentrated. Like the sun momentarily breaking through afternoon cloud cover, his expression brightened, flashing a gleaming smile after finding some small reason to celebrate.

"Oh, good, Good... Not too deep at all. This one will heal up quickly," he mumbled while poking Ishayu's neck.

Piercing green eyes scanned over Ishayu's chest as his weathered, cracked fingertips gently poked about, testing the severity and depth of wounds. His clothing was as old and dirty as the hills, with multiple layers and random patches covering holes and tears. A beautiful necklace aligned with cranberry-colored beads swung from side to side as he maneuvered about. Gracien looked up to see that the man's companions, two boys a bit older than Gracien and probably brothers, each brandished a similar necklace. The old man's boots were wrapped tightly with multiple strips of twine and were quite soiled, as were the bottoms of his pants. He was the embodiment of a Nepali mountain man; rugged to the core yet radiating an inner knowingness of peace and joy.

Ishayu released his hands, the uninjured one trembling as it backed away. The old man scooted in closer as the two younger boys hovered over his shoulder.

He took hold of Ishayu's wrist. "I've saved this for last as to wait for the wound to stop bleeding... I had to make sure there wasn't a more serious issue hiding under the veil of shock. Now let's have a look."

He turned Ishayu's hand by the wrist as he examined the wound. Gracien held in a wince, looking from the old man to the boys, to his hand, and then back to the boys. He anxiously scanned their expressions looking for any signs of disgust or worry.

"Three left and pretty clean tears, not bad... considering," the old man spoke with a surprised tone as he gave a satisfied nod.

He then pulled Gracien's arm into his lap as one of the boys handed him a wineskin of water. "Drink."

The water felt cool and crisp going down but then his stomach churned with its arrival. "A little more... You'll need it," the old man encouraged before looking Gracien dead in the eye. "Ready?" His bushy eyebrows lifted with the question.

The boy nodded, then winced, squeezing his eyes shut as the water trickled over the mutilated stumps.

Diluted blood mingled with saliva, hair, and dirt as the mixture washed down Gracien's hand and wrist. "Ohhh...Rrrrahhh!" he groaned then growled as the pink water exposed the mangled damage beneath.

"Are you left-handed?" the old man inquired. Gracien shook his head no.

"That's good news. And this is actually a very clean amputation, especially from a wolf. It won't need much, but I'll need to clean things up a bit. And then we'll get you all bandaged up. I'm going to get started... You may um, want to look away."

For the first time, the old man's piercing green eyes met Gracien's before releasing a comforting smile and nod of encouragement.

"It's okay, it won't hurt for long and then we'll be done. Ready?" he said as one of the others handed him a knife.

Gracien held his breath. Worry and panic bubbled up as he considered the impending pain. His glare took in the man's genial presence before consenting with his own nod. Gracien's gaze met that of the two boys for a moment before they both turned away. His wince was constant now, tensing his body while trying not to squirm. But overall, the pain wasn't nearly as bad as he feared. The sound of the knife whittling away however was rather unsettling and much louder than he cared for.

"Almost done, you're doing very well. I patched up these other wounds too, nothing too bad but you'll be sore in the morning and for a few days after," the man said while wiping his hands with a rag.

"Bubā, we'll gather his goats," one of the boys said.

The two could have been twins, but one was clearly taller and wider than his younger counterpart. They both had silky long hair that shone with the richness of lamp oil. The taller, fuller one had his hair tied up in a bun on the top of his head while the younger one's fell about his neck. He kept placing loose strands back behind his ear – bringing Gracien back to the days when he would do the same in his previous life as King. Both of them bore similar sunburnt cheeks and hazel-colored pupils. Their youth beamed from wide-eyed gazes, like a lantern's glow at twilight. Their clothing was not as worn as their father's, and it was much tighter around their bodies, giving them an agile, graceful appearance as they moved about with swift, natural fluidity.

"Good idea, we'll catch up. Your home, it's in the direction of your goats, yes?" The man looked to Gracien for a moment before returning to his work. "You can look now." He slowly wrapped several pieces of a torn shirt around the boy's hand.

"Yes, a small hut, about a thirty-minute walk if the goats aren't too much trouble." Gracien couldn't help but wince through his speech.

The two boys looked to one another before picking up their large packs, as well as their father's, then dashing off towards the herd.

"They're good boys, a bit older than you, I'd guess. The goats won't be much trouble for them. And hopefully they're a bit more settled with the wolves having made their retreat. Let me help you up." He rose to his feet, sighing with the buildup of ache in his body. "Old knees… Lots of miles. The older, taller one, he's called Yajat. And the other, Yajin." He chuckled before gently pulling Gracien up to his feet.

"Thank you for helping me." Gracien cradled his hand as he back-stepped.

"No need to thank me, we heard the commotion while passing through. First the frightened calls of the herd, then the screaming," the man spoke casually while dusting himself off.

"My hand, my fingers… should I…?" Gracien didn't know how to proceed.

He paused for a moment while scanning the scene of the fight.

"Should you what? Find them?" He shook his head. "They're of no help to you now, best to leave behind what's not helpful. And who knows… You could spend half a day looking and the whole time they're inside the belly of a one-eyed wolf!" He chuckled again.

"How did you know it lost an eye?" Gracien's face washed over with confusion.

"We saw its retreat, its frantic behavior… It was clawing at his face and rubbing it into the ground. And there's no blade lying around so how else could you have managed to injure it?"

Gracien pictured the blade in his rucksack, thinking himself a fool for losing it on his way down the hillside. The old man bent down, picking up the bloodied staff and washing it off before handing it back to Gracien. Then the two of them walked over to the dead wolf, standing over and staring at it.

"He's beautiful. It's not too often you get to see one up close."

The old man pulled out a knife then bent down, cutting one of the canines from its mouth before turning his blade on the wolf's hide.

Gracien watched as he made quick work of removing the wolf skin before wrapping it up and cleaning his blade. He was slow to stand while washing off his hands again, using the water from the wineskin carefully. The man nodded with satisfaction before walking a few paces and pausing, turning back towards Gracien.

"My name is Bandhu… That's something I usually share much earlier when meeting someone." He chuckled with his eyes squinting over. "But I guess either way, it's nice to meet you…?"

"Ishayu. And thank you, Bandhu."

"Let's check in on the boys, I'm sure they've got your herd all bundled up by now."

And with that Bandhu began making the trek back up the hill, the fresh wolf skin tossed over his shoulder. Gracien followed in his wake, clenching the staff with his good hand as if to check that all his fingers were still there.

The call of his goats rang out in the distance.

Gracien moved to attend their call before stopping himself short with a wince. *Bandhu, and the boys... They're taking care of them,* he thought before slumping back into his seat.

The hills rolled out before him like billowed bed sheets and the tall, lush grass appeared so perfect and still that he could have been looking at a painting. Gracien sighed, leaning back against the firm trunk of the bodhi tree, a favorite of his mother's. The extensive, intricately shaped tree trunk was molded by time's artistic hand, hiding secrets and tales of antiquity in its multitude of crevices. As if it had been carved out solely for this purpose, Gracien fit snuggly into a little pocket of the trunk. While picking at a newly wrapped, partially bloodied bandage, he winced as he prodded and tested for any reduced soreness. Several days had passed since the wolf incident and he had yet to make much progress in improvement. He was ready to be done and healed, but even with Bandhu taking care of him and the boys attending to the goats, it seemed impossible for his hand to improve. He unconsciously grabbed for this or that and constantly bumped into just about anything, each time wincing over, gritting his teeth, and squeezing the wrist of his injured hand as if it were a hissing viper.

As he picked at the bandage he muttered, "You don't realize how much you rely on something until it's gone." The statement settled within his gut like a swallowed stone.

A wave of anxiety built within his chest as his mind raced with an endless array of wandering thoughts. He exhaled, slumping into himself, and allowing the tension to pour from his body. For some reason he began visualizing Aya being there with him. He pictured her leaning up against the other side of the tree trunk as if they had decided to rest in the shade after a long stroll. Visualizing her beside him helped him to feel more comfortable speaking out loud.

"Aya... I miss you and I feel utterly lost without you. I miss having you around, and I miss your kisses. I miss your affection and your compassion..." Tears began gathering but he quickly wiped them away. "I miss being your husband. I miss being the man I once was. But now... now everything's been ripped away. And I don't know what to do with myself. A shepherd." He sobbed, stuttering a bit. "A boy minding goats in the middle of this, this nothingness." He motioned to the sprawling landscape. "I just don't... I just don't know Aya, and I need help... Please guide me. Help me with some direction. I'm so, so lost and..." He held up his injured hand, sighing. "I'm a mess, just look at me..." His hand dropped to his lap, sending a surge of pain rippling up his arm. He grabbed for his wrist again, choking it until the pain abated.

Gracien gently placed his hand into his lap like it was a cup of tea before dropping his head in despair. The boy sobbed for several moments before thinking something over. The idea seemed a bit crazy, but it wouldn't leave his mind.

He wrestled with the notion, teetering back and forth... *Don't be a fool, that's impossible. Yes maybe, but what could it hurt? No one's here.* He checked his surroundings then began to think his request, *Ayadonna...* Again he stopped, inhaling courage before speaking out loud. "Aya, my love, can you hear me?" He checked the tree canopy as if she could've been up there listening.

His gaze dropped, scanning the windless, grass covered hills. "Hey you..." Gracien paused, breathing in deeply before continuing. "Please can you give me a sign? It's been so calm today... A gust of wind, a breeze, anything... anything to let me know that you're here with me, listening in on my silly requests."

Deep within himself he felt that she was with him, but he wanted something more, he wanted to see *it*. He missed her response, the affection of her sweet voice and this void made the moment eerily quiet. Gracien recalled one of the thousand times Aya had heeded his requests.

"Tell me you love me," Gracien had casually requested in the middle of a quiet stroll.

Aya smirked, keeping her head down before placing a strand of hair behind her ear. Ever so slowly she looked up at him from the corner of her eye, her head tilting to the side as she considered him. Gracien, maintaining a smirk, stared at his feet while they walked.

"I love you," she said.

Simple, sweet, and pure. Like a schoolboy finding out his crush liked him, he couldn't help but fall into a full smile. Something he knew with every ounce of his soul, but something he still longed to hear every day. Gracien had asked her this a thousand times over, and Ayadonna never disappointed him.

He liked to hear that she loved him even though he knew more than anyone. He needed to hear it, see it, and feel it. And so, after asking his sweet Aya for a sign of her love, Gracien found himself holding his breath as he looked to the skies, hoping for the arrival of a butterfly. He scanned the leaves and branches above, wanting them to shudder. His eyes fell upon the grassy hill just before him and found only stillness, only silence. Some time passed as he sat with expectancy, searching the area for any abnormalities before finally giving up.

Just then something moved on the summit of a hill directly in front of him. The grass on top began to sway. Not from side to side like a

dancer, rather it bowed forward like something was pressing it from behind. A sudden wind arrived. The grass covering the downward slope of
the hillside continued to bow forward as the wind rolled down like an
ocean wave building momentum. Gracien's eyes went wide as the howl
of the wind arrived before its embrace. The unexpected gale continued
rolling down the hillside until meeting the ground then charging towards him. Then, the wave swallowed him up.

His mind blushed with visions of Aya as he heard the sound of her
sweet voice whisper, "I love you, my Beloved."

Gracien's eyes teared over as a stimulating vibration rippled over his
skin. The gale blew past, shaking the branches and leaves just as he had
desired moments ago. It had chilled the wake of tears streaming down
his face as he inhaled air sweeter than goat milk.

His spirit had surfaced from the abyss, and he couldn't help but don
a schoolboy smirk while holding back a laugh. "Thank you, my Beloved," he whispered while basking in the beauty of emotion.

"Ishayu?" Bandhu's voice rang out from the other side of the tree.

Startled, Gracien jumped. "Over here," his raspy voice returned as
he wiped away tears before poking his head out from the tree.

"Agh, there you are. We've been looking for you, supper is almost
ready. You haven't eaten much today and if you expect those fingers to
grow back then you'll need to fill that belly." Bandhu chuckled as his
hands rounded the massive tree trunk before poking his head out. "You
seem to be in rather high spirits. I don't think I've seen you with such an
aura of satisfaction before."

Bandhu knelt, sitting cross legged on one of the exposed roots with
his hands resting on his lap. Gracien smiled then recoiled into himself,
trying to hide his tears. He returned his gaze to the hill; the grass having
returned to a painting.

"A beautiful day, just perfect," Bandhu's words poured out in a trickle. "A bit of a breeze would be nice but I'm not complaining." He chuckled again.

Gracien looked at him, curiosity washing over his face as Bandhu rocked in his seat, adjusting himself a bit before straightening his spine and beginning to breathe very slowly.

"Do you mind if I stay here a while and sit with you?"

Gracien shook his head, then resumed scanning the horizon as Bandhu's eyes closed with him teetering in his seat several times before settling. Somehow Bandhu's presence added a level of peace which had not been there prior. As the minutes went by the boy couldn't help but glance at the old man out of the corner of his eye. Bandhu had yet to move a muscle other than his diaphragm, which rolled his breath in and out of his body like someone kneading a mound of dough. The setting sun began consuming the idle stalks of grass as the crisp blanket of dusk settled over the landscape. After over forty-five minutes Gracien wondered whether he should wake Bandhu before returning to the hut for supper or if he should let him sleep.

Without opening his eyes, Bandhu suddenly spoke up, giving Gracien a start. "You've been squirming the entire time, is everything alright?"

"You startled me, I thought... I thought you were sleeping."

"I wasn't sleeping but meditating. It's nice around new energy." Bandhu's eyelids peeled open and he stretched, pulling his shoulders back and cracking his neck from side to side. "I love a good sunset meditation." He ingested the final moments of daylight with a deep breath and a contented countenance. "Ahhh... I feel refreshed." He looked over to Gracien.

Bandhu's words and expression intrigued the boy. "What... How... What do you *do*, while meditating?" Gracien asked.

Bandhu didn't chuckle as Gracien had predicted but became rather serious, turning towards the boy but with an amiable, partial smile.

"Meditation... Well, there are many reasons and many intentions. Tonight, I was trying to still my mind and soak up the last of the day's radiance, kind of like a nap but more efficient and no groggy feeling after." The old man chuckled once again. "But typically I want to be without thought, to give my mind a rest so to speak and allow my true self to reign over awareness." Bandhu huffed with a smirk at Gracien's expression, which resembled a mindless goat.

"Was that a bit confusing?"

Gracien nodded, his furrowed brow and bewildered look cemented as Bandhu released his meditation posture, slinking down the tree root and facing the boy.

"It's easier if I teach you. Just the beginning part. There's nothing to worry about, it's just breathing at first, okay?" Bandhu smiled.

Before the boy had a chance to counter, Bandhu proceeded. "Keep your spine straight and place your hands on your lap with your palms facing upwards, like this. Make sure to keep your shoulders back and then take a deep breath. Good, now close your eyes." Gracien looked to Bandhu, but his eyes were already closed.

"Now feel the breath being pulled in through your nostrils, feel the rim of them flare ever so slightly as they tug at the inhalation. Be sure to breathe with your belly, not your chest... Feel the air fill your diaphragm like wine into a wineskin." Bandhu's voice was as clear as the wind, firm but sweet.

Like a brisk breeze, it reached beyond the boy's exterior, chilling his core like the pluck of a harp cord.

"Settle into the moment like a ripple rolling over then merging with the surface of a pond. Feel the air retreat, deflating your belly as the breath is released back into the world. Notice how the air is slightly warmer as it passes over the rims of your nostrils."

Gracien's nostrils came alive as if Bandhu himself had somehow warmed them. Like wind sweeping dirt from a stone road, Gracien's breath had cleared his mind, making it cleaner and focused, lighter even.

"That was just one breath." Bandhu's voice seemed to come from within Gracien's mind, vibrating with the sincerity of a revelation.

"Let's do that several more times, I'll guide you. Another deep breath..." Bandhu instructed, and Gracien heeded without hesitation.

The two of them breathed in unison beneath the great bodhi tree as if they were part of the root's structure.

Sometime later, the duo sauntered back to the hut as Gracien inquired, "where... where did you learn to do that? To meditate like that?" He felt himself walking slower, as the two of them were trudging uphill but without any effort.

"I didn't discover it by myself. There was one who helped me. A wise, noble teacher who gave me the lessons I couldn't create on my own. Muktinath, that's my teacher's name." Bandhu smiled.

Gracien pictured what this wise, noble man must look like: a short, long bearded man with silvered hair and deep-set eyes. He walked with a cane and barely spoke, but when he did, pearls of wisdom trickled from his mouth through a voice as creaky as an unoiled door.

Gracien moved to ask another question before Bandhu answered it. "In the mountains. Up in the mountains." He stopped, turning towards the peaks slicing into the nightscape.

Bandhu inhaled deeply, his eyes narrowing on the peaks glowing under the lingering daylight as if they had been dipped in honey. Gracien exchanged glances between Bandhu and the majestic Himalayas, finding both equally impressive.

"Do you smell that?" Being pulled from his reverie, Bandhu turned to Gracien with eyes as wide as saucers. "Supper must be ready! We shouldn't keep two growing boys from a meal unless we want to face the wrath of puberty. HA!" Bandhu roared as the two resumed their stroll, Gracien mindfully considering the mountain's secret teacher in place of visions of supper.

He looked over his shoulder, seeing that the grass within his wake had been flattened by footsteps as he counted the herd. Gracien's hand swept over the soft tips of the waist-high grass, watching as his fingers mingled with the flowing blades. He was a king again with his gleaming eyes and manicured beard. The stalks careened with the weight of the wind. His head tilted to the side as he studied their movement. It seemed as if the pasture performed a choreographed ballet, swaying and pitching around him like a meadow of synchronized dancers. The emerald-colored winds howled over the grassy hills, which weren't one huge rolling mass but rather a series of soaring islands. His ear caught the ripple of a new howl, one that sounded not of the wind, but something more like a hymn sung far off in the distance.

As the echo of the beautiful sound faded, Gracien resumed his stroll, his feet slicing through the grass as if he was wading in the shallows of a peacock-feathered sea. His attention returned to the goats, whose mouths chewed the grass while hovering over the hills like clouds. An ocean of greenery flowed along the hillside, its surface being tugged by an unseen current. Gracien squinted, focusing on the rich, chestnut-colored summits expanding along the horizon. They were crested with a pearled icing that sliced into bulbous, pastel clouds. Like warmer lands inciting migration, the Himalayas beckoned him with a near palpable force.

Gracien walked uphill, one hand leaning on the shepherd's staff while the other glided over the careening spires of grass tickling his palms. The sensation stirred a memory of his childhood which layered over his vision like a sheet of ice. A boy's hand, his own from many years prior, had skimmed over the surface of a pond as seaweed danced just beneath. His little hand felt the slimy, wet tickle of seaweed, stirring a giggle from him as small waves rippled out. The surface of the pond rippled out while reflecting the forest surrounding him. As his hand skimmed the water's surface, Ayadonna appeared over his shoulder in the pond's reflection, somewhat blurred yet radiant as ever. The child spun around, only to find himself back in the hills, surrounded by goats, the wind howling about, and back in the body of a shepherd.

Gracien smirked at the ancient memory, turning again, and resuming his stroll until nearing the summit of the tallest hill in view. The heavens were painted with embellished features and impossible colors. The clouds glowed with an inner cobalt while the outer edges faded in vibrancy like diluted sapphires. The sky behind the clouds bore the pink hue of blooming cherry blossoms. Gracien inhaled like a liberated prisoner as he pushed off his knee with one hand and gripped his staff with the other, climbing the last few steps of the steep incline. Like it does after a heavy rain, the air felt dense yet cool and comforting. It embraced the man as he crested the earthly platform overlooking a great expanse of sailing hills. His hair flailed in the wind as the grass below rippled out like the miniature waves on the pond from his boyhood.

Gracien looked to his free hand, making a fist then splaying out his fingers and examining them. He then looked at the staff with all its wear and scars. It looked so tired, so worn and defeated, like an elderly man beckoning death's sweet embrace. His father's staff suddenly felt too heavy, and his hands were so small – the hands of a boy once more. The shepherd's staff was so heavy that his boyish hands could barely hold it up. He rolled the great staff into the nooks of his elbows, as if it was a mighty tree branch.

And then she called to him. "Grayyy - Sea - Ennn…." His name swirled over the landscape as if Aya herself was the wind blowing about.

The bottom of the heavy staff fell to the ground, and the boy leaned on it as he peered over the landscape, searching for her.

"Grayyseaenn.... Let it beee...." she howled as he pulled the staff upwards, allowing the great weight to balance on itself.

He knew it was time.

He couldn't help but weep. This old shepherd's staff held so much sorrow. "So heavy... so weighted with grief," he whispered as tears streamed down his cheeks. The wind swiped them away as it embraced the boy before helping him to push the staff over the ledge. "Goodbye father," he said out loud as the staff pitched forward like a toppling tree.

It groaned out as it plummeted downwards before being swallowed up within the cloud clover below. He stared into the miniature swirl of clouds, watching as it healed over and feeling a weightlessness reside within. He looked to his hands again, the hands of a man clenched into fists before splaying out his fingers. Gracien stood taller, gazing out into the expanse sprawling out before him. One thing and one thing alone stood out amongst the rest: the peaks of the Himalayas glowing with the luster of gold. The wind whipped about, that hymn along with it, tossing his hair and rolling over a stretch of grass towards the mighty mountain range as if it was carving out a path.

Gracien's eyes popped open, the sound of twilight welcoming his return. The boy rose from the bedding as slowly as he could. The glow of the sleepy embers crackling within the hearth provided enough light for him to move about.

He couldn't make out their forms, but he could hear the others sleeping. One of the boys chastising his dream. "The lost sheep, down in the valley..." he mumbled, "who will save it?" He rolled over with a slight moan.

Gracien kept still, holding his breath as Yajin settled back into a peaceful slumber. Like a stalking snow leopard, he crept about the hut packing his things. He filled a large satchel of supplies then added extra layers of clothing over those he was already wearing. One more small satchel was filled with food and a few spare effects, and he was nearly ready. Rising from his cowering position he stood tall for the first time since waking. Gracien adjusted the strap of the satchel with his good hand while approaching the hearth. The flooring groaned out under his extra weight, making him pause and lessen the pressure of his foot before applying it again and stepping forward.

His injured hand extended, reaching out for his father's staff before pausing. The pop of an ember leapt from the hearth with the wind howling down the chimney, stirring the glow into a flame. Gracien's bandaged hand hovered in front of his father's staff. Examining his hand under the newborn firelight, he saw that it was not the hand of a boy any longer, but one that had grown into the hand of a man. Gracien looked over the mess of soiled dressing and before he knew it, his good hand was stripping away the bloodied bandage, unspooling it as several stings of pain cut through him. He didn't allow himself to wince as he stared down at the deformity, a determined man accepting his fate. He tossed the bloodied rag into the fire and waited. A moment later the flame bulged as the bandage ignited, illuminating half of Gracien's complexion in a golden luster as the other half lay veiled in darkness. He stared at the bandage until it was all but consumed before shifting his gaze to father's staff.

His hand did not grab the staff but caressed the polished wood. "Goodbye father," he whispered before turning, echoing his dream. He tiptoed towards the door and paused, speaking under his breath, "thank you my friends." He gave them a nod before pulling the door and making a silent exit.

He pressed the door closed then walked backwards from it, exhaling a great breath. The night sang out around him as his breath released like steam from a boiling kettle.

"Nice night for a walk, aye?" Bandhu's face illuminated under the glow of his pipe, causing Ishayu to topple over as he gasped in fright.

"What... what are you doing out here?" he spat.

The glow of the old man's pipe lessened as a quiet chuckle rang out. "Shhh... shhh... shhh. We don't want to wake the boys. I'm out here every night. I enjoy a good pipe after a long meditation, helps me center. And I was waiting for you..." His face lit up as he sucked on the pipe.

"I wasn't going to let you go without providing some directions. Well at least the best I can do with all these years mushing up the details. But I should be able to get you there just fine."

The smoke from his pipe billowed around the old man's head, cloaking him from Gracien.

"How did you..." Gracien began.

"I know my mind, boy, and therefore I know *the* mind. I knew the moment I spoke about my teacher that you'd take off trying to find Muktinath. Egh-ha!" Bandhu coughed, leaning over. "This... this is also why I smoke in the nighttime," he croaked, laughing. "The boys, they think I'm killing myself with this stuff." He recovered, sitting up straight. "Why do you think I mentioned my teacher in the first place?" he questioned.

Gracien could hear the old man's smirk. "Why are you helping me?" he asked.

"Because I was you. At some point in the soul's evolution, everyone is. But don't mind that now." He rose from his seat, approaching Gracien.

"I shouldn't... I shouldn't call you, 'Boy.' You have the spirit of a man and the hardened grit of one too. Your journey will prove to soften that over time, and I wish you a fruitful quest. I hope you find what it is you're looking for." Bandhu pointed towards the north, sharing his directions with Gracien before placing his hands on both of Gracien's shoulders. "Fourteen days or so, depending on the weather. This is the best season to trek through, but that doesn't guarantee a safe journey." He sighed. "The Himalayas, as majestic as they are, they've taken many seekers from this world too soon. So be cautious and stay present." Bandhu then mumbled a silent prayer over Gracien before returning to his seat.

Gracien backstepped. "Thank you Bandhu. And one other thing, I won't be returning. I'd like to leave this place, and my goats to you and your sons. A gesture of my gratitude. Thank you Bandhu. Please tell Yajat and Yakin I wish I would've had more time to get to know them. Namaste." He turned, avoiding Bandhu's response, stepping quickly into the darkness.

A few days into his quest, Gracien found himself scaling a rugged dirt path dividing an enormous expanse of rice fields. He paused, taking a moment to catch his fleeting breath while patting his sweat covered brow. It didn't do much good as the rag was too wet to mop up any more sweat. An unrelenting afternoon sun beat down on him, making the reddest patches of his weather-beaten skin throb with irritation. A thin shirt worn only to separate his skin from the satchel straps was also soaked with perspiration, as were the straps themselves. The stifling air was thick with moisture and the temperature seemed to challenge what could be achieved on a clear summer's day.

He took out a wineskin, weighing the lightness in his hand before downing the last of the water. *I'll need to stop soon, to fill up,* he thought, his intense gaze scanning the landscape.

His bulging cheeks took their time swooshing the water around before swallowing. He picked at a lentil stuck in his tooth from the afternoon meal, dal bhat with a spicy chutney, and yellow curried veggies with a side of pickled cucumbers. Gracien ate this meal or a similar version of it each day of his life but along this adventure he discovered some rather tasty alterations. The rice in this version had a sweet basil flavor while the lentils were a bit saltier than usual. As he resumed walking, Gracien considered which preparation he preferred, but it was just too damn hot to think about food. The wind, a seemingly rare commodity this afternoon, finally made an appearance, blowing in and cooling the wet spots on his skin. The sweet breeze provided a much-needed refreshment to the tune of mildly aggressive rapids flowing in the distance.

"I do need more water." He looked for the sapphire river but couldn't make it out from where he stood.

Sweat had already reformed across his brow, he instinctively swiped it dry with his forearm. "An hour or so more and then I'll take a dip and fill-up." He smirked, adjusting his satchel before resuming his ascension through the vibrant stalks of grass.

"Follow the river. Ascend the rice fields until you think you've reached the last of them… then climb some more." He repeated the first part of Bandhu's directions as his wide gait placed one new step in front of the next.

Three days into his journey and his legs were sore and heavy with an ache he had never before experienced. His lower back felt as bent as a banana and his feet had each developed a string of blisters. Reddened lines of irritation ran across his shoulders from the satchel straps rubbing into his flesh. His hands and feet were pudgy and bloated from countless steps. The first two days he found himself annoyed and even angry at times with the various aches, bruises, and mild scratches. But this third day there had been a shift: he was working on Bandhu's instructions for meditating throughout his walks, keeping his eyes open, and focusing on his breath. And so, he had noticed a change. He wasn't nearly as upset with the aches and pains, as the physical sensation drew him into awareness like a moth to a flame. This newly discovered concentration, coupled with the beautiful and undistilled sound of nature, drew him into a presence on a level he had never before experienced.

One thought arose: *it's kind of like a meditation in its own respect: stillness, focus, an underlying feeling of peace.* He inhaled, drawing in the humid breath, and holding it as he continued to trudge onwards.

A moment later and that peaceful thought morphed into something else completely. Suddenly, he was overwhelmed with the surrealness of Aya's passing and his current situation. The thought then evolved, highlighting the complete uncertainty of what he was doing in this very moment, escalating his anxiety like a twister whipping across an open landscape.

One anxious thought led to another, which then doubled his angst by highlighting his utter lack of reason for this journey.

This is utterly insane. Thoughts like this blossomed from nowhere, enraging his budding panic like a furious wind provoking a forest fire. *What the hell are you doing, Ishayu… Leaving your hut, your house like that without any kind of plan or destination and just giving everything you own away to complete strangers? You fool! What an idiot!* His breath doubled as he blinked his surroundings into focus.

His heartbeat raced as his vision began tunneling, feeling as though an icy hood was being pulled over his head. Like a blind man inspecting the floor on which he stood, Gracien patted the earth before sinking into its cool embrace.

Stop, stop, stop… pa-lease stop… his mind pleaded with itself as the panic swept in, whisking away his outer senses as his pulse surged with budding terror.

And then his grief awakened like a mythological beast rising from the sea.

"Aya my love… Why did you leave me?" Gracien pleaded with her while cradling himself.

He lay crippled with the torrent of panic and grief dueling for dominance when something mysterious suddenly occurred. He felt or rather noticed a presence of some sort, something new yet familiar. It lingered in the backdrop of his mind, watching or attending to his thoughts like the sea watching ships sail across it. This new presence merely observed the thought that raced through, examining the incessant stream of panic-filled, grief-brimmed thoughts, yet it remained unmoved and indifferent. Beyond that even, this force was at complete peace with the moment.

For an instant, his discovery of this mysterious presence banished all his fears and anxiety in one quick swoop, leaving him feeling still, quiet, and settled. But in the very next, the previous tidal wave of panic rebounded, expelling his peace like beggars upon a stoop. He resumed rocking himself and yet through this immediate change of temperament, Gracien's external environment remained the same. No threat came forth, no change in the sun's brilliance or the wind's gentle touch, even the birds continued their song. It was his mind, and that alone, which had shifted like an instant storm, ushering in terror, then instilling peace for a flash, then allowing the terror to rebound.

With this realization, Gracien slowly pushed himself off the ground as echoes of mental chaos dwindled. His observance narrowed, penetrating the soul of this newfound truth, and replaying the episode as if he was rereading part of a book.

Like a strike of lightning, a bold and illuminating thought rippled through his mind. *While I focused on my body's ache and discomfort, I sensed the wind's touch and the sun's warmth, and concentrated on the struggle of each new step…* His brow furrowed over as his tear laden gaze narrowed in on the distant horizon. *I had no thoughts, my mind was blank. I felt…* He paused, sitting upright as he searched for the correct term. *Only… presence. And then for some reason, without choice, my mind filled with thoughts of…* Like a hunter he began retracing tracks before feeling his angst and panic creep in from the shadows of his mind. *No, no, no… Stay here, stay present.* He took a deep breath, standing and scanning the landscape with all the concentration he could muster.

His head dipped backwards, and he closed his eyes. Gracien smelled the air, felt his body's ache and the radiating warmth of his sunburn. He listened with all his might to the surrounding harmony of critters moving about: the birdsong, the rustle of grass, and the wind's migration. All this happened in an instant as Gracien exhaled, releasing his breath as slowly as the oldest tide to ever have been. He was back, united with this new state of being, with presence.

Gracien stood tall, formulating the right sequence of words with exacting focus. "No thought meant stillness and peace. Thoughts of dread, uncertainty, and loss… They drummed up despair and panic." He nodded, tilting his head, and finding himself ascending back up the path as if the previous episode had all been a dream.

Gracien couldn't put the particulars of this discovery into words, but he certainly knew that something very profound had just occurred. As he resumed his trek, Gracien's mind replayed the events repeatedly, trying to discover some small new detail at every pass. A few minutes later and his mind was busy juggling an endless stream of useless thoughts. Just then he heard the subtle lull of rapids. Picking his head up, he smirked at the beauty of the river rounding a bank. He ran up to it, tossing his gear to the side and quickly undressing. He jogged into the shallows, wading into the calm bend of the river. Scooping up water and dowsing himself under the coolness, he enjoyed the shudder of pleasure rippling through his being.

As the days progressed forward, the seasons drifted backwards. The stifling hot and humid summer abated into the refreshing embrace of spring. Rice fields and thick jungle vegetation thinned into pockets of forest along the trails with rejuvenating breezes toting floral scents and crisp river aromas up the maturing foothills. His irritation with the difficulty of the trek and the varying terrain dwindled as he continued. Gracien found himself questioning why he ever had irritation and annoyance in the first place. Maybe it was the cooling and now tolerable temperature that had allowed him a whole day's trek before needing to rinse off in the river. While the temperature dropped, the elevation soared. Testing the young man's lungs, his breath ebbed with a bit more difficulty with the passing of each new day. The tradeoff, however, was that with the thinning air and reduced humidity, it was much easier to breathe and the air even tasted fresher. Gracien took more time to catch his breath, finding himself edging a cliff to take in the majestic beauty of an untouched landscape.

The snowcapped Himalayas bloomed as he ascended, the rocky terrain enlivening as the crispness of snow mirrored the sun's radiance. Gracien saw blankets of pines peeking through the horizon whenever he had a good line of sight through the valley ahead. Thick forests engulfed him one moment, swaddling the young man in a crisp, shaded chill before thinning to nothing and giving way to the sun's unbridled warmth. Gracien trudged uphill through the heavy vegetation, then one innocent looking switchback later and he was overwhelmed by a view so majestic it stole what breath he had left. The sparkling river was a constant companion but, like any good sidekick, it departed for a portion of his journey. Gracien's path would diverge around a steep cliff-side for a few miles before reuniting with the winding river like two old friends. The fluid chorus of moving water kept his mind present as he walked alongside it, but he also enjoyed the fading of its lull as their paths diverted. True silence was a rare commodity, as the retreat of the rapid's acoustic lull allowed for the hymn of the wind and the song of birds. Gracien didn't mind nature's choir, as the silence typically proved too much for him. Empty silence was too thick, too loud, and most of the time made him feel uncomfortable in his own skin. It highlighted his reality, his solitude, darkening his thoughts and beckoning grief's return.

There were, however, some unexpected treats which lightened the mood when his anguish and suffering seemed to veil the blanket of beauty surrounding him. Passing through the various villages was an absolute joy. The children's smiling faces, dirty and worn down by the elements, expressed the highest state of joy while they toyed with sticks and stones, acting out some playful drama with invisible friends and joyful laughter. The host families of the teahouses bustled with activity and energy. Mothers shouted commands, deploying a multitude of children out to complete various tasks while finalizing the finishing touches on a supper which would be delighted over by migrating trekkers or shepherds. The nomad's hardened faces, unmoved as they migrated over the difficult terrain, softened as the aromatic stew billowed steam beneath immense smiles and gleaming eyes. Tales and myths were shared alongside rice-wine toasts and communal laughter. Gracien kept to himself for the most part, but the corner of his smirk extended often enough as he eavesdropped on swapped stories of adventure and mishap.

As if they had been expecting his arrival, animals frequented Gracien along his journey. Goats encircled him as they shared the same path for an afternoon, chewing mouthfuls of grass on one end and dropping pellets of waste out of the other. He had never seen such massive herds. Hundreds, or maybe thousands, scattered themselves over the hillsides, blanketing the river's shore or clogging up the narrow mountain passes. Enormous bulls as big as huts flaunted horns borrowed from the depths of Naraka. Magnified muscle spilled down their limbs while strutting along like undisputed warriors. Yaks with fur caked in nature and excrement frequented his path when they weren't camouflaged in the grassy plains. Their noses trickled gunk like sap from a tree wound. Massive slug-like tongues licked and picked inside their nostrils as if digging for some unknown delicacy. Packs of wild horses migrated over the sprawling hills, slowing time as Gracien marched along in selfish awe. Their color patterns amazed him: mountain grays speckled with mud, shiny caramel ones, spotted cow look-alikes, and a few as black as night whose sheen radiated its own vibrancy rather than the reflection of the sun. And then there was, 'the one.' A shooting star illuminating a murky night. She was pure white and an utter spectacle with her long flowing mane tantalizing the winds.

"Wow." He couldn't help but feel like he was seeing something not meant for his earthly eyes. Gracien knew then and there that he would one day adventure along these mountains on horseback.

The sound of Gracien's footing along the gravel faded as he took in the pageant-like horse parade. It was a dream, their hair fanned out as they raced about aimless and free, nudging, and caressing one another. The tall grass swept about their delighted gaits as the wind blew through, encouraging them like the whip of a charioteer. It was the ideal, balanced existence. One free from strife and worry with nothing preying upon them and an endless bounty of nourishment, which also padded their galloping hooves. Gracien felt envious of their livelihood, but as they danced along the open prairie with one another like carefree children, he couldn't help but smile, adjusting his satchel straps and taking a deep breath before nodding in recognition. He didn't know what he understood or even why he was nodding, but something new had settled within him which wasn't there moments ago. His eyes narrowed as he focused in on the last of them overtaking a hill and disappearing on the other side. Suddenly, the white one stopped short. She turned towards him and met his gaze, a moment which felt like a sign. Gracien wanted her to come to him, to leave the others or rear up and make a spectacle of herself, but she just stood there taking him in before disappearing over the hillside. He exhaled, allowing his smile to melt away before resuming his own voyage.

Hawks and eagles screeched out, interrupting Gracien's deep thoughts. He could watch their soaring flight for hours if he didn't have to mind his steps through the tricky, ever-changing terrain. Squirrels and other darting rodents scampered about, stopping to share a brief exchange while boasting bulging cheeks. The insects seemed to be having a reunion, celebrating the feast of flesh making its way right through their kitchen. Creepy crawlers, buzzing brutes, stinging suckers, wiggling wretches, tickling titans, and squishy scoundrels – each of them gave him the heebie-jeebies. But none were worse than the eight-legged adversaries.

Spiders, holy spiders. Spiders for days and then more spiders. Rickety bridges extended over sections of raging rivers, simple constructions that swung with the sneeze of a breeze. But at least they were reinforced with all the funnel webbing running their length. He ducked, quick stepping over the bridge, only looking up briefly to see a starry sky on a moonless night. Except that the starry sky was spider webbing, and the stars were the spiders.

"Oh-shit, Oh-shit, Oh-shit," he sputtered, squirming like a child as he imagined the spiders running the length of his body.

The rapids below the bridge raged, adding to his anxiety as slippery planks, thinning, and rotting from wear, made for the worst possible footing. Ropes anchored to trees and rocks along the banks creaked and squealed, moaning out in revolt for their imprisonment which had lasted over a generation. Any other spider-free bridge was a delight. He'd lean on the rope, stick his hands out in front of him and pretend he was flying. Gracien usually took his time soaking up the river's spray, appreciating the lush, winding valleys or nearby waterfalls spouting rainbows.

On one special occasion, Gracien had spent the night sleeping outside of a teahouse all wrapped up in the navy of twilight. He couldn't fall asleep, the image of the countless spiders seared into his mind's eye. If he counted them up, their numbers would have exceeded the number of steps he took throughout the day. Gracien woke early the next morning, checking his clothing and hair, thinking some creepy crawler had found a place to hunker down for the night. As he made his way to the latrine he checked, doubled checked, and then triple checked. The old rotten door swung into the small enclosure like a piece of bark swinging from a derelict tree. It slammed shut behind him, extinguishing the daylight. Per usual he held his breath for as long as possible before breathing only through his mouth. He dropped his pants, positioned himself to hover directly over the hole, then exhaled with a smile. Gracien loved getting this done first thing in the morning, it made the day's trek lighter. A minute, then two, and then three went by before something caught his attention. Out of the corner of the door crept the biggest goddamn spider he had ever faced off with. "You've got to be kidding me." His jaw dropped. The beast flaunted golden brown hair as thick as pine needles, legs bigger than Gracien's fingers, and the bulk to take down squirrels.

"Aghhh-Huh!" He shivered, "I'll be over here, just doing my thing… and you, you just go about doing your thing. I'm minding my own business and that business has just concluded."

Gracien was trapped. His pants were shackled around his ankles, the space to maneuver was only a bit bigger than he was, and the spider stood between him and the rickety door which swung inwards.

"Why would the door swing inwards, who makes a door swing into a freaking cavity this goddamn small," he muttered through clenched teeth.

His brow began to bead over with sweat as it suddenly got very warm inside the latrine. The spider hadn't moved a hair and all eight of its eyes glared at Gracien.

"Not like this… Please not like this," he prayed not to die before trying to stand.

The spider shifted in a flash, spinning itself a hundred and eighty degrees back and forth three separate times. Gracien screamed bloody murder, rocketing to his feet, barreling through the door, and blasting it off its hinges. He landed a mere foot from the exit.

With his pants still wrapped around his ankles, he had no choice but to army-crawl away like a frantic crocodile. "Aghh! Aghh!" he screamed, thinking the spider was going to yank him back inside the latrine.

He finally jumped to his feet, sprinting away, all the while struggling to pull his pants over a very messy bum.

The only wonderful bugs from the lot were caterpillars and butterflies, both of which checked in on him from time to time. Every time they did, he couldn't help but feel that Aya had sent them to do so. A gift, a little tug for his attention.

"I'm with you my love, keep on going. I'm proud of you and I believe in you… In us."

It's like he could hear her voice ring out just beyond the tree line, within the rustle of leaves, the flutter of rapids, the kiss of the wind. At times he felt her there with him, just a few steps behind him, listening as he talked. When he laughed, she laughed with him. When he cried, she was there to comfort him. When the loneliness and despair swept in around him like an ominous storm, she was his shelter. Aya was the embrace of warmth through the cooler nights, and she was the river's current washing him clean after a day's progress. She was the song of twilight lulling him to sleep. Ayadonna pulled him into presence, she was his meditation and his mindfulness. He couldn't help but relive some of his favorite moments while burying the darker ones deep within himself, even pretending they had never occurred. But for most of the journey, his solitude helped to keep his mind in a good place, as did a few of his favorite memories.

Gracien found himself resting on a hillside, picking apart a stalk of grass and working his maimed hand to move beyond the ache of deformity. He took these breaks more often as the days progressed, realizing he wasn't in a hurry to be anywhere.

The young man spoke to the unadulterated nature surrounding him as if it was created just for that purpose. "She was late, like very late... We were all waiting. The entire city seemed to be waiting on her." He chuckled to himself before resuming the story. "I was sitting on the throne and had a million tasks thundering through my mind as we waited for the proceedings to begin."

Gracien's deep set eyes scanned the crowd for familiar faces as the Great Hall radiated with an afternoon sun. Light reflected through the polished window cutouts, flooding the large chamber with warmth and creating a comfortable setting. The windows were brilliantly engineered and angled just right so as to perfectly illuminate the inner hall no matter the time of day or season. The gaze of Ninurta, Gracien's father and former King for many decades prior, fell upon the guests from the top tier of a magnificent tapestry hanging near the throne. The fidgety thumb and forefinger of Gracien's right hand alternated between pulling at the tail of his thick, blackened beard and replacing a strand of hair behind an ear after its escape. The massive pair of thrones glittered from the light pouring through the windows, the Queen's even more so as it was currently unoccupied. Birds fluttered above, chasing each other from one ceiling support beam to the next as high pitched chirps echoed about. Everyone in attendance whispered as they waited. A few hundred people filled the endless row of pews while waiting for the proceedings to begin. As they leaned in and over one another, passing quick messages and whispering hushed gossip, their expensive and extravagant attire glistened under the afternoon sun. The Babylonians took these Reconciliation Proceedings seriously, an opportunity for the who's who to be seen and heard, but mostly seen as the show was focused up front. The pews were like mining belts, distributing the wealthiest and most influential gems upfront, closest to the action. Many of them mingled with the senators in attendance, exchanging news and pleasantries.

These senators discussed issues of the state while donning their best expressions of dignified concern. Their flowing robes were various shades of gray depending on their tenure. The novices wore robes of tinted silver while brandishing enthusiastic expressions. The most seasoned senators looked more like bearded storm clouds. Witnesses fidgeted, looking out of place, and confused as to why everyone seemed to be waiting for something. And the king's advisors, Tamuza and Shenbar, looked like two old men sharing a pleasant conversation as they waited patiently, volleying a quickened laugh and a charmed smile.

Gracien exhaled then sighed as his patience thinned. Glances over his shoulder were now happening every minute or so before returning to the sprawling masses with an overly pleased smile and an assuring nod.

He considered sending Shenbar to go check on Aya before the clacking of footsteps rang out. *Finally,* he thought.

Queen Ayadonna approached with a quickened double step every third stride. Gracien didn't look back this time. A genuine smirk, which seemed impossible moments ago, spread across his face as Aya made her entrance. Her left hand tugged at her gown, pulling it free from her hasty feet as her other hand swung like a pendulum, slicing the air for balance. While approaching she inhaled, slowing herself and rounding the throne platform before stepping up towards Gracien, whose smirk matured into a smile.

Aya leaned in to kiss his cheek. "Sorry I'm late… These damn leggings are a nightmare," she spat out quickly before squinting one eye and blowing a length of hair free from her face.

Gracien let out an entertained huff as Aya backed away an inch or so, gazing into his eyes with her smile suddenly extending to its fullest width. "Hi!" She let out a slight giggle as her eyes penetrated his.

"Hi," he returned. "Glad you could make it." Gracien rolled his eyes.

Aya let out a loud chuckle that startled him, making his smile even larger. Her laugh was famous, like a battle horn it gave anyone within earshot a start. The notorious roar didn't bruise but elevate her already wholesome character. Booming throughout the Great Hall, most people may have felt embarrassed wielding such a bellow. Aya however, remained proud of it. Confused and startled bystanders eventually became delighted with the contagious sound after experiencing it up close. This brief chuckle was just a tease, and so with it Aya took her seat.

With their innocent and adorable affection, the two of them resembled teens having to play it cool after having a romp in a nearby stable. Like someone lighting a hundred candles in an abandoned cave, the energy within the Great Hall changed in a flash. The smiles of everyone, especially the women, radiated with delight as they watched the royal couple greet one another. The King radiated his adoration for Ayadonna, and she radiated it right back. A sweet and playful voice further amplified her nurturing character. For many of the attendees, their relationship proved more entertaining than most of the plays performed in one of the city plazas.

Like any individual, Aya and Gracien each had their own personality flaws, but as a couple they were perfectly imperfect. For their love, with all its flaws and blemishes, was everything a loving relationship was meant to be. It was vulnerable but invulnerable, perfect but genuine, raw but seasoned. It was ordinary but at the same time dreamy and unattainable. This is what made it so perfect. The way they acted with one another was authentic, not some practiced performance. It's like they couldn't help themselves, whether within the company of others or not, they couldn't help but be absolutely and completely head over heels in love with one another. The two were wrestling kittens, anyone watching couldn't look away. The love shared between Aya and Gracien was not some story book, fictitious tale. It was the inspiration for such stories, something to be idolized and recreated by all the couples throughout the kingdom. And this was expressed within the hundreds of delighted smiles watching the couple be themselves.

Gracien inhaled, glancing towards Aya, who nodded with a, *yes I'm ready now, thank you,* smile before Gracien knocked on his armrest three consecutive times, gaining the attention of his two advisors as their bushy eyebrows shot up attentively.

The murmuring throughout the hall dwindled as Shenbar, Gracien's short, plump advisor stood and flexed forward as if waiting to belch. "Your Excellencies, this reconciliation concerns the matter of an unclaimed mass of land between the east and west banks of the Euphrates River," his voice squeaked as if mumbling in his sleep. "We have the honor of hosting senators representing both sides of the disputed land in question. From the West Bank we have Senator Eudorus of Ur." Shenbar nodded towards the elderly gentleman, receiving a slight nod in return. "And we also have Senators Brabazon and Kishnar, both of Ur." Shenbar gestured again.

"And from the West bank we have..."

"UP!"

The pop of a hiccup interrupted Shenbar mid-sentence as Aya's hands shot to her mouth while her face blushed over. Gracien took his time looking over to his bride, biting his lip as he did so.

Aya's hands fell to her lap as she straightened. "Excuse me," her voice carried through the hall. "UP!" Again, she hiccupped loudly. "Oh my!" she said as her hands again shot up to cover her mouth.

As the crowd chuckled with delight, Shenbar looked at Gracien who was still fighting off a smirk.

He shrugged his shoulders, leaning over and putting weight on his elbow as his hand moved up to hide a smile and muffle a chuckle. "Hhutttt…" His peripheral vision glanced at Aya who was overcome with embarrassment.

"UP! UP!" Aya bounced on her seat with the force of the involuntary spasm as her hands now pressed down on her mouth as if she was kidnapping herself.

And with that the audience gave up their humble attempts at muffling their chuckles and allowed themselves to laugh out loud. Gracien's eyes teared over as he sunk into his throne like a delighted child. Distinguished senators, seasoned advisors, and noble Babylonians entertained the front rows with hordes of socialites gathered behind them. But as Queen Ayadonna continued to hiccup, each audience member reverted back into school children enjoying a teacher's rare mishap. They couldn't help themselves, seeing their beloved queen lose any thread of composure, through a mere hiccup attack led them to lose their practiced composure.

"UP!" Her small frame bounced from the throne as both hands cupped over her mouth while her large, alarmed eyes searched for a way out.

"UP!" Aya was frozen, running away would only make her look worse and she couldn't exactly excuse herself and go hide somewhere within the Great Hall.

All the while Gracien was delighted with amusement.

"UPPP! up!" This time it was a big strong one followed by a mousy one.

This is how out of hand it was getting; people were now mentally cataloging the type of hiccups. The audience had never been this entertained. Not only was Aya imprisoned in this hilarious situation, but their king was absolutely losing his shit: he couldn't breathe, his vision was blurred with tears, his face was the color of wine, his cheeks burned with strain, and his stomach ached with delight. Everyone in the room was laughing in hysterics as Aya continued to randomly bounce on her throne with a force that seemed equal to one and a half times her own weight.

"UoooPP!"

"That sounded exactly like a donkey fart," Shenbar said before giggling like a schoolboy with Tamuza.

"Hold, hold your... hold your breath," Gracien finally uttered through a torrent of muffled hysterics.

Aya nodded, taking an overly dramatic inhalation as if she was preparing to dive for pearls. Everyone's boisterous laughter immediately simmered like boiling water removed from a flame. Something equally entertaining but more so thrilling was afoot. Gracien straightened, leaning in towards Aya with a narrowing gaze. The senators and advisors straightened up, elbowing one another as the crowd composed itself, settling back into proper etiquette as an unspoken wager gained momentum. Would she hiccup again after this great breath? Ten seconds in and people began leaning in to get a closer look. Murmurs grew along with a slight blush in Aya's face as she reached twenty seconds, twenty-five, then thirty.

It looked like she was about to let it go but then someone from the back of the hall shouted, "Keep going!"

With those two words the audience united in support, cheering her on as if they were attending a chariot race. Her face crimsoned, her fingers drummed the armrest, and her eyes widened.

Gracien became antsy, squirming in his throne as he inched closer to her. "Honey… haha… You okay?" His head dipped forward as his eyebrows ascended with concern.

Aya's big, ballooned cheeks nodded as her hand began rhythmically beating the armrest. She suddenly sprang to her feet, startling everyone before pacing back and forth while slapping her hips. The atmosphere resembled a brothel during Games Week. Aya bent over, her eyes pinching together and her hands drumming her knees, all the while the crowd continued cheering her on. Gracien shook his head in utter disbelief while slapping his own knee.

GASP!!! Aya shot up to a full stance, drawing in a breath so loud it rivaled the crowd's chants.

"Wow," she squealed as her lungs recovered and the entire hall erupted with her triumph!

Aya steadied herself with one hand on the throne while the other tapped at her chest. She took several deep breaths before offering an embellished bow and returning to her seat. Gracien clapped slowly while rolling his eyes.

As the audience slipped back into composure, Shenbar took a step up, resuming his place at the podium. "Aghh… Let's see here, yes, yes. Your Excellencies...the um….the ugh…" The parchment ruffled between his fingers as he secured his prior spot. "...Yes, let us proceed… and from the East Bank we have Nicogoras of Erech and Soloman of…"

"UP!" Aya bounced in her seat with a look of annoyed defeat spreading across her face.

The audience chuckled as bets were settled. Aya turned to Gracien who gave her a, *you poor thing* kind of look.

"I think it would be better if I excused myself before this gets any more out of hand," Aya spoke as she rose.

"I think that's best," he returned.

Queen Ayadonna rose, walked to the center of the throne platform, pinched her gown at her hip, and offered one final bow. The audience rose, granting her a well-deserved standing ovation. She smiled, turned, and made her way towards the exit.

"UP!"

"The way she commanded a room, even through something as insane as a hiccup attack, was inspiring. They absolutely loved her for it. We all did," Gracien spoke to the nature surrounding him.

He inhaled, looking up from his feet for the first time. The boy suddenly realized he had been mindlessly walking all along and was now headed right into some new village. As soon as he realized this, angst mounted with the thought of having to be around other people. It was so easy opening up to nature that the idea of having to be normal again engulfed him in a wave of anxiety. He felt like a stranger wearing another's body.

Ever since he had left Bandhu and the boys, Gracien felt uncomfortable and awkward around others. Trying to act normal and even trying to remember how he used to be once upon a time was difficult. How did he ever uphold that confident, charming charisma that once came so naturally? Running into other people was infrequent, except in the villages of course. Even here, most people were busy managing their migrating livestock, hosting guests in the teahouses, or like him, migrating through this magical land on a spiritual journey. He did his best to avoid them all. As a result, Gracien found himself spending more time with the wild dogs than he did with people. It was easier to speak with them. They seemed to understand him more as he didn't need to pretend. A few scraps of food, a couple head rubs, and he had himself a temporary traveling companion. The pups usually sported thick, mangled manes and amiable demeanors. They were prepped for the elements and relied on the charity of people more than living off the land. They'd trot along with him each morning as he set out, excited over nothing and happy with it too. On Gracien's departure however, the dogs would reach a point beyond the village, arriving at an invisible border of sorts, and ponder whether to continue with him or head back. He loved watching their hesitation, the way they suddenly stopped, barking for him to return, and tapping their excited paws. Or maybe they were happy to have spent some time with a new friend, and just saying goodbye. Most times they'd just stop and wait, tails moderately wagging as they watched him leave. He preferred this, feeling important enough for them to take their time and see him off. It always made him smile and usually meant a good day was ahead.

As Gracien approached this new village, he took a mental inventory of the aches and pains in his body. His breath felt deeper, truer. Or maybe he was suddenly more attentive to it, observing the ebb like one taking in the serenity of a subtle sea tide. The young man's ache and soreness had also abated as he racked up distance. The blisters deflated like failed dough, his shoulder flesh roughened up, defending itself from the assaults of the straps by hardening under the pressure. His leg muscles took much more of a beating before screaming out in protest, even along the steepest of inclines. Achy feet and ankles however, still pleaded for a break, and so he felt he had no choice but to grant it to them.

I'll stay an extra day to rest and recover a bit, he thought as he approached what seemed to be a suitable option for his two-day stint.

He pushed the door open, noticing the rustic but charming feeling that was typical for all the teahouses. The echo of his footsteps rang out as he walked through the hollowness of this new dwelling. During the first few days of his journey, he preferred sleeping outside with the cool summer nights soothing and comforting him after the long, harsh days. But as the chill of elevation began to sweep in with dusk's arrival, Gracien favored the coziness of a hearth and a hot meal. His nostrils flared, checking for any sign of a stew.

Shirisha, the innkeeper, suddenly blurted out, "hey you. One night? All alone? Hungry?" The old woman sputtered out the questions like a rock tumbling down the hillside.

Gracien tensed with fright. She had silently crept up right there next to him before making herself known.

He stammered, not knowing which question to answer first. "I... I..." The woman chuckled and as she waited for him to compose himself. "Two nights, and yes just me." His eyes widened with the hearth's alluring warmth and hypnotizing blaze.

The teahouse host was wrapped up in a thick yak fur coat, with a hood twice the size of her head and equally generous sleeves. Her ink black hair sucked the light from the room, and was pulled back so tightly it resembled taut reins restraining a horse. The redness in her weather-beaten cheeks made her look like a doll. Deep, amber pupils glimmered through slices for eye openings as the freckles around her nose, eyes, and brow resembled a constellation on a moonless night. Her teeth were abnormally misaligned, and her lips were chapped with deadened skin.

"That may need two days at least before the swelling gets manageable." She pushed him to a bench, making him sit down before kneeling before his foot.

She took Gracien's ankle within her hands and examined it. "Your hand, it's missing fingers. Seems recent, wolves I bet," she mentioned casually.

Gracien moved to respond but she was already onto the next point while removing a small jar from her coat pocket.

"Can't be too safe, especially when traveling alone, you're alone right? Well, this should help get you back on your feet. Ha!" She paused, waiting for a reaction but all she saw was Gracien's dead frozen glare. He was completely taken aback with the woman's eager assistance. "Really though! It... will... help... get-you-back-on-your-feet! Aghh-haha!"

Her hand slapped down on Gracien's ankle, and he bit down on his lip, tensing his whole body as his eyes teared over. All the while the tea-house keeper roared in laughter while beating down on his ankle like a treacherous husband.

"Whoo-Wee, that was funny." She wiped tears from her eyes before resuming. "Well here we are... Let me finish up." She slathered more of the minty smelling ointment on Gracien's left ankle before dropping his leg to the ground and grabbing for the other.

Gracien began to relax as a cat jumped out of hiding, landing with the silence of nightfall on the bench beside him. His brindle coat swelled as he rubbed up against the boy, all the while the woman continued to lather up his ankle. As Gracien's deformed hand pet the creature, it purred with satisfaction while he took a visual inventory of the room. The monster brick hearth continued to crackle and pop, books and lanterns served as decor, a fleet of eccentric chairs sat empty, several small tea tables with dirty glasses and ash trays waited to be cleaned, a few mismatched rugs were worn and battered beyond use, dusty climbing gear hung from the walls, and an unattended tobacco pipe seeped smoke, filling the room with a pleasant, earthy fragrance. Everything in the room orbited around a long wooden table, which looked like a marooned ship toting a mess of dirty dishes and no guests. Dampened sunlight slithered through three large windows as the sun dipped into the snowcapped Himalayas, which stood much closer now compared to ten days prior.

"How much further... How far until the pines? I'm supposed to look for him once I reach the pines... a... a blanket of pines as thick as a beard? About four days, correct?" He recalled Bandhu's colorful directions.

"What's awaiting you in the pines?" Shirisha spread the leftover paste between her fingers onto Gracien's hands. "Rub this into your temples, it will help you sleep easier with the thinning air."

"A teacher, Muktinath. A friend of mine told me of him." Mindful of not wanting to appear desperate, Gracien chose his words carefully as he rubbed the salve into his temples.

"Ohhh… Muktinath, well let me see now…" A sole eyebrow rose, and she smirked, quickly standing with the agility of someone half her age.

Gracien sensed her sarcasm, a look of confusion washing over his face. "Yes… Muktinath. My friend, Bandhu… he mentioned that this teacher may be able to, umm, help me with something," he spoke slowly as if he had said something stupid.

"I'm not sure that will be possible, but you'll have to see for yourself now won't you. But I can tell you this, there's a quicker way. It's through a steep canyon but it will save you two days' time. There have been many bandit attacks on the longer trail, so this is safer too." She scooped the cat up into her arms. "Two days with less elevation gain over the first day but the last portion of the second is a bit rough, many hours of uphill trudging. You're young though," her eyes narrowed as she gazed at Gracien, "but… seem older, more mature than you should be." Her gaze let up, "don't go left at the riverbank, but right. You'll descend for a couple hundred meters before beginning your climb back up, this is why no one finds the path." She shook herself from an unwelcome flashback then motioned to ask him a few questions before noticing his unease. "Remember. A right at the riverbank not left," she mentioned indifferently while walking from the room, caressing the cat, and humming an old Nepali tune.

Gracien's body deflated, slinking off the bench and onto the fluffy yak rug. He placed his arms behind his head, gazing up into the ceiling as the firewood popped and sizzled. He took a deep breath and couldn't help but feel kind of special. Even though his life was so surreal and extremely difficult at times, Aya was still sending people at just the right time to help him along his way. His eyes teared over as he debated what new level of craziness he had just reached. Or maybe he just missed his wife. Darkness filled not only the room, but his heart. He missed her there beside him, even in her sickest of times, breathing life not only into her being but into his as well.

The innkeeper was right, the first day was a breeze compared to the extremely difficult hike Gracien was ascending now. But his mind rejoiced knowing he saved himself two days of work, even though he hadn't considered it work since the third day after his departure. Yesterday was an amazing experience as the pine forest, thin and sparse at first, welcomed the young man into an ever-thickening blanket as he progressed upwards. The smell was as thick as the congestion of towering trees, which moaned out like a group of cranky old men when especially strong gales blew through. Mounds of pinecones littered the ground with some being bigger than his head. The shade that cast down on his journey was quite welcomed as the thinning air and steeper inclines proved to test his endurance. He used the pointy-sappy branches of the trees as supports, pulling himself up the steep slope like the Nepalese honey hunters using ropes to gain access to enormous hives buried under the cliffs. The terrain was tricky too, consisting of large, apple-sized rocks mixed into soft and unstable earth, which was pitched at a forty-five-degree angle in some parts. His steps were timid, placing only half his normal pressure before allowing his full weight to press into the earth and only then bringing the next foot forward and repeating the process. Occasionally, the earth gave out, causing him to slide down several meters before he caught hold of a tree or large boulder. Gracien couldn't help his frustration, growling and blowing hair from his face then clawing his way back up the unreliable soil. His sweat drenched clothing was proof he had been at this all afternoon. The carrot on the stick however was that Gracien felt like he was nearing the prayer wheels of the temple that Bandhu had mentioned, he just had to be.

"Once you arrive... Take your time and walk around the prayer wheels and make sure to move in the opposite direction of the sun's rotation. As you circumnavigate the wheels, spin them one by one and pray for that which will heal your heart."

Gracien remembered the sweet old man squeezing his shoulders for emphasis. He also knew that Bandhu had stopped himself from wrapping him up in a big hug.

As he summited this final stretch of steep incline, his ears perked up with the arrival of an unusual sound. It sounded like a chipmunk squealing out after being captured by a hawk. The high-pitched whine was followed by a clacking sound, like boat oars knocking into one another. Gracien pulled himself up onto the top of the hill, looking back and not feeling very accomplished, as this last haul didn't seem that far down. The clacking and whining rang out again, causing him to spin his head towards the sound which must have been just beyond a wall of pines. He cautiously stalked forward, being gentle and precise when pushing the branches from his path. These parts were known to have snow leopards and he had heard legends of tigers exploring the upper regions of the mountain range as well. The sun broke through the branches, blinding his efforts as the sound of clacking wood rang out again. His hand attempted to shade the sun's intensity as he stepped through, entering a clearing. A large circle stood before him with a hundred or more prayer wheels running along a brick wall about waist high. He recalled Bandhu mentioning there were one hundred and eight in total; he had thought that was an odd tally at the time but now he wished there were more.

181

The wall formed a decent sized circle which was covered by a very handsome, golden roof with three gilded towers also painted a vibrant gold. Several bulky beams boasted a rich crimson color while supporting the impressive roof by crossing over a massive wooden support beam centered in the middle, making the entire roof and support system resemble a gigantic ornate umbrella.

The summit temple, he thought as his deformed hand fell to his side while he approached the temple.

He had envisioned this temple every day of his trek and looking upon it now, he realized his imagination had fallen very short. The hand crafted, rustic beauty standing before him was an awesome sight to behold. His three fingered hand extended towards the first wheel as he approached but he hesitated, trying to think of a prayer of healing. Multicolored Tibetan prayer flags, signifying good luck and fortune, fluttered in the wind. They purified the air and pacified the gods as the prayers planted within them were lifted to the Heavens. But no prayer crossed Gracien's mind or heart as he read the inscription carved into the prayer wheel.

It wasn't written in traditional Newari, but Sanskrit. "Om Mani Padme Hum," he whispered the inscription out loud.

Each wheel held the same mantra but in different colored paint. His fingers nearly grazed the wooden surface as he tried with everything he could to think of a prayer which could heal his heart.

But only one word and one sound came forth. "Ayadonna." His fingers retracted, his hand retreated.

"It's difficult to find the right words sometimes, isn't it?"

Gracien jumped back from the wall. "Who's there?" he shouted, scanning through the spaces between the wheels.

"Just me, who else?" she said.

A woman with long black hair gleaming in the sunlight rounded the wall.

She held a serious expression for a moment until a smirk broke through. "Namaste." She placed her hands in prayer before offering a humble bow. "My name is Muktinath."

"But, but you're a, a…" Ishayu muttered as he followed Mukti while she strolled along.

"A what?" She smirked, smiling with her lips pursed together as if she was experiencing a slightly sour flavor.

Mukti's ink black hair was thick and full but perfectly clean and tidy, pulled together in a tight, uniformed ponytail which swept across her lower back as she walked. A band of light gray hair bloomed from the corner of her forehead, causing a steak of silver to slice through the blackness like a lightning strike through twilight. Slate gray eyes held uncompromising compassion, like she had already known the pain in Gracien's heart before he spoke of it. She carried herself with the grace of a sixty-year-old and the vigor of someone half that age. Gracien guessed that she was probably forty-five, give or take a dozen years. Her lips were thin and almost non-existent as they stretched across her teeth, hiding them as she smiled.

"Not a man… I mean… See, I was expecting something, someone else," Ishayu stammered while trying to recall if Bandhu ever mentioned this teacher of his being a woman. "I'm not sure why but I just thought… and not that there's anything wrong with you being a…" He immediately felt like an ass, exhaling his frustration with a sigh.

"Ahh, so you expected something, and it didn't come to be? And this upsets you?" She continued to walk, passing him as he stopped to consider her question.

Mukti was taller than Ishayu by a good foot or so and her presence was ten times his. Like an endless, grayed sea, she was calm and collected, graceful and reticent. Ishayu caught up with her, moving to speak but unable to find the words. His brow lifted with a thought before quickly dismissing it. Again, he motioned to say something before surrendering to embarrassment and choosing to silently stroll along as they ventured deeper into the unspoiled remoteness. His shame faded quickly, crediting this to Mukti as her presence was kind and comforting. For some reason he felt like she was unable to judge him or at least she didn't put forth that kind of energy. Mukti bore a dark complexion, which highlighted the beginnings of middle-aged wrinkles along her brow and corners of her eyes. She was slow in everything she did, as if performing the embodiment of grace for an audience. Pausing her stroll and reaching out a hand, she knelt down then began petting the petal of a jasmine flower with the knuckle of her index finger.

She leaned in, inhaling the aroma. "I love that smell. It makes me feel cleaner, lighter." Her lips stretched across her teeth as she gave a smirk of satisfaction.

"Are you more upset because you expected me to be a man... or because of the embarrassment of allowing me to know your unmet expectations?" Mukti questioned as if speaking to the flower.

For the third time in a row Ishayu's mouth moved to answer before closing as his brow wrinkled over with consideration, "I'm not sure... I don't know what I was, am feeling. Maybe both?"

She stood, looking towards him. "Not knowing is good... So many people defend without thinking first, as if they must know everything and never be wrong."

She turned from him, resuming her stroll. Her footing was slow and calculated, as if she was tiptoeing around broken glass. She adjusted her long, beige colored robe, pulling it up as she made her way through a puddle. Ishayu noticed she was barefoot with the tail end of a tattoo snaking from beneath her robe and down her ankle. A white knit scarf, heavy and dense, laid across her shoulders, cascading over her chest. Her delicate, feminine hands tugged at it like a person pulling in their pillow during a pleasant dream.

"My friend, Bandhu, he um, he told me to come find you. He told me that you may be able to help me." He surveyed the forest encircling them, "where are you taking me?"

"I'm not taking you anywhere," she casually returned.

A pang of angst shot through him as he instantly considered this whole trip an utter waste of time. Immediately after, a wave of stress roared through him as he considered what he was supposed to do now.

Mukti paused. "I mean it's your choice to come with me, but I'm not taking you anywhere." Seeing that he was stressed she continued. "It's okay." She calmed him with her eyes and allowed some idle silence to fill the space.

"What I intend for you to understand is that you are free to join me. I live a ways further but the walk is nice, especially with this perfect weather."

Ishayu exhaled relief, feeling his heart pound in his chest as the wave of stress and anxiety poured from him like water from a broken dam. "Thank you, thank you," was all he could manage.

Mukti's small nose twitched with delight, it was spattered with light colored freckles which extended over accentuated cheekbones.

"You're welcome to stay with me as long as you wish. I have plenty of room and I'm currently not hosting another. I will however ask you to help maintain the space while you live here, can you agree to this?"

"Of course!" Ishayu blurted out before clearing his throat. "Of course I can, and thank you."

She smiled in return. "Then let's enjoy the sound of nature as we walk… We'll have plenty of time for questions and such later."

Her eyes narrowed on the forest canopy, smirking at something unseen. As they walked, Gracien frequently found himself holding his breath from fear of saying the wrong thing.

They walked into a clearing of grass leading up to a massive garden. The beautiful, expansive space served as a centerpiece with several quaint structures encircling the communal area. One of the first things Gracien noticed was how amazing everything smelled. Whatever flourished in the garden acted like a natural incense blanketing the area in a floral glaze.

"This way," Mukti directed as she strolled through the grounds and Gracien followed, his eyes as wide as saucers.

Mukti's sanctuary was a buffet of aromas, flavor, and sensations. The duo cut through the communal area, walking along perfectly round stone pavers curving through a gauntlet of vegetation. Mukti splayed out her fingers, allowing her hands to caress the leaves and flowers as she walked. The garden featured several dozen kinds of plants aligned in perfectly symmetric rows and designs. Even peering into the space above was a treat as towering pines encircled them to the melody of running water in the distance. Gracien had never seen such an array of greenery.

Fascinated with the never-before-seen shape of leaves and plant structures, he leaned down to investigate before Mukti urged him along. "This way."

They eventually exited the garden space, walking through soft, padded grass leading up to one of the small cottages. It was a charming little bungalow with walls made of stone and thick logs serving as support beams in each of the four corners. The roof was thatched, with a little chimney sticking up from the back corner. He smiled at the indigo-colored door.

"And here is where you'll be staying." Mukti swung the massive wooden door open, leaning on it with a smirk as Gracien entered, ducking his head under the arched stone frame.

He took a deep breath after stepping through, allowing his eyes to adjust to the darkness before making a visual inventory of the space.

"It's perfect," he said, grinning as his hand swept over the curved arm of a wooden chair placed in front of a small, stone hearth.

Muktinath followed him in. "You may find yourself within the comfort of that chair quite often. Many," she inhaled as her hand swept over the backrest, "many guests of mine and ones before me even, have gained great value within this very same chair. I hope it serves you well during your time here." She picked up a hammered bowl of bronze and a padded mallet, "this is a Tibetan singing bowl." She moved the mallet around the edge of the bowl which stirred it into sharing its song.

The vibration rippled through the small space like the subtle tremor of a distant earthquake. Gracien couldn't help but smile as the tone bathed him in pleasure. It felt as if the bowl or rather the song was speaking to some deeper, ancient part of him and the sensation he felt was that part of him responding back.

"You may come to use this quite often as well. The technique can be easily learned, and the song is rather soothing after a long day's work." Her eyebrow peaked suggestively. "Supper will be ready in an hour. I'll give you some time to yourself." Mukti placed the bowl down and bowed, saying "Namaste," before placing her hands in prayer then making her exit.

"Namaste," Gracien said, placing his hands in prayer and giving her a slight bow in return.

A moment later the two fingertips of his bad hand grazed the jackets of several books nestled into a nook carved within the wall. The books were small more like manuscripts and so he removed three at once. The covers weren't leather as he suspected, but rather some kind of organic plant material hardened and glazed.

He read the titles out loud. "*The Noble Eightfold Path, The Four Noble Truths, The Nine Dhyānas.*"

His eyes tried taking in some of the passages, but he just couldn't focus. Exhaustion rolled over him like a morning fog and Gracien sighed, feeling a bit emotional as he pulled the chair back and took a seat. It groaned out, the wood joints flexing as he settled within its embrace. The young man scanned the rest of the room, a sparse bed lay off to the side with a small wooden table and one stool tucked into the corner. Several unlit candles of various heights melted into the table's top. A slight stream of air blew through the gaps in the stone walls as well as the wood flooring. He closed his eyes and listened intently as the hearth seemed to answer the call of the breeze with a howl of its own. Then came the tears. He didn't understand why he was crying but they came, nonetheless.

"I ache for you Aya. Why did you have to leave me to this life… This struggle, all by myself? It's so, so difficult to walk this path, honey, and sometimes…" He sniffled, clearing his nose. "Sometimes, even though I feel and even know I'm doing what's best for me, it's so damn hard to learn how to live without you here by my side. It's more than hard, it's impossible without you."

He leaned forward, crying into his open palms, and letting the stream of emotion pour from him as the room howled in return, matching his mourning.

The next morning his eyes peeled apart, yawning, and stretching Gracien scanned the unfamiliar space. As he blinked his new reality into existence, it took him a moment to recollect exactly where he was. He looked over the room before pulling the blanket to the side, swiveling his feet off the bed, then plopping them down on the cold flooring.

Gracien yawned again before a realization hit him like a sack of bricks. "I've forgotten all about her," he whispered while turning back to the cool, empty spot next to where he slept.

In a flash he recalled all the times he woke up previously feeling the agony and the misery upon realizing she was dead. But now, for some deranged reason, he missed that anguish. And here he was, waking with no immediate thought of her, no instant wave of utter grief crashing down over him with his first conscious breath. At some point, he must have gotten used to waking up without her.

The realization was devastating, like he had somehow dishonored her, dishonored their love. "This is where it begins... This is where I begin to forget," he spoke to himself like a scornful wife berating a deceitful husband. He stewed in the mix of resentment and disbelief for several minutes before his eyes focused beyond his self-loathing, centering back on the foreign dwelling. Then a surge of excitement crested.

"Mukti! The sanctuary!" He leapt from the bed, nearly tearing the door of its hinges.

The wilderness welcomed him with a chorus of birdsong, sunshine splashing through the forest canopy, bringing the freshest breeze he had ever tasted. Colossal pines stood with open arms as the wake of twilight raced towards the opposite horizon. The remnants of a brisk dawn swaddled him up as he placed his bare foot on the grass outside the hut. The cool, sharp sensation rippled up his leg. He couldn't help but smile then snicker before he was laughing out loud with his eyes tearing over.

"I'm here! I'm here," he managed through a bonded smile. "It begins here, it begins now." His lips trembled the words forth as his eyes teared over.

Outside of a few shared meals together, Mukti kept to herself for three days straight. She allowed Gracien the time he needed to investigate the grounds and settle himself into the new space. He slept, he rested, he meditated, and he wandered a lot. Most of that time was spent ruminating over his journey here and analyzing his ever-changing perspective, which shifted like the seasons. Gracien thought about Aya almost constantly. Like a drunk wrestling withdrawal, he yearned for her mentally, emotionally, and physically. Not only did he grieve Aya's loss, but the loss of his friends and family from previous lives. His mind couldn't help but highlight all that was missing from his reality instead of what was right there before him.

Over the first few days he found himself pondering Mukti's past; wondering how she came to live here, when she arrived, and why she dedicated herself to this garden and to helping others. She was a natural teacher because of her keen sense of their struggles. Like a dog sensing an intruder, Mukti knew of Gracien's suffering. He knew she wasn't aware of the source of his suffering… how could anyone ever guess at such a thing? But there was something in the way that she looked at him, with such sympathy and patience, that didn't soothe his suffering but aggravated it. All it did was draw more focus to the fact that he *was* suffering, which would then double his attention on why he was so sad in the first place. It was salt on an already painful wound. Even though he'd only known her for a few days, Gracien knew this wasn't her intention. But it didn't matter, it still stung every time. Like a guilty dog he'd avoid making eye contact with her while feeling his worst. He'd excuse himself from meals when the tension became too thick or make a quick getaway when they'd be in the garden together.

It's not that Gracien didn't yearn for someone to share in his grief. He wanted to scream or cry about it then be comforted like a child after a nightmare. What he really wanted though, was to meet someone who had lost the love of their life. It was selfish and horrible, but he yearned to share in that unspoken bond of sorrow known only from the partner left to live a life without their Beloved. Once or twice he even moved to reveal his secret to Mukti just so that he could free the words from his soul.

"My wife, my Queen… She died." He dreamed of saying it, repeating the words in his mind like he was practicing lines for a performance.

But each time a wave of fear washed over him. "What will she think? What will she say… What could she say?"

With his next breath, a deluge of terrifying possibilities played out: Mukti's diabolic laugh booming through the gardens at Gracien's utter insanity, having someone come and take him away, mocking him for being a liar, or the worst of them all, "that can't be true, it must all be some kind of dream," and with those simple words, she would dismiss him altogether.

His fear over what would happen to him if he shared his insane tale was a monster hiding under his bed. Nothing could be done except to live with it. And for this reason, he kept his story buried deep within – making his and Mukti's time together very quiet.

It wasn't all so bad as Mukti urged him to listen to the forest and the river as they ate. "Allow yourself to melt into the serenity, merge with nature and focus on the sounds just as you did along your adventure here."

She spoke between small finger-fulls of rice. Gracien couldn't be certain of how she knew that's exactly what he did along his trek, but he followed her instructions and saved his questions for another time. On the fifth morning things shifted with Mukti's instructions the previous night.

"Tomorrow morning please water the garden earlier than normal and then wait for me there. Get some rest, Ishayu, goodnight."

Like bathing in a chilled river, the morning weather was cold but refreshing at the same time.

"How do you feel?" Mukti asked as they sat crossed legged in front of one another.

Mukti's legs seemed twisted in an uncomfortable position with her feet pulled into her lap while Gracien's were partially crossed and already aching. They sat on the ground in a tiny communal space between the various huts adjacent to the gardens. The stone pavers were still a bit wet from Gracien spilling water as he carted buckets up from the river. The various plants and herbs Mukti cultivated for trade needed to be watered daily and so this was one of his chores.

"Tired." He laughed, "so many steps down to the river and then back up again. After trekking here I'm used to the steps by now... But carrying a bucket of water perched on either end of a staff, *while* trying to balance it across my shoulders, whew. It was hard with my hand and all." He raised his deformed hand, "and I had to make a few separate trips, I'm definitely not used to that, but..." he interrupted his own train of thought. "How many steps are there anyway?"

"I'm sure you'll find out soon enough." Mukti smirked as she replied sympathetically. "It's important to keep yourself strong. I also wished for you to be physically worn out a little so that your mind would settle faster. Seems like you're still a bit excited though."

Gracien's brow squished over with confusion as he moved to ask what she meant before Mukti continued. "I'll explain a bit more later. I mean how do you feel with your posture?" Her thin eyebrows rose with interest.

"Oh, that. Fine I guess." He teetered back and forth in his seat with the rolled-up mat underneath his butt providing a bit of leverage.

"How about you walk me through the steps again please?" Mukti asked.

Gracien inhaled, "Okay sure… Sit and settle. Then wiggle my butt into the mat and get comfortable while keeping my legs crossed." He mimicked adjusting as he spoke. "Or if I decide to sit in the chair then with my knees bent at a ninety-degree angle." He inhaled with his eyebrows rising as he thought.

"Spine?" Mukti helped.

"Yes, spine straight and my head balanced on my neck and settled without tension. My hands like this?" He picked his hands up then placed them back down. "Cupped within one another or I can do this too, right?" He moved then placed each one on a thigh, palms up.

Mukti nodded. "Very good. Go on."

"Shoulders back like this, chin parallel with the ground and then let the tension pour from my body… Take three deep breaths, trying to breathe with my diaphragm, and on the third exhalation close my eyes." He closed his eyes.

"Very good. Now let's cover the next steps."

"There's more?" Gracien opened one eye.

Muktinath actually laughed out loud for a split second before settling.

"Not much for today. Close your eyes and keep your mouth slightly open. A little more… There. Good. And now keep your tongue touching the ceiling of your mouth as you breathe through solely through your nostrils."

She allowed him to try it out for a few breaths before continuing.

"Very good, Ishayu. And now I want you to keep track of your breath. With your diaphragm. Remember, feel your belly ebb with each inhalation and exhalation like watching a great pine rock back and forth in the wind. And that's all for now."

Gracien's one eye opened again. "That's it? But what else? Should I say something in my head? What should I think about?" he sputtered off the questions.

"Just observe your breath and watch your thoughts, and I'll come get you once it's time." Mukti rose, placing a hand on Gracien's shoulder.

"Time for what?" he asked with his eyes closed but his brows rising with expectancy.

She patted his shoulder once more before the sound of her departing footsteps faded into the distance.

For several weeks Gracien adjusted to his new routine. He managed the garden in the mornings and early afternoon, then meditated followed by lessons with Mukti. Some days he'd take the day off, resting and searching within for answers and meaning. He ate well and slept well, as the demanding garden work kept him incredibly exhausted but fit. At first his constant water runs up and down the stairs were not only physically challenging, but also mentally. Gracien found himself bickering over exactly why he was doing such laborious work and what the reasoning of all, 'this' really was.

Without the distraction of the ever-changing scenery or the thrill of adventure, his mental angst and anger was a near constant companion.

He was angry with the hard stone steps, with the number of them, with his deformed hand and having to function normally, at being hot and sweaty, every time he spilled water. And he was furious that Aya was dead. His mind raged throughout his chores for the first few weeks until he began implementing Mukti's meditation techniques. After doing so, he began noticing a subtle shift in his demeanor, in his peace. The stairs became easier with each passing day, all one hundred and eight of them. Now he bounded up without spilling much water and the buckets teetered back and forth less frequently. The pound of his footing became tender and gentle with all the repetition. He even noticed a difference in the way he watered the various plants, taking his time and being gentle with the deluge as it spilled into the garden bedding. While doing so he focused on his breath, exhaling while pouring, then inhaling while moving onto the next plant.

Like enjoying the company of an old friend, something about working with nature, especially plants used for food, was grounding for him. He'd talk to the plants as his hands refreshed the earth, turning it over like a baker with his dough. Even his deformed hand felt good raking through the cool, fertile soil. Internal laughter rang out as he hummed and danced about, paying compliments on a particular herb's growth while encouraging another's. He listened to the garden speaking to him as he trimmed wilting growth, cleaned and managed the body and leaf system, and of course plucked the bounty with a grateful bow. He enjoyed taking his time to look over his work, to marinate in the pride of a job well done.

He never really spoke out loud throughout his morning chores, for fear that Mukti would be listening in, but his mind was rampant with conversation. As his fingers and hands tussled with pruning, an endless stream of negative thoughts ran through him. They ranged from delusions of impossible realities and anxiety riddled worries, to anguished grief and penetrating depression. When the wave of grief became too much, he retreated into his cottage, cloaking himself in darkness and allowing the depression to wreak havoc. Muktinath checked in on him from time to time but for the most part gave him space. Gracien figured she had helped quite a few people already, so he was doing his best at allowing himself to be helped. The sanctuary enabled this as well as helped him to finally feel safe somewhere, something which hadn't happened since leaving Babylonia.

He didn't feel alone all the time though. Speaking to Aya along his strolls while marching through the forest or by the river's edge gave him a sense of comfort. He shared many of his worries as if she was just a few paces behind him or just on the other side of the tree trunk he leaned up against. And he knew she listened as well as spoke through the lull of the river, the groan of the towering pines, the howl of the wind, and his favorite, visiting butterflies.

One was fluttering around him this very moment after he decided to settle next to the river and practice his meditation.

He smiled, toying with it when suddenly the thought *time heals all wounds,* surfaced in his mind.

Along his trek, Gracien had overheard one of the teahouse matrons say it to her sister who had miscarried a child. He remembered becoming angry enough to pack his bags and storm off.

What does she know about it, about losing someone! He had riled himself up during the morning hike, hosting a furious inner debate which blinded him from the beauty of the terrain.

Now as he sat on the riverbank just down the path from Mukti's sanctuary, the memory managed to send a ripple of anger through him. He exhaled in a huff, then adjusted his posture before trying to calm himself.

Again, the woman's words rang through his mind, *time heals all wounds.*

As he meditated on the well-known saying, with his hands cupped in one another atop his lap, the ghostly sensation of his former fingers tingled.

His eyes popped open with a sudden realization. *My fingers will never grow back and so my hand will never heal. I'll simply learn to live without them… It's the same with losing someone. No one heals from losing a loved one, we simply learn to live without them.*

He was proud of his insight before his eyes began tearing over. The deeper meaning of it materialized, and it was about as depressing of a thought as possible. The truth of it crushed him, causing his throat to swell. In the very next moment, he realized that his entire life, or rather his entire existence, teetered on his ability to live without Aya. Like an overly efficient drain, his spirit washed right out of him. He laid down in the grass, pulling his knees up into his chest as the sorrow plugged up his throat. How he missed her. The agony of her death sucked the will to heal from him as he sobbed like a defeated child. Gracien sat there for some time, allowing the buildup of grief to pour from him before something caught his attention.

Movement. The sound of something wading in the river pulled him from his despair. Gracien pushed himself up ever so slightly to investigate. It was Mukti, her back was to him, as she washed herself with a sponge. Gracien let out a little gasp, then sank back down into the cover of the tall grass. Mukti glanced over her shoulder, scanning the area where he laid before resuming her bath. Gracien pushed the blades apart to get a better look. He wasn't spying on her because she was naked, but because Mukti's skin was a canvas covered with the most beautiful tattoos he had ever seen. He held his breath as he squinted in on the amazing designs and various scripts. Mukti was kneeling in the water so only her back and upper buttocks were visible. His eyes couldn't look away. The gaze of the tattooed masterpiece encompassing her entire back was nothing less than transcendental.

Gautama Buddha, his heart whispered.

Mukti had spoken about him on a few occasions. "There is one who achieved perfect oneness… He is called Buddha," her words seemed to ring out ten times clearer as Buddha's expression shifted with Mukti's movements.

He knew it was Buddha's face because the same one was chiseled into a few dozen statues scattered about the sanctuary and on the pages of the books in his room. As Gracien gazed in awe over the perfection of the art, he couldn't help but feel utterly mesmerized by Buddha's presence. Vibrant blues and greens bordered his golden complexion with his lustrous gaze penetrating the depths of Gracien's soul. For the life of him he couldn't understand how a man whose eyes were serenely shut could bestow such a powerful gaze. Buddha held a sliver of a smirk, like he was the only one to understand an existential secret. That illustrious smirk was cradled in the embrace of an expression overflowing with compassion, serenity, knowingness, and divinity. The image was godly. A purification of being and in an instant, it banished Gracien's anguish. Witnessing Buddha's calm, all-knowing expression gifted the young man with something he had not experienced in a very long time, possibility and purpose. Knowing that an all-pervading peace and oneness was attainable, and possibly attainable for him, made him shudder with hope. He finally exhaled, quickly inhaling, then realizing his hands were squeezing the grass as if he was hanging from it. Careful not to alert Mukti, Gracien crawled backwards from the concealed spot. Like staring at the sun too long, Buddha's face was seared into his mind.

"This, this is what I desire," he whispered.

"Desire is the root of all suffering. Yes, that's what I said. But more on that later. We're supposed to be deepening your meditation. As discussed, your goal is, no thought," Mukti said while walking circles around Gracien.

He was sitting on a flat stone near the river's edge trying to find just the right spot in his posture. The sun broke through the tree canopy, flickering down over them with each passing breeze. The river's current was minimal as the water level was the lowest of the season with winter's approach. A breeze danced through, sprinkling aromas of fall.

"Here's an example for you. Consider the river. Its current is thought. It's not that you stop the current, you watch it flow by with indifference. Stopping the thought is as impossible as stopping the river's current using your hands, so don't waste your time trying to stop your thoughts. Observe the stream of thoughts flowing through your mind and then observe your reaction to these thoughts." She spoke as intently and slowly as possible, like Gracien was reading her lips.

Frustrated with this afternoon's third, unsuccessful attempt, Gracien squirmed in his seat. "No thought… What a joke," he mumbled.

Mukti picked up on his frustration. "This might be a bit too challenging for you at first. Please look at me." Mukti adjusted her robe and sat down next to him. "I know you suffer so therefore your mind suffers." Her eyes looked deep within his as she spoke.

Gracien swallowed, then averted his gaze.

"Fine let's discuss it further. It's not only you who suffers. Every one of us suffers because we have desire… which is the root of *all* suffering. When we desire life to be other than what it is, we suffer through these desires not being fulfilled. So," she paused, rolling up the sleeve of her robe and exposing her bare arm. Gracien's eyes went wide, his hand jutting out and his fingers hovering over Mukti's painted arm.

It was completely covered with tattoos, as if her arm was a scroll of scripture.

"I am painted, yes. I have many symbols stained into my skin, but the reason I'm showing you this is because of one script in particular." She pointed to a scripted tattoo.

Gracien spoke the words out loud. "Om Mani Padme Hum."

He looked up, questioning her with his eyes. "Those are the words written on the prayer wheels."

"Yes, the jewel is in the lotus." She nodded before pointing to the first word. "Om. Pronounced, A-U-M." Gracien felt the vibrations as she pronounced the word.

"This sound symbolizes our impure body, speech, and mind. It also symbolizes the pure exalted body, speech, and mind of a Buddha."

Gracien whispered the word and then they said it together, letting it carry longer.

"Ommm."

"Then we have Mani." Her finger moved upwards with her lips over-embellishing. "This means jewel, and symbolizes the factors of method – the altruistic or unselfish and benevolent intention to become enlightened and to embody compassion and love."

Gracien's lips silently repeated the word.

"Here we have Padme. These two syllables mean lotus and symbolize wisdom. You have seen the lotus flowers blossom from the mud, but without being tainted by the faults of the mud… This is so with wisdom."

"And finally, Hum. Indivisibility of method and wisdom. Wisdom affected by method and method affected by wisdom. One consciousness with wisdom and method as one unified body." She rolled down her sleeve as Gracien scanned her arm fascinated by the various, whimsical designs and scripts.

"Instead of focusing on your thoughts and observing them, I'd like for you to reflect over these six syllables and their meaning. Like training a drunk to cease drinking, we must remove the bad influence by compensating it with a positive one. We can temporarily banish your negative, anguished thoughts with beautiful ones." Her hand patted his shoulder as Gracien reflected on the mantra.

"I'll let you begin." She rose, dusting herself off then taking in the beautiful river scene. "What a wonderful companion the river can be. It listens or speaks depending on what you need."

A chill blew through, causing Mukti to wrap herself up as she looked to the tree canopy.

"Winter, she's stirring. We'll need to replenish our supplies sooner than expected." Her gaze fell back on Gracien as she turned to make her exit, humming, "Om Mani Padme Hum."

Gracien took a deep breath inward, tensing his entire body for several seconds then exhaling. He repeated this three times before bringing his hands into his lap with one upon the other and settling into his posture. He closed his eyes. The river current trickled by, the sound of which intensified as his focus centered on it. The forest awoke: critters bounded about, the stretch of swaying pines rang out, insects whistled, and birdsong lulled him into its chorus.

He began. *Om… Mani… Padme… Hum…* The mental sound sent a vibration throughout his body.

He didn't know how this was possible with the mantra being thought, but he felt an inner shiver each time he repeated it. *Om Mani Padme Hum.*

His body felt the atmosphere as if he had been dropped into it; the denseness of the air, the coolness coming off the river, the fresh breeze of the forest. It was all a treasure chest of sensation.

Mukti snaked along the bank of the river, being careful with each footstep as she placed it into the forest flooring without giving off a sound. She made her way down to the first of several, modest waterfalls.

The sound of the trickle was a delight as her feet crossed a slick tree trunk running over the river. She kept Gracien within sight, checking in on him as he seemed to have finally settled. His diaphragm ebbed just as she had instructed, and his posture was near perfect. She sensed the slightest movement from him as her feet navigated around a large, broken branch sticking up in the middle of her makeshift bridge. She braced herself, using the branch as a railing as she approached the other bank before stepping off into the soft mud. Mukti couldn't tell what was causing his slight movement, so she made her way back up the opposing bank.

Gracien's focus held steady on the third eye, his eyes lifted and centered on the spot as the inner mantra harmonized with the forest's chorus. "Om... Mani... Padme... Hum..." His belly ebbed as he observed his breath for a few moments before thinking about Muktinath.

His mind revisited the fascinating tattoos before he noticed he was latched onto a thought. He gave his mind an inner shake, pulling it from the thought then refocusing on the mantra as well as the forest. Something shifted as he re-settled within the several anchors. Like the parachute of a dandelion being plucked from its stem and floating off into a new expanse, it felt as if his mind had untethered itself from his body. His senses were pulled away from the river, the birdsong, and the forest as his focus converged into this new space.

Mukti crept along the bank with the stealth of a snow leopard, watching Gracien as she neared the direct spot across from where he sat. A crack sounded out, as her foot stepped through a hidden tree branch and she froze, watching to see if he noticed. Her smirk extended as he remained unmoved, for she could see he was exploring something special. She crouched down onto a patch of grass directly across from him, settling within her meditation posture and watching him.

Like a spirit soaring through nightfall, Gracien felt as if he was flying through twilight. His eyeballs flickered under his eyelids like someone in a deep sleep. Breath, bodily sensation, sound, smell, the third eye, and the mantra – they were no longer. Liberated from his cumbersome body and free to explore, to expand, he merged with self, bathing in the bliss of a reunion.

Mukti's head tilted with curiosity as her gaze finally narrowed in on the slight movement that she wasn't able to see while crossing the river. Gracien's hands, one placed on the other in the seat of his lap, remained as still as the stone on which he sat. But his thumbs unknowingly twitched, ticking away like an untuned heartbeat. Mukti watched for several minutes as Gracien held fast within his meditation. Other than his thumbs ticking away every so often, he was rather statuesque. She smirked before allowing her own eyes to close, joining him.

An embrace of color splattered across the open expanse he traversed. It was thrilling. He was a hawk diving out of the night's sky and blasting through a valley rich with life and abundance. His body was no longer, only self, only experience without senses. He soared like a wind-blown cloud merging with eternity, drifting back into the ether before time had ever been. It was the dream of an angel, the embrace of spirit. And here is where Gracien stayed until suddenly remembering his life back on earth.

And just like that his earthbound awareness returned: first to his lungs with the coolness of a breeze and then to his ears with the chirp of a bird. The forest chorus rebounded along with the river's lull. His chest heaved breath like a man pridefully claiming the summit of a mountain. Gracien's eyelids peeled apart, revealing Mukti sitting across the river, a Devi, or goddess of the forest.

Mukti's face was the embodiment of composure, of serenity. As the sunlight danced across her face, she seemed to smile but didn't. In that moment she resembled a mother looking over her child. Buddha's serene expression was a near perfect reflection of her own. As Gracien looked her over, he realized she was Buddha. His head tilted as he drank in her semblance, taking her in like she was a rainbow stretching over a valley.

A subtle grin split his face. He felt grateful for her, for this setting, and for Aya too. As he inhaled, his eyelids fell closed and he resumed his meditation, searching for that place from which he just came.

A month or so had passed and the days continued getting shorter. Today, however, felt longer than most, as it was the third and final day of harvesting the garden. What was once a thriving and abundant nursery of plants and herbs, now lay barren. The rich, vacant soil gleamed with contrast compared to the former blooming vegetation. With earth smeared over their arms and hands, Mukti and Gracien were finishing the last of it. The air was fragrant with the healthy harvest and sharp from the chill of winter's stir.

"Right understanding, right thought, right speech, right action, right livelihood, right effort, right mindfulness, and right concentration. The noble eightfold path. Which, if any, do you believe we are *not* practicing while working together in the garden?" Muktinath asked.

Gracien smirked, knowing the answer wasn't in the pages of the books he had been reading, but rather in his cleverness. He remained silent.

"Well? What's your answer?" She tugged at top of a stubborn root.

While his hands stayed busy, his lips stayed silent, wit pulling at the corners of his smirk.

Mukti paused her work. "You're not going to offer me a reply?" She questioned as a confused look washed over her face.

Gracien stood upright looking to her, nodding, and pointing to his immovable mouth.

Mukti's head titled as she pondered his response before unleashing a bellow of laughter.

It was so abrupt, so large a force from such grace that it physically moved Gracien back a step.

"AGH-HAHA! Right, speech! Well done, well done indeed."

Allowing himself to laugh Gracien joined her in the delight.

"You really had me confused there for a moment. I cannot remember the last time I laughed like that. Right, laughter. Buddha may have missed one." She giggled.

Returning to his work, Gracien laughed again. "Right laughter it is... I'll add it to the books when I return."

"You know I'm more than happy to make the journey. Three days only and I'll return. You can have the sanctuary all to yourself," Mukti suggested regarding the upcoming supply run.

"No, no I would prefer to go. I miss traveling, the mindful presence of the open road, and trekking through such beautiful scenery. If you don't mind, of course," he returned while tying a cord around the last of the bundles. "There we are, good to go."

He stood up, standing next to Mukti as they looked over the final yield.

"We did well, a plentiful season indeed. Maybe the river water, fresh and transient, made a difference this time around," Mukti said. She tugged on a cord wrapped around one of the bunches they would keep at the sanctuary before sweeping her hands together with a satisfied nod.

"What do you mean, this time around? What other water is there?" His brow furrowed with confusion as Mukti's full, unadulterated smile gleamed.

Now it was her turn to enjoy the silence of cleverness.

"The well of course, that's what I use to water the garden." Mukti busied herself with tightening a few more strands of cord on the bunches before picking one up and hoisting it over her shoulder.

Close on her heels, Gracien followed. "What do you mean?" He laughed nervously. "You use the well and not the river water?"

"I didn't have you cart that water up all those stairs because it was better for the garden. I did it because it was better for you."

Mukti spoke with a simple grin as she placed the bunch of herbs atop an already impressive waist-high stack.

Gracien moved to rebut but she cut him off, turning to face him. "How do you feel?"

"Wh-what?" he stammered.

"I said, how… do… you… feel?" Her eyes held such sympathy it was hard for him to hold her gaze.

"A little tired I guess, but…"

Mukti grabbed his arm, squeezing it firmly then moving to his shoulder.

"Wha… what are you doing?" Gracien stammered again, stepping back.

"So firm and strong… Like branches and boulders, and these." She poked his legs with her finger. "Tree trunks, sturdy and powerful." Then her finger poked his forehead. "And this… Clear and settled, isn't it?" She waited as Gracien's countenance softened into realization.

"You were training me, keeping me active, making me stronger." The three remaining fingers on his left hand squeezed his own arm as he spoke with a glazed look. "And I am strong, and I feel… I feel wonderful, healthy, and fit." His eyes met hers now, "and my diet, so clean and nourishing… No tobacco or drink. Just water, tea, and good clean food. You've built me up and made me strong. But why?"

Mukti nodded, holding his gaze, and allowing him time to make the connection himself. He continued, his eyes falling from hers as he spoke his thoughts out loud through a slow stream of focus.

"A strong body, a healthy body is the foundation of wellness, of a strong and clear mind. Without that first, a strong and clear mind is difficult, almost impossible." His gaze lifted, meeting Mukti's as his face softened, glowing like a cloud passing over the sun. "You were training me, keeping the momentum from trekking up here, keeping me fit and healthy so that I could make better progress with my meditations?" He questioned but she held her equanimous visage.

"Without physical health, the mind's health is extremely challenging to achieve. Once we feel good, physically, the mind is easier to work on, it's less of a struggle." Mukti spoke as slow as the river's trickle then turned to go fetch the remaining bundle.

Gracien contemplated her words, hovering in her shadow as she walked at her typically casual pace.

"Get some rest tonight. You should leave early tomorrow morning. Heading out at dawn will ensure you arrive at, or just after, dusk. And Ishayu?" Mukti turned to him. "I wasn't making you anything. You made yourself. And another thing, thank you for all your hard work with the garden, and for making the trade run." Her gaze wandered, peering up into the canopy as she spoke, "I do enjoy our time here together… and I also cherish my time here, alone."

Gracien nodded. "I'll get the last bundle and prepare Dhonu for the trip," he referenced the donkey a local farmer leant to Mukti for the supply runs.

Mukti nodded, smirking at some unseen delight. "Looks like you'll beat the snow just in time, this is a gift as the trek is much longer and more difficult with snow hiding the path. Make sure you get rest, nonetheless, thank you again Ishayu. Namaste." She placed her hands in prayer.

Gracien nodded. "Thank you Muktinath. Namaste," he said, placing his hands in prayer as Mukti made her exit.

The door of his cottage felt waterlogged as he pushed it open. Mocking Gracien's exhaustion, it too moaned out with fatigue. The hearth and chair before it seemed to call out to him as he ambled over. Gracien moved several of the books before plopping down into the seat, forgoing a proper meditation posture, and melting into the chair. He exhaled, his body feeling the wear from the long day of harvesting.

"Light the fire, light the fire, light the fire," he encouraged.

An hour later the crackle of fire sounded out as he cleaned the dishes from supper. Wiping his hands with a rag, he tossed it over to the table before taking his seat in the chair for his evening meditation. The padded mallet dinged the singing bowl three times and the small space flooded with an entrancing vibration. Gracien rounded the outer edge with a padded drum and like wind rising at dusk, the howl of Heaven swirled about him.

After several moments of tuning his spirit, he placed the bowl down. The old wooden frame of the chair groaned out as he settled in, his body sinking into it with the weight of exhaustion. The fire exploded with those intense, stirring pops that come with fresh wood. The wave of heat just felt lovely as Gracien melted into his posture. He began focusing on his breath and attending the fire's chatter as it rambled on. Gracien considered what Mukti had mentioned earlier regarding his physical fitness, noticing a trickle of thoughts instead of the typical deluge while being so tired. He mentally shook his head, recapturing his anchors and trying to focus on observing thought while not engaging it. As the fire's pop and crackle dwindled, his head began to bob. His eyes felt heavy even with his eyelids closed. Gracien's mind darkened further as the lull of sleep pulled him in like a steadfast current.

His bare feet walked along the wooden flooring as the hearth's embers glowed in his wake. A moment later Gracien was outside, his hands, complete with ten fingers, wrenching up the loose garden soil. It was cool in temperature but warm with life. Gracien couldn't help but think that the soil was light and radiance in physical form. The garden sounded much louder than normal, like he could hear its pulse. It was brighter too, he looked around to investigate, finding both the sun and the moon illuminating the sanctuary at the same time. His smile extended as he stepped onto the earth, his feet sinking into the rich soil. Gracien looked around again, finding himself transported to the river's current, smiling at the mighty pines as they swayed and spun like great dancing giants.

"The garden, the herbs, the supply run," he thought as his feet raced up the stone steps, bounding up one, then three, then several at once.

He glided up the long winding stairway as it ascended into the Heavens. Gracien was light and free. Like a bird discovering flight, he soared upwards before landing with a gentle thud back in the garden. He had never felt so strong. His feet were the roots of a mighty tree. His legs, the trunk. His toes extended, burrowing themselves into the welcoming earth.

Then he heard her call. His head rose, he floated forward looking through the garden. The scintillation was unworldly, he could see the vital energy pulse and migrate through the leaves and branches. The plants coiled and snaked in place as he sought her out, it was a labyrinth of flora as his feet stalked over the warm earth. He and Aya were mere children now, caught up in a game of hide and sneak. Her giggles rang out into the night as he gave chase. Aya's glorious hair billowed in her wake as she evaded him, ducking, and dodging through the garden as Gracien gave chase. Her laugh evolved, maturing back into Aya's womanly form as Gracien stepped out from behind a great sunflower stalk, catching her and wrapping her up in his arms. They fell towards the earth, then through it like an embracing couple falling through the surface of a pond. As they fell, they swung back and around like a pendulum until they were tipped back onto their feet, finding themselves standing within the barren garden holding one another in an embrace.

Hello, my love, Gracien thought with a smile.

Hello, my love, her voice returned within his mind.

I've missed you, why haven't you been to visit? How can I get you to stay with me? His mind rattled off questions as Aya's laugh echoed within it.

Aya looked up at him as his arms wrapped around her petite frame. *Gracien, my love… I'm always with you… Always watching over and guiding you. How do you think you arrived here, in this sanctuary? You exist with me, my love.*

Her words stirred emotion and life within Gracien like dawn's first light breathing life into a forest.

It may not be enough… but I'm the breath in your lungs when you wish for a windstorm. I'm the river diverting around your feet as you pray for an ocean. I'm the warmth of a fire when you desire the sun. She looked at him from the corner of her eyes, then nodded to the sky.

Gracien gazed upwards, taking in the cloud covered evening as it began to snow. Large, fluffy snowflakes cascaded downwards as he and Aya delighted in the unexpected event.

Like stars hidden from cloud cover, I'm always there… watching over you whether you feel me or not. The snow fall accelerated as clouds began to thin and disperse like time had sped up, revealing a starry, jubilant vibrancy not of this world.

Gracien gasped as the divine landscape swirled and bulged before him. Suddenly he and Aya were lying down on the earth with their heads next to one another and their feet heading in opposite directions. They looked up into the sky, feeling the world spin slowly around them. The last of the cloud cover withered away, exhibiting the glory of space. They soared up into the Heavens as the snowfall fell through them.

Stars glimmered and sparkled as if performing for the darkness. Indigo, violet, and emerald streaks raced across the sky as galaxies swirled like swarms of rainbow-colored birds. The moon glowed like a wet, marbled sphere. Gracien could hear it turn, the low hum rippling through him as Aya's hand squeezed his. Stars glistened as they darted about, cast through the sky like stones skipped over a reflective, moonlit surface.

They were lying next to one another now, hands and arms embracing. They careened through the open universe on a chunk of grass covered earth as if it were an iceberg floating off into space. The garden, Mukti's utopia, the Himalayas, and all of Nepal never were just a novelty in a story long forgotten. Gracien and Ayadonna soared through space like mated stars. He merged with something bigger, something eternal as he clutched Aya's arm.

Don't be scared, this place, it's our home. It's within you, within us both. It is us, our very being. We are not in space, Gracien, we are within you, within us both. The universe, which we are... is One. It's this moment and yet at the very same time it's every moment and everything... that ever was.

Her arm held his so completely that it felt like a snake coiling around him. *This... this is why we are never apart. I am your stars, and you are my space, you are my light, and I am your sun.*

Gracien no longer floated through space but was space. Like expanding fog, he felt his body disperse while merging with all the celestial splendor surrounding him.

We are eternity Gracien, we are the beginning and the end. Aya's voice became murky and faded as if the strength was being sucked from it. *...as is everything which has ever existed... forrr... weee... arree...*

POP! The hearth's fire snapped out like a mini explosion, launching Gracien's head upwards as his chest heaved with breath. He looked down, seeing that his hands were not in his lap but gripping the chair's armrest as if someone was trying to pull him from it. His head turned towards the door as he heard or rather felt a presence just outside. Like a dehydrated fern soaking up overdue rainfall, Gracien uncoiled himself off the chair. His tight, achy body groaned as he stood with his joints audibly popping. His frame slackened as he pulled the door open. Large, fluffy snowflakes had canvassed the sanctuary, creating an immaculate wonderland. He smiled, stepping into winter's inauguration as snow-flakes fell on his face, instantly melting while he strolled mindlessly. Gracien giggled at first then laughed out loud, spinning around like an unfettered child.

He approached the garden, the blanket of snow illuminating the space even under the shadow of a moonless night. Gracien paused, star-ing at what he thought looked like two imprints in the snow. He slowed as he approached, crouching down to investigate as the snow had accu-mulated around the spot with the forms, but not as much in the middle of it. It appeared as if a couple had been embracing. There were no tracks, just the cutout.

"How… it can't…" His hand hovered above the impression, but he didn't dare disturb it.

Gracien shook his head in disbelief before looking to the Heavens with a modest grin. His neck cringed with the effort before he relaxed, lying down inside the imprint. He stared up into the vibrant, starry sky as the snowflakes continued cascading down around him. Once again, he felt as if he was floating up into the sky with Aya by his side.

Gracien tightened the straps around Dhonu as the donkey chomped away at whatever delight Mukti fed him. The garden bounty stacked atop him was about five feet high, but light compared to what Dhonu would be lugging back to the sanctuary after making a trade with the general store.

"It's still teetering a bit, make it tighter on the left side, and make sure he can't turn his head and snack along the trip, or we won't have anything left to trade," Mukti said while rubbing the white stripe running down the center of his grayed, furry nose.

The snow surrounding Dhonu had been trampled into non-existence, with only a thin layer leftover from the nightfall, "are you sure you don't want me to accompany you?" Mukti asked as she examined the sky for the third time this morning.

"If I didn't know any better, I might venture to think you're a bit nervous or scared even, Mukti," Gracien returned.

"I'm not nervous about you going, I'm being cautious about the snowfall. It's early, too early and can prove..." She inhaled, thinking her words over, "challenging. The snow, it steals away the trail and once the path is gone, you're either somewhere safe or you aren't. Being cautious before crossing a river is looking to make sure nothing is coming along to sweep you away... fearing it... is avoiding the river altogether because something bad *may* happen. Knowing the difference between these two perspectives can lead to a life of fulfillment... or one of regret."

Gracien nodded in understanding but still felt the urge to assure her. Stopping his task, he turned to her.

"Muktinath, I will be as quick as can be and I've been through more challenging things than a bit of snowfall. Let's finish up so I can get a move on it." His maimed hand patted her arm. "Let me grab my bag and I'll be off."

Mukti exhaled, nodding her consent.

Twenty minutes later, and the two of them were guiding Dhonu through the forest. The huge stack of harvest tilted from one side to the other with each step as they retraced the same path Gracien and Mukti took into the sanctuary many months prior.

"Remember, a day's journey there, then make the trade. Rest while Chantin and her husband, Batsal, prepare Dhonu for the return trip. They'll be expecting you. He too will rest for a bit before they load him up with everything, we'll need to make it through the winter so there's much to bring back. Here's a bit of extra money for something you'd like… a gift for your help." Mukti grinned, her face appearing between steps over Dhonu's neck as they neared the clearing with the prayer wheels.

"I can't accept…" Gracien began before Mukti cut him off.

She placed the pouch of coins into his hand. "I insist… it's a cold, long winter, you'll need something to bring about a bit of sunshine." Mukti stepped towards him, placing her hands just before Gracien's head as she bowed her own head in prayer.

Her thin lips quivered for several moments before settling into a grin as her hands fell back to her side.

"You are not your thoughts," she said.

Gracien's face washed over with confusion. "What?"

"You," Mukti poked him in the heart, "are not," her hand rose to her own temple, and she tapped it twice, "your thoughts."

Gracien motioned to respond but Mukti shook her head. "Ponder my words as you journey. All you need to do is examine what I've said, and we'll discuss it when you return."

She pulled him into an embrace then quickly turned and began walking back to the sanctuary. It all happened so fast he didn't even have a chance to hug her back.

"You are not your thoughts, think about it!" she called back, and Gracien could hear the pleasure in her cleverness.

He smirked, tugging at Dhonu's reins while approaching the prayer wheels. The sound of Mukti's steps faded into the strum of the forest as

Gracien paused, preparing his mind and heart. As his footsteps neared the wall of prayer wheels, only one prayer thrived. Gracien's fingers reached out to spin the wheels, but he hesitated, stopping short.

"My only prayer is for us to be together again, and it can never be."

His fingers retracted and a moment later Gracien's footsteps retreated along the path heading from the temple.

Four hours later with eight more to go, Gracien was feeling wonderful. He wasn't the least bit winded as he ascended another slope with Dhonu close behind. The donkey was a master of tempo, taking his time in the steeper areas while attending to the supplies stacked up on his back. Gracien encouraged him over the more difficult terrain, smiling and congratulating Dhonu with each little accomplishment. The snowfall was minimal and the trail clear as the two traversed the winding paths towards the village.

As the cluck of Dhonu's hooves rang out along the gravel path, Gracien's mind spoke, "om," with an inhalation then, "mani" with an exhalation followed by, "padme," with the next inhalation and lastly, "hum" with the final exhalation.

That mantra was repeated end over end while trying to sweep any other thoughts from the stillness within. His senses delighted in mother earth like a dog reuniting with its owner. Gracien missed the smell of various terrains, the wind cooling him off under the sun then chilling him in the shade. The majestic landscapes swept him up into their embrace like a lover, the ever-changing color of the river wooed him, the sense of freedom under the open sky made him blush. His mind was at ease, something he attributed not only to being back on the road but also due to the mindfulness work these past few months with Mukti. He felt excited, thrilled, and not for what was to come but for what he was already experiencing. Gracien knew a quicker pace was important, but he couldn't help but take his time as Dhonu strolled along close behind.

A few hours later, Gracien's hand shielded his gaze from the sun as it gazed back from its highest point. The temperature was cool with winter winds blowing down from the north. The pair withdrew from a pine forest, walking into the embrace of warmer temperatures and narrowed paths as Gracien hummed a Babylonian tune. Dhonu seemed to really enjoy the parts Gracien whistled as the creature chewed on a few snacks slipped to him from the harvest.

"Okay let's take it slow here Dhonu," Gracien said while surveying a path narrowed further by a minor landslide.

They were common throughout these parts as the rock face was a bit more brittle. "Nice and slow, that's good... easy does it my..." and just like that the ground beneath his feet gave out.

Gracien screamed as he plunged then scraped along the cliffside before being jerked to a stop by Dhonu's reins.

His chest heaved breath. "OH MY! HOLY SHIT!" he screamed as his feet dangled over a bottomless canyon.

Gracien peered upwards, following his arm which flexed with rippling muscles and pulsing veins. His left hand, or rather the three remaining fingers, clenched at the leather reins hanging down from Dhonu's face as the donkey screeched and wheezed.

Gracien took a deep breath, trying to poke about with his toes looking for a ledge as his free hand steadied him from spinning. "Easy boy easy!"

No luck, his feet kicked at the open air, infuriating Dhonu, and causing Gracien to plunge downwards. "Aghhh!" he screamed while clenching his eyes closed and bracing for the fall.

His plunge stopped an instant later as Dhonu caught his footing, dangling Gracien over the edge like a spider from his web. One of Gracien's eyelids peeled open, he gulped, looking below him then up to Dhonu who screeched and snorted as his feet slid over a mixture of loose earth and snow.

"Dhonu? Dhonu, my boy... Back up boy. Back up."

Dhonu snorted, spittle dripping from his flaring nostrils as he shrieked.

"Please Dhonu... paaa-lease... take a step back, just one!" Gracien's mind raged with terror but somehow his voice was calm while coaxing Dhonu into retreat.

Gracien's fingers were purple yet in that very moment he thanked the heavens for having the remaining three.

"Easy now... go for it but slowly," he encouraged Dhonu as well as himself while his other hand reached up.

Wincing with the effort, Gracien grabbed the reins with his good hand and steadied himself from spinning. Dhonu screeched with what seemed anger now, the awful sound echoing throughout the canyon. Then a more pleasant sound rang out, the scratch of leather along the rocky surface as Dhonu took one slow step backward after another.

"That's right... Good boy, Dhonu! Keep going!" he shouted through gulps of air.

Dhonu continued his acoustic tantrum while stepping backwards as if he was backtracking on a frozen lake. As the scrape of leather sounded out, Gracien discovered he was holding his breath while wondering if Dhonu was saving his own hide, or Gracien's. Then the leather began to tear along the brittle rock face.

"That's right Dhonu, good boy!" he yelled, holding on for dear life as the cliff's edge approached.

As carefully as possible he placed his feet along the cliffside, then released his good hand and took hold of what seemed like a stronghold, a large rock slicing back into the mountain. As one of the reins splayed and snapped, Dhonu continued pulling. It all happened in a second, and Gracien closed his eyes.

With all their strength, the duo yanked Gracien over the cliff, dragging him onto the safety of the gravel. Dhonu stomped and shook triumphantly as Gracien rolled over to his back, heaving breath as he tore the leather reins from his deformed hand. He made a fist then splayed out his fingers, squeezing blood back into his hand. Dhonu was already chomping away at some of the escaped harvest lying about his feet.

"Well done my friend, well done." His breath spilled from him as he rolled over to his stomach, looking up to Dhonu. "Thank you Dhonu… Thank you so much." He held his hands in prayer, saluting the heroic creature.

Gracien's face contorted as he pushed himself up, feeling a scorching burst of pain catapult up his bloody leg. He looked down at the source and found a crimson pool spreading along the fabric of his pants with several gashes in the material.

"Shit."

He winced, pulling a few stones from his flesh through the fabric. His fingers, raw and tender from the climb, tore the hole wider so he could examine the wound. It wasn't horrible, but it wasn't good either. Gracien's mind welcomed a torrent of anxiety as he was halfway through his trip and now had to deal with this.

"Go back or carry on?" he questioned but the answer plunged into his head from above: "Clean yourself up, and get moving. Keep heading towards the village because without the winter supplies, we're doomed." He sighed then took a deep long breath, inhaling the courage to continue.

Twenty minutes later, and the pair had successfully navigated beyond the narrowed landslide. Gracien hobbled every so often as the side of his calf raged with pain when the path sloped downwards. But when the path ascended, which it did quite often, the pain was minimal.

As they walked along like retired workmen, Gracien treated his companion to quite a bit more of the harvest than he should have. The crunch of footsteps in the snow and the cluck of donkey hooves were the only sounds until the bustle of a community stirred in the distance. As the sun began settling for the night, casting its amber blanket over the vast, mountainous terrain, Gracien and Dhonu approached the village entrance three hours later than planned. Snow was trampled into the trail by wheel tracks and a stream of footprints. Mimicking the river, the unceremonious path wound downwards into the quaint, narrow town. A sole man, rugged and dirty with adventure, leaned against a dead tree while amusedly eying Gracien and Dhonu. Several painted animal skulls decorated the supports of the village entrance, the bone white color gleaming under the golden hour radiance. The stranger's pipe glowed with his inhalation before a cloud of smoke veiled his weather-beaten face. Gracien met his gaze as the smoke cleared.

"Namaste. The store… Batsal, Chantin?" he inquired, carrying himself like a defeated soldier returning home.

The stranger looked him over before pointing down the road with his pipe. "Third on the left, green door." His pipe returned to his mouth, then he tongued it over to the other corner. "You've seen better days, boy," he declared with a nod.

Gracien returned, "Haven't we all?" Nodding thanks, he and Dhonu walked under the archway of flapping, multi-colored prayer flags welcoming them into Manang.

Chantin was a tiny woman, with the top of her head barely reaching Gracien's chin. The storekeeper was petite but quick as a fox as she darted around the shop grabbing this or that. She shouted out the various items on the supply list as if she was auctioning them off. Gracien looked around, listening for who he expected was her husband, Batsal, heeding her directions from some hidden nook of the quaint shop. A pair of chickens bobbed their way in front of Gracien, causing him to leap back in fright and almost knock over a stack of eggs.

"Whoa... sorry." His hands braced the side of the teetering egg stack as both he and Chantin held their breath.

Batsal's head popped out from behind a tower of rice sacks. A wisp of silvered hair careened about his bald head like a belly dancer, then his eyes narrowed and he made an instant retreat. From the sound of it, he seemed to be wrestling a bear as he grunted behind the curtain.

"Whoa... that was close, sorry. It's... it's a little tight in here." Gracien swallowed nervously then smiled. "Mukti said you'd have everything we need?" His eyebrows rose with hope.

Chantin's smile broke as she realigned the stack of eggs. Deep wrinkles and age spots cascaded along her aged face, the only characteristic keeping her from looking like a twelve-year-old girl. Her hair was still black as night, with a faded sheen but not a single gray in sight. She was highly energetic, shooting out dynamic hand gestures to accompany her orders like a retired general.

The shop was a labyrinth of items with no apparent structure other than chaos. Long ladles and other assorted cooking utensils hung from the ceiling, spinning like ornaments with the help of a gentle breeze. With all the visual stimulation and Chantin darting about, Gracien felt his head spinning too.

"Yes, yes! Everything you need and some things you don't. Bastal!" She stopped to listen, her head tilting like a dog's. "Seven cartons and three sacks, not the other way around!"

She began stacking supplies on the counter while speaking with Gracien. Huge clay pots lay haphazardly atop baskets brimmed with various grains. Bushels of vegetables were nibbled on by an obese bunny with a fluffy, chocolate colored coat.

"Some of these... oh and two of these. Eight, no nine pounds should do it... maybe eleven, looks like a long winter." She poked her head outside to examine the skies.

Gracien eyed the doorway while scratching his neck. The energy in the shop felt like a brewing volcano and he wanted out.

"A few hours and we'll have you all sorted, we'll make sure to include a few sweets as we know Muktinath loves her sugar." Gracien's face squished over with confusion and Chantin laughed. "Everyone's got their secrets, haven't they?"

She grabbed him by the arm, ushering him towards the door as if he'd missed several cues to leave. Chantin and Gracien approached Dhonu and the massive tower of harvest.

"Oh wow! Great harvest this year... river water I bet! Always a bigger harvest when she has someone doing all the hard work for her." Chantin pointed up the road, squinting her eyes and crooning her neck. "There's a teahouse, just up the road, a quaint but friendly place, ask for Dhirti, she'll put you up for the night and get you all patched up." An eyebrow hinted towards his injury. "And we'll take care of Dhonu here." She mindlessly rubbed Dhonu's ears, "then you can make your way back and hit the road, quickly too." She peered up into the skies again. "Yup, a long winter indeed... and in a rush to get started."

Chantin tugged at Gracien's sleeve. "Six or seven hours. Get some good rest... try the ginger chai, that's my favorite."

A thunderous clamor sounded out inside the shop and Chantin dashed up the steps, cursing Batsal as she disappeared into the chaos.

Glad to be free of the shop, Gracien shook his head. "I need a drink… and something stronger than tea. Good luck boy."

He gave Dhonu a pat before picking up his satchel and heading towards the teahouse. He was utterly exhausted half an hour ago but felt a sudden surge of excitement. Twenty steps in and the clamor of celebration met him along his stroll. His senses followed the cheer, men singing to the tune of colliding mugs, stomping feet, and a set of drums. Two men stumbled from the tavern, singing as they departed while Gracien approached. Gracien adjusted the strap of his satchel as he came in for a closer look, his fingers thumbing Muktinath's coins. He poked his head through the doorway, his eyes going wide with the celebration.

The raucous debauchery put a grin on his face as memories of rowdy Babylonian feasts arose. He recalled times he had abandoned sobriety for days at a time. As the multitude of indulgent memories blended into one another, he tried recalling the last time he actually allowed himself a few drinks in the company of like-minded men. With a nod he adjusted the strap of his satchel before stepping into the festivities.

Five hours later and Gracien had yet to step back out. "And that was, was that, that was the battle of Ur… the battle… we won!" Gracien slurred, slapping his newfound friend on the back as if sharing the punchline of a joke.

Dust plumed from the man's thick coat as his scruffy, sweat covered face jiggled with a near silent, wheezing laugh.

"Another! Another for me, and another for HE!"

Gracien said to no one in particular as his full mug collided with the man's. The tavern was busier than before, bustling with grizzled characters trekking their way through the mountain pass. A trio of musicians played in the corner while patrons sang, danced, and celebrated. A plump, shiny headed server carting an armful of mugs wiggled his way between tables and lumbering drunkards.

Gracien stumbled while turning around, tripping over a stool and then pointing and frowning at it before backpedaling. "Shhh…" he said to the stool before bumping into a beast of a man.

Even leaning on a table, he was a foot taller than Gracien.

"Forsaken fool!" the man bellowed, turning, and slapping Gracien on the chest with the back of his hand.

"That's not the second but the third time you've spilled my drink, boy. Grrr," he literally growled, and loud enough for his three seated friends to bellow with laughter before exchanging excited elbows.

"One time, that's to be expected at an inn like this." He picked up his own mug and took a gulp, what didn't make it in his mouth trickled down his full, rust colored beard.

Gracien frowned with his hands bobbing apologetically. "Listen, listen I'm… I'm going to, sorry I had bumped…"

The behemoth cut him off. "Once, once is acceptable, expected even. But two times, well that's…" He placed his mug on the table nice and slow then grabbed Gracien by the collar. "That's a THREAT!" Their faces were mere inches apart. "But three! Three makes me think you're trying to flirt! AHGHA-HA-HA!"

All the men roared with laughter as Gracien tried shaking the blurriness into focus.

"You big tease!"

The man bellowed before his giant fist slammed right into the side of Gracien's head. Everything went black as he collapsed to the ground like a sack of rocks.

"Ughhh…" He rolled to his side, falling off the bedding and crawling towards the window. Gracien pulled back the curtain, the white glow of the accumulated snow stung his eyes as if it were an unabashed sun.

"Ugh. More like *wrong* conduct." He tried swallowing, rubbing his temples only to find a large knot of swollen flesh where his right one should have been.

"Ughhh."

He deflated, sitting back against the bed. An entire day had passed before he could even take a piss without wanting to wretch. That was several hours ago. Chantin had left several messages with Dhirti who just now appeared in the doorway.

Gracien's one eye sliced open and he groaned, dismissing her with a wave of his hand. "Bring more water, tell her I'll be over when I can. I fell, hurt my head." His muffled speech poured out with ache as he spoke through a musty pillow.

Dhirti rolled her eyes then disappeared. Gracien tried sitting up but the pain throbbing through his head was ruthless, rising like a tsunami every time he moved. He looked outside again, squinting with the brilliance then looked back at the bed, inhaling like someone preparing to undertake some bold physical feat. Gracien grunted with the effort of pulling himself back into bed before melting like seared butter; he was snoring like a banshee two minutes later.

The chirp of crickets welcomed him back to consciousness with the growl of his stomach chiming in shortly after. His body was as tight and dry as a sunbaked rope. Gracien gulped down the remaining water and felt surprisingly good, the headache had all but passed but the wounds in both his temple and leg throbbed for attention. He moved quicker now with the anxiety of his predicament coming to life. The curtain whipped back, revealing a decent amount of snowfall with more accumulating. It was just before sunrise.

Eat, then hit the road you goddamn idiot, his mind raged with a flare of guilt and fury as he began searching the room for his shoes and gear.

Thirty minutes later and he couldn't tug Dhonu from the general store fast enough, pulling him through the few inches of snow as if they had stolen all the goods stacked on top of the donkey's back. Batsal had been great, knowing all too well the wrath of his wife and doing his best to get all the supplies secured atop Dhonu as fast as possible. Like a furious mother, Chantin had berated Gracien for being gone so long, even poking his temple and asking what happened. As he tugged at the reins fastened around Dhonu, he couldn't believe she had threatened him with a sandal after smelling the booze. Gracien reeked like a Sunday morning brothel. Dhonu was also disgruntled with their departure, grunting and screeching more than usual as his hooves trudged through the sloshy muck along the path leading from the village. The snowflakes continued to flutter down, melting on Gracien's cheeks as he felt the difficulty of the trip weighing down on his dehydrated limbs.

"What an irresponsible idiot, come on, Dhonu!" Gracien tugged at the reins as his patience thinned.

"Mukti will be so disappointed," he yelled, as Dhonu struggled in the snow while grappling with what must have been triple the weight stacked on top of him compared to before.

The village disappeared only a few hundred meters from where they stood. Gracien paused, staring up at the snow-covered trail as it ascended before him. He couldn't help but pace back and forth while yelling at himself.

"Through the snow, with this storm brewing, all this extra cargo, and I'm still hungover. I can't believe this, what kind of mess have I got myself into?"

Gracien finally tugged on Dhonu's reins and the two started traversing the difficult trail upwards. It would be a few hours of uphill climbing before even beginning the great descent back down to Mukti's sanctuary. At least the trail was stomped and battered from all the trekkers and various animals making their way through. The only thing was that all the prints were headed the other direction back to town. The sky growled as a murmur of distant thunder resounded through the ominous sky. Gracien looked up as Dhonu screeched his displeasure.

"We'll have to move quick Dhonu, this can't be good for us," he spoke slowly as his frustration fled with the arrival of something much worse, fear.

He felt the persuasion to head back to town deep in his gut.

He nodded. "Just nerves and all the drink."

Several hours in and the snowfall had thickened with the wind picking up, reducing their visibility to only about twenty feet or so. The chill whipped right through Gracien's clothing as he had delayered just before successfully ascending a steep, rocky incline. The trail thinned or rather melded with the terrain hugging it. Minimal traffic meant minimal prints to follow. Most of the other trekkers and herds had found their destination or at least found somewhere to hunker down until the storm had passed. Gracien wasn't alone though, as his anger with himself had not dissipated but strengthened. He let a good amount of it out on Dhonu, pulling and cursing him along while slapping the sacks of rice. Being furious with more than just the situation, Gracien just couldn't shake the anger.

His hangover still lingered, and his mind was a torrent of toxic, horrible thoughts as he berated himself and Dhonu. "C'mon dammit, hurry up!" He whipped the reins and Dhonu screeched while quick stepping up the path.

Gracien blamed the tavern for getting him so drunk, the behemoth man for sucker punching him, and even Mukti for sending him on this voyage in the first place. He was pissed with each of these, but he was furious over one thing more than anything else: for God taking away his Aya while placing him in this hell. He frequently fell into bouts of grief, slowing his stride and feeling the urge to give up entirely.

"What a complete ass, what's the point of it all? A few hours of celebration followed by three days of misery, what a shitty trade-off. Before it was fun because there was nothing to mourn over or grieve... but now, now all it does is highlight all the pain."

He felt like crying but instead, rubbed snow on his swollen temple while managing the cumbersome limp, which had rebounded, making the grueling trek that much harder. Gracien was letting Dhonu lead as this section of the path was especially thin, bordering a steep cliffside without any railings. Dhonu's hooves clattered over the tricky rock terrain, as it was impossible to see what was beneath the snowy surface. The fluctuations of the trail were extremely deceiving, as gaping holes filled with snow only looked to be slightly different from the ground surrounding them. Several times Gracien fell more than a foot or two as he stepped into a hole. Other times he nearly twisted an ankle stepping on the side of a stone or uneven step.

"C'mon Dhonu, I said HURRY UP!" His deformed hand cracked the reins again.

"BA-BOOM!" A sole thunder strike boomed, and with it, Dhonu's terrified screech.

In an instant Gracien found himself face-planted in the snow with the donkey's sudden retreat. Gracien heard his screech, the quickened patter of his hooves, then nothing at all. He pushed himself up, wiping snow from his face with his fingerless gloves before scanning the area.

"Dhonu?"

He stood, looking at the expansive openness before tracing Dhonu's tracks along the snow. His heart thundered as Gracien scrambled up the thin path, falling over twice and bracing himself with his hands.

"Dhonu!" he screamed, and the echo resounded through the canyon.

"DOUGH - NEW!!!" he screamed again with both hands cupping his mouth before returning his attention back to the tracks.

They led up another steep incline for a few meters before completely disappearing. Gracien walked up the last of them, gasping as he peered down into the canyon below.

"Please, no."

The canyon was sprinkled with all their supplies, as well as Dhonu's carcass.

Gracien fell to his knees. "No, no-no-no!" Was all he could manage as he stared blankly at Dhonu's lifeless form lying on the pearl white canvas.

His panic raged. Gracien motioned to speak, to ask someone what he should do or where he should go. He felt so alone, abandoned, and betrayed as he continued to stare at the supplies peppered about the canyon. He sank into himself while kneeling at the cliff's edge.

"Now what?" He felt the coldness of snow seep beyond his clothes as the minutes crept by.

Time stopped as Gracien sat with a deadened glare fastened to the morbid scene below.

"Go back now? But Mukti, what will she do? It could be days or weeks before I'm able to get to her… and without anything at all. Now, now she has nothing."

Gracien racked his brain, trying to think if Muktinath kept a storage of supplies or if what lay scattered below was all that she had.

"I can't go back to the village and just leave her without knowing what happened. This…" He began to cry with the buildup of insurmountable guilt and frustration. "This is all my fault. I can't leave her to die."

Gracien stayed there for a while, allowing himself the time he needed to purge his guilt before standing and wiping himself off. The chill of the storm suddenly cemented as if he had stepped into it from a warmed hut.

"I'll go get her. We'll return to the village together and resupply ourselves. We can work something out. Go back Ishayu, and just tell her what happened. This wasn't your fault."

Even as he said it the words betrayed him. He tried his best to shake off the guilt and the dread of having to come clean to Mukti.

"Go back, tell her what happened and together you'll figure this all out."

His eyesight returned to him after the mental exchange, highlighting the freshly fallen snow piling up on Dhonu's carcass.

"His burial. I'm so, so sorry Dhonu, you deserved better," he muttered as an unconsidered realization arose.

The financial cost of his stupidity, of losing Dhonu – it all came crashing down on him like another thunder strike. Gracien deflated, shaking his head with defeat before backtracking out of the large body print left in the snow before him. He brushed himself off, instinctively trying to wrap his coat around him only to remember that it too was with Dhonu. As he rubbed his arms while hugging his chest, his predicament darkened further. Gracien looked to the nonexistent trail heading towards Mukti, then towards the one leading back to town. He considered both but a tug of intuition persuaded him back to town. His mind dismissed the palpable force with a dozen analytical reasons why he should head back to the sanctuary instead.

They'll all laugh at me, a drunk fool who killed his donkey, he thought.

With the tower of blame and mental angst of having to face everyone in town, he turned toward the trail heading to Muktinath and began his march through the unmolested snow. A pang of angst rippled through his heart's center, he ignored it and carried on.

An hour or so in and Gracien's arms felt frozen to his body as he shivered while carefully placing each step to avoid falling over again. He was drenched from tripping and falling over in the snow several times and new snowfall continued to accumulate on his body. The visibility wasn't even ten feet now as the storm raged with aggressive winds whipping into exaggerated swirls. The skies sunk into darkness with the clouds dropping down on top of him and the plummeting temperature. After another hour or so it was impossible to tell which direction he was going or whether the trail was under his feet or not. Never before had he felt such unbridled cold. His fingers and toes vibrated with the bitter, freezing intensity before completely numbing over. Bearing the brunt of the winter winds with nothing to shield it, Gracien's face felt like it had been separated from his head.

"S-s-s-sooo c-c-cold-d-d." He trembled through his clenched teeth.

With his fingers unable to clutch his arms anymore he looked around for shelter.

Anything to sh-sh-shield me from th-th-the wind, even his thoughts stuttered.

He swallowed, or at least tried to as he investigated the forest for protection. The only warmth within was fueled by the rage of his circumstance. His mind screamed and spat blame and evidence as to why he was such a complete fool. Anxiety-ridden speculation tore his mind into two, then three, then multiple conflicting personalities. They blamed and bashed one another over what steps should have been taken while berating Gracien over all the mistakes.

Through his almost blind rage Gracien stumbled over the terrain, slipping and falling, but this time taking forever to push himself back up to his feet. His body, or rather the parts of it he could still feel, throbbed with frozen ache and stinging pain. Through the perfectly white snow, a dull purple color shone, it was coming from his fingers. And in the moment, he couldn't help but think that his old fingers were fortunate not to have experienced such a fate. Something caught his eye, an outcropping of pines. He rushed towards them on all fours. Several massive tree trunks stemming from one root system formed a partial, protective hut. Gracien collapsed into the middle trying to climb through. His body gave up, going limp with exhaustion, as all he could do was hunker down and clutch his knees into his chest.

The middle of this protected nook was free of snow, filled instead with a bedding of pine needles which bounced with his weight. Even if he could have cried it was impossible with the freezing temperatures. He was so angry, so furious with what came of this trip, yet in the moment he seemed to accept his fate.

"This… this is the end of the path, isn't it Aya?" he whispered to himself as he rocked, betrayal brewing in his green eyes.

A moment later the fear overwhelmed him, and he pleaded. "Help me Ayadonna, help me get myself out of this mess." He sobbed tearlessly through drawn out gasps.

The tree limbs overhead moaned and groaned out with the snow's accumulated weight as the wind sliced through gaps in the massive trunks. It whistled and howled as Gracien shifted his body, trying to use his deadened hands to scoop a hole from the bed of needles to bury as much of himself as possible. He did so, making a nest and settling in it, the effort of which drained any energy he had left. Gracien was unborn again, clutching his knees within nature's womb.

After an unknowable amount of time, something stirred within him like the song of a singing bowl – Mukti's voice penetrated the moment. *You are not your thoughts.*

Breathlessness. The words stole him from the storm, the cold, the wind, and the pain. Each word resounded in his mind like an echo in a cave. A space between them expanded, and with it an experience, or possibly a presence made itself known. Even the storm seemed to recognize the authority of this new force as it too settled. Gracien's body deflated with the strain of his muscles surrendering as he sank into the embrace of the needle bedding. His teeth ceased chattering as he focused his entire consciousness on this new, expanding presence.

He yearned to escape the hell that surrounded him, and it was all he could do as his body heat dropped further. A new wave of emotion came through, despair and anguish over his cemented fate. His eyelids compressed, pushing impossible tears outwards, rolling down his cheeks before freezing. Gracien's mind raced with thoughts of death as he stressed through impossible options. Waves of violent shivers ripped through him as he felt his life force seep away. An immensity of fear never before experienced erupted as the idea of certain death entombed him.

You are not your thoughts, again her message rang out.

With these words he began centering his concentration on his surroundings. He listened to the symphony of swift gusts and long, drawn-out gales shifting in tone and strength. His mind attended to each change in pitch like someone tuning an instrument. Any thought of fear was instantly banished from his mind as he concentrated. Like an approaching light, the presence between his thoughts intensified and strengthened. Something new arrived and Gracien focused on it – a growing intensity of light just beyond his eyelids. The light moved up-wards into his head. It was a warming presence which he followed at first before it slowly dropped down to the center of his chest. His heartbeat was slow and soft. As if his consciousness had relocated, Gracien felt like he was perceiving the world from his chest and not his head. He stayed in this place for quite some time, unaware of time's passage.

Little by little his awareness retreated from the external world and focused completely within. Gradually, the light began to expand beyond his place of heart, filling his inner shell yet never touching the edges. A constant and profound vibration flourished, providing the first physical comfort since his demise. The inner radiance seemed to expand outside his body, spreading beyond his physical self. He didn't sense the outer world around him but rather merged with it. Like water being poured into water, he felt connected to everything around him yet somehow completely separated. His awareness evolved beyond sensing the world and into unity with it, yet all on a level beyond the physical – the light of a sunrise merging with that of a sunset.

His consciousness traveled deep within himself, falling yet expand-ing down an eternal abyss, one which was both thrilling and familiar. An energy not of himself bloomed, something primal and ancient. It warmed and intensified, swelling and flowing about like untamed fire before suddenly exploding like an orgasm of spirit. With the ethereal climax his eyes shot open, breaking the frozen seal of tears. An impossibly glorious radiance shone before him. No trees, mountains, or forest – just a perfectly white canvas of untouched creation, winter winds sweeping through and swirling snow into form.

"Gracien," and with her voice calling out, Aya's body formed within the swirling snow. He gasped as she shone with an inner radiance not of this world. A Winter Queen, her glorious hair and dress flowed like snowy drifts, but her expression was far from icy. Ayadonna neared, looking him over with a serene smile and supreme compassion. He felt her breath on his neck, her hands on his shoulders. Gracien's lungs sucked in a frozen breath and held it – then the last of his warmth retreated with a final exhalation. Aya stepped to him, the fullness of her beauty overwhelming his vision as Ishayu's eyes closed.

FIVE

His eyelids flickered like candlelight before fluttering apart, revealing a towering, beamed ceiling with moonlight pouring through several open windows. A symphony of slumber resonated around him as Gracien's pulse raced alongside his budding realization. The sound of his short-lived inhalations grew louder as he worried over where, or rather who he was. A moan rang out from one of the others nearby who must have been bargaining with a bad dream. Across the room a sudden tussle of bedding rippled through the expansive space.

Gracien's ears came alive, twitching like a dog's sensing some distant disturbance. "Get out," his raspy voice croaked.

With the flick of his wrist, he whipped up the sheet, mushrooming the thin fabric and making his escape before it caved back down to the bed.

"Hey!" He froze with the call, holding his breath like a mouse pleading not to be discovered.

Nothing followed. *It must have been a cough.* His mind was already messing with him.

He inhaled a deep breath of courage before resuming his retreat. As his gently placed toes navigated the mess of beds, a disharmonic choir of slumbering hisses, wheezes, and whistles rang out. Like a prisoner given a chance of escape but without any inkling of where to go, Gracien scanned the darkness for an exit. Framed in moonlight, the thin lining of a door glowed from a foyer just beyond the main room.

He raced towards it but then a floorboard unleashed an eerie groan with the weight of his footing. His teeth clenched as he sucked in air with a hiss, sending a chill down to his core. No one seemed to notice. A rapid, nimble bound followed by a quickened patter of footsteps led him down the hallway and through the glowing exit. As he catapulted himself into the courtyard, Gracien drank in the twilight through flaring nostrils. It was all too much. He collapsed to his knees, shielding his moans with hands as his heart ached with legions of pain. His muffled cries rattled his muscled frame like fierce autumn winds shaking an ado-lescent tree. He tried moving further away from the door, but his limbs wouldn't work. In the next breath, he found himself crawling over cold stone pavers instead.

The fresh air of the courtyard tempered his panic, allowing the time he needed to catch his breath and scan the area. Chilled summer winds rustled the pink leaves of a cherry tree centered in the middle of the quaint space. The vibrant leaves shone with an unnatural radiance as a few of the blossoms tumbled downwards, collecting around the trunk. A Chinese gable-and-hip roof bordered the beautiful canopy, jutting out in a perfect square and cloaking the walkways beneath in darkness. Pro-nounced, dragon-spine ridges worked their way down the seams, leading to the dragon's scaled head and slithered tongue while its bulbous eyes kept watch over Gracien from the upturned, flying eaves. The night was sharp with the aroma of an unseasonal chill. Centered like a watchman's lantern hanging in the night, the glowing moon shone down on the en-closed garden. The courtyard was a place of comfort and prayer, a sanc-tuary in which Gracien felt safe enough to be as he was. With the wave of anxiety behind him, he was able to stand, albeit slowly.

He walked over to the cherry tree before taking a seat. The blanket of blushed blossoms was cool and soft, sinking with his weight as he found comfort leaning up against the trunk. A new space opened with anxiety's departure: fear. Muffled cries poured through his fingers as he allowed himself to mourn without suffocating the outpouring of grief. He sucked in a labored, sputtered breath before releasing one drawn out moan as his body sunk downwards.

"Whyyy… why, why, whyyy-aghhh..." he cried, surrendering to fate, and allowing himself to grieve the finality of Ishayu while accepting this new awakening.

His frigid death seemed to accompany Gracien into this life as he endured a wave of chills and violent shudders. Gracien slowly became aware of his current athletic body curled over his two compressed knees as he buried his head between thin, muscular arms. Smooth, feminine hands, five fingers on each, covered his gleaming black hair as if shielding himself from the cascading petals.

"Suyin what are you doing out here? Are you alright?" a voice whispered from the darkness across the courtyard.

Gracien's head popped up, spinning towards the source. "I needed some air, I… I had a nightmare," he stuttered like a frightened stage performer.

"Again? Do you want me to stay until you're better?"

The young woman's whisper was the warmth of fire on a frigid night. She stepped out of the darkness. Framed in ink black hair, her pale complexion glowed like that of a ghost under the moon's radiance.

"Ning," Gracien mouthed. He was taken aback by the appearance of his friend and fellow disciple.

"No… no I'll be alright. I just need a bit more time, the cold air helps." He swallowed.

Ning frowned. "Okay, but come back to bed soon, try to get some rest before morning, it's an early training session."

Gracien nodded, failing at a smile as Ning lingered before stepping back into the darkness.

Gracien gulped down air as if he had surfaced from a freezing lake. His despair surged, causing a physical ache in his chest as his mind obsessed over all the struggles in each of his past lives. A living nightmare, a cruel fate twisting and wrenching love from his soul with no escape in sight. His head fell back as he sobbed while staring through the branches and leaves. As the moon flickered between the dancing pink blossoms, Gracien couldn't tell if he was dreaming or not. The wind picked up, shaking dozens of petals down atop him, which only muddled his confusion while time slowed.

As the petals fluttered down around him like fledgling butterflies, Gracien inhaled. "Aya, please help me escape."

A cluster of pigeons cooed, vehemently flapping their wings, and bouncing between the wine-colored beams running along the impressive ceiling of the training hall. As a sole, white colored feather tumbled downwards, some of the newer disciples attended the distraction. Master Chi cleared his throat, tugging at the leash of their attention and pulling them back into focus. They refocused, watching the more seasoned disciples up in front while trying to mirror their form and flow. From the pigeon's perspective, the rows of practitioners resembled perfectly aligned crops performing a choreographed dance under the weight of a stern wind, Master Chi. The age of the disciples ranged from seventeen to mid-twenties, the latter for those who needed extra time conforming. There was a decent balance of boys and girls, with the females barely tipping the scales.

Master Chi was a shorter man who boasted impressively wide shoulders and a full frame of muscle. His bulbous physique bulged beneath his free-flowing robes as he demonstrated a form or executed a maneuver. All his robes were tailor made from the finest silks, and he was never seen in the same one more than twice. With hands clasped behind his back and buried within the intricately patterned sleeves, he glided through the students like a hawk searching for mistakes. A two foot long, ink black braid protruded from the very back of his head, with the rest of his scalp being clean shaven and gleaming like polished marble. The notable weave ran the length of his back and was sectioned off with red ties every couple of inches. At the tip hung a bronzed arrowhead ticking back and forth as his slippered feet stalked along the glossy, auburn-colored flooring.

Master Chi floated between tiers of disciples sectioned off by rows. The class of the disciple was evident by the color of their robe: chartreuse being first years, second year bearing teal, emerald green for third years, royal blue for fourth years, and indigo for fifth year. This left the coveted violet sheen for disciples with six or more years of apprenticeship. The graduation of color darkened from the back of the room to the front, thinning with numbers as it progressed.

"Shhh-kkk," the communal slide of scraping slippers rang out as the mass of martial artists swept a foot across the flooring, keeping one leg straight while the other bent at the knee.

Their guards were situated; with one hand reaching out a foot and a half in front of the chest while the other hovered inches away in a defensive pose with fingers pointing towards the ceiling. The elbows of the advanced students were firm and tucked inwards while those of the novices were lax and unkempt.

A communal whooshing sound resonated through the great hall, "Phusshhh…" The mass exhalation filled the room like a crashing wave.

The disciples pressed a fist forward with the exhale as the other hand retreated, latching onto their ribcage.

Gracien's brow beaded over with sweat, the droplets dripping down onto his royal blue robe as he flowed through the Form. The vibrancy of his robe accentuated that of his sea-green pupils, which darted to the side as Master Chi swept behind like a phantom. Dark circles hung beneath his eyes from a sleepless night of cold sweats and reliving Ishayu's arctic demise. His own mocha-colored ponytail whisked from side to side as he frantically checked his peripheral vision for Master. He was short for an eighteen-year-old woman, but his frame flaunted strong, stocky legs and a muscular butt.

Just get through this session, focus, and keep it together Suyin. You can do this, he thought, igniting his vision into focus with a quickened shake of his head.

His right arm circled, directing it into the next position while blowing another focused exhalation through pursed lips. "Whhh-Huh!"

The communal sound was jarring and aggressive, scaring the pigeons through a massive yin-yang shaped window centered under a pitched ceiling. The bird's hasty retreat kicked up dust from the top of a rich, cranberry-colored beam running the entire length of the room. The clamor sent the dust cascading down through the sunlight like miniature snowflakes. The room was flooded with light, as an additional yin-yang shaped window complemented the other wall. Below the yin-yang windows stood massive wooden folding doors that had been pulled open, exposing a well-maintained courtyard on either side. The adjacent walls housed dozens of radiant, white scrolls. Plum-colored calligraphy quoting Sun Tzu and his teachings from the *Art of War* gleamed from the stark white canvas. The space between the scrolls was draped with different training tools, sandbags, and weapons. Several wooden dummies guarded the walls like listless gargoyles. At one point the wooden arms, belly, head, and sole leg were as polished as the rest of the body but now were worn down and dulled from all the wear.

Gracien tried to maintain composure, breathing like a woman

through labor as his inner monologue panicked over the lingering effects of Ishayu's death. The only thing helping keep his shit together was the familiar feeling of the training room. He couldn't help but feel like he was back in the Great Hall of Babylonia. Like a hearth warmed blanket, the room wrapped him up in the comfort of familiarity. Considering he was fighting off a budding panic attack, this served as his saving grace. The Forms were typically his favorite part of training, as the focused concentration coupled with the grace of fluid movements lifted his spirits and calmed his mind. They were the closest thing he had ever experienced to meditation in movement. This morning however, he was nowhere near that place of peace and tranquility.

What I wouldn't give to be back in Mukti's sanctuary right now, he thought, blowing a strand of hair from his face just as someone's hand wrapped around his elbow.

Master Chi's hand redirected Gracien's elbow inwards. "You seem to be distracted, Suyin. Remember, keep this tight against your ribcage. Recall the exercise squeezing the tea leaf against your side while holding the position. It's always there, try…" Noticing that he was on the brink of tears, he released his hold and softened his eyes.

"This isn't a matter of proper technique, is it?" Master's gaze burned right through him as he awaited a response.

Gracien's anxiety boiled over with the weight of everyone's attention crashing down on him. He swallowed, looking around for a moment before returning to Master Chi and nodding yes.

"Would it be better if you sat out for the rest of Forms and returned later?" His eyebrows pitched with expectation. "Maybe until afternoon classes?"

Master flashed an encouraging smile, his cratered skin buckled with the smile lines and his coffee-colored eyes softened further. His jaw barely offered a chin, but prominent jaw muscles flexed as he leaned in, wrapping an arm over Gracien's shoulder then leading him from the room. He was grace in motion and his steps were a panther's stalk.

"Take some time in one of the courtyards, the air will freshen your spirit," he urged Gracien from the room as if he was a prayer lantern.

Feeling a new surge of embarrassment as he made a hasty exit, his lips began trembling. Gracien's hand clutched over his chest as his labored breath intensified. But a thought arrived as if dropped into his head from above.

What do you fear?

The question seemed not to belong to him, as if it was spoken by someone standing over his shoulder. It extinguished his budding panic, slowing his gait and straightening his posture. The fresh air of the courtyard was a massive help for the second time in some hours, extending his breath as his eyes narrowed on the thought as if it was hovering before him.

Gracien probed the depths of his mind, looking for a reason to be afraid. Silence, no thought. Like a morning meadow veiled in a predawn fog, his mind was muted and still. His senses activated, taking his focus into his body and all the sights, sounds, and smells surrounding him; escorting him into the presence of the now. The bellow of nature expanded as if everything had come to life with his arrival. Gracien's ears picked up the enduring silence under all other noise, the hum of reality. His eyes adjusted, observing the texture and grain of the bark, the fluidity of a leaf's tremble, the shade of green painted onto the grass.

He left the immediate courtyard and continued walking as far as possible from any prying eyes. Like a desert mirage, a patch of grass settled beneath a grand, ancient looking willow beckoned him. He trotted over then settled within his meditation posture. As soon as he found himself comfortable, the mental silence fled. In its wake swirled thoughts of dread, loss, and regret. He began shifting as the irritation swarmed, but like a triumphant warrior, that sole thought returned.

What do you fear?

The thought rang out like a funeral bell, sweeping away debris from the shore of his mind and smoothing the sand into stillness.

As he pondered the question, Gracien pinched a blade of grass between his fingertips. He then placed his hands within his lap, blowing out a long exhalation through pursed lips while closing his eyes. His smooth, pale features softened as the tension poured from his face. Thin, expressive eyebrows relaxed as nostrils speckled with light brown freckles flared with breath. An accident seven years prior had left a thin scar slicing across his face from his bottom lip to the side of his chin. It ticked as he dove back into the depths of his mind searching for the root of this fear. He sighed with frustration, which was common practice for him. Gracien couldn't help himself, his mind centered around the memory of his last passing, the snow whipping about and the wind's frigid bite.

And then there she was, Ayadonna's approach during the final moment. The mere memory of his Beloved's arrival sent shivers down his spine. Aya's gaze was powerful and penetrating, stirring Gracien's spirit into excitement. But then the gaze of another merged with Aya's before consuming it.

Master Chi's compassionate eyes bore through him as Gracien was pulled from the memory of his Beloved. His master's gaze had everything his fathers didn't: compassion, patience, and understanding.

Father's baritone voice and final words stung like an old war wound, ringing out in Gracien's mind like the clang of a broken gong. "I'll know my daughter after she's proper, after she's been re-*adjusted* into what a daughter to a man like myself should be. I've got a reputation to uphold Suyin, you know this and yet you jeopardize our entire way of life with your *choices*."

Gracien recalled not only the sting of father's words but also mother's dismissal of them. The entire time he spoke, it wasn't to Suyin but to her mother, who attended his speech with her back turned on them both.

"Like her sister... why couldn't she just have been like her sister! They're twins! Same body, same home, same face, same everything. But no, different *insides,* different *desires.*" He spun around, catching the glare of Suyin's sister who watched from an adjoining room. "When she's better... yes, then she can come home. When she's better, when she's adjusted!"

Her mother had cried, but it didn't matter because Suyin never knew if she had cried for herself or for her daughter. No farewell embrace, no promises of paying a visit, or encouragement to return home for breaks. Suyin had tried to believe that her mother wasn't strong enough, that she didn't have the courage to face her daughter and hold her gaze. And for that she pitied her, she pitied them all.

Gracien's agitation bubbled over, squirming, and shifting as if ants were crawling about his body. He had made his peace with father and the family's neglect but being in this school, in this place, it was better than home and somehow worse in the same breadth. Gracien didn't know where this feeling came from as the Zen Reformation Academy had treated him well, besides the scars of course. The resemblance to the Great Hall of Babylon was a tremendous comfort. He had a few friends, more like acquaintances but the other students were kind and sympathetic for the most part, especially Ning. He didn't know why an ominous feeling overcame him, but something didn't feel right.

Like a stone tipped over a hill's ledge, his mind sputtered with one random thought after another. He found himself shaking his head trying to re-center and focus. It was too much, too difficult with the flurry of wavering thoughts and emotions. He deflated, feeling alone, and lost.

"How did I end up here? Why am I here... What's the reason, Aya?"

His head dipped down, bobbing between his knees as he pulled them into his chest. He was sick and tired of crying and feeling bad for himself so instead held his breath. The tails of branches swaying about from the great willow cried out but something else rang out too, a trickling beyond the towering perimeter wall just behind the tree. Gracien stood, walking over to the wall, and sliding a hand across the smooth, stone surface. His fingers grazed on the padded moss growing over the mortar as he pitched his ear, holding his breath and listening.

A stream or a creek, just beyond the wall.

He looked up some thirty or so feet before stepping back to get a better look. The colossal barrier loomed over him like a stone Goliath.

The scar on his face extended with that of his smirk. "Now to find a way over."

"If you want to be reborn, let yourself die. If you want to be given every-thing, give everything up."

Gracien read Lao-Tzu's passage for the third time in a row, allowing his mind to chew on the words. He gazed up from the *Tao Te Ching*, his fingers holding down the worn pages as his vision dulled out of focus, veiling the room around him. The classroom was a subtle symphony of disciples turning pages and volleying secret chatter as birdsong rang out just outside the windows. A quick snort sounded out followed by a communal giggle as one of the other fourth years groaned in his sleep.

The tutor's aid watching over the class, Jia, was a 'Beyond.' That's what everyone called a disciple with seven or more years at the Zen Reformation Academy, or Zura for short. Jia kept herself busy with her own study, and so didn't care much what the class was working on. And every person there knew it, and so took advantage of the free time not doing anything related to their studies. Gracien didn't notice any of them, all his senses were dulled as his focus centered on the *Tao* passage. He felt that it was somehow written just for him; that somehow Lao-Tzu knew of his future situation and scribbled these few words to help him in some small way. But he couldn't for the life of him grasp the deeper meaning. He sighed for the fourth time in two minutes, stopping to scan the room. Gracien found that he loved studying the *Tao*, realizing the flow and deeper meaning to be his favorite kind of poetry, the kind which stokes the embers of your spirit. It was his sacred creed and never far from reach.

The fourth year's lessons were highly focused on the *Tao*, yet unlike the others, Gracien spent a great deal of time pouring over the book in his free time too. Their schedule allowed for quite a bit of free time, as every disciple was required to excel within everything they studied. The Academy didn't weigh them down with a dozen subjects, just a couple at a time so that no one had an excuse for not mastering the material. They weren't there to be educated on the typical subject matter taught in most advanced schools, because the Zen Reformation Academy was much more than a school: it was a program for rehabilitation.

Although Master Chi never used this word when meeting with potential parents or sponsors, he as well as the parents knew all too well that rehabilitation was the academy's main concentration. You don't use the word disciple rather than student for no reason. If your child enrolled, they vowed to serve under Master Chi and dedicate themselves to his curriculum of rehabilitation.

Wealthy parents, distinguished sponsors, and prominent caretakers, typically, high ranking officials, affluent landowners, or successful capitalists, sent their debilitated children to Zura so that they could "adjust to the expected and proper role in which they are meant to fill," as Master Chi put it during an initial tour of the grounds.

If Zura was a bush, Master Chi was beating very far around it.

Through word of mouth and excellent results, these guardians knew exactly what they were paying for. Their children were messed up in some way: law breakers and delinquents, disobedient and perverse, sexual degenerates or homosexuals, outright rebels or "a ruthless villain with an evil spirit," as one especially charming parent put it while referring to her seventeen-year-old son. And it didn't matter. Eventually they all broke, that's why there wasn't a cap on how long a student could or, more likely, *had* to stay – crowning them with the title of, 'Beyond.' Through enough commitment, enough determination, enough schooling, enough kung fu training, enough reprogramming of the heart, and enough mental, emotional, and physical discipline – no one stood a chance. Master Chi broke them all, and he was very well compensated for doing so.

"Suuu-Yinn, Suu-Yinn, Suyin!" Ning called with graduating intensity until finally stirring Gracien from his daydream.

"Oh sorry," Gracien replied, shaking himself from a daze.

"Haha… a little distracted, yes?" Ning pulled a chair up to his table, then took the *Tao* from under Gracien's hands.

"Which passage are you reading? Ohh… I like this one, but I wonder if he's talking about reincarnation or giving everything up in this life?" Ning spoke to the book, glancing up at Gracien with a smooth smirk.

Ning's hair was short in the back, even shorter than some of the boy's and as thin as spider silk. Her bangs were long, swiping just over her hazel-colored eyes. She bore a pleasantly surprised look most of the time and was notorious for her nervous smile-giggle combo. While Ning kept chatting away and flipping through the *Tao*, Gracien examined her beauty: her ivory-colored face, the way she moved her thin lips by over-pronouncing words, the sound of her laugh, which she only shared with the right company. Her best feature was her attentiveness. When Ning listened to you, she seemed to understand with her gaze, nodding in comprehension and really connecting. Gracien loved that about her, everyone did. She was a few inches taller yet just as strong and fast as Gracien but bearing a thinner frame. And she had several nervous ticks, one of which was constantly hiding her knuckles, which were ashy and cracked from punching bags of uncooked rice to deaden the nerves.

"We should get out of here," Gracien blurted out, blushing over as Ning let out one of her nervous laughs.

"What do you mean, like go into town? We can't, break isn't until next week."

"I'm not talking about town, have you ever..." Gracien leaned in. "Have you ever snuck out?"

Ning pushed herself back, a wave of fear washing over her face. "No, no way. Suyin, that's not smart... we can't..."

Gracien interrupted, "okay take it easy. Take it easy, it was just a question." Gracien leaned in, closing the gap between them "But have you ever heard of anybody who has?"

"Of course, there's a hundred stories of people sneaking out and each one of them involves discipline, you know discipline, right?" Ning looked to Gracien before a wave of embarrassment washed over her, causing her to avert her gaze.

"Everyone here knows discipline, Ning," Gracien said while rolling his eyes. "All the stories involve disciples sneaking out in the middle of the night through one of the exits. They almost always got away with getting out, it's when they tried getting back in is when they got caught."

Gracien realized his voice was getting a bit too loud for this particular conversation. "Sorry, sorry," he resumed in a whisper. "I'm not talking about sneaking through the front door, Ning." He looked over his shoulder.

"Could you be any more suspicious?" Ning huffed with a smirk.

Gracien sighed. "I know a way. Well, I think I know a way. I can't be sure but I'm pretty sure it's legit. And nobody, I mean nobody, knows about it."

Ning leaned in, she was doing that intense whisper now. "That doesn't make any sense, how can you not be sure... but also be, pretty sure?"

"I just need a bit of help is all, and I figure you and I can figure this out together." His eyes went wide with embellished seriousness, making Ning laugh and then Gracien too.

"Okay fine Suyin, but where? And when? And how?" Ning sputtered off.

"Let's start with the when. We need to wait a couple of weeks, give ourselves some time for things to settle down after the lantern festival."

"What happened to, 'we should get out of here'... huh?" Ning asked with a smirk.

Gracien laughed. "I was a bit hasty. But we should go after a morning sparring session. You'll follow me after class and I'll head to the northeast courtyard off the west wing, but I'm going to take the long way and go down a few unnecessary corridors. Just bear with me, okay?"

"Are you sure about this?" Ning spoke slowly, over-pronouncing the words.

"I'm not sure about anything these days... but I'm sure I want to... 'be given everything,' so I'm giving everything up." Gracien poked the *Tao* then gave Ning a wry smile.

"Okay, we can cover the details again after the festival," Ning said before rising.

The two exchanged a smile before returning to their busywork.

With hands clasped behind his back and buried within the sleeves of a lavender colored robe, Master Chi meandered through the aisles of disciples as they stretched in unison, warming up for the morning training session. Their gleaming robes swooshed about as their arms swung back and forth. They twisted side to side, occasionally touching a toe, cracking their joints, and jumping in place. Master was especially quiet this morning, not having shared a single word of encouragement. Moments later he cleared his throat and with the subtle command the disciples instantly aligned themselves for Forms. While the tutors handled the classrooms, Master Chi was the sole instructor for what he considered their true education; kung fu. This training involved four pillars: Maneuvers, Application, Forms, and, his favorite part, Contention.

Master Chi lifted his head, pausing his stride as he inhaled while scanning the room of students.

"If the mind is willing, the flesh could go on and on without many things."

Sun Tzu's words were the only others Master relied on when providing the encouragement he saw fit. He spoke softly and he never raised his voice, but his rate of speech always quickened at the end of each sentence like the sting of a whip. Master's footsteps resumed, causing some of the old wooden floorboards to creak out. The disciples bowed to the front of the room and began First Form.

Their training sessions began with Forms, followed by Maneuvers and then Application. On some days they had Contention, but they always concluded with another round of Forms. The open palm of Gracien's left hand extended forward with an almost reluctant speed. He exhaled as his arm reached its furthest extent. His wrist rolled his hand into a fist, then paused for a moment before bringing it back and securing it next to his ribcage. A palpable weight seeped from his being as tension poured from him. Forms had this effect on most of the disciples. It was their way of playing with, or rolling their energy, cultivating the positive and releasing the negative. In essence, Forms were interlaced Maneuvers enacted with heightened concentration and a passive pace.

Maneuvers were kung fu movements consisting of either an attack, a defensive block, or a simultaneous combination of both. A practitioner strikes and blocks using their hands, fingers, palms, fists, shoulders, and elbows. But there weren't any limitations on what could be used depending on the circumstance and the disciple's mastery of the art. The more advanced practitioner also used their feet and knees to strike and block. Every maneuver is launched or thrown from various stances, something practiced and maintained through the entirety of their training.

Application was for practicing one maneuver or a chain of them repeatedly, focusing on the exact positioning to optimize force, power, placement, and simply put: the total devastation of an opponent's strikes and blocks. The disciples practiced using wooden dummies, the sandbags hanging from the walls, with another student, or alone. Application was a workout in its own right, helping to keep them strong and fit. This was another aspect of the art which Gracien not only enjoyed but appreciated, as it paid generous dividends to his mind, body, and spirit.

"The greatest victory is that which requires no battle."

Master's voice poured over the mass of students from the back of the room. Gracien had heard this quote a dozen times, as it was one of Master's favorites. His mind pushed it together, then pulled it apart, manipulating and molding meaning from the ever-changing form of his circumstance.

How can I win; how can I be victorious without ever engaging in combat?

At first the words drew him into a martial arts frame of mind before the meaning migrated to his situation – his seemingly never-ending existence.

What does it mean to win… what is victory?

Immediately, his heart revealed a memory, not just one but many all meshed together like a ten course meal served on a platter. The jumble of memories unfolded, then exploded all at once: laughing, playing, loving, and living a fulfilling life together with Ayadonna.

This would be my victory, an impossible one, he thought before shaking himself into focus.

His concentration returned and with it he launched a punch out in front of him with the fierceness of a viper's strike. *Stay here and focus on the Form, Suyin,* he encouraged.

Gracien believed Forms were the core of kung fu, a meditation in motion. And like meditation one could sometimes get lost in thought while forgetting themselves and their motives.

First through Third Form were like a choreographed dance consisting of maneuvers and stances all flowing from one to the next. Some disciples practiced Forms with a rigid, shaky power – flexing their muscles and exacting the position of a strike or block as if there was a weight pressing down on it. But for Gracien, Forms were a choreographed dance, one performed with the pace of a swan floating across a stilled lake. No matter your approach, the focus was to deliver the different moves using proper technique and an almost elegant, graceful fluidity – all the while relying on the flow of qi. Every disciple began with First Form, needing to master it before advancing to Second, Third, then Weapons. Their advancement was proven with an annual proficiency evaluation which tested not only their mastery of the Forms, but also the Maneuvers, Application and finally, Contention.

"Know yourself and you will win all battles."

Master's words reverberated through him as his footsteps approached. Feeling as if some unknown presence watched him, Gracien looked over his shoulder only to find Master three rows away. He shook his head in confusion, scanning the room before refocusing on his next move.

What battle am I fighting? he thought before the idea of Contention sent a spike of anxiety through his chest.

Contention was a battle for sure, a battle to implement everything they've learned by fighting another disciple. Master Chi knew full well that to be capable in a real-world scenario, his disciples needed to fight without holding back.

"Contention can be brutal, yet all the better for proving your worth in battle… and therefore worth, in general." Gracien recalled Master's jarring words from years ago.

Master Chi's baritone voice sounded out again.

"There are not more than five musical notes, yet the combinations of these five give rise to more melodies than can ever be heard. There are not more than five primary colors, yet in combination they produce more hues than can ever be seen. There are not more than five cardinal tastes, yet combinations of them yield more flavors than can ever be tasted."

His words flowed like honey as the disciples progressed through the Form. Gracien focused, shutting his eyes as his breath deepened. His concentration intensified on the sweeping motion of his hand swinging out to the side like an ax ascending into a tree branch. Master's quotes as well as the mass breathing began to fade as he took himself within, deepening his internal focus. He shined during Forms, losing himself and flowing like a tempered ballerina while executing the movements with instinctual precision.

There. There it is, his mind thought before going blank. This was the place, he had found it once again, a ship without destination, a sole tree on a sprawling hillside. It took a bit longer this time, but he was finally there, all alone as if no one else was in the training hall. He flowed like water and breathed like the wind. Gracien didn't perform the Form but *became* it. Like a tree gradually leaning, twisting its limbs and turning its leaves towards the light of day, he achieved oneness – unification of mind and body, fusion of Creation and Creator. It only lasted a moment or two, but like a perfect kiss, it lingered. The sensation of something more, something beyond him pulsated within and he cherished it.

Sometime later, his ears tingled with the sound of the communal breath coming back to life as Master's footsteps audibly sounded out from the front of the room. He couldn't help himself, Gracien smiled like someone waking up from a nap while on holiday.

He as well as the others finished the last few movements before simultaneously slapping their hands on the side of their hips, giving off a mass, "HUH!" then bowing towards their Master.

His eyes narrowed over his disciples as the corner of his mouth pulled up into a satisfactory smirk.

The subtle lake waves lapped onto the pebbled shore as the crunch of footsteps rang out. The entire discipleship walked along the lakefront, positioning themselves for the ceremony. Gracien clutched the two rice paper lanterns in his arms. One had a small wooden bottom made for floating while the other was light as a feather and made to fly. His sandaled feet pattered over the shore's pebbles as he followed the others lining up along the water's rim. Flaming torches, held by the Beyonds, bobbed with their gate, glowing brighter as the last of the sunlight melted into the brisk dusk. On a sunny afternoon, the opposing shore boasted matured pines crawling up grayed hillsides. One could easily make out the speckled, foamy rocky outcroppings too. Standing only a few thousand meters from where Gracien and the others chose their spot, the opposing shore was being swallowed up by nightfall, the sable-colored lake now a boundless ocean.

He was hesitant, not sure of what he should be looking for, his white, full robe catching repeatedly around his ankles. The crunch of steps grew louder with the budding darkness but like crickets with dawn's arrival, their busy work fell silent. The lapping of the waves filled the void as Gracien watched the others prepare. He followed their lead, bending down and readying the lanterns for their voyage.

The water lantern was shaped like a little house with four rice paper walls and an open roof. Gracien knelt, just at the furthest extent of the lake's reach, avoiding the chill of its kiss. He looked to his left and several dozen disciples lined the rounding shore with a few feet between them. To his right stood seven others, including Ning. The two were separated by another student, a first-year boy who pushed his water lantern around like a toy ship. Gracien smirked at his antics before his focus shifted to Ning, who prepared her lantern with the utmost attention and care. Gracien found himself wondering what Ning was going to pray for as Master's words sliced through the moment.

"The water lantern is for the past, for what was lost… to honor and cherish it. The sky lantern is for the future, to pray for what you wish to come. Take your time with each and allow the sacred power of prayer to humble your spirit."

Gracien took a deep breath as two of Master's most trusted disciples made their way around the shore lighting the lanterns with a candle. The candle's glimmer jumped from one lantern to the next until a crescent moon glowed along the shore, painting everyone's face with a golden glow. Some were already praying with heads bowed and concentrated expressions while others fidgeted with their lanterns. Like a settling fog, a sullen energy fell upon the shore. Some of them were shrouded in grief, weeping for the past with tears trickling down their cheeks.

Observing their grief made Gracien recall his own, swelling his throat and constricting his chest. It's all he ever thought about; his Beloved Aya, her suffering, her death. Their shared life flashed before him, slowing with the approach of Aya's sickness then playing out with deliberate reluctance.

"I pray for her, I pray for my love..." He sobbed, tears dropping down onto the glowing lantern as it trembled within his hands.

Gracien took his time, marinating in his suffering before continuing. "To be at peace, to be free of suffering, to be whole and healed... liberated from pain and sickness, free from death's cold embrace."

With his eyes still closed he leaned forward, placing the wooden base onto the lake. The chilled water tickled his fingertips. He opened his eyes. His hand nudged the lantern over the hump of the first small wave. It lingered for a moment before catching the current and sailing out from shore.

Gracien watched the blackened surface of the lake recede from utter darkness into midnight blue as a hundred lanterns sailed across it. A plain of starry ships speckled across the lake, ferrying their prayers to a place of sympathy. Gracien's vision veiled over with images of Aya singing and dancing, laughing while telling a story, the stillness of her face as she read, the joy of it as she enjoyed a stroll, living life in all aspects. Then a cry stole Gracien from his reverie. He looked over to the first-year boy with his sky lantern already floating ten feet before him. Being too young and too excited to embrace the gravity of such a ceremony, his footsteps scurried over the pebbled shore as his lantern ascended. The boy's retreat revealed Ning kneeling in her pearled robe, absorbed in what seemed an insurmountable grief. Her cries carried down the shore as did many others. Gracien looked over to his left and only one other lantern was already sky bound. The pale, pure faces of all the others were cloaked in sadness. The darkness made them smaller, and as their shoulders shuddered as their tears fell, they looked to be mere children again. They purged their sorrow and in doing so, revealed to Gracien that everyone has a reason to grieve.

As his water lantern's glow shrunk like that of a shooting star, he rose, taking his second lantern and walking over to Ning. The crackle of Gracien's footsteps sounded out as he approached. He stopped, hovering over the unobservant girl as she cried into her hands. Gracien placed his lantern next to Ning's then wrapped her up in an embrace.

"It's okay, it's okay. You're not alone," he said to Ning what he himself longed to hear.

Gracien looked up to the sky. "They're somewhere beautiful, somewhere unimaginable. Somewhere where pain and suffering have no place, an eternal sanctuary with endless glory and radiance."

Ning's cries abated and her head rose through Gracien's arms as she heeded his words. Gracien continued, describing the Heavens as if he could see all the detail before him.

"A place of unending possibility and radiance, of eternal peace and unbound joy, an everlasting life filled with love. A place with windows into our world, where they see our suffering and hear our calls."

As he spoke, Gracien took Ning's hands, helping them to prepare her second lantern. While their faces flickered under the flame's dance, they each held their lantern like it was a sacred offering.

Gracien continued, "A place where they're able to send us signs of their love, of their presence in our lives. A place where songs of their joy and love ring out here in our world… but within the scent of a flower, the flutter of a butterfly, the harmony of birdsong… within the embrace of friends. Their love is the glory of a sunset and the stillness of dawn."

Their fingertips nudged the lanterns into flight, watching as they ascended out over the lake, merging with the floating mass of stars budding across its surface. The girls bathed in the silence as the lanterns progressed onward, speckling across the perfect skyscape. It looked as if the stars descended to kiss the earth before retreating back into the cradle of creation.

Gracien grabbed Ning's hand. "They're waiting for us in this place, waiting for the day when our suffering too has been washed away with our spirit's flight."

They watched, hand in hand, as the lanterns twinkled off into the distant heavens.

The lantern ceremony served as the impetus for what would be a full week of break for Zura, but with rules and curfews in place. With bags packed and classes concluded for the season, none of the disciples wasted a moment of their time off. Many of the youngest headed home to be with family the morning after the ceremony. Having already enjoyed their fair share of trips home or to the big city, the more seasoned students stayed behind, spending their time training with one another, studying, or keeping to themselves.

For everyone else, there was such a buildup of excitement leading up to the ceremony that they couldn't wait to experience the hustle and bustle of Beijing. For the most part the students were able to do as they pleased. Well, not so much for the first and second years as they had supervised leave. Tutors chaperoned them throughout the break: timetables, tours, scheduled meals, and even bathroom breaks. But the third years and up were free to do as they wished, as long as they were back before curfew.

Daily transportation was arranged to several points of interest. Ornately designed carriages were pulled by hulking stallions boasting manicured manes, sweet dispositions, and black, glistening coats. Their shoulder muscles rippled, and they smelled of earth, barley, and manure. They weren't inclined to refuse affectionate pets and tasty snacks before carting everyone off to one of the select destinations across the city and beyond. Accompanied by a handful of fellow disciples, Gracien and

Ning found themselves bobbing off the plush, chartreuse-colored carriage seats as the massive wheels weathered the unforgiving stone. The bunch couldn't help themselves, smiling and giggling away as they tumbled like dirty laundry while making their final approach into Beijing. A symphony of city life sprung up like birdsong at dawn. The enormous wagon pulled into the meeting point on the outskirts of the second largest market in all of China. The meals at Zura were nothing to turn one's nose up at, but they could be repetitive and sometimes sparse. So, the first task on the docket was to delight in some new, tasty treats.

The market spilled out into the cobbled street like a cornucopia as the crew poured out of the carriage like madmen, laughing and delighting in the immediate abundance. The girls held hands and skipped into the entrance as the boys sprinted like marathon runners, each jumping and slapping one of the multicolored lanterns strewn across the open gates. They landed like expert tumblers, bounding forward a few strides then disappearing into the hubbub. Overcome by the communal excitement, Gracien and Ning followed suit, swinging their joined hands through the air as they raced forward.

"What should we have first, something sweet or something savory?" Ning asked, the thrill of excitement heightening her already high-pitched voice.

"Savory, something salty... and spicy too!" Gracien replied as they approached the first merchant. "Fried fish and rice, bore-ing!"

With their mouths already salivating they dashed from one cart to the next.

The market was much grander than anything Gracien had ever experienced before. He was accustomed to markets with the typical rows of vendors aligned on either side of the street. But with the road being so wide, an additional row of vendors sliced down the middle. The market space was so huge that in some places two tents stood back-to-back in the middle section while other times there was only one massive tent taking up the entire belly. The market never seemed too thin, going on and on with a mild pause at busy intersections while being peppered with carriages and pedestrians slicing through.

Thirty minutes in and Gracien sucked at his fingers, lapping up the last remnants of a sweet, red bean bun. Ning's head bobbed as she removed another sweetened cranberry from the lengthy skewer.

Her eyebrows elevated as she questioned Gracien with an "Mmm?" while poking him with the Tanghulu.

Gracien declined, shaking his head before dashing over to the pumpkin pancake cart. The sweet aroma struck them like an unexpected punch.

Like any good market, the sections varied by purpose; services leading off to the west while household items snaked down a nearby stream. Personal as well as labor related items took up a large central hub while groceries, herbs, spices, and prepared food dominated the current area. Endless rows of steaming pots, brimmed with a plethora of tasty delights, extended further than the eyes could see. Mountains of rice accompanied towers of seafood; some being dumped into rich golden broths that plumed aromatic ecstasy. Strips of chicken, beef, pork, and a dozen unknown meats encircled stacks of sautéed vegetables with various seeds sprinkled on top. Thick, weighty noodles were pulled from bowls of broth like enormous anchor chains being hauled up from murky depths. People slurped, sucked, slobbered, and salivated.

The girls kept the conversation light, focusing instead on stuffing themselves with all sorts of delights. They split meals, laughed over embarrassing stories, swapped tales of Zura and Master Chi, and relished in the splendor of the market. Ning bought a few trinkets, some incense, and a handful of snacks for later in the week while Gracien mainly perused, feeling uninspired by the options and even a bit sad with no one to shop for. Here and there they'd run into fellow disciples, exchanging tips for the best sweets, or stopping to share a kettle of jasmine tea at one of the many quaint teahouses.

Masses of people drifted through, toting baskets of groceries, their choice of meal, or both. The more successful food carts dished out meals with such rapidity it was a flurry of color, aroma, and commotion. Lines of customers snaked out into the communal walkway with pedestrians slicing through without issue. Idle cooks busied themselves with a game of dice or dominos before launching themselves into action with a patron's arrival. Some people ate as they shopped, bargaining with a pinched dumpling between chopsticks while negotiating with a mouthful of noodles.

One section of the market seemed more like a sketchy petting zoo. Razor footed roosters battered their rivals for supremacy within circles of wide-eyed men and heated bets. Goats bleated while testing the limits of twine leashes as schools of small fish circled shallow pools in makeshift basins. Massive groupers stricken with a final gasp lay strewn across red stained chopping blocks. Turtles paced in place, mounds of snakes writhed in barrels, lizards snatched up crickets, and gleaming salamanders searched for salvation as the strengthening glow of lantern light grew with the setting sun. Gracien squirmed, his face souring over as skewered scorpions fought to escape their fiery fate.

"Toasted scorpions! Want one?" Ning teased as the girls hurried past a hundred towers of the writhing creatures and their protesting pincers.

With all the people navigating the bustling market, the disaccord was expected. Queues of people argued over succession, abandoned children screamed for mercy, merchants battled over customers, and customers over inventory. Untamed pets preyed upon the situation like pickpockets. Filthy street dogs looted toppled plates as cats stalked the awnings like seasoned thieves. Uninterrupted lines of lanterns zig-zagged just overhead, with merchants playing their part and lighting the nearest by climbing rickety ladders and makeshift platforms. They wielded bamboo sticks with glowing metal tips, which ignited candle wicks centered within the multicolored, rice paper shell. As dusk swept in over the market, yellows yawned, greens glimmered, blues bloomed, indigos ignited, and reds radiated the darkness away.

This is definitely an escape, Gracien thought as he felt a palpable release of anxiety while tilting his head back and inhaling some new delight.

This felt good, whatever *this* was. More than that, it felt important. As Ning chatted away with a merchant selling vintage coin necklaces, Gracien considered how important it was to find this balance, to feel as if he was living life instead of just thinking about it all the time. It felt real, it felt visceral – like he knew he was going to open his memory vault a long time from now, in this life or the next, and relish a diluted version of this exact moment. The memory might be vague, with the aromas diluted and the sights blurred, but he knew with utter certainty that this was a wonderful moment. And recalling this moment one day would incite a smile, usher in a sensation of having lived life and embraced it for whatever it had been. He inhaled, feeling life course through him with a vigor that was unmatched throughout his daily routine back in Zura. He continued inhaling deeply, scanning his surroundings as if he was seeing color for the very first time and surrendering to the sensory magic embracing him from every angle. His unblinking gaze made its way about before landing on something familiar, something intimate.

It was a couple. Gracien watched them from behind. The man was husky with wide shoulders and an erect posture. The woman had long, beautiful black hair and her hands were wrapped over him as if they had been posing for a painting. They weren't doing anything out of the ordinary, the man was paying for a dozen nian gao while the woman scanned the market. Gracien's forehead reddened as his hardened gaze scrutinized the couple. The man placed the change into his pocket, took the bag of cookies, then grabbed his wife's hand and disappeared into the masses. A wave of envy washed over Gracien as his hands began clenching into fists.

He moved forward to give chase before realizing his madness. Like a sleepwalker shaken to reality, he awoke from the blinding bitterness.

A wave of embarrassment washed over him. "What was that? It wasn't even a choice... It was a reaction, an instinct even."

He felt the embarrassment pour from him as shame surfaced. Gracien scanned the market, looking to see if anyone noticed while wiping away a bit of sweat between his eyebrows. As he began his retreat, something caught his attention from the corner of his eye. Just across the way an elderly woman sat somewhat removed from the market's clamor. She wasn't out in the open like the other vendors but off to the side of a dimly lit alley. Some odd trinkets, two empty turtle shells, and several candles with wax piled up at the base were spread about a makeshift table between her knees. Her old, wrinkled hands toyed with what looked like a stack of sticks, mixing then rearranging them like a deck of cards.

Gracien felt drawn towards the mysterious woman as she glared through the passing crowd. She noticed, pausing her shuffling routine, and turning her attention towards Gracien. Her translucent, milky eyes locked right onto Gracien before shooting him an acknowledging nod. Gracien looked around as if someone behind him was being summoned before turning back and taking a hesitant step forward. The spell of envy still lingered, so he tried shaking the nerves from his hands while cutting through the market's traffic. As he stepped into the alley, Gracien noticed a little sign hanging on the wall.

"Divination - Discover your Fate."

Disputing the appearance of her aged hands, the fortune teller resumed rearranging the twelve sticks with impressive speed and agility.

"Your fate... You come to discover your fate?" she asked in a creaky voice, her milked out eyes didn't look at Gracien but just above his head as if he was two feet taller.

Gracien didn't know what he came to discover, only that he felt pulled there and so kept quiet.

"Ahh yes… Too timid, too frightened to learn your fate?" she asked while preparing the various elements scattered across the miniature table for Gracien's reading.

As if she hadn't washed it out in ages, her hair was a twine of brownish grays and dulled blacks. It swirled down her back in a tangled weave. Wrinkles and liver spots littered her face, and her nose was as sharp as a blade. Her eyebrows danced as a clutter of golden earrings chimed out with each turn of her head. She seemed to be wearing at least six layers of silk, each dulled and weathered. Several rings adorned her aged hands and Gracien imagined how long ago she got them over those bulbous, bulky knuckles. The skin stretched over her hands was tired and thinned with seasoned maturity.

I'm not frightened, I don't know what I am… but I'm not frightened, Gracien thought as he shifted his weight and toyed with his fingers.

The woman let out a sinister giggle as if she had read Gracien's mind.

Her feeble shoulders bounced with delight. "A small reading then? This one is free but the question which comes of it will cost you, agreed?"

"What question?" Gracien asked.

"Well, I don't know… that's for you to ask," she responded with a smirk.

Then something quite strange happened. The fortune teller's smirk as well as her entire face froze as if time had stopped. Gracien sensed the bustle of the market flow behind him, but this old woman just stood there as if she was a statue. Gracien glanced around, wondering if he was the mark for some stupid scheme to scare him into paying more. Then a chill overcame him. A familiar sensation, one of comfort and affection, washed over him and with it the fortune teller's smirk began to extend. And something else occurred along with it; the woman sat up straighter then her face softened and brightened as if youth was being poured into it. The wrinkles retreated and the liver spots melted back into what was now an olive, glowing complexion. Prominent cheekbones extended, her lips bloomed, her nose softened, and her hair thickened – growing darker and richer as if it had been washed and tousled. Her hands too became those of a younger woman. With the sudden change, Gracien let out a gasp as the woman's eyes transformed, the milky blindness fading and giving way to a rich honey color.

Those mystical eyes fell on Gracien with a smile. At first, he wanted to flee, to pull a stranger into this scene and ask if they saw what he did. But something about the woman tugged at his very soul.

The creaky voice abated and with it a golden tone rang out from her perfectly plump lips.

"You are no girl, but something older… something more," her young hands placed down the sticks, and she turned her full attention to Gracien. "Listen closely, we haven't much time."

Gracien's head shook with disbelief, he felt like running away in one moment and bear-hugging the woman in the next.

"It's okay there's nothing to fear, you're perfectly safe. But like a migrating ship without a starry night, or an adventurer without a compass, you're lost in a place so very familiar. Yet your compass shines so clearly, so brightly… you must follow that light and that light alone, for that's your heart trying to guide you. But a broken compass cannot guide, just as a broken heart cannot lead one to their destiny."

Gracien's head trembled as he leaned in closer, hovering over the table and soaking up every word seeping from the woman's perfect mouth.

"You have a purpose much larger than what you think. Your purpose is a forest... yet you long for a sapling. Your purpose is an ocean... yet you crave a raindrop. You desire to *be* loved when your purpose is to *become* love." The woman's soft hands slid over Gracien's, who was now kneeling before the table in utter amazement.

"*Become* love. Whatever that takes, this is your purpose. Do not be fooled by circumstance, your broken heart will be such no matter the circumstance. *Become* love, believe in yourself. Believe... in... us..." The woman blinked reassuringly and with it someone grabbed at Gracien's shoulder.

He screamed, spinning to his feet only to discover Ning standing before him.

"I'm so sorry! I was looking for you and didn't know... Is everything alright? I didn't mean to scare you," she rattled off her own fright as Gracien instantly spun back around.

The old fortune teller looked up to him. "Your fate... you come to discover your fate?" she croaked out as if they hadn't shared this same conversation moments ago.

Her seasoned appearance had returned as well as that sinister giggle. Shaking his head in disbelief, Gracien took three quick steps backwards, bumping into Ning.

"Let's go... these fortune tellers give me the creeps," Ning said as she guided Gracien from the alley.

Gracien turned to her. "Did you... did you see her? Did you see what she looked like?"

Ning's expression muddled before looking back at the old woman who had already lured in some new sap.

"Did you see her face, the young one?" Gracien asked impatiently.

"What do you mean the young one? Was there another, her daughter maybe? I only saw the old lady, the one you were talking with. Did you pay her any money? Did you drink or eat anything she gave you? You're acting weird, Suyin," Ning said, shaking her head. "Oh look! There's Lian and Jiahao over by the games, let's go see if they've won anything."

Gracien looked back over his shoulder as Ning tugged him by the hand. The old woman was running her boney finger down a man's palm, poking it, and revealing his fate.

The following day Gracien decided to pass on another field trip, as he couldn't stop obsessing over the fortune teller experience. It wasn't just that either, the wave of envy he experienced after seeing the happy couple still bothered the hell out of him. From the moment he opened his eyes in the morning he was infatuated with the mystery of it all. Gracien couldn't help but hide under the covers until the commotion of others embarking on some new adventure ceased. Ning was nowhere to be found and hadn't made a stop over to check in on him before taking off. Gracien couldn't tell if he was happy or hurt by this, but didn't dwell on it too long as his mind was wrapped up reliving the fortune teller's cryptic message. Like a rusty anchor being pulled from its watery grave, it took everything for him to function both mentally and physically. He was slow to leave his bed, slow to clean up, slow sipping his tea, slow as he walked and slow in his thoughts. It was like being hungover but without any of the fun the night before.

Still donning his bed robe, he settled himself by squirming into the nook of a bench looking across one of his favorite courtyards. This was the quiet one with the mighty willow tree where he had discovered the sounds of a stream just beyond the wall. Four times in a row he moved to take a sip of tea, yet it never made it to his lips as confusion weighed down the cup.

"My purpose is to *be* love… What does that even mean? How can someone *be* love? Maybe she said be *in* love?" He negotiated but the fortune teller's words rang out with perfect clarity as he mulled them over for the hundredth time.

"You desire to *be* loved when your purpose is to *become* love." He sighed with frustration.

"How can I *become* love if Aya isn't here to love me anymore? How can I *become* love when Aya's not here for me to love?"

His confusion abounded as frustration boiled over into anger.

"It's not like I chose this… like I wanted her to die and for me to be left with nothing!" Gracien hadn't realized but he was yelling out loud.

He nearly screamed the word 'nothing,' which shook him from his enraged trance. He looked up, scanning the courtyard to see if anyone had heard him.

"Okay calm down, it was just a message and it felt good. That's where the importance lies, I don't have to figure out her message just yet. All I know is that it felt good, like it had come from Aya herself and that's important. Time, I apparently have time to figure out what it meant and hopefully I will… eventually." He rolled his eyes.

Giving up, Gracien laid down on the bench with his wrist lying on his forehead and his knees pointing up in the air. The anger trickled from him, but still, he couldn't help feeling defeated.

"The further one goes, the less one knows." Another well-timed quote from the *Tao* dropped into his mind as if gifted from another.

He began to cry, wondering what Ayadonna would tell him, how tight she would hold him, how much better he'd feel after enjoying Aya's supportive gaze, her comforting touch, her heartfelt affection. He missed everything about her and just missed the person who was his best friend. And with that notion, he thought of Ning. The thought dried his tears, bringing a small smirk to his face and then a smile. Before he knew it,

Gracien was giggling at their shared adventures. She was a good friend, more than that too… maybe a best friend? His expression matured with the idea of him and Ning being so close. He sat up as if suddenly discovering the solution to a lengthy problem, leaning forward he realized that Aya's importance was fading, and Ning's was blooming. The sense of betrayal was immediate; a rogue wave hurling him into a frigid, tumultuous sea. The tears returned as betrayal, shame, and disgrace washed over him. The beauty of his friendship with Ning darkened, rotting away as a familiar hollowness intensified in his chest. He laid back down on the bench, allowing the curtain of despair to cement as he wept. Quite a bit of time had passed until the sanctuary of sleep overcame him, allowing him to drift off into the refuge of dreams.

Gracien woke a few hours later, feeling the gravity of sorrow and the weight of sleep in his eyes, cheeks, and throat. He pushed himself up, his muscles rebelling against his migration. His defeat and depression awoke along with him, tears budding up.

"No, no, no snap out of it… I can't, I can't do this to myself all over again." A slight moan rang out as he stood, taking a deep breath, and detangling his hair as he sighed three times in a row.

He looked over the courtyard, which was still empty, but it somehow mirrored his energy, appearing dark and grim. His stomach rumbled. He felt unclean, like the grief was slathered over his skin, so he gathered his things and made for the showers.

After a good long shower with water hot enough to poach an egg, some more tea, and a full meal, Gracien felt renewed, but not enough to venture out.

It's so quiet here, so empty and almost eerie without all the activity of a normal day.

The echo of his footsteps down the empty hallway was his sole companion as he strolled along. He didn't have any destination in mind, just exploring as he made his way around the expansive grounds. Without obligations and grief veiling his senses, Gracien felt as if he was fully *seeing* Zura for the first time. Something was so familiar as he sauntered about like an adult visiting their childhood schoolhouse.

The academy was impressive for an institute such as this, even rivaling many of the manors and estates of the wealthiest nobles within a hundred miles. Gracien's hand drifted just above the highly polished stone lining a desolate corridor. He was pulled into the reflection of his hand, seeing not that of a Chinese girl but that of a Babylonian king. This place was familiar because he couldn't help but feel as if he was touring the palace of old. The feeling should have been beautiful and encouraging, but it was nothing close to that. With a gasp, he realized why.

"It's like home... but after Aya's death." His eyes widened as the connection cemented.

His unblinking gaze stared down that long corridor, unable to see the intricate architecture and design particular to this country and time period. All he saw was the Babylonian palace yet cast in the shadow of its queen's passing. As if death itself stalked the corridor, a heavy chill embraced him from behind. He spun around, enclosing his arms around himself. He didn't see anything down the other way but felt as if some unknown entity was approaching as he walked backwards. He tried swallowing the dryness in his throat.

"Maybe it's time to venture outside after all, visit *the wall* perhaps." The echo of his whisper hissed down the hallway just before the patter of his quickened retreat.

A couple of hours later he was all alone, walking along a section of the Great Wall of China which wasn't hosting any other visitors at the moment. The afternoon was glorious, with a nice warm sun and those big puffy clouds from children's stories. Having dumped his depression along the ride, he felt immensely better, lighter, and free.

"Maybe the carriage ride shook it from me?" He snickered, holding his head up high as he scanned the horizon. "Or maybe it's this place, this spectacle," he said while trying his best to absorb the magnitude of this man-made creation.

The Great Wall surpassed the capability of his eyesight, seamlessly melting into the distant horizon. It was impulsive too, snaking along in some sections then suddenly kinking at a ninety-degree angle like a lizard's broken tail. Gracien thought the massive wall resembled the upright scales running down the back of a slumbering dragon, making the lush rolling hills the body of the beast. It seemed so small, as he looked at it from such a distance away. Yet as his two small feet stood atop a massive, grayed stone, dirty and weathered from the elements, his mind struggled imagining the herculean force it took to achieve such a feat. He recalled the Great Pyramid and its impressive stature; it was like comparing a grain of sand to a desert. The recurring towers jutting up from the slithering mass were impressive castles in their own right, some with multiple levels and a dozen or so windows. And not to mention the terrain, it was like building a thousand pyramids on the slopes of a mountain. He recalled the overwhelming feeling of standing on the shores of Babylon and taking in the sea's endless expanse. The Great Wall was the only man-made creation capable of generating a similar sensation. Gracien found it difficult to rub the amazed smirk from his face as he strolled along its vacant canopy.

He almost jumped with an idea. "I'll do First Form on the wall!" he squealed.

Gracien climbed up on top of one of the lower rails, losing his sense of self as a wave of vertigo overwhelmed him after peering down the very long drop-off.

"Whoa, whoa, whoa!" he cautioned as his feet slid backwards on the stone.

The rails of the wall were four feet thick, so he had plenty of room, but it was still frightening standing on top. One added value with this higher vantage point was that the greens of the rolling landscape really came alive.

"The world belongs to those who let go." Lao Tzu's words poured from his heart as his gaze wrestled the might of the horizon.

He wanted Aya to be there with him and he imagined holding her hand and both peering out into the expanse.

She would have loved this, he thought, feeling a bit guilty using past tense.

Gracien inhaled. "And she *wants* me to love this, to be present and enjoy the moment, which I will do in your honor, my love."

And with those final words, he began First Form. As he began with the first of the moves, it felt sensational. The unification of his rich, ancient culture embraced him. The Great Wall in all its glory, coupled with the sacred art form which poured through him, was almost too much to handle.

I'm practicing kung fu on one of the most culturally significant creations of all time… this is a dream. Gracien kept his eyes open, as he didn't want to take any chances overstepping the edge.

As his feet scraped and slid through the movements, he couldn't stop the memories from flooding his mind. Flashes of his and Aya's earliest times together arose as his arms gracefully flowed through the movements of First Form. The first time he laid eyes on her, the first time he heard her thunderous laugh, the first time they shared that earth-shattering gaze, and the first time Gracien knew that there was something more to this woman, something different, something beyond his understanding. As Gracien's wrists rolled with the strikes extending then retreating with sloth-like speed, his heart burst with the memory of their first kiss.

Hand in hand, they had strolled through the Palace gardens, exchanging small tugs, stifled laughs, and timid smirks. Aya's beauty was thrilling, her hair resembled the flowing locks of seafaring sirens. Her gaze made him feel not like a man, but a boy. Under the cover of darkness, they walked in the more hidden parts of the gardens as their courtship was still a secret, at least to all of Babylon. After hours of incessant conversation, his voice was raspy and his cheeks sore from smiling. They wordlessly walked along with their arms swinging in unison. He kept busy wiping his palms on his pants with the constant buildup of nervous sweat. This was the seventh time in a row it crossed his mind.

Kiss her. He dismissed the notion as the possibility of rejection bubbled up.

The space between them narrowed as the time spent looking anywhere but at one another dwindled. Gracien calculated his steps as if he was crossing a narrow bridge; they echoed throughout the empty sanctuary.

Kiss herrr, he taunted himself like a serpent.

The sound of Aya's exhalations strengthened, as if she was breathing for them both. He could almost feel her heartbeat. Was it him or was she radiating heat like a hearth?

Gracien pulled at his collar. Looking to her, he giggled nervously.

Aya smiled, it was too large for the moment. Her embarrassed eyes retreated to her feet.

Kiss her you coward! his heart screamed like a battle clad warrior charging down an enemy hillside.

A wave of confidence washed over him; he stood taller, his eyes narrowed, his chin muscles flexed – then and there he became a man.

Gracien tugged at her arm, rolling Aya towards him and with it she leapt into his arms. Their lips locked within the fullness of a very hard kiss, the kind in which the passion extinguishes the pain. Neither had control, nor any desire for it. They surrendered to their connection, allowing the attraction to steer them. Aya released the sweetest, softest, most intoxicating moan. Gracien, having never experienced the magnitude of such a moan, was crippled by it. Something so slight, so insignificant, yet bearing the power to liberate or destroy an entire civilization was a rather profound experience – a moan such as this had caused the Trojan War. Their heads swayed, their hands clutched, their body's flexed for a moment, for two, then three more before deflating like windless sails. With their eyes still closed, their lips parted, a tether of saliva extended then tore. Both had released a breath of utter satisfaction, one rivaling the final exhalation of a life well lived.

Gracien's arms snaked through the air like serpents ascending a tree. His breath was slow and calculated, his body completely in tune with the final parts of the Form, but his mind was lifetimes away. As he exhaled, the memory faded with reality flooding his senses. His eyes opened and the majesty before him nearly brought him to tears.

"What a kiss, huh my love? What a kiss indeed." As he whispered into the winds, his hands dropped down to his side and his posture took on that of a regular stance.

More memories arose, flashes and sections of them flickering like a candle flame. Zura and its sprawling campus reminded him so very much of the palace with its courtyards and endless corridors. Even the Great Wall brought him back to episodes of strolling the palace walls while peering out into the endless landscapes. Ning somehow reminded Gracien of Aya, or maybe she was a reminder of intimacy, of attraction. Gracien's memories darkened, weighed down with Aya's disease, with the grief of the battle and the fated conclusion. The eerie feeling returned, that sensation of being watched by malicious eyes. He swallowed and his heart raced as he stepped backwards as if being threatened by some invisible force. The memories grew clearer, narrowing in on the corridor just outside of their chamber room and the hundred times Gracien had raced down it, bringing healers and medicines. Then images of being back in their bedroom and the endless miles he paced while Aya, gaunt and yellowed with disease, fought for her life. The memory of his budding worries and relentless fear, the excruciating thought of her death, it all rippled through him like a raging fire.

Gracien gasped. "No, no, please... I'm not ready, I can't... I can't," he mumbled as the memory dragged him into darkness like a punished child. "Please no... Don't take me back there." He shook his head, clenching his eyes closed as if he was drowning in the memory.

His eyelids burst open and his nostrils flared with breath. He hurriedly scanned the Wall as if it was the very last thing he would ever see.

"Stay here, focus on the now," he begged.

After a few moments his quickened breath finally began to settle.

"It's okay, it's okay... I'm not ready, I'm just not ready."

His heartbeat steadied and not knowing what to do, he tried to pick up where he left off within the Form. It was useless, his technique faltered, and his limbs abandoned him.

"Bad form, keep your elbows in!" someone shouted, saving him from the moment.

It was Ning. Happy with the intrusion and the opportunity of escape, Gracien inhaled deeply, wiped away his tears and smiled. He delayed, refusing to turn towards Ning as her hurried footfalls approached.

"And your knees are hardly bent, sit down in your stance more!" Ning yelled with a laugh.

Gracien returned with one of his own, wiping the tears from his cheeks. "Sorry, I'm having a moment." Gracien attempted a smile, but Ning was too busy trying to climb up the wall to see it.

"How? How the hell did you man…" Her footing slipped. "Mannn…iggge…" She recovered, pulling herself up.

"Whoaaa… that's a far drop." Ning swallowed before retreating. "Nope, nope, nope… Not for me, not for me." She jumped back down to the main walkway.

"Afraid of heights? Really?" Gracien teased and Ning moved to respond but he cut her off. "I'll come down." Gracien dismounted like a cat.

Ning froze, seeing Gracien up close. "What's wrong?"

"Nothing, honestly. I was just having a moment, you know?" he responded.

Ning nodded. "Yeah, I do. I was just…" She exhaled before becoming emotional herself. "I was just having one myself, down a way. It seems like this is the place to do that."

They both shared a nervous laugh.

"Or maybe the beauty out here somehow encourages the pain to surface." Gracien scanned the horizon before looking at Ning.

Gracien moved to say something more before hesitating and looking away.

The two sat silently for a few moments as Gracien wrestled with his mind, trying to summon the courage to ask her a question.

With a rush of bravery, he looked to Ning, blurting out, "what was your moment about?"

Ning's head dropped down as she avoided Gracien's eyes. Her chest inflated as if she was going to speak but then nothing came. Gracien could tell she was preparing herself, trying to find the right words as well as the necessary courage.

Ning began, using the faintest of whispers. "My mother, and sister... It was an accident. They drowned."

Gracien let out a little gasp. A moment passed, then two, then three. Ning said nothing more and Gracien suddenly came to, realizing she wouldn't be adding anything else.

"I'm so, so sorry Ning... I can't, I mean I can..." he stuttered, not knowing what to say.

Gracien placed his hand on Ning's shoulder. "I don't know what to say other than I'm sorry."

Even as the words poured from him, he knew they lacked any true comfort. Ning shuddered as if a great chill rippled through her and then her head rose ever so slowly. Her eyes didn't meet Gracien's as her head rolled back and tears streamed down her cheeks. She scanned the heavens and allowed herself a full, unbridled cry. Gracien realized that sometimes no words are needed, just one's attention and presence. His hand squeezed a little bit tighter as Ning's torment poured from her, taking extended gasps of breath as she navigated the grief.

Then, like a flower surrendering to nightfall, her head dipped back down until her gaze met Gracien's. "Thank you for listening, for being here," she whispered, but this time her words were stronger, ripened, and free.

Gracien nodded and the two embraced. With his chin tucked over Ning's shoulder and his arms tugging firmly, Gracien's eyes teared over as he scanned the horizon, happy and proud that he could serve another, even if he wasn't quite sure of how he had.

"Okay, okay. Phew!" Ning sat up abruptly, inhaling and straightening her posture. "Enough of this nonsense, let's... let's chi sao, yes?"

"Good idea," Gracien agreed, Ning smirked.

The two popped to their feet before placing their hands in guard and connecting at the wrists. Chi sao, or rolling hands as it's called, is a technique for strengthening one's reaction time and sensitivity to an opponent's energy. A practitioner can try different maneuvers within a continual, fluid state – all the while their opponent does the same. Each person tries to get a leg up on the other by landing a strike or tying up the opponent's hands and arms. All of this is done without breaking a bonded, physical connection. It can be practiced with a somewhat aggressive, intense energy or a tranquil, graceful one. Gracien and Ning preferred the latter, especially for such an occasion.

They began, keeping their feet planted for the first couple of minutes and concentrating on the hand work instead. Their hands and arms coalesced, looking like two bakers whirling the same dough. Moments later, the dance began, stepping and moving around to gain position. They were a spectacle to see, grace in motion and nimbler than house cats. It looked like they were performing a choreographed dance while their hands and arms manipulated some shared, invisible orb of energy. Gracien closed his eyes, and Ning followed suit.

In the beginning, the goal was to outmaneuver one another, land a strike or find an opening. But now they had a wordless agreement to merely try and maintain the flow and energy of the exchange without giving or taking too much from the other. Their performance was the grace of Forms multiplied threefold, sending a ripple of energy over the terrace. Like lava beginning to bubble in a volcano, Suyin felt something deep within herself revive. The physical touch, the intimacy, the mutual affection, it was thrilling. Unlike a quick hug or encouraging pat, their exchange lingered well beyond anything Gracien had received in lifetimes. As their hands and arms danced with one another's, the energy shifted. Amplified by sensuality, their connection evolved into something more.

And how Suyin appreciated it. She would have never known unless it came to this, but her very being longed to be touched, to be embraced and swaddled within the caress of another. The lack of this very thing nearly brought tears to her eyes as she realized how long it had been. And how wonderful it felt. Her desires flamed as Ning's touch somehow healed a part of her which, up to that point, had felt inoperable. The light and warmth of a summer's day banishing the dark chill of shadow. Like a child experiencing some newfound joy, she let out a little giggle as the pleasure poured over her flesh and down into her soul. It was magnificent, and she could tell Ning appreciated the exchange in a manner more than just practicing her technique. It continued for longer than anticipated until like clouds parting after a subtle rain, the two girls separated, stepping back with a salute and a bow.

Suyin's smile gleamed, Ning's was even brighter.

"That was spectacular!" Ning shouted.

Gracien laughed, then smiled again. He could tell Ning had improved since her cry.

"Have you eaten anything; I brought some fruit?" Ning questioned as she retrieved her satchel. "We should head out pretty soon if we want to be back in time for curfew." She shielded her eyes while gazing at the sun.

As Ning gazed out into the landscape, Gracien stared at her, watching the sun's shimmer race along her black hair.

"Starving, yeah. We should start back. We may already be running a bit late."

Three hours later and the carriage ride was finally bumping along the unmanicured road heading back to Zura. The two had gotten turned around on the Great Wall going in the wrong direction for almost an hour before realizing it. Curfew aligned with sunset, so they were racing back to Zura and losing. Gracien felt his nerves bubble up with the thought of returning after curfew, but Ning was a complete maniac. She couldn't sit still, fidgeting and picking at her fingernails while constantly peering out the carriage window every ten seconds as if they would magically appear back at the academy.

"What if we're late, and the doors are shut? What if Master is out there waiting for us? Do you think they'll do a headcount, maybe at dinner? Suyin what are we going to do!" Ning sputtered off the questions before shoving her head through the carriage window. "Can you hurry please!" she shouted to the driver who completely ignored her sixth attempt at encouraging him.

Gracien pulled her back into the cabin. "Ning sit down, sit down. I'm worried too but we're doing all that we can. You've asked him to go faster and he's doing what he can. Try to settle down some, maybe…"

"You settle down! Don't tell me to settle down! You're the one who got me into this mess!" Ning erupted.

Gracien's eyes went wide and his whole body constricted with the unexpected outburst. "I'm sorry… I just," Gracien tried to respond before being cut off.

"Some of us are actually concerned with doing well at Zura and *not* getting into trouble!" Ning was shouting now, even with the rumble of the wheels over the rocky terrain, her voice roared.

"I *am* concerned…" Gracien moved to respond before being cut off again.

"No you're not! You don't care a bit, ha! Please Suyin everyone knows you're checked out… maybe you never checked in!" She fake-laughed again.

Gracien's cheeks flushed red, and his teeth clenched down as his anger began matching Ning's.

"Ning let's just see if we're late first and then take it from there. There's no need to rip each other apart right now… We're both very concerned." Gracien stood, staring her down. "I don't need any more scars along my back either!"

They held their silent, furious glares on one another before the light rapidly retreated with the setting sun. They both jumped to the window, poking their heads from it, and glaring at dusk as if it had just betrayed them. They looked to the road ahead, seeing it wind up the hill with Zura being a mere speck in the distance. Gracien and Ning slipped back into the cabin, slumping back down on the bench without saying a word all the way back.

The carriage didn't even have time to stop as the girls leapt from its door. Like stalking predators, they instinctively snuck up to the front entrance. The massive doors towered over the girls like disappointed parents. Gracien gave them both a little shove, it was like pushing stone.

"Locked," he hissed to Ning who immediately tucked her head into her hands and fell to her knees.

Gracien couldn't help feeling annoyed with the drama.

"Now what…" Ning wailed softly.

Gracien paid her no attention, examining the doors and looking for a hidden key or anything to keep them from knocking. His hands felt around the stone wall, seeing if any of the bricks were loose and concealing their salvation. As his fingers tricked down the cold wall, he experienced a flash of brilliance.

"The willow in the courtyard." He stared blankly at the door as a grin extended.

He spun towards Ning. "The courtyard tree… The one I told you about when I was talking about sneaking off," his words spilled out. "Remember? The one I thought maybe we could climb?" He knelt, shaking Ning.

"See… you are checked out, already trying to escape somewhere we can't get into!" Ning snarled.

"No, no… think! If we can sneak out, then we can Sneak! Back! In!" He grabbed Ning by the shoulders, watching her eyes grow wide with realization.

"But what if they catch us, what if…"

Gracien cut her off. "How much worse could it be! We're already in line to receive one lashing! If this works, we're in free and clear, if not then we come back and knock. Late is late. Ten minutes more won't make a difference." Gracien couldn't help but smile as Ning jumped to her feet.

"Then what are we waiting for! Let's get to it and stop standing around!" Ning cheered, and the two scattered like frightened cats.

The crunch of footsteps and dense chirp of crickets sounded out as they walked through the dead brush piled up against the perimeter wall. Without the moonlight breaking through the forest canopy, it was difficult to see. Gracien scanned the top of the wall, looking for the recognizable willow branches from the other side. He suspected they'd be hanging over the wall like a mass of rope draped down the outer side, or at least he hoped. Ning was at it again, talking herself into a state of frenzied panic but this time it was at least through hushed whispers. Gracien's hands were shaky, and his stomach felt queasy with the intensity of budding nerves, but he kept to the task at hand, giving his head a quick shake every time he needed to recenter. The sound of running water grew louder the further the wall extended out into the surrounding forest. Gracien couldn't get a good scope of the layout under the swelling darkness, but it seemed that the stream bent inwards just twenty or so paces out.

"There! There it is," he exclaimed, leaving Ning in his wake as he raced towards the cascading willow branches.

It was exactly as he imagined, the branches dangled over and down the incredibly tall wall but with one problem, they weren't long enough.

"Crap!" Gracien shouted, deflating as Ning caught up.

"What! What is it?" Ning asked, exchanging glances between Gracien and the willow tree. "That's it right... Now what?" Ning was radiating stress.

"Give me a second." Gracien surveyed the top of the wall, it was crumpling in certain parts. He began walking along looking for an opportunity to climb up.

"You said we could get in from here! So now what? Hello!" Ning was breathing down Gracien's back as he paced along the wall.

Gracien spun on her. "I never said anything of the sort! I'm trying to save us from some punishment here and you're not helping! Get off my back and give me some space!" Gracien yelled, stepping forward and stopping short an inch from Ning's face.

Ning stepped back, "I'm... I'm sorry." She shrunk. "I just..."

Gracien sighed. "We're not knocking on any doors just yet." He placed his hand on Ning's shoulder. "Let's just keep it together and continue looking."

"Looking for what?" Ning asked.

"I don't know, anything to help us get over this stupid wall!" He turned, kicking the stone.

"Like that?" Ning pointed.

Gracien turned, looking down Ning's finger to see a huge, fallen tree leaning up against the wall a hundred feet farther down. A cave of roots and dirt stood at the side of the uprooted base facing the river like an enormous shield. The main hunk of the tree ascended the wall with an endless array of dead branches crushed up against it.

"That may work!" Gracien exclaimed as they ran towards it.

The tree couldn't have been a better fit for their escape, or rather, invasion. Dozens of broken branches served as steps and ran the entire length of the trunk. They were children again, getting lost in some imagined fantasy while scaling the castle walls. Hand over foot, they scampered up the tree like two monkeys.

"Careful, there's some slick moss up here," Gracien whispered below.

As they approached the top of the wall, the humid forest air thinned, and the hum of crickets lessened. At the very top of the tree most of the branches just stopped. Gracien climbed up onto it and peered down, they were at least thirty feet up. There was nothing on the other side of the wall so the top portion of the massive tree must have fallen into the courtyard and been cleared some years prior.

Ning joined him, grunting with the final part of the climb before immediately kneeling.

"You've got to be kidding me!" she faintly screamed while peering down, "I'm not great with heights, Suyin. And this wall is a lot thinner than I thought it would be!"

Gracien knelt, taking Ning by the shoulders. Something within him came alive, something protective and courageous.

"We're already there Ning, we've made it this far and you're a nimble, graceful warrior! This is nothing. You can do this, and I'll be by your side, or rather your front every step of the way."

With her eyes squeezed shut, Ning shook her head. "Nooo I can't, I just can't," she begged.

"Yes. Yes, you can and you will. Just like Forms, nice and slow with intense concentration. You got this Ning. Now take a deep breath and let's get the hell off this wall."

Gracien spoke with such vigor and encouragement Ning couldn't help but meet his gaze. She took a deep breath and nodded.

Gracien helped her stand. "Focus on your feet and hold my shoulders as I walk, we're not going far... a hundred feet or so, right there." Gracien pointed to where the willow clutched the wall.

Ning nodded, then took a deep breath and nodded again. Gracien took Ning's hands and placed them on his shoulders as he slowly turned towards the willow.

"Just continue breathing, keep your knees bent, and follow me." His first step slid over the stone with a scrape.

The stones running along the top were crumbling where the tree had crashed into it, with big gaps where stones should have been. The girls made good progress considering the height, darkness, and treacherous footing. But as they neared the willow, Gracien saw that there was a big dip in the stone catwalk where the wall had worn and fallen away.

"Okay we may have to change our plan a bit."

"What? What do you mean?" Ning said, tightening her grip on Gracien's shoulders.

"It's okay. Ning, we're almost there but I need you to walk on your own here. Just this little stretch and then we're at the tree. Then we're home free," Gracien spoke as slowly as he could while breathing with Ning as if she was having a baby.

Ning nodded. "Okay."

Gracien nodded, repeating, "okay," before turning back towards the tree, taking a step, and then screaming, "Aghh!"

Before he knew what happened he was hanging on the inside of the courtyard wall. Ning was clutching him tightly by the hand and gripping his shirt, her own legs dangling over the forest side of the wall. Gracien instinctively tried to pull himself up.

"NO! NO!" Ning yelled before Gracien realized that if he made it up, Ning would fall.

After a full moment of panic, Gracien said, "it's okay, we can do this! How's your grip?"

Gracien surprised himself with how calm he was.

"What?" Ning screamed.

"Shhh! Not so loud. I asked how's your grip? We're each going to walk a leg over this broken part and pull ourselves up."

"What?" Ning whisper-screamed again.

"I said…"

"I know what you said, I'm freaking out!"

"Ning, we have to do something, and quick. On three kick your right leg up and simultaneously pull yourself up, okay?"

"Are you serious? I hate this!" Gracien could hear her breathing heavily on the other side of the wall, before finally agreeing. "Fine, okay!"

"Onneee… twooo…" Gracien counted.

"I CAN'T!" Ning screamed.

"THREE!" Gracien screamed back and prayed Ning would match his kick.

She did. In a flash they shot themselves upwards, scrambling back on top of the wall. Bearing surprised expressions, they froze. With Gracien hugging Ning from behind, they looked like two wrestlers fastened to each other. Gracien pressed off Ning and stood, then quickly made his way over the broken, sunken section. He stopped, bracing himself on a willow branch before turning to Ning.

"Okay now your turn… We're almost there."

Ning had watched Gracien dart across the section like an old dog staring down a youthful pup. She inhaled, dropping her head in defeat, and peering down the side of the wall.

"Why'd I do that?" she moaned after noticing the drop off.

"Ning, come on, let's get the hell off this wall already!" Gracien whisper screamed.

His adrenaline was in overdrive as a sting of pain began trickling down his arm. He looked to find a large scrape cascading down his forearm, then looked back to find Ning was already crawling along the top of the wall like a novice cat burglar.

"That's it... that's it... You're doing great, almost there..." Suddenly more stones gave way. "Agh!" Ning's hand pushed through the mess of loose stones before catching herself and hunkering down on the wall like a frog. As the stone debris disappeared into the soft brush at the base of the wall, Ning released a low whine.

"Ning, listen to my voice. You are five feet from me. Five feet. My grip and stance are secure. This tree is strong. And we're ready for you. Come on, you can do this." Gracien crouched down with his hand reaching out and his fingers fanning the open air.

Ning lifted her head up. Her chin was scratched from the fall. She blew her hair from her eyes and resumed her crawl.

"Four feet, that's it, that's it... three feet, there you go almost there... two feet, YES!" Gracien grabbed her hand, pulling her into a one-armed embrace as her other hand held fast to the willow.

They nearly jumped with glee at their triumph.

"Well done! Now for..." Gracien turned, preparing to engage the next obstacle. "The easy part," he said before Ning tugged his arm.

Gracien turned back around and for the second time in some moments he was unaware of what was happening as it was happening. Ning had pulled him in for a kiss. The sensation was an explosion of sweetness, a sensual concoction of adrenaline, fear, death, and romance. After some moments later their lips parted, slowly pulling away with their closed eyelids resting peacefully. The corner of Ning's mouth drew into a smirk as her eyes opened. Just like that she had vanished into the mass of willow leaves and down the impressive trunk.

Gracien was stupefied, careening like a drunk taking in the last bit of the night. He took his time surveying the crescent moon and starry night before he too disappeared down into the safety of the courtyard.

All the disciples were back in Zura and had eased into their first week of normalcy. After getting away with sneaking back in scot-free yet feeling a little worried someone may have witnessed their underhanded spectacle, Gracien and Ning had decided to lay low for the last few days of break. Ning was especially worked up, having almost let the cat out of the bag on two separate occasions, had Gracien not stepped in. The first instance by coughing loudly and the second by pretending to trip and shoving Ning. However bad Gracien's anxiety was, Ning's was tripled. But if Gracien had anything, it was sympathy for the madness brought on by anxiety. It wasn't hard to recall the overwhelming dread and debilitating angst he had endured while caring for Aya. Anxiety isn't a choice and Ning wasn't choosing to be this way.

Things had changed since Gracien accidently tripped and plowed into Ning, as it wasn't the passing of time which diminished Ning's anxiety over their sneaky trespass, but rather her nature to find some new reason to worry. Gracien decided to take it all in stride, as he appreciated his relationship with Ning, even with her aggressive, anxiety ridden outbursts. Gracien did his best trying to comfort and assist Ning in discovering a more peaceful mindset, but in doing so also discovered that his own anxiety was sometimes triggered by Ning's. And not so much by what triggered Ning's anxiety, but by Ning's anxiety or the energy she was putting out. But let's not forget, Gracien had plenty on his plate already and now he found himself wrestling two new streams of emotion. On one hand, he was grateful for Ning, for their shared connection and reliance on one another as allies through harsh times. The tide of affection and intimacy was exciting and even refreshing, but the other stream teemed with feelings of betrayal and shame. Like a cheating spouse, the very instant an unfaithful act concluded, Gracien felt swept away by a tidal wave of remorse and guilt for even glancing at Ning with Aya still residing in his heart.

As the weeks rolled along, Gracien wrestled with the nature of their relationship. His struggle aligned with reality, as the two couldn't appear more than just friends, even though their attraction was evident. But through well planned rendezvous, they allowed themselves to be as natural as two impassioned lovers. For Gracien, that was the part he valued most. After Aya's passing, the ensuing void of intimacy had been one of the most difficult aspects of the grieving process. But as many seasoned couples come to understand, affection and intimacy alone cannot sustain a relationship.

So as the year continued unraveling, Gracien discovered that like a pristine silver platter, his relationship with Ning began to tarnish – and not because of anxiety. It was Gracien, he found himself constantly analyzing and judging Ning: her personality, her beauty, her body, her intelligence, even the way she laughed or the way she looked while she slept. No matter what Ning did, or how beautiful and affectionate she was, she could never hold a candle to Aya. It was an impossible competition, like weighing an ocean against a puddle or the moon against a stone. Ayadonna was a goddess, not to every eye that had perceived her, but to Gracien's. And it was his eye which scrutinized every aspect of Ning's personality, all the facets of her appearance and all the minutiae of what she wasn't. He had yet to make the connection, but Aya had attained a godlike rank. Gracien had martyred and glorified the image of his Beloved well beyond what was just.

See the thing is, memory has its limitations. Whatever we recall, whether it's an experience or a person, it's a watered-down version of the experience and a silhouette of the person. And the memory of the person or event becomes more diluted as more time passes. This is a well-known and agreed upon fact. So why is it that when Gracien recalled the sound of Aya's laugh, the smell of her hair, or the gleam in her eye, he didn't experience some diluted version but one that was enhanced and almost immortal? Because grief can expand the limitations of memory, breaking down barriers and pushing boundaries. Aya had become Gracien's God, and there was no competing with one's God. All of Aya's guidance, the signs and love she poured into Gracien's life, the visitations within dreams, the angelic receptions, the encouraging omens; they had added up, tipping the scales beyond reality. Aya's scale plates were tipped so far over they may as well have been nailed to the table. Gracien had also found himself, unintentionally or maybe subconsciously, imagining things which had never occurred, making up fantasies in his head to serve as solace and fill that bottomless void of intimacy created by her death.

Neither of the girls understood the looming challenges of maintaining such an innocent relationship, so as was typical, their bond teetered between extremes. One day they'd be in awe of one another, utterly bound by infatuation and embraced in some new shared hysterics, then two days later they'd be sworn enemies. Things weren't made any easier with the challenge of keeping their relationship a secret. With the threat of physical punishment or even the possibility of expulsion, neither could bare the aftermath of being discovered. But neither of them was strong enough to put an end to their affair. The secrecy however, with all its danger and significance teetering on the edge of a blade, was a thrill in its own right: sneaking off to hidden corridors for a quick make out session, passing passionate notes to one another in the middle of class, slinking into each other's bed for an hour of predawn cuddling, or canoodling in a clandestine spot while taking turns reading poetry. It was romantic as can be, especially with their constant, aggressive mood swings thrown in the mix.

They were two peas in a pod when the moons were aligned. Gracien was always able to help Ning see the positive side of things and Ning had an uncanny knack at getting Gracien to laugh no matter how depressed he felt. For as much as her anxiety made her look like a cauldron about to explode, Ning sure did know how to let off a bit of steam. And Gracien loved that about her. Ning was spontaneous, adventurous, and as entertaining as could be when her mood was in the right place. She was a necessary and appreciated support through Gracien's continued struggle. And he needed all the support he could get, for Gracien believed that life was purposely trying to overwhelm him.

Sometimes it felt like he was hiding an evil twin version of himself. This dark doppelganger tried to sabotage all the hard work Gracien had invested into relationships as well as his goals of growth and healing. Every step forward seemed to come with one the other way. So, at times, progress was glacial and gut-wrenching. Zura didn't help much either, as the more time Gracien spent within its confines, the more it made him itch. At first the similarities between Zura and the Babylonian palace were a comfort, like returning to mother's house for a home cooked meal. But without mother there to add her final touch, the recipe could never be the same. So as the familiarity between the darkened palace and Zura strengthened over time, he began resenting not just Zura but his entire life there. The corridors closed in around him, the training room took on an eerie semblance, the lectures irritated him, the quietness of the whole place annoyed him, the other disciples left him feeling judgmental, and Master Chi seemed like somebody else entirely. He couldn't quite put his finger on it, but something about him was inauthentic, maybe even corrupt. Like the wooden dummies trying to impersonate a real-life opponent, Master seemed like he was doing everything he could to appear like some consummate, kung fu sage. When he contemplated it further, Gracien couldn't help but recall several faces from the Babylonian Senate, two-faced scoundrels who played the role of loyal confidant in one moment only to sell Gracien out the very next. With all these opposing forces, Gracien was getting more comfortable with the idea that maybe he didn't belong locked up behind Zura's walls anymore – so that's why he began spending more time beyond them.

"Even the finest sword plunged into salt water will eventually rust."

Master Chi stated as his footsteps slid across the rich, polished flooring with the communal breath of Second Years mimicking a seasoned tide. Like the hypnotizing dance of blue-green algae swaying in a subtle current, flashes of teal robes gleamed under the sun's embrace as the mass of students swept, swerved, and drifted in unison. Master, donning a vibrant orange robe with pearl white fluting and an ever-watchful gaze, flowed through the mass of students like a clownfish through his faithful crop of anemone.

Just outside the main training hall in the southeast courtyard, a group of Fourth Years encircled two Beyonds sparring below a bare cherry blossom tree. The onlookers were the pupil of an eye, contracting and expanding with the brilliance of the inner feud. Amethyst ribbons flared, whipping about as the Beyond's robes struggled to match the pace of exchanged strikes. The untuned inner drum of grunts, huffs, and growls coalesced with the outer lurch of cheers and jeers. In an instant, a stutter of several events unfolded: a lightning strike, its grim audible crack, the thud of collapse, the "Ohhh..." of defeat, and the settling of rank.

Back inside, down a length of corridor followed by two lefts and a right, the hum of First Years reading aloud sounded out in their class, Ancient History. A brief pause followed suit, then the crisp flick of a communal page flip as everyone but the tutor turned to chapter twenty-one. The gap in sustained murmur poked her shoulder, stealing her away from dreams of an unfettered romance. The chorus of tepid speech resumed while she scanned the sea of unenthused expressions. All was as it should be. She slumped with a sigh before shifting her gaze to illusions of intimacy.

Two cooks scrambled, exchanging glances between a mealtime schedule bearing faded calligraphy, a rich golden swirl of spiced beef and potato stew, and their head chef, who smoked a dingy cigarette while leaning against five crates of stacked eggplant. Every thirty seconds, the brief ember illuminated the unlit storage room and his unshaven face as he fantasized about the tutor in Ancient History. A clatter of stacked plates jingled as the senior runner, the chef's daft nephew, carted the heap through the small confines of the kitchen while a pint-sized runt of a boy followed closely in his wake, toting a basket of utensils weighing more than him.

Trembling rakes, rusty shovels, and muddied boots scraped, scooped, and stomped through the extensive grounds as a crew of groundskeepers moaned over the previous night's quarrel between violent gales and dead tree branches. Horsemen brushed shimmering blackberry-colored coats, flicked muck from reused horseshoes, repaired wagon wheels, and pitch-forked hay into stalls; sipping on home brewed rice wine to keep the autumn winds at bay.

And off in the distance, balanced on two glistening river rocks, completely removed from the bustle of Zura's daily life yet only fifty paces beyond the perimeter wall, Gracien executed First Form while repeating a new *Tao* quote.

"Be content with what you have; rejoice in the way things are. When you realize there is nothing lacking, the whole world belongs to you."

The Tao Te Ching lay over to the side: its words circled, starred, and underlined, its pages earmarked, and its cover bearing as much wear and tear as was normal for a decade of fixation.

While his body gracefully migrated through the maneuvers of the Form, his mind wrestled with the quote. As critters ran about, preparing for winter by stockpiling supplies, the stream's soothing lull ferried Gracien to previous incarnations. But that was not his goal during today's secret retreat, his fourth this month. And so, his mind parried, repeating Lao Tzu's boundless sentiments out loud this time, steadying the critters in their tracks and seducing the stream's current. He dissected and analyzed the entire sentence but found it too vast to pioneer in whole.

An idea arrived. *Separate the two sentences and meditate over each.* He nodded with his decision.

And as they tend to do, the sun drifted, and the day ripened. The winds, exhausted from the previous night's debauchery, merely hissed, and huffed. Yet even through their shallow attempts they tickled the last remnants of summer, enticing the most stubborn of leaves into fleeing from their branches. A frustrated sigh matched that of the wind's hiss.

"Be content with what you have; rejoice in the way things are."

His mind unraveled it, his heart flirted with it, his spirit danced with it, his emotions surrendered to it – his entirety rejected it.

An impossible task, rejoicing over Aya's death. *Never*, he thought. With the declaration Gracien shook the irritation from himself and dove into the abyss again, trying to deepen his intimacy with the passage.

His arms twirled like the wings of a windmill before retreating into guard as the fifth consecutive run of First Form concluded. The scream of ache in his shoulders sounded out as his arms slapped down to his sides. Gracien leapt from the river rocks to the leaf covered shore, kneeling like an injured soldier as the ache of his legs joined that of his arms. He settled himself into his meditation posture, pulling his legs into himself with the struggle of a sailor hoisting waterlogged rope.

His back straightened, his hands cupped within one another, his shoulders bled out the last of ache before being pulled back, and his eyes closed with the release of a slow and steady exhalation. He pulled Mukti's voice within himself, hearing the mantra sound out as if his old teacher had whispered it.

Om Mani Padme Hum.

And as he settled into the meditation, he allowed the pooled emotion to empty like swirling muddied waters down a drain. His mind wandered like a bird on its first flight: the sound of Ning's laugh, the coolness of his seat, the trickle of water, Master's ridiculous robe today, what would be for lunch. It was an endless stream of petty considerations. His eyes opened, he focused on his third eye location, took a deep inhalation, and tried again. After several more unsuccessful attempts sprinkled with unwavering determination, the place he hoped to find, found him.

"To a mind that is still the whole universe surrenders." Lao Tzu's words were a gong of heightened awareness.

He mentally smirked at the irony of a stilled mind thinking up quotes about a stilled mind, therefore un-stilling the mind. Gracien released the thought, followed his next breath into a newfound depth, and recentered within the stillness.

Ten, twenty, then thirty minutes passed and still the comfort and solace he experienced continued to congeal. And within its embrace he found liberation from his strife. And just as Ishayu's had over a hundred years prior, Suyin's thumbs unknowingly ticked away as a temporary smirk of harmony replaced a discontented frown.

The clap of his bare feet racing over the marbled, palace floor rang out. His readied hands swept back and forth, trying to maintain his balance as Gracien chased Aya, his laugh hunting hers. The echo of both resounded through the arched corridor safeguarding them from the elements and the courtyard just beyond it. Sunlight flashed on Ayadonna's face, the pillars spacing out the radiance every time she passed a new one. Her face glowed with a full serving of afternoon sun and her eyes were watered over with delight. Gracien's heels flaunted vibrant grass stains from chasing Aya through the garden moments ago. Her hair was a breadth away, his fingertips kissed the tip of her fluid mane before she rounded a corner, sputtering on her heels while her arms swam in circles trying to maintain the momentum. Aya's burst of nervous laughter startled birds into retreat as Gracien bellowed out his own delight. They were children again, wide-eyed, and full of glee.

Tamuza and Shenbar peered from the other side of the courtyard, halting their exchange to encourage the couple like gamblers at a chariot race. They clapped and whistled, Tamuza's piercing shrill causing a palace worker to grab at her chest in fright while steadying herself on the courtyard railing. Gracien beamed with joy, his feet were phantoms, never touching the stone while effortlessly catapulting him over the pristine flooring as he basked in Aya's jasmine scented wake. Her white linen dress billowed out behind her like an untethered sail. Palace workers clapped and cheered them on, delighting in the festivity. Gracien enjoyed the encouragement before noticing something strange. A disciple from Zura appeared, Xuilan, she considered him with a slight scowl as he raced by. His eyelids fluttered and his head shook in bewilderment.

Gracien returned to the race, shaking his vision into focus, and centering on Aya, who had a much larger lead on him now. He gritted his teeth, speeding up as they raced along a new corridor. But this one was strange, not from the palace but from Zura, the Chinese architecture standing out like a black wolf in a flock of sheep. He slowed, pausing to examine it before Aya's enticing beckon rang out. He sprinted ahead, trying to catch up but she was rounding corners and flying up steps like a loose sheet whipping about in the wind.

"AYA! Wait for me! Aya my love, slow down!" Gracien called after her, chasing the echo of her laugh.

Two more disciples from Zura appeared, both holding books and scrutinizing scowls. He blew past them in an instant, but their faces were embedded in his mind, Daiyu and Mingxia, Fourth Years he knew from training. It became colder, like the warmth of this place had fled for higher ground. As Gracien screamed after her, Zura's halls merged with those of the palace.

"Ayadonna! Where are you? Come back to me!"

He cursed as his panic surged. Like a team of ghosts, disciples poured from the walls. Gracien caught sight of Aya's fingertips as she rounded another corner, the back of her heel, or the breadth of her hair as she escaped down a flight of stairs. She was the flash of a bird, the scurry of a lizard, the last bit of a setting sun.

"Aya, stop! Please wait!"

He screamed to the emptiness sweeping in behind her. She was nowhere but everywhere. Her laugh resounded from multiple places at once. The palace was no more; he was back in Zura but somewhere new, a wing or section he had never visited before.

Aya's calls became more urgent, layered with stress and even pain.

"Gracien? GRACIEN! Help me, my love. Please!"

"Aya! Tell me where you are! Aya, please!"

He settled on a direction, sprinting, and screaming for her. Aya's screams seemed to be coming from just beyond a corner and so he raced around it, slipping, and falling to the ground. Gracien instantly recovered, picking himself up.

"No," he cried, stopping dead in his tracks.

He was a statue of fear staring down the dark, horrid corridor leading to their chambers.

"She died there," he muttered as breath launched itself from his lungs.

"Gracien, oh Gracien… please help me," Aya called from beyond the pitch-black opening leading to their bedroom.

The corridor extended, reaching further and further away as if the door was falling down an abyss.

"No, no, no… please… not this. I can't bare this again. Please no, don't make me endure this again. Aya please… PLEASE!" His hysterical pleading rang out as the darkened doorway leading to their chambers morphed into the angel of death.

"Gray-sea-ennn…" Aya called to him, her frantic beckoning weaker and frailer now as if spiked with death's kiss.

"Gracien… will I be okay? Am I going to die?"

His throat closed as his very soul seemed to wither and die.

"No, please no," he begged.

The memory of her final conscious moment pulled him under the surface of existence. He was a man drowning in the twilight, catching glimmers of a blurred moon while wrestling the fury of a merciless current. The stone corridor beneath his feet began to tilt forward, slanting towards the passage of darkness awaiting him.

"NO! Nooo!" He scrambled towards the wall, his fingertips scraping along the stone as the floor continued pitching downwards.

It was too fast, and suddenly Gracien found himself sliding down the floor while clawing at the stone.

"NOOO! Aya, help me!" he screamed while free falling towards the doorway, plunging downwards and protectively throwing his arms before his face a moment before hurtling through the blackened passage.

Gracien launched upright, holding his arms in the same protective position. He tried swallowing the dryness as sweat dripped down his brow. His thin shirt was soaked through, as were the sheets. The communal bedroom was a mass of undulating hisses, snorts, and moans. Flashes of Aya's death flickered in his mind and he squeezed his eyes closed as if to escape the scene. Gracien cursed, holding his breath, and shaking his head.

No, no, no… not again. I'm not going there, he thought. He began to speak out loud, his voice gaining strength "NO! NO!" he yelled.

"Suyin, Suyin, you're having a nightmare, Shhh…"

Ning's hushed whispers embraced Gracien as her arms did.

"It's okay… it's okay. You're safe, you're safe here with me."

Ning rocked the poor girl back and forth. Gracien puddled, melting into the embrace as his face contorted into a silent cry.

"It's okay… it's all okay. It was just a dream, it's all just a dream." Ning stroked his hair, pulling him in closer.

It had been nearly a week since his nightmare and Gracien still felt the lasting effects. He had been purposely avoiding Ning and her relentless prodding over what had happened, figuring it was easier avoiding the issue than causing yet another dispute. There was no easy way to explain it and *it* wasn't just a dream. Gracien so wished he could find the courage to finally talk about the entirety of his past, the details of Aya's death and his own fateful leap.

Rather, Gracien pondered over another masterful *Tao* quote as he walked down a lonely corridor. *"To understand the limitation of things, desire them."*

He clutched a few books in one hand while tipping his thumb to each of the four fingers in his other, having two extra fingers over Ishayu still felt a little strange.

"Maybe Ning is the closest thing I'll find to someone who can and *will* understand me without thinking I'm a raging lunatic."

As he imagined how the conversation would go, an image of Mulungwa suddenly appeared in his mind, then Kaleef and the orphan crew, then Bandhu, and finally Mukti. It wasn't so much an image of each of them but rather a sensation. Gracien felt Mulungwa's bold, understanding gaze, Kaleef's eager attention, the affection of the orphans, Bandhu's radiant smile, and Mukti's unmatched perception. It was more than just a memory but a force of nature, something beyond his understanding – as if their spirits were paying him a visit.

I could have told them; I could have told any one of them… but I wasn't strong enough. I was too afraid, and everything was too fresh, too raw. I didn't know then… what I know now.

That thought stopped him dead in his tracks. His head rose as he considered how much he had changed. His growth was a gulf; from wanting to die and choosing to do so, all the way to who he was here and now; not just wondering how to tell another soul of his plight but yearning to share it with someone special. It felt almost sad to think about his growth, his evolution. Some small part of him felt as if he was leaving the past behind or even forgetting it altogether.

No, it doesn't have to be that way. I can continue to honor Aya and our love for as many lifetimes as I'm granted, for eternity if that's what it takes.

He stood taller, taking in a deep determined breath, and picking up the pace of his stroll. He was heading for the willow tree, and not as a means of escape but as a companion. He loved reflecting, meditating, or reading under its protective embrace.

A few minutes later he was all nestled up next to the great trunk like a mouse curled up next to a slumbering dog. The wind blew through, stirring all the branches into sweeping the ground. The vibrant green leaves and vine-like nature of the tree had migrated to an otherworld, leaving a lifeless, sandy color in their wake as winter approached. All this recent reflection over past lives brought him right back to the first. It wasn't that he couldn't just speak about Aya, but that he couldn't speak *with* Aya. How he missed opening up to someone else, sharing his heart and allowing himself to be open to the idea of advice. Losing Aya meant so much more than just losing a wife and best friend, it also meant losing *being* a best friend. Gracien's mind began serving up examples of their casual time together before finding one moment in particular.

The waves of the Euphrates had rippled up the shore as they had strolled along hand in hand, trying to avoid the soggy soil. Other than the royal guards looming about, they had the entire shoreline to themselves.

Gracien had spoken with his free hand, casually gesturing, "I understand your point and I agree with you, in a sense – but Aya, Tamuza raises a valid argument. We have those budgets for a reason. Please just consider it, I told him I'd speak with you so now I have."

She motioned to respond, but he cut her off with a quick wave of his hand. "I'm not really concerned with all that..." Gracien deflated after he was finished talking.

Aya's expression morphed from one of hurt to confusion. "Something else is bothering you then?" She slowed their stroll, angling herself towards him as they continued to walk.

He nodded. "Honestly... I needed to get away from the palace, the people there, the work, the numbers, the constant pleas, and requests from senators, all of it..." He let out an overwhelmed sigh while rolling his eyes. "It's all just so much... too much and I feel like I'm never making any progress. The moment, the instant I wake up my mind rages with everything I must do that day." His tone was thick with passion and the pace of his words began accelerating. "And I can't even fall asleep some nights because my mind obsesses over everything I need to get done the *next* day. Not to mention feeling like... well that everything I did that day wasn't enough, that I could have done more!" he gave a frustrated shout, turning towards her. "I can't win!" His fingers flexed before him as if he was squeezing an invisible watermelon.

"Whoaaa... Where is all this coming from?" Aya rubbed his arms, speaking with a calmed composure.

"Raw-Ugh!" Gracien shouted as frustration boiled over, his hands slapping down on his hips.

Aya pulled him into her embrace like a mother pulling her overgrown son in for a much-needed hug. They swayed together for a while, Gracien settling in like a well-fed baby as the anger drained from him.

After several moments he said, "I needed that." Then let go of the hug but held her at arm's length. "Is it too late to run away together?"

"Ha!" Aya let out an amused laugh.

"I'm serious! We could be soaking up the sun on some beach in Africa with nine adopted children by now!"

"Nine children, Ha!" She laughed again, taking his hand as they resumed their stroll. "It's been a while since you've spent some time with the orphans... and you think you can't sleep now?" Aya laughed, swiping a strand of hair behind her ear.

Gracien huffed a smirk, his fingers intertwined in hers while their hands swung back and forth. Their footfalls sank into the mixture of sand and soil as their aimless stroll curved around each new wave crest.

"Maybe we need to break away for a bit, go somewhere, anywhere. Nothing too long, just a few days, a few days without any work. Just you… and me." His eyebrows rose with expectancy.

Aya leaned over, bumping his shoulder with hers as she smiled. "And several dozen guards of course."

"We…" Gracien considered for a moment, "can glue palm fronds on them and make 'em hold coconuts?"

Aya's bottom lip curled with consideration. "That may work actually." They both shared a laugh.

"But you really need a break. I wish I had some sage-like wisdom to share, but I'm just a pretty face," she said and Gracien snorted out a chuckle.

"Could you get away, maybe after the summer solstice festival?" she asked.

"I don't see how… and I know it would be nice, lovely to slip away for a few days but my mind…" Again he released a large sigh, "it just doesn't know the difference between here or there, palm fronds and coconuts or senators and reconciliation proceedings. No matter where I am, or what I'm doing, it's incessant, obsessive and it just won't…" He paused to consider the best way to put it, "simmer. Yeah simmer, like a boiling cauldron spilling over with thought, I just want it to simmer and settle down. I want silence. And you know something?" He looked at her. "It only ever stops chattering away when I'm alone with you. You're my simmer."

"Really?" she asked.

"Yes, really." He nodded.

"So maybe a break will be good after all, so long as we can…" He jerked his head towards the guards, "keep the palm trees at bay?"

Aya twisted into his arms, facing him, and looking up as he placed his hands around the small of her back. "I think that can be arranged… I'll probably need to have a little chat with Tamuza and um, explain some stuff and *possibly* apologize for stealing funds from a few of his infrastructure endeavors." She made a cute 'my fault' face. "Then I figure he'll be pretty happy with himself, and we'll ask to steal away while he watches everything over." She smirked.

"That may work, except we won't ask… you'll ask." He laughed.

"If not, I'll just sleep with the King and get what I want from him… Supposedly the King can do whatever he wants, right?" She tickled his waist while gazing up at him. "And from what I hear, he's a total pushover after a decent romp."

"Oh, is he now? Well either way I think we should go with plan B and then take it from there." He squeezed her tightly as the river's reach extended, kissing their feet before fleeing back into itself.

Aya smiled, closing her eyes, and tightening her embrace while resting her head on his chest. "You're my simmer too."

Gracien sank into himself, into her, into gratitude – settling deeper into his love for her. In his mind and in his heart an unspoken prayer of gratitude radiated as he rested his chin on her head and they began to sway for several, silent moments.

"Ready to head back?" his deep tone rumbled.

She nodded, they kissed. Gracien turned, resuming the aimless stroll as Aya stopped to pick something up from the sand. His feet dug into the soil, allowing the cool squishy mixture to rub between his toes. His senses seemed heightened, intensified, and somehow elevated. As he continued walking, the water wading in around him looked clearer and sounded crisper. His chest slowly expanded as the fresh air filled his lungs, enjoying the sensation as if just now noticing breath for the very first time. Color exploded across the horizon with the setting sun, and so he turned to take in the majestic scene.

His heart felt full, as if its capacity expanded. "Aya, one other thing…" He turned to her, his feet sinking deeper into the wet sand as timid, river waves crested up and over them.

"Aya?" he inquired, but she was gone.

No footsteps were in sight, all of them including his own had been washed away by the lapping waves. "AYA!" he shouted.

Like a child separated from his mother in a bustling market he spun, searching as the panic overwhelmed him. "AYAAAA!!" he screamed as guards began racing down the grass covered hillside.

"Over here!!" she called, immediately settling his dread with the mere sound of her voice.

"Oh Marduk!" Gracien slumped over with relief, resting his hands on his knees, and recovering his senses as the guards encircled him.

"Nothing to fear boys... Just Queen Ayadonna being, Queen Aya-donna," he said.

As the guards began backing away, Aya splashed in the meager wave break, the radiance of her smile rivaling that of an unabashed sun. Her boisterous laughter sent nearby ducks into flight as Gracien's own smile broke open, extending into its fullest capacity before finding himself racing along the shore. The water crashed in and around his feet as he sprinted through the shallows, then his ankles, his shins, and finally his knees before diving through the glimmering surface. He covered the final distance underwater then emerged just before her.

"Rawr!! Hahaha!" He roared and laughed, sweeping her up in his arms as they both burst out into laughter.

Her fingers swept the wet hair away from his eyes as their bodies swayed together in the current.

"Never leave me like that again," he warned with a smirk and a wink.

"Impossible, we're together... forever," Aya whispered back, embracing his face between her hands before leaning in for a kiss.

Their mouths merged, not with a kiss but with teeth and excited smiles as Gracien had held her tightly, falling backwards like a tipping oak tree.

"Aghh!" Aya laughed as they fell into the river's welcoming embrace.

Gracien could feel Aya's embrace and the warm rush of river water as he sat under the protection of the massive willow. The memory was a full meal and he felt fat and lazy after it.

"I miss you so much, honey. I just wish we could sit here together and share stories, laugh, and tell jokes, or nothing at all. Just sit here quietly, stare into one another's eyes… and simmer."

Just then an especially brisk wind swept through. The willow rattled as if chilled to the bone. The sound of ravens squawking in the distance grew as if they were alarming the forest of some impending doom. The sound grew louder as they circled overhead before landing in separate parts of the tree. The flimsy branches bobbed with their great weight and heavy glares.

He strained his neck trying to get a good look at each. "They're just so odd and mysterious."

As he moved to get a better look at the third one, he couldn't help feeling that something beyond casual, idle time was occurring. There was a weight in the air, like he was being spied on or a storm was brewing in the distance. He sat up, his eyes scanning the courtyard while his ears perked up too. A tingling sensation enveloped him and then the ravens began squawking loudly. Gracien slowly stood, using the tree to press himself up as he continued investigating his surroundings. He exchanged glances between the birds and the courtyard as the sensation of alarm morphed into one of comfort. Gracien couldn't make sense of it or even put the shift into words. It felt as if the invisible presence spying on him had suddenly pounced, wrapping him up in warm, notable vibrations. His mind flooded with images of Aya: laughing, sleeping, eating, and her glorious gaze. It was as if Gracien had no control over what he thought. He was taken over by thoughts and visualizations of Ayadonna as his body trembled with an overwhelming sensation. His lips quivered out the question,

"Aya? Is... is that you?"

An explosion of confirming tingles rippled through his being. Gracien fell to his knees, his smile pushing the limits of its reach as he explored the feeling.

"Aya my love... It is you, isn't it!"

The ravens squawked, startling Gracien back to reality as all his visions faded but one. It was as simple as could be, Aya sweeping a strand of hair behind her ear while sharing a casual smile. The image was blurred, frozen in time. Time ceased to pass, and he melted into the moment.

Having temporarily abandoned reality, his mind slowly returned. And with its return, came thoughts of how what just happened couldn't be real, a delusion of grief, a farce he played on himself. Gracien shook his head, trying to keep that one simple image of Aya in it as he smiled. His mind could think what it liked, but his heart knew the truth. He didn't need to understand the particulars of what just happened, all he had to do was accept that it did happen.

"She just paid me a visit... She came to me."

His smile exploded into a laugh, giving the ravens a fright, and sending them off. With their departure, a bundle of toasted leaves showered down around Gracien. The excitement was almost too much, he felt like dancing. And so, as the leaves rained down around him, that's exactly what he did.

Three days later, and now it was the metaphysical experience under the willow that lingered. Gracien felt better than he could recall himself feeling in quite some time. He stood taller when he walked, paid more attention to his surroundings, and smiled quite a bit more too. He also engaged with other disciples more, finding himself maintaining eye contact and enjoying the interaction. He was extra nice to Ning and not to butter her up for anything, although he did have a special request which might make Ning recoil with dread. But he genuinely wanted to be kinder. His bubbly energy had even managed to pull a slight smirk from Master Chi as he tinkered with Suyin's form earlier that morning. Though his bubbly energy was not very helpful in preventing a raspberry sized knot and one inch cut from forming over his left eye. He had kind of asked for it when he requested to spar with a Beyond, as all the cheerfulness had given him a false sense of confidence. During Contention, he had routinely bested Fourth Years. And on five separate occasions a Fifth Year too, three of which were men. But today would not be the day he bested a Beyond. It wasn't even close.

After missing a block, catching a center-line strike to the forehead, then a, "oh my gosh Suyin! I'm so sorry!" followed by a stream of blood cascading over her eye – that was that.

Twenty-seven minutes later, which was eighteen minutes longer than it took Master Chi to hurriedly rush Gracien to Zura's infirmary, his short legs dangled over the gurney as he awaited treatment.

The nurses there were usually quick to attend any injury within minutes, if not seconds. But today they seemed to have their hands full, and Master Chi had yet to leave as he watched them from the infirmary's door. There was a First Year man, or rather boy, across the room and three beds down. Gracien was unable to get a look at him while putting pressure on his cut and being hurried to the furthest gurney. A paneled divider was partially extended so he couldn't see the boy's face either, but he sounded young, and he sounded scared. Gracien exchanged his right arm for his left as the ache of placing pressure on his cut was taking its toll. Something wasn't right, he felt it in his gut. The boy's feet kept kicking out and tensing, but his arms and hands seemed glued to the side of the gurney. Suddenly Master Chi yelled from the doorway, startling Gracien as he had never seen him so angry. Gracien's hand dropped, ripping at the crusty blood, and tearing a new hole in his wound. The pain didn't even cause him to flinch, as what transpired across the room numbed his senses.

Master rushed over, pushing one of the nurses aside then administering something into what Gracien guessed was the boy's mouth. His wrists were strapped to the gurney and his muffled cries and screams chilled him to the bone. Gracien's mouth hung open in disbelief as his legs kicked about like someone being choked to death, striking Master right in the gut after several moments of aimless bursts. Master grunted in response then pressed forward, slamming the gurney into the wall while the two nurses backpedaled as if trying to sneak away. Both donned appalled expressions, one even allowed a hand to slowly rise, cupping her mouth in terror. The boy gasped, choked, screamed, and then fell silent – his legs slowing into an eerie idleness. Master backed up, pulling at his robe, and petting away wrinkles as his gaze remained fixed to the boy.

"He'll wake in ten minutes or so, make sure he finishes the rest of the serum. Clean up the scrapes and burns from the straps and tell him that if his insubordination continues, he'll suffer a much harsher punishment compared to this," Master spoke as calmly as if he was discussing the weather.

As Master spoke, the nurses kept their heads down as if they were praying. Then both bowed and leapt into action, their perfectly white attire flashed as they bound around trying to keep themselves busy. Master moved to leave before catching sight of Gracien from the corner of his eye. He must have forgotten he was there. His head slowly twisted towards his other student. Gracien felt himself wanting to flee. As Gracien met his master's gaze, it bore through him like fire through a hayfield. Any previous notion of compassion, love, or sympathy was completely gone. A cloak of deceit had been pulled back before his very eyes and he saw Master for what he was. No more disingenuous smiles, sympathetic nods, or comforting expressions – just darkness. What may have been even worse, was that he knew Gracien was seeing his true form. His trembling gaze narrowed, and hate slithered from it like smoke from an extinguished oil lamp. He heard his teeth grind and felt the room darken. Gracien suddenly realized he shouldn't be meeting his gaze at all, and his head promptly dropped. Having bested his glare, Master disappeared through the door in a flash of radiant teal.

Gracien's eyes opened half a minute later to find several droplets of blood in his lap and the boy's legs giving off slight twitches. One of the nurses attended Gracien a moment later, making quick work of his wound then sending him off without a word exchanged between them.

"The wise man is one who, knows, what he does not know," Gracien mumbled under his breath.

Gracien and Ning sat with a group of Fourth Years reviewing sketches of a new maneuver they'd be adapting tomorrow. Master Chi had an artist sketch out Master holding the various maneuvers perfectly, so he was more than willing to share the drawings with his dedicated apostles. He also had several perspectives captured so that everyone would know the exact angle in the bend of his knee from both the front as well as the back vantage point. As the loose sketches were passed around the table, little was said beyond someone pointing out a small detail others may have missed.

Ning elbowed Gracien. "How's your cut?" she inquired while leaning her head from side to side as if the sketch was 3D.

"It's fine." Gracien's fingers padded the bandage as he recalled visions of the boy's feet kicking wildly. "Listen, I need to talk to you," he whispered just loud enough for Ning to hear.

"Good, I still have a bad bruise on my ribcage from two weeks ago. I'd rather have a cut, heals faster," Ning mindlessly returned without removing her eyes from the sketch.

"I said I need to talk with you." Gracien noticed his voice was much louder than he wished with the wave of frustration washing over him.

One of the Fourth Year's looked up from his sketch.

He had Ning's attention now. "About what? Is everything alright?"

Gracien nestled himself closer to Ning. "Not here, not now." He scanned the room. "Meet me at the willow tree after sunset," his words were the hiss of a newborn snake.

Ning's face was a statue of concentration, as if there was a delay in her interpreter deciphering the message. Gracien's eyes trembled as they scanned Ning's.

"Okay, after sunset," Ning whispered back before they both fell silent, resuming their work.

An eager dusk blanketed the landscape. Gracien teetered back and forth, flexing the build-up of ache in his knees before settling with a sigh. His knees were tucked into his chest with his arms wrapped around them. He was perched on one of the mighty willow branches like a watchful owl but traded its stoic nature for one of impatience.

"She's always late. Why is she always late?" Gracien grumbled.

He could feel the irritation bubble up like a geyser. He had been waiting for over thirty minutes and every minute after the first fifteen was sending him further down the rabbit's hole of delusion. His mind rattled off one reason after the next for Ning's tardiness: Ning wanted to show up late on purpose, Ning got into an argument that escalated into a fight with that arrogant Beyond, Jiahao, Ning sat around talking shit about Gracien, someone told Master about their relationship, Master got ahold of Ning and was choking something down her throat, Ning ran away, Ning, Ning, Ning...

"Enough!" Gracien shouted loud enough to startle himself.

The night came alive: crickets chirped in harmony, frogs sporadically croaked, night owls cooed, the stream's trickle serenaded the wind's caress, and the branches trembled with delight. He had been masked in delusion this whole time, completely cut off from reality as his mind untangled one new negative delusion after the next. Gracien sat upright, his face tilting from side to side as he reflected.

Why is it that my mind only contrived negative or scary delusions? All of them made Ning look bad and made me feel horrible. Why didn't I imagine her helping a fellow student who hurt himself, or teaching someone a new maneuver and just running late? It didn't have to be a noble reason either. Why didn't my mind conjure up some neutral reason like she stubbed her toe or just lost track of time and was now rushing to meet me?

He continued pondering this curiosity before hearing a crunch ring out in the deadened leaves. His hand squeezed a branch as his eyes latched onto the empty courtyard. The crunch came again so he needlessly leaned behind the tree trunk and its umbrella of branches. Like an investigating gopher, Ning's head popped out from a wall of bushes then instantly disappeared. Gracien laughed as Ning's cautious expression pulled the irritation from him like an uncorked drain before scrambling down the tree.

"Pssst!" Gracien hissed.

"There you are!" Ning rushed him. "I've been waiting here for over thirty minutes! You said meet you at nightfall! I thought something happened to you! Maybe Master caught you or you ran away!" Ning rushed Gracien, pointing a finger as one accusation after the next sliced through the night.

"Easy! Easy Ning, I've been *here* the whole time! I was up in the tree! Waiting for *you* for thirty minutes. Calm down, it's okay," Gracien pleaded with his hands up defensively.

Ning moved to rebut then another crunch sounded out. Both girls froze before making a silent dash for the willow. They climbed up high enough to stay hidden then waited for the source to reveal itself. The glow of a lantern peeked past the stone wall first, followed by the scowling face of a groundskeeper. Ning and Gracien held their breath as the man aimlessly stalked the courtyard scanning the night. Three weaving laps later and the lantern's glow was swallowed up by the night.

"Let's go," Gracien whispered and the two made their move.

It should have been a two-minute escape, but with the wall's decaying platform, Ning took three times longer just working up the courage to cross. They eventually made it through the gauntlet of difficulty and down to the safety of the forest. The sharp edge of a crescent moon sliced through the canopy as stars shimmered brightly with the moon's diluted luster. The girls sat next to one another on a fallen tree trunk a few paces off the stream's edge.

"I've been coming here for months now. It's nice, it simmers me."

"Months, why... why didn't you ever tell me?" Ning asked.

Gracien could tell she was hurt. "I..." His eyelids flickered as he dug for a lie. "I just thought you wouldn't want to come?" he volunteered while knowing he was simply possessive.

It's my time to be alone with the river, with Aya, he thought.

"Why would you think that?" Ning shot back defensively.

"Well with all the height issues, the broken wall and then having to escape over it… and then having to do it all over again to get back in. I figured it was all too much for you." Gracien's eyes widened like a fisherman's tensing a bite.

"I guess that makes sense," Ning replied.

"But that's not important now. I asked you out here to tell you something strange… but saying that out loud, it's not that strange." Gracien shook his head in confusion as Ning's expression puzzled over.

"It's Master Chi. He's not who we think he is. Although lately, I feel like I've always known this… somehow. He's not some wise sage guiding us all to enlightenment or something," Gracien spoke slowly, trying to find the right words.

"I probably could have told you that," Ning replied.

"What, really?" Now it was Gracien who was sporting a puzzled expression.

"Yeah… isn't it obvious? What sage beats people for not abiding by his rules?" Ning huffed.

"Well, I guess that's true. But they received discipline for falling out of line," Gracien said as Ning moved to interrupt. "Wait, wait it's okay. I think we're both on the same side of things. Just let me tell you what I saw," he continued without Ning's consent. "Master choked one of the First Years while I was waiting to get this treated." He pointed to the forehead bandage.

In typical Ning fashion she gasped then sputtered off a handful of questions "Choked a First Year? Who was it? What did he do? Is he okay?"

After Gracien relayed the entire experience at the infirmary, Ning sat with a glazed look on her face.

Gracien audibly swallowed the dread as the horrid image of the boy's twitching legs replayed in his mind.

"I'm just glad you didn't have to see it, it was horrific, Ning."

Ning sat with a hand cupped over her mouth, gasping in disgust at every turn.

"Oh, my Suyin, I'm so sorry you had to see that. Are you okay?" Ning placed an arm around him.

"Yes, I've... I've seen worse," he trailed off before coming back. "I was fortunate actually, to see his real colors, to experience the true nature of our horrible *Master!*" His teeth ground down as his anger rose.

"Okay, okay let's take a deep breath now and try to relax." Ning took a nice deep inhalation as Gracien stewed.

"It's okay, I'm fine. It's just so horrible. He acts so noble but he's nothing but a fraud. He's a big part of the reason I asked you here to-night." He grabbed Ning's hand. "I have something to ask you." Gracien swallowed.

Ning softened further, turning her full body towards Gracien. "Okay."

Gracien inhaled. "Let's leave this place, together?" His eyes widened with expectancy.

"Leave? But we just got here?" Ning returned with confusion.

"Not here, Ning. Not this forest. Zura. Let's leave Zura." Ning moved to pull her hand away, but Gracien held it firmly.

"It's okay... I know it's a lot to ask. But I've thought it through, and I know, I just know we'd be fine out there." His head nodded to the horizon as he pulled Ning's hand into his lap.

"You mean leave, like really leave?" It clicked for Ning, "Aghhh... you mean escape, just like this but never go back." Her eyes examined Gracien for several silent moments.

"Yes, that's exactly what I mean," Gracien spoke to the sky. "I don't want to stay here anymore... I feel like I'm just not right for this place.

That I'm meant for another life... far away from here." He sighed. "But you could go with me!"

Ning's brow ascended and then all at once dropped. "Aghhh... I see. It's not that you want to run off with me... You want to run off and wouldn't mind a companion?" Her glare fell on Gracien.

"No. I want both." Gracien turned his entire body towards Ning, scooting closer. "I don't want to be here anymore, this place... There's just something about it, something strange." Gracien struggled to find the words without going into his past. "It's eerie for me, uncomfortable and awkward. It feels like I'm wearing my sandals on the wrong feet or like my robes inside out. It's hard to explain, but all I know is that I need to leave." He sighed.

"Everyone wants to leave Suyin!" Ning shot back. "This place is okay at times I guess, but it's a cruel, cruel place... Forcing us all to be something we're not, to *conform* into what *they* want us to be."

"Exactly. So, let's leave Ning! We can do this together!" Gracien took Ning by the shoulders.

"And as for leaving here and only wanting a companion, that's not true. Ning, you're the only reason I *haven't* left yet... and I'm not leaving without you." Gracien's passion melted Ning like a flame to butter.

Ning's eyes welled up and the two collided into an embrace, feeling something more powerful and true for the first time in a very long time. Both squeezed one another harder, their hands trying to regain mass on the other as if slipping away.

Allowing himself to be vulnerable was cathartic and empowering. Gracien hadn't experienced this feeling since long before Aya's sickness. The words would eventually come, and his story would be told, but for now this was a milestone of growth. The strength in their arms gradually deflated and the tears came forth.

"Do the difficult things while they are easy and do the great things while

they are small. A journey of a thousand miles must begin with a single step?" He phrased Lao Tzu's sentiment as a question.

Ning looked to him, nodding in understanding as she breathed deeply, grabbing, and squeezing Gracien's hand.

They marinated in the silence of trust and love for several moments before Ning croaked out, "okay... okay let's do it."

Gracien grabbed Ning by the shoulders. "Really? Are you sure? I mean... You're serious, right?"

Ning nodded, wiping her tears. "Yes, of course," she exclaimed before Gracien yanked her back into an embrace.

"Ohhh yes-yes-yes! Thank you!!" Gracien responded as they both cried, hugging, and swaying like reunited lovers.

Taking this all in, the gaze of another glowed under the pale moonlight. The groundskeeper from earlier stood hidden behind a tree. He chose his hiding spot well, far enough not to be discovered but close enough to hear their entire conversation – and he had heard more than enough. Moments later his silent footing retreated into the safety of the darkness as he withdrew.

As they warmed up, stretching, and shaking their limbs into readiness, Gracien and Ning toyed with each other, exchanging flirtatious smiles and funny faces from across the training room. This day seemed just a bit more beautiful after their successful rendezvous the previous night.

"Everyone, make your way into the courtyard," Master Chi's voice boomed throughout the hall followed by the thundering of his quickened footsteps.

Several disciples gasped. His instructions were a death announcement, sending a chill through the entire room. Some began shuffling towards the door while others stood frozen in fear. He had only uttered those words one other time this year, which was a rarity compared to last. Master's eerie omen meant one thing and one thing alone: Reparation.

Gracien recalled Master's speech on his very first day of orientation. He was so casual and almost charming about it all.

"This room..." He had gestured with a graceful sweep of his hand. "This is our sanctuary, a temple of the mind, body, and spirit. Within these walls we will learn the sacred art of kung fu, and honor this space with constructive, inspiriting energies. Anything falling outside of this paradigm... must fall outside of these here walls." He gestured again, peering up at the ceiling before his hand swept along, pausing on the open door of the courtyard.

"We conduct our discouragement training there, in the courtyard. Reparation must be made for any offense. And I alone distinguish when an offense is owed restitution."

Suyin had exchanged confused glances between Master Chi and the doors of the courtyard.

"We conduct Reparation within the courtyard so that the evil energies released can escape our sanctuary without impediment."

He had looked so smug, as if he was proud of how clever he had been without revealing enough for the new disciples to grasp the true meaning of Reparation. That meaning cemented with the crack of a grass reed striking the back of a Second Year three weeks later. Gracien could still hear the echo and see the red lacing race across the boy's pale flesh.

Gracien was pulled from the memory with an immediate wave of fear washing over him. His mind struggled with all the secret wrongdoing he and Ning had gotten away with over the past few months. So many reasons for him to be the one making Reparation, but he wasn't alone. Everyone there wrestled with similar thoughts as they trotted forth like shackled prisoners making their way into what was once a glorious morning. The sun's radiance still shone down but it couldn't lift the internal gloom of their own minds. Each of them sifted through various offenses, the most severe of them arriving first and then scaling down to something stupid like leaving an unwashed plate in their bed. Eventually they all ended up on the same dreadful thought, the same question that turned their chests to stone and sent their spirits into hiding.

Will it be me?

This was followed up by a second thought.

But why would it be me, it couldn't be me?

This initiated a flurry of reasons why it would be someone else. They mentally ticked off all the offenses they knew full well were committed by their fellow classmates. They began tossing narrowed glares or timid glances towards one another as they marched along. Master had played them perfectly; in an instant they were pitted against one another and all for good reason. Reparation was a cruel, soulless act. It was no wonder their heads hung like prisoners being led to the gallows.

As Gracien and the others filed into position, he was hijacked from his frantic worry by a very strange event. He caught it from the corner of his eye and had to do a double take, squinting as he kept pace with the others. Three men wearing dirty, charcoal-colored cloaks carried what looked like a rolled-up rug through a side door of the courtyard. They were about a hundred feet away, but for some reason it just didn't sit well with Gracien. The load they carted didn't bear the rigidity of a rug as it kind of sagged in the middle. One carried the back end while the two others stood on either side toting it like a log.

"Suyin. Ning. Square up!" Master's words sliced through the moment like a sword, stealing the breath from Gracien's lungs.

The air wouldn't come. The others began backing away from him and Ning as if they were two lepers disrobing in the market. Gracien was a statue. His feet wouldn't move, his throat wouldn't swallow, and his face began flushing before Master Chi breathed life into him.

"NOW!" he roared.

Ning and Gracien didn't have to move, as the others formed a circle around them. Both girls knew they had been discovered, and it didn't matter for what. This wasn't a trial; it was a sentencing. But Master had never before asked two disciples to square up, and so the terror of uncertainty was an added layer of dread. Ning's feet slid towards Gracien's. The stone beneath them screamed as they made the final approach, standing a foot away from one another. Neither had raised their guard. Gracien finally picked his head up, only to discover Ning's eyes drowning in tears. Just over her shoulder, Gracien saw the fresh reed leaning up against the cherry blossom tree, with the groundskeeper from last night standing off in the distance. The shadowed man took everything in like he was betting on a sure winner. In an instant everything clicked.

It was him. We were careless and he must have seen us, he thought.

A tower of guilt crashed down on top of him.

Poor Ning. I'm the one who got us into this mess. It would've never happened if I didn't ask her to sneak out.

His vision refocused on Ning as the groundskeeper faded into the background. Ning was a mess; she couldn't have looked any worse if she had just been sentenced to death. Her guard rose, it trembled as if she was suffering hypothermia. Gracien didn't raise his guard but instead stared at Ning, wordlessly begging for forgiveness.

"SQUARE UP!" Master's voice boomed, his face twisting with rage as spittle shot from his mouth.

"No." Gracien didn't think he had uttered the word loud enough, but the communal gasp confirmed that he had.

"What! How dare you!"

Master's Zen tone had devolved into a menacing growl as he raced forward like a rabid dog. He stopped short, instantly composing himself and wiping a slight beading of sweat from his pristine scalp.

"No matter. I had other plans for you two. It will be better if both of you are at your best, uninjured and strong."

He shared that very same, smug smirk. Gracien motioned to go after him, but Ning had grabbed him by the arm. Luckily, Master's back was already turned as he approached the reed.

"Just fight me, put up your guard!" Ning shouted.

Gracien never let his eyes leave Master as he replied through clenched teeth. "It's too late for that now." He took his time speaking as his hand moved to peel Ning's off his shoulder.

"Very well indeed... For today I won't be the one who collects the reparation. Instead... it will be both of you."

Master tested the integrity of the reed, slashing the air with three successive swipes. He took his time as if he was a boy trying to amuse himself. Satisfied, he approached the outer rim of the circle while trying to bend the ash-colored reed, but it was strong and eager to return to its true form.

"Three lashes each, dealt by the other of course." He threw the reed into the middle of the circle, it rattled on the stone just before Ning's feet.

"And for every lash that doesn't draw blood... an additional three lashes will be added."

Another communal gasp sounded out. The judgment was ruthless, but everyone knew this wasn't the first time Master Chi had devised such heinous theatrics.

"Go first." Suyin tried reassuring Ning with an encouraging nod and a softened gaze.

Ning shook her head, but barely. Suyin bent down, picking up the reed and handing it to Ning.

"Don't waver with your strike... Make it true and make it count."

Their hands touched as Suyin handed over the reed. Everything in the courtyard stilled as time slowed. Suyin didn't give her a moment more to think, turning away from Ning then immediately removing the top part of her robe. She was slow and meticulous in her movement, carefully hiding her breasts within her arms. Somehow the awareness and grace of her movement made her think of Mukti bathing in the river. As the robe fell around her waist, three pink scars crept down her back from a debt already paid.

Ning looked to the reed, glaring at it for far too long. Her hands trembled as the awaiting horror crippled her.

"Begin!" Master yelled, startling Ning back to reality.

She looked at him and Master nodded, encouraging her with that self-righteous smirk. Finding his arrogance more repulsive than her awaiting punishment, she averted her gaze.

Her eyes landed back on Suyin. Ning's hand raised like a shaky kite on frail winds. She squeezed her eyelids closed as tightly as possible, pushing another wave of tears from them as her hand came down with a scream resembling that of a tormented prisoner. The crack of the reed on Suyin's flesh reverberated throughout the courtyard as Suyin winced, a sole tear escaping.

"Five more lashes!" Master Chi's horrid command chilled the scene as the sting of a bloodless abrasion incinerated Suyin's flesh.

"Aghh-huh!" Ning cried out as if it were her on the tail end of the strike.

Suyin's fingers dug into her arms, her fingernails nearly drawing blood.

"Ning! Draw blood!" she screamed without turning to face her.

The next few minutes were unbearable. The younger disciples cried while the older ones brandished distant glares, looking beyond, or burying the horrid reality. Everyone could feel the palpable weight of trauma being branded onto Ning's soul. She wasn't made for this, she wasn't some callous soldier but a timid, fragile girl.

Then, it was done. Suyin's trembling fingers tried covering herself up, but it was impossible. Master stepped through the circle, taking his time to approach. His confident fingertips grabbed the ends of Suyin's robe then gently pulled it over her shoulders. She winced, pausing her efforts for a moment before finishing. Five violet fissures slowly raced along the blue-colored silk as the material hugged her battered flesh.

Master leaned down, his lips stopping a breadth from Suyin's ear. "Your little escape route will be gone by week's end." He sneered as he retreated backwards.

"Now switch," he over pronounced the words while stepping back through the circle.

Ning cried out as Suyin took three deep breaths, trying to compose herself. She didn't want to cry anymore. She didn't want to fuel Master's sadistic lust by revealing her pain and fear, but she couldn't stop the tears from coming. Ning and Suyin's gazes united, holding fast long enough for Suyin to offer a sympathetic smile.

"It's okay, I promise it will be fast and it won't hurt until the final strike settles. Trust me, Ning."

Suyin reached forward, prying the reed from Ning's lifeless hand.

Ning prepared herself, removing her robe and covering her subtle breasts. She turned as slowly as a migrating moon. Her fingers dug into her arms with anticipation as she inhaled one endless breath. Unlike Suyin's back, Ning's was as bare and pure as a newborn's. A wave of remorse washed over Suyin for having to destroy such a beautiful, untouched canvas.

Suyin's hand regripped the reed, and she lifted her arm. The anticipated lashings shrieked with agony and her arm nearly fell. She gritted her teeth, raising it higher as she screamed with rage. With a flurry of instant violence, she began. The disciples gasped in disbelief, their circle billowing outwards as if a fireball had erupted.

Ning was so riddled with adrenaline and trauma that she barely felt the sting of punishment. But just as Suyin had promised, the pain came roaring through. It muted Ning's surroundings but everyone else was shaken by Master's roar.

"NINE MORE LASHES!"

"NOOO!" Ning cried out.

Master bellowed a mighty laugh before being gagged by what he saw. Ning's back bore three, clean lacerations which all began pooling with blood. He darted forward, pushing the others out of his way then spinning Ning around.

"If you want to lead them you must place yourself behind them." Gracien, barely standing and heaving breath, spoke as if Lao's words were his last.

No one had ever dared to speak to Master Chi like this. A demon seized his face. His eyes went wide, his nostrils flared, and his teeth flexed. His hands crushed Ning's shoulders before spinning on Gracien. Like a cobra he moved to strike just as Gracien's hand dropped the reed, his eyes rolled into the back of his head, and he collapsed right before Master Chi's feet.

Before his dream had even ended, he felt it. Her hand, the softness of the back of her fingers rubbing down his cheek, a breath of time, then another ran down his cheekbone and into his thick beard. Gracien's eyelids struggled to open as his mind wrestled with the meshing of consciousness. His eyelids fluttered into an embrace of absolute whiteness; a purity so intense it beat his vision back into retreat – but it was all for nothing. A flash, an instant so short no amount of time could have captured it, but that was all it took. A sliver of a glimpse and his eyes shot open like someone thrown into a pool.

"Aya, is it you? No, it can't be?" he stuttered as his eyes adjusted to the extreme radiance enveloping them both.

Aya's gleaming smile and quick giggle confirmed his senses were true, causing Gracien to leap up.

"Aya! Oh, my sweet, sweet love!"

His arms flew around her, pulling her into himself as if she had been brought back to life. Her laugh ignited something within him born long ago, something words alone could never define. He was praise – birdsong with the arrival of dawn. He was adoration – the tide's endless pursuit of the moon. He was love – the abounding, ethereal connection shared between two souls unbound by space or time.

"Aya! I can't... I just can't," Gracien stumbled over his words as Aya's translucent appearance solidified.

"Is this real or is this a dream?" He pushed her away, examining her at arm's length.

"Yes, this is real and yes, this is a dream." She smirked.

Her unblinking eyes gazed into the depths of him, her smile gleamed, her face beamed with veneration. But a moment later the luster of her radiance dulled; her face sank, her smile retreated, her eyes teared over.

"Gracien, I see how hard it is for you. I feel your pain and the depth of your grief. I'm here to remind you, my love, that we are bound together forever. I am always there with you. There's nowhere to run to. There's no escape to be made as we are united no matter where you are. Stay and breathe... Allow yourself to heal. Allow yourself to learn."

Aya's hand rubbed down his bearded face as his eyes pooled with tears.

"Learn what? What am I supposed to learn that will replace you? What could I possibly learn to banish the darkness?"

"To love again." Her head tilted as her brow furrowed with concern.

"I don't want to love another Aya... Only you," he spoke like a man pleading for his life.

He and Aya drifted about, floating through a never-ending sea of pearled luminescence.

"Love yourself, Gracien. Learn to love yourself, truly and completely, and you will love in a way that magnifies your very being. Always remember, believe in us and trust that you are exactly where you're meant to be."

Her fingers rubbed his cheek again but this time pressing through like a mountain's peak pushing through cloud cover. She smiled, embracing him as he sobbed into her arms like he had done so many times before.

"Believe in us and learn to love again." Her words became an echo and her form merged with his as the two united with a wonderful flash of brilliance.

Gracien's eyelids fluttered open, and he was back. Aya's image was there one moment but then, as if painted on a puddle, it dissipated into nothingness. Her words lingered, echoing from a place beyond the world of dreams.

"Learn to love again."

Then something hissed, followed by a grunt and Gracien's eyes went wide.

The infirmary was extremely dark, but he could hear Ning's labored breath while battling a nightmare. Gracien tried to recall more of his dream, but it was already beyond the horizon. Ning gasped, her body tensing as her legs kicked out.

She yelled, "Aghhh!"

Gracien's whole body tensed in fright before moving to react. He was stupefied by the fury of his own wounds tearing through his back like a raging fire. His hands tore at the sheets as if his legs were being severed. Nearly a minute later and his lungs finally sucked in a breath. Ning yelled out, violently tossing to her side. Gracien saw the blood soaking through her bandages as she thrashed about, rebelling against the night terrors.

Gracien took a deep breath, bit down on his lip, and pulled himself up into a sitting position. The adrenaline kicked in, but the pain was excruciating. Sweat beaded over his brow as he gasped for air. Ning was close, only one bed over and she continued thrashing against her sheets. Gracien spun his legs over the bed, placed his feet on the floor then sucked in a deep breath and stood. That was a huge mistake. Like sunburned skin being pulled and slapped, the flesh on his back revolted against the movement. The fatigue and faintness returned as blood neglected his head but poured into his legs. He steadied himself for a few moments, focusing his entirety on his breath as Ning continued wrestling with her nightmare. Gracien's eyelids blinked three times and he inhaled, standing up a bit taller as a wince washed over his face before taking three steps forward. He arrived at Ning's bedside. Gracien noticed that neither of their wrists were strapped down, recalling the boy from before and feeling grateful for this small gift.

He pressed Ning's shoulders down, knowing the wave of pain she was about to experience.

"Ning, wake up. Ning!"

Several shoves later and Ning's eyes exploded open. The very next instant a wave of anguish washed over her face. Gracien held her shoulder down with one hand and cupped her mouth with the other. Ning screamed through it. The sound of her muffled moans didn't spread more than a few feet, but they sent shivers down Gracien's back. Gracien moved his hand and Ning drew in a quick, deep breath before clapping it back in place. Ning followed up with another defeated moan.

After a whole minute, Ning's eyes finally began to relax.

"I'm going to move my hand away, don't scream, okay?"

Ning nodded and Gracien peeled his hand away as a leash of saliva sagged then broke. Gracien's head dropped onto Ning's chest as the two heaved labored breaths in unison. They sat there for five minutes trying to gather their sanity.

Gracien's head lifted, and his gaze fell on an empty gurney, the one where the boy had laid two days prior. It was bare and rustic: no sheets, no pillow, no comfort, no nothing. The rawness of it screamed.

Where is he? He should still be there, sleeping or at least watching us right now.

His jaw flexed before he gasped, his mouth falling open as the little color that was left poured from his face.

"The three cloaked men… Just before the reparation."

He murmured to himself as the scene replayed in slow motion: the men's cautious stride, their soiled cloaks billowing in the light breeze, the sag of the bundle, the awkwardness of how they lugged him about.

"It wasn't a rug, it was the boy," he whispered.

He fell to his knees with the realization. His mind raged with the thought, the truth tearing right through him. It numbed his body and suffocated his spirit.

Ning noticed, trying to sit up before a deep wince turned into a groan. Gracien shook his head, gathering himself as his jaw muscles flexed with hatred. His teeth clenched as he pressed himself up, pushing through a wince before taking Ning's hand and squeezing it.

"We're getting out of here, Ning. We're getting out of here right now."

Their unblinking gazes held firm for several silent moments. Without the slightest gesture they each knew the other was fully committed. They were going through with their escape, not eventually, but now.

Their bare feet stalked through the corridor leading to their bedroom. It had taken them twice as long sneaking about weathering waves of pain and impaired dexterity. They were each half themselves, but together they made a whole, leaning on and pulling one another along. Besides the occasional grunt, neither of them had uttered a sound since agreeing on an escape plan just before leaving the infirmary. It wasn't the best of plans either.

"Grab only what we need and make for the willow."

It took Ning a few seconds to realize that was the extent of Gracien's plan before biting her bottom lip and nodding nervously.

They were almost there but stopped just short of the communal bedroom. Ning felt as if her heart was going to burst through her chest and Gracien's frenzied pulse was making her dizzy. The hisses and grunts coming from the sleeping mass grew louder as they neared. Gracien stood just behind Ning.

"Only what you need," he whispered into her ear while giving her shoulders an encouraging squeeze.

Ning's head dipped in understanding and they both made for their beds. As Gracien tiptoed through the maze of beds, he couldn't help but recall his awakening in this room many months ago, then making a similar escape. He grabbed his satchel, shoving anything he could fit inside. His mind raced with worry, feeling like he moved too slowly and that Ning might leave him behind. But he could only go so fast while keeping quiet. His hands suddenly froze as the realization took a moment to register. Someone was screaming. Like an underwater shriek the sound was muffled and incoherent.

"WUHH! WUNNN! RUHHH! - RUNNN! RUN SUYIN!!"

Gracien's eyes went wide. He dropped to his knees, cowering at the foot of his bed. It was Ning.

She screamed again, this time it was eerily clear and impossibly loud. "Suyin Run! Ruu…"

Her shriek was cut short with a sharp whack then a loud thud. Someone knocked her out and let her fall. Gracien cupped his own mouth in terror, sitting there like a deer just before an arrow pierces its neck.

Chaos erupted.

"Get a lantern! Find her!" someone yelled, and the room exploded into a frenzy.

Gracien's mind exploded with panic, but one word surfaced through all the chaos.

Run.

The room was cloaked in darkness. He grabbed his satchel and sprinted towards the corridor, not even feeling his wounds as the adrenaline masked them. A dozen confused students littered his route but he bound through them. He sprinted through the corridor, stumbling, and falling into a slide, then popping back up to his feet and bounding through the courtyard door.

All he heard was the sound of his rapid exhalations as he made for the willow. His feet galloped across the cold grass like that of a hunted gazelle. Gracien's pupils were as wide as an addict's as he approached the tree, the fear and remorse of leaving Ning already tearing through her.

Go back for her! his mind screamed.

Only he knew it was hopeless.

His saving grace swayed in the wind as the great willow beckoned him. His arms and legs scampered up the massive trunk, making quick work of it before hopping over to the stone wall. He could hear them, whoever *them* was as they scoured the grounds. He glanced over his shoulder as his feet traversed the stone. Lanterns danced through the courtyard like enormous, drunken fireflies. His arms shot out to the side while balancing across the broken section of the wall. Some of the stone crumpled beneath his feet as he dashed over it much quicker than usual. His body fought the strain of injuries as it struggled keeping up with the pace of his tyrannical mind.

The dead tree trunk was only a few paces away and he was already planning his return.

"I'll come back for her," he pleaded with himself.

In the very next moment Gracien's arms were flailing through the air as he plummeted towards the ground. His frantic gaze looked up to see not to the top of Zura's stone wall, but the Babylonian cliffside as he fell for what seemed a lifetime. The thud of his body smashing into the forest floor came first, then the crunch of flesh and bone, then the shriek of death.

The weight in his chest was unbearable, the air wouldn't come, and blood oozed from his mouth and ears. His body lay sprawled over some

light forest debris, which helped to break his fall but not enough to prevent its undoing. He couldn't move any part of himself as the burn of
airlessness terrorized his being. Gracien's head erupted under the pressure of death's crushing force before bloody bubbles burst through his
nostrils. A rush of air finally came. The gasp that followed was so inhu-
man it shouldn't have been birthed into the forest night. The air wheezed
through his nose as he struggled to draw another. His chest felt like it
had been smashed through his back and everything below it felt gone.
As the darkness crept in, so did the search party. Their expressions solidified Gracien's gruesome fate. As he lay paralyzed, Master Chi's face slid
in over Gracien, examining the petrified casualty.

*"One with outward courage dares to die; one with inner courage dares
to live,"* Master whispered Lao Tzu's words. Then an expression of indifference crystalized before fading into a smirk and disappearing into a
tunnel of darkness.

His arms flailed in the air as the roaring sea raged towards him.
Gracien's anguished demise came screaming in and he longed for it. His
last thought was of Aya and then – it was over.

Gracien's eyes popped open, and his breath struggled to come. The
confusion was suffocating. He moved to check his surroundings, but his
body wouldn't budge. It was a blessing, as seeing his state of being would
have been a shock so harsh it may have prematurely stolen the last of his
life. His muscled physique had been mauled by the forest bedding, leaving him paralyzed from the neck down with a slew of internal injuries.
There wasn't the torrent of pain as he had expected, but rather the an-
tithesis of it. His body was a cocoon of anesthesia, like being swallowed
whole by a snake after receiving a dose of its paralyzing venom. His eyes

wept with misery as a frenzied escalation in his breath boiled over. A moment later a crippling realization accompanied it. The memory of his falling was a flash.

The aftermath however, played out in slow motion; lying on the forest floor as darkness waned in and out while one disciple after the next filled the circle above him. It was a nightmare. Their expressions were a death sentence, their pity the noose, and Master Chi's smug smirk, the executioner. This was it. He knew this place all too well. His time had come.

Like the flicker of a final ember igniting one last flame, his pupils renewed with a thought. "Ning!" he sounded the word out loud.

"Suyin! Suyin, you're awake!" Ning's frantic voice sounded out right next to him.

"Can you hear me? Are you in pain? Can you move?" she sputtered out the questions before crying out. "What happened, Suyin? What happened?"

Ning sounded like she had been crying for hours and Gracien couldn't understand why she wouldn't come closer. As if Ning read his mind, she began grunting and wincing. The sound of stretching leather squeaked out as Gracien realized that Ning was strapped down to her own gurney.

Gracien tried moving his head to look but it barely shifted. The mere thought of it sent his vision tunneling as the air retreated from his lungs. His mind raged with panic as the sensation of being held underwater entombed him.

"Suyin!" Ning cried out as she tore at the wrist straps like a bound dog.

As Gracien strained to breathe, Ning strained for escape. Her hand was just too big and the leather too strong. With a sudden flash of inspiration, Ning stopped trying to pull her hand through the vice-like grip and instead pushed it forward, walking the leather up her forearm. She pushed and pushed, driving the restraint beyond her elbow and further still. Now she had some room to play with. She rolled to her side and began unbinding the restraint fastened around her other wrist.

Gracien wanted to kick at the bed, to strike it with all his might and scream into the night. He could almost feel the internal corruption stealing the last of his life. In an instant everything changed as Ning was there, cradling and kissing his head. Her affection was a torrential rain dousing a raging fire.

"Breathe… there, there, there. Shush…"

Ning pleaded as she swept Gracien's hair to the side just as she had done through all of his nightmares. Ning pulled on his lifeless body, tugging at Gracien as if he was being pulled away by an unstoppable current.

"Please breathe Suyin… Please breathe!" she wailed, losing herself in anguish.

Gracien, in all his own fear and anguish, felt the presence of something he had never known before: comfort through death. Like a pond thawing with spring's warm embrace, he relented, surrendering his fight, and allowing the solace of love to ferry him to the Beyond. The love they had shared was immense yet partial, resolute yet wavering, passionate yet fickle. It was infinitely more than the darkness of solitude. And as the very last of this life flickered out, Gracien allowed the prevailing presence of their love to evict his fear. As his eyelids fluttered, as a final breath seeped from his chest, as Ning's cries faded into the distance, Suyin's eyes closed and Gracien felt himself thrust outwards, soaring through the Heavens.

As if his body was being pulled, pressed, and stretched, an expansion of his being commenced. He was a cloud thinning into obscurity, watching his hands and arms fade into translucency as a sense of familiar acceptance crept into his awareness. Too much was happening at once, but in the same instant time had no place here. Like being greeted by his family after a lengthy voyage, the sensation of home suddenly pierced him like an arrow as his upward ascension accelerated without the protest of earthly elements. Something embraced him, something like silence but deeper and older.

His ascension erupted, blasting him through sapphire blues and silvered pearls. Like curtains for an opening act, the skies opened, revealing the vastness of eternity. Cemented within a harmonic void, an infinity of stars hailed, planets bowed, and galaxies beckoned. In the foreground a presence stirred, something formidable, unseen, and supreme. He felt it within, felt it filling him, or maybe he was filling it. This force wasn't making itself known, rather Gracien's capacity to feel it had awakened. Like a phoenix, sound was reborn. Surging from the funeral pyre, a hum of ethereal vibration rose from the ashes, kindling the very essence of his soul.

As if light had morphed into sensation, a perceivable melody rippled through him like a winter's chill, a lover's moan, the perfect bite, the scent of dusk, a lasting embrace, a child's smile. All earthly senses were now one, Being. Gracien rejoiced as the limitations of sense abounded, bursting with an ever-blooming eruption of euphoric love. Bliss. Gratitude. Compassion. Humility. Virtue. Honor. Kindness – mere notions incapable of capturing the glory of triumph or the valor of love. The weight of the universe embraced him, cradling his beingness like a babe.

His body, forever gone, merged with this celestial Force like ice into water. The limitations of his being now expanded with inconceivable speed. There was no fear, only the excitement of a carefree child racing through a meadow. Liberated from confinement, his spirit twirled, swayed, and leapt – frolicking in a bath of eternal oneness.

Gracien's soul rode the wave of expansion as a dandelion pappus rides an unfettered wind. Separation dwindled the further he soared to whence he came. Suddenly her presence bloomed. In an instant Aya's ripple merged with his. He guzzled her laugh, inhaled her aura, cradled her gaze, consumed her aroma, and melted within her spirit. The birth of creation, the invention of love. The two tumbled through existence, bathing in a lagoon of immortality. The hum of Source caressed their souls but then the vibration flickered and popped – crackling like the fires of earth. The soul known as Gracien awoke, then remembered. With this remembrance came a new force, a gravity that longed for his return. Plucked from divinity and pulled downwards like a lightning bolt, he thundered back to earth.

Here's a preview of Book II

S IX

The crackle of the fire was loud, too loud. His eyelids jutted apart as an instant anxiety entombed him. Distant screams sounded out as the dread morphed into confusion, then alarm. Or was it all just part of the lingering dream? Gracien pushed himself up from the bedding, perking an ear to discover reason for his angst. A mocha-colored hand with dirt under the nails swept a tangled mass of black hair from his concerned expression. His teenage face hosted generous cheeks, deep-set eyes, and a broad nose with small, perfectly round nostrils, which swelled as he smelled the air. The humid forest air didn't carry the typical scent of a lowly midnight. The night felt different, and the hut was too quiet. Except for the twins being sound asleep, the hut was empty

Where is everyone? he thought.

As his thin, toned arms pushed himself up, the crackle of his bedding's dried grass coalesced with an aggressive, distant crackle from beyond the hut.

"Davi?" His older brother was the first he called out for. "Mama, Papa?"

Gracien pulled a tunic over his shoulder as he dashed over to the hut's doorway, hanging on one of the flaps and peeking outside. A gust of wind blew through, and with it, a foreboding presence. It hung in the air like an unwanted stench. Everything felt so strange that he hadn't considered Suyin's death.

"Where are they?" He felt stupid asking out loud as a scream of horror rang out. "Aghhh!"

Gracien fell back into the hut as if he had been struck. He scrambled back to the twins, the pair of three-year-olds hadn't stirred. Like crickets bounding in a meadow, screams sounded out through the village. *It wasn't just a dream after all.* He retreated inwards as the alarm boiled over into full blown panic. His instinctual mind cried for him to run, to flee and save himself. His lungs heaved breath as a mass of dread choked his bosom like an anaconda.

Those perfectly round nostrils flared, something about the air, it was thicker and heavier. It tasted of ash.

"Fire," he whispered as his sea green pupils splayed with the realization. "Find them Lamiana!" he encouraged himself to act.

Gracien dashed back to the doorway before stopping dead in his tracks. His hand shot to his mouth, muffling a gasp as the shadow of some creature, some gigantic beast crept along a neighboring hut. The silhouette couldn't be cast from any human form as four twisted horns stabbed upwards into the smoke-filled night. The flame of its torch whipped about in the wind as it stalked forward.

Gracien crept back to the bedding, huddling over the twins. The doorway flap whipped about as the creature's shadow grew larger, expanding beyond the canvas of the neighboring hut. His palm pressed firmly atop his mouth as his lungs screamed for air, but he dared not breathe. A man's bloody hand grabbed the flap of the hut as a blackened spear tip penetrated the entrance followed by a torch. The demon's face appeared and with it Gracien screamed as the fullness of the man filled the entrance.

Framed in lapis war paint, the warrior's eyes bulged like a thief's appraising a room full of gold. His lips parted and a full smile revealed blackened teeth. His eyes closed as his nostrils flared, drinking in the fear.

Gracien dragged the twins backwards as if the entire world was tipping them forward. The man's eyes reopened. The enormous spear tip inched forward, dribbling blood down the head and onto the shaft. His unblinking eyes widened as he unleashed a triumphant, menacing laugh. It spurred the flame of his torch into toasting the ceiling. The twins screamed for mercy as they struggled under Gracien's weight. He dragged them under himself like an eagle hoarding its hatchlings, all the while his scream matched theirs. The warrior's massive foot stepped forward as he knelt, placing down his spear and torch before rising like a mountain with dawn's approach.

To be continued…

ACKNOWLEDGEMENTS

I'm immensely grateful to...

Ryan, for allowing me to talk about this project, sometimes relentlessly, and for taking the constant time and energy to provide exactly what I needed. Thank you for being there for me in the very beginning.

Charna, for the time you gave while managing a million other priorities.

Chris, for your feedback, help, and unwavering excitement. It's almost too much man – dial it down a bit, would ya?

Sarina, for polishing this into something pristine and for being a total stranger who believed in the power of this story.

My mother and father, for being a true testament to what parents can be in a time when someone has no other option but to ask the impossible. And you never hesitated, you never let up. I love you Mamabear, we miss you, Dad.

My siblings, for being such a resolute force of love, not only to myself, but to our parents through our struggle and beyond.

My extended family and dearest friends, for coming together as a true community and for continuing to encourage me through what ended up being a very deep and expansive journey.

Jessica Marie, for allowing me to care for, encourage, inspire, support, and love you through your greatest challenge. It was an honor that

I will cherish forever. I'm equally grateful that you never gave up on me, even after your passing. Your ethereal dedication revealed to me a whole new world. My words do no justice for how much I've grown and for what I've become through this quest.

Suzy, for your sincerity, your patience, your understanding, your steadfast love, and your unwavering support and belief in not only me, but in our family. You are the strongest woman I know, and you inspire me to be better and love deeper. Oh, and thanks for that little angel too ;)

Oliver Holden, for being the embodiment of joy, gratitude, and love. Thank you for teaching me a deeper understanding of presence and for slowing down time.

Everyone, everywhere who helped to inspire and who breathed life into this story – some of you know who you are, while others may not. Regardless, thank you.

And lastly, I'm grateful to you, the reader, for allowing me to share this story with you through this book and the ones that will follow. Thank you for your patience and dedication as I continue my work.

I'm rooted in humbled gratitude,

Joe

Made in United States
North Haven, CT
11 March 2023

33915993R00211